Abraham Lincoln

The Martyr's Monument

Being the Patriotism And Political Wisdom of Abraham Lincoln

Abraham Lincoln

The Martyr's Monument
Being the Patriotism And Political Wisdom of Abraham Lincoln

ISBN/EAN: 9783744732048

Printed in Europe, USA, Canada, Australia, Japan

Cover: Foto ©Raphael Reischuk / pixelio.de

More available books at **www.hansebooks.com**

THE

MARTYR'S MONUMENT.

BEING THE

PATRIOTISM AND POLITICAL WISDOM

OF

ABRAHAM LINCOLN,

AS EXHIBITED IN HIS

SPEECHES, MESSAGES, ORDERS, AND PROCLAMATIONS, FROM THE
PRESIDENTIAL CANVASS OF 1860 UNTIL HIS
ASSASSINATION, APRIL 14, 1865.

"I have builded a monument more enduring than brass."—HORACE.

NEW YORK:

THE AMERICAN NEWS COMPANY,
119 & 121 NASSAU STREET.

PREFATORY.

A FEW days after the assassination of President LINCOLN, the publishers of the present volume received the following letter from the distinguished gentleman whose name it bears:

GENTLEMEN:

You have it in your power to erect a monument of its own kind to the memory of the President, who, but a few months ago, was elected by one of the greatest national acts known in all history, and has now been taken off by foul assassination, as the chief representative of our national existence, and by an assassin who represents in this deed the ruthless evil against which we contend.

Collect and publish, in the speediest possible manner, the inaugural and other addresses of ABRAHAM LINCOLN, his proclamations, messages, and public letters; indeed, all he has written as President, and you will contribute to the mournful celebrations of the American people your share of lasting value, and of far more impressive eloquence than the most fervent orator could utter.

You would thus make the martyr rear his own monument, which no years, no centuries could level and cause to mingle again with the dust.   Your obedient,

FRANCIS LIEBER.

NEW YORK, *April* 18th, 1865.

In accordance with this suggestion the following pages have been prepared ; their object being to present in a convenient and easily accessible form, and with chronological arrangement, the writings of which Dr. LIEBER speaks with such well-merited admiration.   But the editor has included in the collection somewhat more than all that Mr. LINCOLN wrote as President.   The pith of his remarkable speech delivered at the Cooper Institute, in April, 1860, all of his speeches of any importance while he was President elect, and other expressions of his purposes and his convictions, not uttered exactly *as* President, will be found in the collection, which is well worth the thoughtful perusal of every citizen of the Republic.

THE MARTYR'S MONUMENT.

THE memory of ABRAHAM LINCOLN is now fresh in the hearts of his countrymen. It is hardly a memory. The grass which we would keep ever green has not yet had time to spring upon his grave. But already we are taking measures to erect monuments which will preserve that memory, and show the honor in which we hold it to after generations. This is right, and proper, and becoming; but it is almost superfluous. The name and the fame of him who fell by an assassin's hand, a martyr to his devotion to his country, to the duties of his high office, and to his conviction that "if slavery is not wrong nothing is wrong," will endure without the help of stone or bronze. It was what he did that will make our dead President immortal; and his deeds will of necessity be recorded upon one of the grandest and most stirring pages of the world's history. But beside the record of his acts he left behind him in his spoken and written words, which were but the expression of the motives of his deeds, a monument more enduring than any, however splendid, that will ever be erected to him by wealth and taste inspired by gratitude. To present his character in these fitly and completely to his fellow citizens, that they may be enabled to see how wise and good he was, how entirely he was devoted to the cause of his country and to freedom, and how skillfully he performed one of the most difficult tasks that ever man was called upon to undertake, how by forbearance and by patient waiting, no less than by vigorous and decided action when the time had come for action, he led a great nation through a crisis of unequaled peril, until he fell a victim in the very hour of its complete salvation, is the purpose of the following pages.

This collection presents a complete view of Mr. Lincoln's public life from the time when he was chosen as a candidate for the Presidency by those who were determined that slavery should no longer be extended by the authority and under the flag of this Republic, until the very day when that flag was formally raised again upon Fort Sumter as a sign that the Republic was preserved in its integrity and Slavery was utterly destroyed, and when he, having accomplished his great mission, closed his labors and gave up his spirit. Of all his speeches, messages, proclamations, public letters, and orders during that eventful period, only such parts have been omitted as were of a merely formal and business character. All that displayed his patriotism, set forth his principles, or illustrated his personal character has been solicitously retained. We have here Abraham Lincoln's portrait painted, and his monument raised, by his own hands.

THE GREAT ISSUE.

Rarely, if ever, was the issue to be decided by a great war so simple and so clearly defined as in the case of that war of which Abraham Lincoln's election was the immediate occasion, and which his administration conducted to so triumphant a close. That issue was whether the Government of the Republic known as the United States of America had the right, and the power, and the will to prevent the extension of negro-slavery over the common territory and under the authority of the Union. That right was asserted, and the intention to exert it declared, by the party whose votes made Mr. Lincoln President. It was denied, and the purpose based upon it was denounced, not only by a large majority of the people of the Slave States but by a powerful minority in the Free States ; which majority and minority, working together, had for many years directed the councils and swayed the power of the Government. Upon this issue Mr. Lincóln delivered an address at the Cooper Institute in New York on the evening of February 27, 1860, at a time when he had no notion that he should ever be President. Senator Douglas, then the leader of the Free State minority above mentioned, had taken the position that the fathers of the Republic had denied the right of the Government to interfere with the question of slavery in the Territories or common landed possessions of the Union, adding, as a conclusive argument against such interference, that "our fathers when they framed the Government under which we live understood this question just as well and even better than we do now."

This doctrine of Mr. Douglas Mr. Lincoln took as the subject of his address, and by careful historical research he brought to light the remarkable and pregnant fact that, with one or two exceptions, the fathers of the Republic, meaning those who took part in framing the Constitution and in establishing the Government, had, on every occasion of the consideration of the subject of slavery in the Territories, shown by their votes that in their judgment Congress *had* the constitutional right to exclude slavery from or admit it to the Territories, or to modify the form under which it should be admitted, or declare the conditions under which it should exist. Mr. Lincoln brought forward contemporary record of such action by the fathers of the Republic in 1784 and in 1787, before the formation of the present constitution; in 1789, in 1798, in 1804, and in 1820. Mr. Lincoln thus summed up the facts which he had brought to light.

Here, then, we have twenty-three out of our thirty-nine fathers "who framed the Government under which we live," who have, upon their official responsibility and their corporal oaths, acted upon the very question which the text affirms they "understood just as well, and even better than we do now;" and twenty-one of them—a clear majority of the whole "thirty-nine"—so acting upon it as to make them guilty of gross political impropriety and wilful perjury, if, in their understanding, any proper division between local and federal authority, or anything in the Constitution they had made themselves, and sworn to support, forbade the Federal Government to control as to slavery in the federal territories. Thus the twenty-one acted; and, as actions speak louder than words, so actions, under such responsibility, speak still louder.

   *   *   *   *   *   *   *   *

The sum of the whole is, that of our thirty-nine fathers who framed the original Constitution, twenty-one—a clear majority of the whole—certainly understood that no proper division of local from federal authority, nor any part of the Constitution, forbade the Federal Government to control slavery in the federal territories; while all the rest probably had the same understanding. Such, unquestionably, was the understanding of our fathers who framed the original Constitution; and the text affirms that they understood the question " better than we."

It is surely safe to assume that the thirty-nine framers of the original Constitution, and the seventy-six members of the Congress which framed the amendments thereto, taken together, do certainly include those who may be fairly called "our fathers who framed the Government under which we live." And, so assuming. I defy any man to show that any one of them ever, in his whole life, declared that, in his understanding, any proper division of local from federal authority, or any part of the Constitution, forbade the Federal Government to control as to slavery in the federal territories. I go a step further. I defy any one to show that any living man in the whole world ever did, prior to the beginning of the present century, (and I might almost say prior to the beginning of the last half of the present century,) declare that, in his understanding, any proper division of local from federal authority, or any part of the Constitution, forbade the Federal Government to control as to slavery in the federal territories. To those who now so declare, I give, not only "our fathers who framed the Government under which we live," but with them all other living men within the century in which it was framed, among whom to search, and they shall not be able to find the evidence of a single man agreeing with them.

In this speech Mr. Lincoln set forth, in a very note-worthy manner, his appreciation of the relative positions of the Free and the Slave States upon the great question then agitating the country. After saying that the Republican party only asked that slavery should be marked as "the fathers" marked it, "as an evil not to be extended, but to be tolerated and protected only because of, and so far as, its actual presence among us makes that toleration and protection a necessity:—let," he continued, "all the guaranties those fathers gave it, be, not grudgingly, but fully and fairly maintained." Then, addressing himself to the propagandists of slavery, he said as follows :

And now, if they would listen—as I suppose they will not—I would address a few words to the Southern people.

I would say to them :—You consider yourselves a reasonable and a just people ; and I consider that in the general qualities of reason and justice you are not inferior to any other people. Still, when you speak of us Republicans, you do so only to denounce us as reptiles, or, at the best, as no better than outlaws. You will grant a hearing to pirates or murderers, but nothing like it to "Black Republicans." In all your contentions with one another, each of you deems an unconditional condemnation of "Black Republicanism" as the first thing to be attended to. Indeed, such condemnation of us seems to be an indispensable prerequisite—license, so to speak—among you to be admitted or permitted to speak at all. Now, can you, or not, be prevailed upon to pause and to consider whether this is quite just to us, or even to yourselves? Bring forward your charges and specifications, and then be patient long enough to hear us deny or justify.

You say we are sectional. We deny it. That makes an issue; and the burden of proof is upon you. You produce your proof; and what is it? Why, that our party has no existence in your section—gets no votes in your section. The fact is substantially true; but does it prove the issue? If it does, then in case we should, without change of principle, begin to get votes in your section, we should thereby cease to be sectional. You cannot escape this conclusion; and yet, are you willing to abide by it? If you are, you will probably soon find that we have ceased to be sectional, for we shall get votes in your section this very year. You will then begin to discover, as the truth plainly is, that your proof does not touch the issue. The fact that we get no votes in your section, is a fact of your making, and not of ours. And if there be fault in that fact, that fault is primarily yours, and remains so until you show that we repel you by some wrong principle or practice. If we do repel you by any wrong principle or practice, the fault is ours; but this brings you to where you ought to have started—to a discussion of the right or wrong of our principle. If our principle, put in practice, would wrong your section for the benefit of ours, or for any other object, then our principle, and we with it, are sectional, and are justly opposed and denounced as such. Meet us, then, on the question of whether our principle, put in practice, would wrong your section; and so meet us as if it were possible that something may be said on our side. Do you accept the challenge ? No ! Then you really believe that the principle which "our fathers who framed the Government under which we live" thought so clearly right as to adopt it, and indorse it again and again, upon their official oaths, is in fact so clearly wrong as to demand your condemnation without a moment's consideration.

Some of you d. light to flaunt in our faces the warning against sectional parties given by Washington in his Farewell Address. Less than eight years before Washington gave that warning, he had, as President of the United States, approved and signed an act of Congress, enforcing the prohibition of slavery in the Northwestern Territory, which act embodied the policy of the Government upon that subject up to and at the very moment he penned that warning ; and about one year after he penned it, he wrote La Fayette that he considered that prohibition a wise measure, expressing in the same connection his hope that we should at some time have a confederacy of free States.

Bearing this in mind, and seeing that sectionalism has since arisen upon this same subject, is that warning a weapon in your hands against us, or in our hands against you? Could Washington himself speak, would he cast the blame of that sectionalism upon us, who sustain his policy, or upon you who repudiate it? We respect that warning of Washington, and we commend it to you, together with his example pointing to the right application of it.

Of emancipation and of such efforts as that of John Brown, Mr. Lincoln expressed these views :

In the language of Mr. Jefferson, uttered many years ago, " It is still in our power to direct the process of emancipation, and deportation, peaceably, and in such slow degrees, as that the evil will wear off insensibly ; and their [the negroes'] places be, *pari passu*, filled up by free white laborers. If, on the contrary, it is left to force itself on, human nature must shudder at the prospect held up."

Mr. Jefferson did not mean to say, nor do I, that the power of emancipation is in the Federal Government. He spoke of Virginia ; and, as to the power of emancipation, I speak of the slave-holding States only. The Federal Government, however, as we insist, has the power of restraining the extension of the institution—the power to insure that a slave insurrection shall never occur on any American soil which is now free from slavery.

John Brown's effort was peculiar. It was not a slave insurrection. It was an attempt by white men to get up a revolt among slaves, in which the slaves refused to participate. In fact, it was so absurd, that the slaves, with all their ignorance, saw plainly enough it could not succeed. That affair, in its philosophy, corresponds with the many attempts, related in history, at the assassination of kings and emperors. An enthusiast broods over the oppression of a people till he fancies himself commissioned by Heaven to liberate them. He ventures the attempt, which ends in little else than his own execution. Orsini's attempt on Louis Napoleon, and John Brown's attempt at Harper's Ferry were, in their philosophy, precisely the same. The eagerness to cast blame on old England in the one case, and on New England in the other, does not disprove the sameness of the two things.·

Mr. Lincoln closed his discourse by the following passage which he addressed specially to the opponents of the extension of slavery, *i. e.*, in his words, the Republicans, although there were many who united with him in that opposition and in these views as to its nature, its right, and its necessity, who had not acted with the Republican party.

A few words now to Republicans. It is exceedingly desirable that all parts of this great Confederacy shall be at peace, and in harmony, one with another. Let us Republicans do our part to have it so. Even though much provoked, let us do nothing through passion and ill-temper. Even though the Southern people will not so much as listen to us, let us calmly consider their demands, and yield to them if, in our deliberate view of our duty, we possibly can. Judging by all they say and do, and by the subject and nature of their controversy with us, let us determine, if we can, what will satisfy them.

Will they be satisfied if the Territories be unconditionally surrendered to them? We know they will not. In all their present complaints against us, the Territories are scarcely mentioned. Invasions and insurrections are the rage now. Will it satisfy them, if, in the future, we have nothing to do with invasions and insurrections ? We know it will not. We so know, because we know we never had anything to do with invasions and insurrections; and yet this total abstaining does not exempt us from the charge and the denunciation.   *   *   *   *

In all our platforms and speeches we have constantly protested our purpose to let them alone; but this has had no tendency to convince them. Alike unavailing to convince them, is the fact that they have never detected a man of us in any attempt to disturb them.

These natural, and apparently adequate means all failing, what will convince them? This, and this only, cease to call slavery *wrong*, and join them in calling it *right*. And this must be done thoroughly—done in *acts* as well as in *words*. Silence will not be tolerated—we must place ourselves avowedly with them. Senator Douglas's new sedition law must be enacted and enforced, suppressing all declarations that slavery is wrong, whether made in politics, in presses, in pulpits, or in private. We must arrest and return their fugitive slaves with greedy pleasure. We must pull down our Free State constitutions. The whole atmosphere must be disinfected from all taint of opposition to slavery, before they will cease to believe that all their troubles proceed from us.   *   *   *   *   *   *

Nor can we justifiably withhold this, on any ground save our conviction that slavery is wrong. If slavery is right, all words, acts, laws, and constitutions against it, are themselves wrong, and should be silenced, and swept away. If it is right, we cannot justly object to its nationality—its universality; if it is wrong, they cannot justly insist upon its extension—its enlargement. All they ask, we could readily grant, if we thought slavery right; all we ask, they could as readily grant, if they thought it wrong. Their thinking it right, and our thinking it wrong, is the precise fact upon which depends the whole controversy. Thinking it right, as they do, they are not to blame for desiring its full recognition, as being right; but, thinking it wrong, as we do, can we yield to them ? Can we cast our votes with their view, and against our own? In view of our moral, social, and political responsibilities, can we do this?

Wrong as we think slavery is, we can yet afford to let it alone where it is, because that much is due to the necessity arising from its actual presence in the nation; but can we, while our votes will prevent it, allow it to spread into the National Territories, and to overrun us here in these Free States? If our sense of duty forbids this, then let us stand by our duty, fearlessly and effectively. Let us be diverted by none of those sophistical contrivances wherewith we are so industriously plied and belabored—contrivances such as groping for some middle ground between the right and the wrong, vain as the search for a man who should be neither a living man nor a dead man—such as a policy of "don't care" on a question about which all true men do care—such as Union appeals beseeching true Union men to yield to Disunionists, reversing the divine rule, and calling, not the sinners, but the righteous to repentance—such as invocations to Washington, imploring men to unsay what Washington said, and undo what Washington did.

Neither let us be slandered from our duty by false accusations against us, nor frightened from it by menaces of destruction to the Government nor of dungeons to ourselves. Let us have faith that right makes might, and in that faith, let us, to the end, dare to do our duty as we understand it.

Thus clearly, fairly and with eminent kindness and consideration towards the slave-holders did Mr. Lincoln set forth the Great Issue which he was afterwards called upon to try before the world. But previously he had expressed more tersely and almost epigramatically his judgment as to the future of this country in regard to this subject. When Mr. Lincoln was nominated to the Senate of the United States, in 1858, he made a speech, in the opening passage of which were these memorable words:

"A house divided against itself cannot stand. I believe this Government cannot endure permanently half slave and half free. I do not expect the union to be dissolved—I do not expect the house to fall, but I do expect it will cease to be divided. It will become all one thing or all the other."

Surely political sagacity and foresight were never more manifest than in this prediction. It has been verified by subsequent events to the letter. The slaveholders were determined that the Government should be *all* "slave." During the years which immediately preceded the attempted secession, they thought that they were rapidly bringing about the end which they so much desired; and there is no reasonable doubt that at first secession itself was but a new and rough method adopted by them to accomplish this same purpose;—that they believed that after they had shown their ability to defy and resist the Government and establish the principle of State Sovereignty, they could reconstruct the Union on a basis which would enable them to carry slavery into the Territories, and their slaves into any State of their reconstructed Union. They were rudely undeceived, and the man who, next to themselves, was the chief instrument of their destruction, was he who only six years before had told them that they must succeed entirely or fail utterly, that the Government could not endure half slave and half free, and that the Union would not be dissolved.

NOMINATION TO THE PRESIDENCY.

Mr. Lincoln, unexpectedly to himself and to the country, was nominated to the Presidency by the convention of 1860, at Chicago. To the announcement of this fact made by a committee, he made the following reply:

"*Mr. Chairman and Gentlemen of the Committee*—I tender to you, and through you to the Republican National Convention, and all the people represented in it, my profoundest thanks for the high honor done me, which you now formally announce. Deeply, and even painfully sensible of the great responsibility which is inseparable from this high honor—a responsibility which I could almost wish had fallen upon some one of the far more eminent men and experienced statesmen whose distinguished names were before the Convention, I shall, by your leave, consider more fully the resolutions of the Convention, denominated the platform, and without any unnecessary or unreasonable delay, respond to you, Mr. Chairman, in writing, not doubting that the platform will be found satisfactory, and the nomination gratefully accepted.

"And now I will not longer defer the pleasure of taking you, and each of you, by the hand."

The response in writing to which he referred, was soon after received in the following words :

SPRINGFIELD, ILLINOIS, *May*, 1860.

Sir—I accept the nomination tendered to me by the Convention over which you presided, of which I am formally apprized in a letter of yourself and others acting as a Committee of the Convention for that purpose. The declaration of principles and sentiments which accompanies your letter meets my approval, and it shall be my care not to violate it, or disregard it in any part. Imploring the assistance of Divine Providence, and with due regard to the views and feelings of all who were represented in the Convention, to the rights of all the States and Territories and people of the nation, to the inviolability of the Constitution, and the perpetual union, harmony, and prosperity of all, I am most happy to co-operate for the practical success of the principles declared by the Convention.

Your obliging friend and fellow-citizen,

ABRAHAM LINCOLN.

HON. GEORGE ASHMUN,
President of the Republican Convention.

These were almost mere formalities. Yet their tone indicated the character of the man. The short speech was uttered in a tone and with a manner full of dignity, and with an expression of a sense of responsibility which almost amounted to sadness. And in both speech and letter there appears that mingling of firmness and self-distrust, that determination and that reliance upon a higher power which marked Mr. Lincoln's words and conduct throughout his public life. When, after his election, the time had arrived for him to leave his quiet home for the capital of his distracted country, he addressed his friends and neighbors in the following few brief sentences. But few and brief although they are, how fully they express a just and large appreciation of the crisis in which he was called to power, how imbued they are with the man's tenderness, and the statesman's trust in God!

PARTING SPEECH AT ILLINOIS, FEB. 11th, 1860.

My Friends—No one, not in my position, can appreciate the sadness I feel at this parting. To this people I owe all that I am. Here I have lived more than a quarter of a century; here my children were born, and here one of them lies buried. I know not how soon I shall see you again. A duty devolves upon me, which is, perhaps, greater than that which has devolved upon any other man since the days of WASHINGTON. He never would have succeeded except for the aid of Divine Providence, upon which he at all times relied. I feel that I cannot succeed without the same Divine aid which sustained him, and on the same Almighty Being I place my reliance for support, and I hope you, my friends, will all pray that I may receive that Divine assistance, without which I cannot succeed, but with which, success is certain. Again I bid you all an affectionate farewell.

His journey to Washington was a progress like that of a monarch in olden time—he, that simple, unassuming, almost rude frontiersman and village lawyer. He was met at every station by throngs of people eager to cheer and encourage him, and to hear a word of cheer and encouragement in return. In what he said he of course repeate d himself often, and on some occasions he merely uttered a kindly sentence or two, which was cut short by the impatient shriek of the railway engine. The following are all the speeches made by him upon his journey, to which the above remarks do not apply:

SPEECHES AT INDIANAPOLIS.

Gov. Morton and Fellow-Citizens of the State of Indiana—Most heartily do I thank you for this magnificent reception, and while I cannot take to myself any share of the compliment thus paid, more than that which pertains to a mere instrument, an accidental instrument, perhaps I should say, of a great cause, I yet must look upon it as a most magnificent reception, and as such, most heartily do thank you for it. You have been pleased to address yourself to me chiefly in behalf of this glorious Union in which we live, in all of which you have my hearty sympathy, and, as far as may be within my power, will have, one and inseparably, my hearty consideration; while I do not expect upon this occasion, or until I get to Washington, to attempt any lengthy speech, I will only say, To the salvation of the Union there needs but one single thing, the hearts of a people like yours. [Applause.]

The people, when they rise in mass in behalf of the Union and the liberties of their country, truly may it be said, "The gates of hell cannot prevail against them." [Renewed applause.] In all trying positions in which I shall be placed, and, doubtless I shall be placed in many such, my reliance will be placed upon you and the people of the United States; and I wish you to remember, now and forever, that it is your business, and not mine; that if the union of these States, and the liberties of this people shall be lost, it is but little to any one man of fifty-two years of age, but a great deal to the thirty millions of people who inhabit these United States, and to their posterity in all coming time. It is your business to rise up and preserve the Union and liberty for yourselves, and not for me.

I desire they should be constitutionally performed. I, as already intimated, am but an accidental instrument, temporary, and to serve but for a limited time, and I appeal to you again to constantly bear in mind that with you, and not with politicians, not with Presidents, not with office-seekers, but with you, is the question, Shall the Union and shall the liberties of this country be preserved to the latest generations? [Cheers.]

The above speech was delivered in front of the Bates House, at Indianapolis, to a promiscuous assemblage, among which appeared the governor and members of both houses of the State Legislature. That which follows was made at the same hotel in the evening, in response to a formal welcome from the Legislature.

Fellow-Citizens of the State of Indiana—I am here to thank you much for this magnificent welcome, and still more for the generous support given by your State to that political cause which I think is the true and just cause of the whole country and the whole world.

Solomon says, there is "a time to keep silence," and when men wrangle by the mouth with no certainty that they *mean* the same *thing*, while using the same *word*, it perhaps were as well if they would keep silence.

The words "coercion" and "invasion" are much used in these days, and often with some temper and hot blood. Let us make sure, if we can, that we do not misunderstand the meaning of those who use them. Let us get exact definitions of these words, not from dictionaries, but from the men themselves, who certainly depreciate the *things* they would represent by the use of words. What, then, is "Coercion?" What is "Invasion?" Would the marching of an army into South Carolina without the consent of her people, and with hostile intent towards them, be "invasion?" I certainly think it would; and it would be "coercion" also if the South Carolinians were forced to submit. But if the United States should merely hold and retake its own forts and other property, and collect the duties on foreign importations, or even withhold the mails from places where they were habitually violated, would any or all these things be "invasion" or "coercion?"　Do our professed lovers of the Union, but who spitefully resolve that they will resist coercion and invasion, understand that such things as these, on the part of the United States, would be coercion or invasion of a State?　If so, their ideas of means to preserve the object of their affection would seem exceedingly thin and airy.　If sick, the little pills of the homœopathists would be too large for it to swallow.　In their view, the Union, as a family relation, would seem to be no regular marriage, but a sort of "free love" arrangement, to be maintained only on "passional attraction."

By the way, in what consists the special sacredness of a State? I speak not of the position assigned to a State in the Union, by the Constitution; for that, by the bond, we all recognize.　That position, however, a State cannot carry out of the Union with it.　I speak of that assumed primary right of a State to rule all which is *less* than itself and ruin all which is larger than itself. If a State and a county in a given case, should be equal in extent of territory, and equal in number of inhabitants, in what, as a matter of principle, is the State better than the county? Would an exchange of names be an exchange of *rights* upon principle?　On what rightful principle may a State, being not more than one-fiftieth part of the nation, in soil and population, break up the nation, and then coerce a proportionally larger subdivision of itself, in the most arbitrary way?　What mysterious right to play tyrant is conferred on a district of country, with its people, by merely calling it a State?

・Fellow-citizens, I am not asserting anything; I am merely asking questions for you to consider.　And now allow me to bid you farewell.

SPEECH AT CINCINNATI.

Mr. Mayor and Fellow-Citizens—I have spoken but once before this in Cincinnati.　That was a year previous to the late Presidential election.　On that occasion, in a playful manner, but with sincere words, I addressed much of what I said to the Kentuckians. I gave my opinion that we, as Republicans, would ultimately beat them, as Democrats, but that they could postpone that result longer by nominating Senator Douglas for the Presidency than they could in any other way. They did not, in any true sense of the word, nominate Mr. Douglas, and the result has come certainly as soon as ever I expected. I also told them how I expected they would be treated after they should have been beaten; and I now wish to call their attention to what I then said upon that subject. I then said, " When we do as we say, beat you, you perhaps want to know what we will do with you. I will tell you, as far as I am authorized to speak for the opposition, what we mean to do with you. We mean to treat you as near as we possibly can, as Washington, Jefferson, and Madison treated you. We mean to leave you alone, and in no way to interfere with your institutions; to abide by all and every compromise of the Constitution; and, in a word, coming back to the original proposition, to treat you, so far as degenerate men, if we have degenerated, may, according to the example of those noble fathers, WASHINGTON, JEFFERSON and MADISON. We mean to remember that you are as good as we; that there is no difference between us, other than the difference of circumstances. We mean to recognize and bear in mind always that you have as good hearts in your bosoms as any people, or as we claim to have, and treat you accordingly.

Fellow-citizens of Kentucky! friends! brethren, may I call you in my new position? I see no occasion, and feel no inclination to retract a word of this. If it shall not be made good, be assured the fault shall not be mine.

SPEECH AT COLUMBUS.

Mr. President and Mr. Speaker, and Gentlemen of the General Assembly—It is true, as has been said by the President of the Senate, that very great responsibility rests upon me in the position to which the votes of the American people have called me. I am deeply sensible of that weighty responsibility. I cannot but know what you all know, that without a name, perhaps without a reason why I should have a name, there has fallen upon me a task such as did not rest even upon the Father of his country, and so feeling I cannot but turn and look for the support without which it will be impossible for me to perform that great task. I turn, then, and look to the great American people, and to that God who has never forsaken them.

Allusion has been made to the interest felt in relation to the policy of the new administration. In this I have received from some a degree of credit for having kept silence, and from others some depreciation. I still think I was right. In the varying and repeatedly shifting scenes of the present, and without a precedent which could enable me to judge by the past, it has seemed fitting that before speaking upon the difficulties of the country, I should have gained a view of the whole field so as to be sure after all—at liberty to modify and change the course of policy as future events may make a change necessary. I have not maintained silence from any want of real anxiety. It is a good thing that there is no more than anxiety, for there is nothing going wrong. It is a consoling circumstance that when we look out, there is nothing that really hurts anybody. We entertain different views upon political questions, but nobody is suffering anything. This is a most consoling circumstance, and from it we may conclude that all we want is time, patience, and a reliance on that God who has never forsaken this people. Fellow-citizens, what I have said I have said altogether extemporaneously, and will now come to a close.

This speech is strongly marked by that peculiar and, as it proved, very wise trait of Mr. Lincoln's policy in the early part of his administration, although it subjected him at first to reproach, and to charges on the one side of lukewarmness, and on the other of levity—a watchful consideration of the course of events, and the tone of the public mind; a determination not to attempt the impracticable, and not to be too far in advance of the general public sentiment.

SPEECH AT STEUBENVILLE.

I fear that the great confidence placed in my ability is unfounded. Indeed, I am sure it is. Encompassed by vast difficulties as I am, nothing shall be wanting on my part, if sustained by the American people and God. I believe the devotion to the Constitution is equally great on both sides of the river. It is only the different understanding of that instrument that causes difficulty. The only dispute on both sides is "What are their rights?" If the majority should not rule, who should be the judge? Where is such a judge to be found? We should all be bound by the majority of the American people—if not, then the minority must control. Would that be right? Would it be just or generous? Assuredly not. I reiterate that the majority should rule. If I adopt a wrong policy, the opportunity for condemnation will occur in four years' time. Then I can be turned out, and a better man with better views put in my place.

But he was not turned out. The heathen raged, and some of the people imagined a vain thing, yet in the midst of this fearful conflict, with such an approach to unanimity as has not been seen since the days of Washington or Jackson, his fellow-citizens declared that a better man with better views could not be found for the emergency.

EXTRACT FROM MR. LINCOLN'S SPEECH AT PITTSBURG.

It is often said that the tariff is the specialty of Pennsylvania. Assuming that direct taxation is not to be adopted, the Tariff question must be as durable as the Government itself. It is a question of national housekeeping. It is to the Government what replenishing the meal-tub is to the family. Every varying circumstance will require frequent modifications as to the amount needed, and the sources of supply. So far there is little difference of opinion among the people. It is only whether, and how far, the duties on imports shall be adjusted to favor home productions. In the home market that controversy begins. One party insists that too much protection oppresses one class for the advantage of another, while the other party argues that, with all its incidents, in the long run, all classes are benefited. In the Chicago Platform there is a plank upon this subject, which should be a general law to the incoming Administration. We should do neither more nor less than we gave the people reason to believe we would when they gave us their votes. That plank is as I now read:

Mr. Lincoln's private secretary then read section twelfth of the Chicago Platform, as follows:

"That while providing revenue for the support of the General Government, by duties upon imports, sound policy requires such an adjustment of these duties upon imports as will encourage the development of the industrial interest of the whole country; and we commend that policy of national exchanges which secures to working-men liberal wages—to agriculture remunerating prices—to mechanics and manufacturers adequate reward for their skill, labor, and enterprise; and to the nation commercial prosperity and independence."

Mr. Lincoln resumed: As with all general propositions doubtless there will be shades of difference in construing this. I have by no means a thoroughly matured judgment upon this subject, especially as to details; some general ideas are about all. I have long thought to produce any necessary article at home which can be made of as good quality and with as little labor at home as abroad, would be better policy, at least by the difference of the carrying from abroad. In such a case the carrying is demonstrably a dead loss of labor. For instance, labor being the true standard of value, is it not plain that if equal labor gets a bar of railroad iron out of a mine in England, and another out of a mine in Pennsylvania, each can be laid down in a track at home cheaper than they could exchange countries, at least by the cost of carriage? If there be a present cause why one can be both made and carried cheaper in money price than the other can be made without carrying, that cause is an unnatural and injurious one, and ought naturally if not rapidly to be removed. The condition of the treasury at this time would seem to render an early revision of the Tariff indispensable. The Morrill Tariff bill, now pending before Congress, may or may not become a law. I am not posted as to its particular provisions, but if they are generally satisfactory and the bill shall now pass, there will be an end of the matter for the present. If, however, it shall not pass, I suppose the whole subject will be one of the most pressing and important for the next Congress. By the Constitution, the Executive may recommend measures which he may think proper, and he may veto those he thinks improper, and it is supposed that he may add to these certain indirect influences to affect the action of Congress. My political education strongly inclines me against a very free use of any of these means by the Executive to control the legislation of the country. As a rule, I think it better that Congress should originate as well as perfect its measures without external bias. I, therefore, would rather recommend to every gentleman who knows he is to be a member of the next Congress, to take an enlarged view, and inform himself thoroughly, so as to contribute his part to such an adjustment of the tariff as shall produce a sufficient revenue, and in its other bearings, so far as possible, be just and equal to all sections of the country and all classes of the people.

SPEECH AT BUFFALO.

Mr. Mayor and Fellow-Citizens of Buffalo and the State of New York—I am here to thank you briefly for this grand reception given to me, not personally, but as the representative of our great and beloved country. [Cheers.] Your worthy Mayor has been pleased to mention, in his address to me, the fortunate and agreeable journey which I have had from home, only it is a rather circuitous route to the Federal capital. I am very happy that he was enabled in truth to congratulate myself and company on that fact. It is true we have had nothing thus far to mar the pleasure of the trip. We have not been met alone by those who assisted in giving the election to me; I say not alone by them, but by the whole population of the country through which we have passed. This is as it should be. Had the election fallen to any other of the distinguished candidates instead of myself, under the peculiar circumstances, to say the least, it would have been proper for all citizens to have greeted him as you now greet me. It is an evidence of the devotion of the whole people to the Constitution, the Union, and the perpetuity of the liberties of this country. [Cheers.] I am unwilling on any occasion that I should be so meanly thought of as to have it supposed for a moment that these demonstrations are tendered to me personally. They are tendered to the country, to the institutions of the country, and to the perpetuity of the liberties of the country, for which these institutions were made and created.

Your worthy Mayor has thought fit to express the hope that I may be able to relieve the country from the present, or, I should say, the threatened difficulties. I am sure I bring a heart true to the work. [Tremendous applause.] For the ability to perform it, I must trust in that Supreme Being who has never forsaken this favored land, through the instrumentality of this great and intelligent people. Without that assistance I shall surely fail; with it I cannot fail. When we speak of threatened difficulties to the country, it is natural that it should be expected that something should be said by myself with regard to particular measures. Upon more mature reflection, however—and others will agree with me—that, when it is considered that these difficulties are without precedent, and never have been acted upon by any individual situated as I am, it is most proper I should wait and see the developments, and get all the light possible, so that when I do speak authoritatively, I may be as near right as possible. [Cheers.] When I shall speak authoritatively, I hope to say nothing inconsistent with the Constitution, the Union, the rights of all the States, of each State, and of each section of the country, and not to disappoint the reasonable expectations of those who have confided to me their votes. In this connection allow me to say that you, as a portion of the great American people, need only to maintain your composure, stand up to your sober convictions of right, to your obligations to the Constitution, and act in accordance with those sober convictions, and the clouds which now arise in the horizon will be dispelled, and we shall have a bright and glorious future; and when this generation has passed away, tens of thousands will inhabit this country where only thousauds inhabit it now. I do not propose to address you at length; I have no voice for it. Allow me **again to thank you** for this magnificent reception, and bid you farewell.

The following brief recognition of his welcome at Utica, is marked by a trait of that whimsical humor which did much to smooth the rugged road over which Mr· Lincoln was called to pass to glory and the grave.

AT UTICA.

Ladies and Gentlemen—I have no speech to make to you, and no time to speak in. I appear before you that I may see you, and that you may see me ; and I am willing to admit, that so far as the ladies are concerned, I have the best of the bargain, though I wish it to be understood that I do not make the same acknowledgment concerning the men. [Laughter and applause.]

SPEECH IN THE HALL OF ASSEMBLY AT ALBANY.

Mr. President and Gentlemen of the Legislature of the State of New York—It is with feelings of great diffidence, and I may say, with feelings of awe, perhaps greater than I have recently experienced, that I meet you here in this place. The history of this great State, the renown of those great men who have stood here, and spoken here, and been heard here, all crowd around my fancy, and incline me to shrink from any attempt to address you. Yet I have some confidence given me by the generous manner in which you have invited me, and by the still more generous manner in which you have received me, to speak further. You have invited and received me without distinction of party. I cannot for a moment suppose that this has been done, in any considerable degree, with reference to my personal services, but that it is done in so far as I am regarded at this time as the representative of the majesty of this great nation. I doubt not this is the truth, and the whole truth of the case, and this is as it should be. It is much more gratifying to me that this reception has been given to me as the representative of a free people, than it could possibly be if tendered as an evidence of devotion to me, or to any one man personally. And now I think it were more fitting that I should close these hasty remarks. It is true that, while I hold myself, without mock modesty, the humblest of all individuals that have ever been elevated to the Presidency, I have a more difficult task to perform than any one of them. You have generously tendered me the united support of the great Empire State. For this, in behalf of the nation—in behalf of the present and future of the nation—in behalf of civil and religious liberty for all time to come, most gratefully do I thank you. I do not propose to enter into an explanation of any particular line of policy as to our present difficulties, to be adopted by the incoming Administration. I deem it just to you, to myself, and to all, that I should see everything, that I should hear everything, that I should have every light that can be brought within my reach, in order that when I do so speak, I shall have enjoyed every opportunity to take correct and true grounds; and for this reason I don't propose to speak, at this time, of the policy of the Government. But when the time comes I shall speak, as well as I am able, for the good of the present and future of this country—for the good both of the North and the South of this country—for the good of the one and the other, and of all sections of the country. [Rounds of applause.] In the meantime, if we have patience, if we restrain ourselves, if we allow ourselves not to run off in a passion, I still have confidence that the Almighty, the Maker of the Universe, will, through the instrumentality of this great and intelligent people, bring us through this as he has through all the other difficulties of our country. Relying on this, I again thank you for this generous reception." [Applause and cheers.]

SPEECH AT THE ASTOR HOUSE, NEW YORK.

Mr. Chairman and Gentlemen—I am rather an old man to avail myself of such an excuse as I am now about to do. Yet the truth is so distinct, and presses itself so distinctly upon me, that I cannot well avoid it—and that is, that I did not understand when I was brought into this room that I was brought here to make a speech. It was not intimated to me that I was brought into the room where DANIEL WEBSTER and HENRY CLAY had made speeches, and where, in my position, I might be expected to do something like those men, or do something worthy of myself or my audience. I, therefore, will beg you to make very great allowance for the circumstances in which I have been by surprise brought before you. Now, I have been in the habit of thinking and speaking sometimes upon political questions that have for some years past agitated the country; and if I were disposed to do so, and we could take up some one of the issues, as the lawyers call them, and I were called upon to make an argument about it to the best of my ability, I could do so without much preparation. But, that is not what you desire to be done here to-night.

I have been occupying a position, since the Presidential election, of silence, of avoiding public speaking, of avoiding public writing. I have been doing so, because I thought, upon full consideration, that was the proper course for me to take. [Great applause.] I am brought before you now, and required to make a speech, when you all approve more than anything else of the fact that I have been keeping silence. [Great laughter, cries of " Good," and applause.] And now it seems to me that the response you give to that remark ought to justify me in closing just here. [Great laughter.] I have not kept silence since the Presidential election from any party wantonness, or from any indifference to the anxiety that pervades the minds of men about the aspect of the political affairs of this country. I have kept silence for the reason that I supposed it was peculiarly proper that I should do so until the time came when, according to the custom of the country, I could speak officially.

A voice—The custom of the country ?

I heard some gentleman say, " According to the custom of the country." I alluded to the custom of the President-elect, at the time of taking the oath of office. That is what I meant by " the custom of the country." I do suppose that, while the political drama being enacted in this country, at this time, is rapidly shifting its scenes—forbidding an anticipation, with any degree of certainty, to-day, what we shall see to-morrow—it was peculiarly fitting that I should see it all, up to the last minute, before I should take ground that I might be disposed (by the shifting of the scenes afterwards) also to shift. [Applause.] I have said, several times, upon this journey, and I now repeat it to you, that when the time does come, I shall then take the ground that I think is right—[applause]—the ground that I think is right—[applause, and cries of "Good, good"]—right for the North, for the South, for the East, for the West, for the whole country. [Cries of "Good," "Hurrah for Lincoln," and applause.] And in doing so, I hope to feel no necessity pressing upon me to say anything in conflict with the Constitution; in conflict with the continued union of these States—[applause]—in conflict with the perpetuation of the liberties of this people —[applause]—or anything in conflict with any thing whatever that I have ever given you reason to expect from me. [Applause.] And now, my friends, have I said enough? [Loud cries of "No, no," and three cheers for Lincoln.] Now, my friends, there appears to be a difference of opinion between you and me, and I really feel called upon to decide the question myself. [Applause, during which Mr. Lincoln descended from the table.]

AT THE CITY HALL, NEW YORK,

Mr. Lincoln was formally received by the then Mayor, Mr. Fernando Wood, in the following words:

Mr. Lincoln—As Mayor of New York, it becomes my duty to extend to you an official welcome in behalf of the Corporation. In doing so permit me to say, that this city has never offered hospitality to a man clothed with more exalted powers, or resting under graver responsibilities, than those which circumstances have devolved upon you. Coming into office with a dismembered Government to reconstruct, and a disconnected and hostile people to reconcile, it will require a high patriotism, and an elevated comprehension of the whole country and its varied interests, opinions, and prejudices, to so conduct public affairs as to bring it back again to its former harmonious, consolidated, and prosperous condition. If I refer to this topic, sir, it is because New York is deeply interested. The present political divisions have sorely afflicted her people. All her material interests are paralyzed. Her commercial greatness is endangered. She is the child of the American Union. She has grown up under its maternal care, and been fostered by its paternal bounty, and we fear that if the Union dies, the present supremacy of New York may perish with it. To you, therefore, chosen under the forms of the Constitution as the head of the Confederacy, we look for a restoration of fraternal relations between the States—only to be accomplished by peaceful and conciliatory means, aided by the wisdom of Almighty God.

Events showed the utter foolishness and presumption of Mr. Wood in thus attempting to dictate to Abraham Lincoln, and in his declaration that New York was the child of the American Union and that the Union in its integrity and prosperity was to be restored only by peaceful and conciliatory means. Mr. Lincoln met these solemn platitudes with the following expression of his clear-headed common sense and patriotism.

Mr. Mayor—It is with feelings of deep gratitude that I make my acknowledgments for the reception that has been given me in the great commercial city of New York. I cannot but remember that it is done by the people, who do not, by a large majority, agree with me in political sentiment. It is the more grateful to me, because in this I see that for the great principles of our Government the people are pretty nearly or quite unanimous. In regard to the difficulties that confront us at this time, and which you have seen fit to speak so becomingly and so justly, I can only say that I agree with the sentiments expressed. In my devotion to the Union I hope I am behind no man in the nation. As to my wisdom in conducting affairs so as to tend to the preservation of the Union, I fear too great confidence may have been placed in me. I am sure I bring a heart devoted to the work. There is nothing that could ever bring me to consent—willingly to consent—to the destruction of this Union (in

which not only the great city of New York, but the whole
country, has acquired its greatness), unless it would be that
thing for which the Union itself was made. I understand that
the ship is made for the carrying and preservation of the cargo ;
and so long as the ship is safe with the cargo, it shall not be
abandoned. This Union shall never be abandoned, unless the
possibility of its existence shall cease to exist, without the necessity of throwing passengers and cargo overboard. So long,
then, as it is possible that the prosperity and liberties of this
people can be preserved within this Union, it shall be my purpose at all times to preserve it. And now, Mr. Mayor, renewing
my thanks for this cordial reception, allow me to come to a
close. [Applause.]

AT NEWARK

Mr. Lincoln uttered the following brief but significant
sentences :

Mr. Mayor—I thank you for this reception at the city of New-
ark. With regard to the great work of which you speak, I will
say that I bring to it a heart filled with love for my country, and
an honest desire to do what is right. I am sure, however, that
I have not the ability to do any thing unaided of God, and that
without his support, and that of this free, happy, prosperous,
and intelligent people, no man can succeed in doing that the
importance of which we all comprehend. Again thanking you
for the reception you have given me, I will now bid you farewell, and proceed upon my journey.

SPEECHES AT TRENTON, N. J.

IN THE SENATE CHAMBER.

*Mr. President and Gentlemen of the Senate of the State of New
Jersey*—I am very grateful to you for the honorable reception
of which I have been the object. I can not but remember the
place that New Jersey holds in our early history. In the early
revolutionary struggle few of the States among the old thirteen

had more of the battle-fields of the country within their limits than old New Jersey. May I be pardoned if, upon this occasion, I mention that away back in my childhood, the earliest days of my being able to read, I got hold of a small book, such a one as few of the younger members have ever seen, "WEEM's *Life of Washington.*" I remember all the accounts there given of the battle-fields and struggles for the liberties of the country, and none fixed themselves upon my imagination so deeply as the struggle here at Trenton, New Jersey. The crossing of the river; the contest with the Hessians; the great hardships endured at that time, all fixed themselves on my memory, more than any single revolutionary event; and you all know, for you have all been boys, how these early impressions last longer than any others. I recollect thinking then, boy even though I was, that there must have been something more than common that these men struggled for. I am exceedingly anxious that that thing which they struggled for; that something even more than National Independence; that something that held out a great promise to all the people of the world to all time to come—I am exceedingly anxious that this Union, the Constitution, and the liberties of the people shall be perpetuated in accordance with the original idea for which that struggle was made, and I shall be most happy indeed if I shall be an humble instrument in the hands of the Almighty and of this, his most chosen people, as the chosen instrument—also in the hands of the Almighty —for perpetuating the object of that great struggle. You give me this reception, as I understand, without distinction of party. I learn that this body is composed of a majority of gentlemen who, in the exercise of their best judgment in the choice of a Chief Magistrate, did not think I was the man. I understand, nevertheless, that they come forward here to greet me as the constitutional President of the United States—as citizens of the United States, to meet the man who, for the time being, is the representative man of the nation—united by a purpose to perpetuate the Union and liberties of the people. As such, I accept this reception more gratefully than I could do did I believe it was tendered to me as an individual.

IN THE HOUSE OF ASSEMBLY.

Mr. Speaker and Gentlemen—I have just enjoyed the honor of a reception by the other branch of this Legislature, and I return to you and them my thanks for the reception which the people of New Jersey have given, through their chosen representatives, to me as the representative, for the time being, of the majesty of the people of the United States. I appropriate to myself very little of the demonstrations of respect with which I have been greeted. I think little should be given to any man, but that it should be a manifestation of adherence to the Union and the Constitution. I understand myself to be received here by the representatives of the people of New Jersey, a majority of whom differ in opinion from those with whom I have acted. This manifestation is, therefore, to be regarded by me as expressing their devotion to the Union, the Constitution, and the liberties of the people. You, Mr. Speaker, have well said, that this is a time when the bravest and wisest look with doubt and awe upon the aspect presented by our national affairs. Under these circumstances, you will readily see why I should not speak in detail of the course I shall deem it best to pursue. It is proper that I should avail myself of all the information and all the time at my command, in order that when the time arrives in which I must speak officially, I shall be able to take the ground which I deem the best and safest, and from which I may have no occasion to swerve. I shall endeavor to take the ground I deem most just to the North, the East, the West, the South, and the whole country. I take it, I hope, in good temper, certainly with no malice towards any section. I shall do all that may be in my power to promote a peaceful settlement of all our difficulties. The man does not live who is more devoted to peace than I am. [Cheers.] None who would do more to preserve it, but it may be necessary to put the foot down firmly. [Here the audience broke out into cheers so loud, and long, that for some moments it was impossible to hear Mr. Lincoln's voice.] And if I do my duty and do right you will sustain me, will you not? [Loud cheers, and cries of "Yes, yes, we will."] Received, as I am, by the members of a Legislature, the majority of whom do not agree with me in political sentiments, I trust that I may have their assistance in piloting the ship of state through this voyage, surrounded by perils as it is, for if it should suffer wreck now, there will be no pilot ever needed for another voyage. Gentlemen, I have already spoken longer than I intended, and must beg leave to stop here.

SPEECHES AT PHILADELPHIA.

Mr. Mayor and Fellow-Citizens of Philadelphia—I appear before you to make no lengthy speech, but to thank you for this reception. The reception you have given me to-night is not to me, the man, the individual, but to the man who temporarily represents, or should represent the majesty of the nation. [Cheers.] It is true, as your worthy Mayor has said, that there is anxiety amongst the citizens of the United States at this time. I deem it a happy circumstance that this dissatisfied position of our fellow-citizens does not point us to anything in which they are being injured, or about to be injured, for which reason I have felt all the while justified in concluding that the crisis, the panic, the anxiety of the country at this time, is artificiaL If there be those who differ with me upon this subject, they have not pointed out the substantial difficulty that exists. I do not mean to say that an artificial panic may not do considerable harm : that it has done such I do not deny. The hope that has been expressed by your Mayor, that I may be able to restore peace, harmony, and prosperity to the country, is most worthy of him ; and happy, indeed, will I be if I shall be able to verify and fulfill that hope. [Tremendous cheering.] I promise you, in all sincerity, that I bring to the work a sincere heart. Whether I will bring a head equal to that heart will be for future times to determine. It were useless for me to speak of details of plans now; I shall speak officially next Monday week, if ever. If I should not speak then it were useless for me to do so now. If I do speak then it is useless for me to do so now. When I do speak I shall take such ground as I deem best calculated to restore peace, harmony, and prosperity to the country, and tend to the perpetuity of the nation and the liberty of these States and these people.

Your worthy Mayor has expressed the wish, in which I join with him, that it were convenient for me to remain in your city long enough to consult your merchants and manufacturers; or, as it were, to listen to those breathings rising within the consecrated walls wherein the Constitution of the United States, and I will add, the Declaration of Independence, were originally framed and adopted. [Enthusiastic applause.] I assure you and your Mayor that I had hoped on this occasion, and upon all occasions during my life, that I should do nothing inconsistent with the teachings of these holy and most sacred walls. I never asked anything that does not breathe from these walls. All my political warfare has been in favor of the teachings that came forth from these sacred walls. May my right hand forget its cunning, and my tongue cleave to the roof of my mouth, if ever I prove false to those teachings. Fellow-citizens, I have addressed you longer than I expected to do, and now allow me to bid you good night.

AT INDEPENDENCE HALL,

In Philadelphia, Mr. Lincoln was present to honor the raising of a new flag upon that time-honored building. He raised the flag with his own hands, and afterward made the following speech, in which he made a striking allusion, which subsequent events gave reason for believing was not made by mere chance, to the possibility of his life being sought by assassins. The purposes of the men who were then seeking to get him out of their way by the knife and the pistol, were frustrated for four years, long enough for him to accomplish the great object of his life—the preservation and the regeneration of his country.

Mr. Cuyler—I am filled with deep emotion at finding myself standing here in this place, where were collected together the wisdom, the patriotism, the devotion to principle from which sprang the institutions under which we live. You have kindly suggested to me that in my hands is the task of restoring peace to the present distracted condition of the country. I can say in return, sir, that all the political sentiments I entertain have been drawn, so far as I have been able to draw them, from the sentiments which originated in and were given to the world from this hall. I have never had a feeling, politically, that did not spring from the sentiments embodied in the Declaration of Independence. I have often pondered over the dangers which were incurred by the men who assembled here, and framed and adopted that Declaration of Independence. I have pondered over the toils that were endured by the officers and soldiers of the army who achieved that Independence. I have often inquired of myself what great principle or idea it was that kept this Confederacy so long together. It was not the mere matter of the separation of the Colonies from the mother land, but that sentiment in the Declaration of Independence which gave liberty, not alone to the people of this country, but I hope, to the world, for all future time. [Great applause.] It was that which gave promise that in due time the weight would be lifted from the shoulders of all men. This is the sentiment embodied in the Declaration of Independence. Now, my friends, can this country be saved upon that basis? If it can, I will consider myself one of the happiest men in the world if I can help to save it. If it cannot be saved upon that principle it will be truly awful. But if this country cannot be saved without giving up that principle, I was about to say I would rather be assassinated on this spot than surrender it. [Applause.] Now, in my view of the present aspect of affairs, there need be no bloodshed or war. There is no necessity for it. I am not in favor of such a course, and I may say in advance that there will be no bloodshed, unless it be forced upon the Government, and then it will be compelled to act in self-defence. [Applause.]

My friends, this is wholly an unexpected speech, and I did not expect to be called upon to say a word when I came here. I supposed it was merely to do something towards raising the flag—I may therefore, have said something indiscreet. [Cries of " No, no."]   I have said nothing but what I am willing to live by, and if it be the pleasure of Almighty God, die by.

AT HARRISBURG.

From Philadelphia, Mr. Lincoln went to Harrisburg, where he was received by the presiding officers of the Houses of Legislature at the Capitol.   To his welcome he made the following reply :

I appear before you only for a very few, brief remarks, in response to what has been said to me.   I thank you most sincerely for this reception and the generous words in which support has been promised me upon this occasion.   I thank your great Commonwealth for the overwhelming support it recently gave, not me personally, but the cause which I think a just one, in the late election.   [Loud applause.]   Allusion has been made to the fact—the interesting fact, perhaps, we should say—that I for the first time appear at the Capital of the great Commonwealth of Pennsylvania upon the birthday of the Father of his Country, in connection with that beloved anniversary connected with the history of this country.   I have already gone through one exceedingly interesting scene this morning in the ceremonies at Philadelphia.   Under the high conduct of gentlemen there, I was for the first time allowed the privilege of standing in old Independence Hall [Enthusiastic cheering], to have a few words addressed to me there, and opening up to me an opportunity of expressing, with much regret, that I had not more time to express something of my own feelings, excited by the occasion, somewhat to harmonize and give shape to the feelings that had been really the feelings of my whole life.   Besides this, our friends there had provided a magnificent flag of the country. They had it arranged so that I was given the honor of raising it to the head of its staff.   [Applause.]   And when it went up I was pleased that it went to its place by the strength of my own feeble arm, when, according to the arrangement, the cord was pulled, and it floated gloriously to the wind, without an accident, in the light, glowing sunshine of the morning.   I could not help hoping that there was, in the entire success of that beautiful ceremony, at least something of an omen of what is to come. [Loud applause.] How could I help feeling then as I often have felt? In the whole of that proceeding I was a very humble instrument. I had not provided the flag; I had not made the arrangements for elevating it to its place; I had applied but a very small portion of my feeble strength in raising it. In the whole transaction I was in the hands of the people who had arranged it, and if I can have the same generous co-operation of the people of the nation, I think the flag of our country may yet be kept flaunting gloriously. [Loud, enthusiastic, and continued cheers.] I recur for a moment but to repeat some words uttered at the hotel, in regard to what has been said about the military support which the General Government may expect from the Commonwealth of Pennsylvania in a proper emergency. To guard against any possible mistake do I recur to this. It is not with any pleasure that I contemplate the possibility that a necessity may arise in this country for the use of the military arm. [Applause.] While I am exceedingly gratified to see the manifestation upon your streets of your military force here, and exceedingly gratified at your promises here to use that force upon a proper emergency—while I make these acknowledgments, I desire to repeat, in order to preclude any possible misconstruction, that I do most sincerely hope that we shall have no use for them. [Applause.] That it will never become their duty to shed blood, and most especially never to shed fraternal blood. I promise that, so far as I may have wisdom to direct, if so painful a result shall in anywise be brought about, it shall be through no fault of mine. [Cheers.] Allusion has also been made by one of your honored speakers to some remarks recently made by myself at Pittsburg, in regard to what is supposed to be the especial interest of this great Commonwealth of Pennsylvania. I now wish only to say, in regard to that matter, that the few remarks which I uttered on that occasion were rather carefully worded. I took pains that they should be so. I have seen no occasion since to add to them, or subtract from them. I leave them precisely as they stand [applause], adding only now that I am pleased to have an expression from you, gentlemen of Pennsylvania, significant that they are satisfactory to you. And now, gentlemen of the

General Assembly of the Commonwealth of Pennsylvania, allow me to return you again my most sincere thanks.

From Harrisburg the President-elect went by a night train, and as privately as possible, to Washington : it having been thought best by his advisers thus to preclude the possibility of any excitement or disturbance, which could have been taken advantage of by his secret and desperate enemies. The day after his arrival he made the following reply to his welcome by the Mayor and Common Council

AT WASHINGTON.

Mr. Mayor—I thank you, and through you the municipal authorities of this city who accompany you, for this welcome. And as it is the first time in my life, since the present phase of politics has presented itself in this country, that I have said anything publicly within a region of country where the institution of slavery exists, I will take this occasion to say, that I think very much of the ill-feeling that has existed and still exists between the people in the section from which I came and the people here, is dependent upon a misunderstanding of one another. I therefore avail myself of this opportunity to assure you, Mr. Mayor, and all the gentlemen present, that I have not now, and never have had, any other than as kindly feelings towards you as to the people of my own section. I have not now, and never have had, any disposition to treat you in any respect otherwise than as my own neighbors. I have not now any purpose to withhold from you any of the benefits of the Constitution, under any circumstances, that I would not feel myself constrained to withhold from my own neighbors; and I hope, in a word, that when we shall become better acquainted, and I say it with great confidence, we shall like each other the more. I thank you for the kindness of this reception.

On the 4th of March, 1861, Mr. Lincoln assumed the office of President of the United States, to which Vice-

President Breckinridge had declared in the Senate that he had been lawfully elected. But in seven States, South Carolina, Georgia, Alabama, Mississippi, Texas, Florida, and Louisiana, his lawful authority could not be exercised, those States being under the control of the rebels, while Virginia, Maryland, Kentucky, and Tennessee were violently agitated upon the subject of secession. In all of these four States there was a majority of the people, including men of high character and ability, faithful to their allegiance to the National Government. President Lincoln's first task was to take such a position as would consolidate the support of that Government in the Free States and confirm the loyalty of the Border States, and if possible, prevent them from falling into the hands of the Secessionist party. This was the chief purpose of his inaugural address, which follows.

INAUGURAL ADDRESS.

Fellow-Citizens of the United States—In compliance with a custom as old as the Government itself, I appear before you to address you briefly, and to take in your presence the oath prescribed by the Constitution of the United States to be taken by the President "before he enters on the execution of his office."

I do not consider it necessary at present for me to discuss those matters of administration about which there is no special anxiety or excitement. .

Apprehension seems to exist among the people of the Southern States that by the accession of a Republican Administration their property and their peace and personal security are to be endangered. There has never been any reasonable cause for such apprehension. Indeed the most ample evidence to the contrary has all the while existed and been open to their inspection. It is found in nearly all the published speeches of him who now addresses you. I do but quote from one of those speeches when I declare that "I have no purpose, directly or indirectly, to interfere with the institution of slavery in the States where it exists. I believe I have no lawful right to do so, and I have no inclination to do so." Those who nominated and elected me did so with full knowledge that I had made this and many similar declarations, and had never recanted them. And more than this, they placed in the platform for my acceptance, and as a law to themselves and to me, the clear and emphatic resolution which I now read:

Resolved, That the maintenance inviolate of the rights of the States, and especially the rights of each State, to order and control its own domestic institutions according to its own judgment exclusively, is essential to the balance of power on which the perfection and endurance of our political fabric depend, and we denounce the lawless invasion by armed force of the soil of any State or Territory, no matter under what pretext, as among the gravest of crimes.

I now reiterate these sentiments; and, in doing so, I only impress upon the public attention the most conclusive evidence of which the case is susceptible, that the property, peace, and security of no section are to be in any wise endangered by the now incoming Administration. I add, too, that all the protection which, consistently with the Constitution and the laws, can be given, will be cheerfully given to all the States, when lawfully demanded, for whatever cause—as cheerfully to one section as to another.

There is much controversy about the delivering up of fugitives from service or labor. The clause I now read is as plainly written in the Constitution as any other of its provisions:

" No person held to service or labor in one State, under the laws thereof, escaping into another, shall, in consequence of any law or regulation therein, be discharged from such service or labor, but shall be delivered up on claim of the party to whom such service or labor may be due."

It is scarcely questioned that this provision was intended by those who made it for the reclaiming of what we call fugitive slaves; and the intention of the lawgiver is the law. All members of Congress swear their support to the whole Constitution —to this provision as much as any other. To the proposition, then, that slaves, whose cases come within the terms of this clause, "shall be delivered up," their oaths are unanimous. Now, if they would make the effort in good temper, could they not, with nearly equal unanimity, frame and pass a law by means of which to keep good that unanimous oath?

There is some difference of opinion whether this clause should be enforced by National or by State authority; but surely that difference is not a very material one. If the slave is to be surrendered, it can be of but little consequence to him, or to others by which authority it is done. And should any one, in any case, be content that his oath shall go unkept, on a mere unsubstantial controversy as to how it shall be kept?

Again, in any law upon this subject, ought not all the safeguards of liberty known in civilized and humane jurisprudence to be introduced, so that a free man be not, in any case, surrendered as a slave? And might it not be well, at the same time, to provide by law for the enforcement of that clause in the Constitution which guarantees that "the citizens of each State shall be entitled to all privileges and immunities of citizens in the several States?"

I take the official oath to-day with no mental reservations, and with no purpose to construe the Constitution or laws by any hypercritical rules. And while I do not choose now to specify particular acts of Congress as proper to be enforced, I do suggest that it will be much safer for all, both in official and private stations, to conform to and abide by all those acts which stand unrepealed, than to violate any of them, trusting to find impunity in having them held to be unconstitutional.

It is seventy-two years since the first inauguration of a President under our national Constitution. During that period, fifteen different and greatly distinguished citizens have, in succession, administered the Executive branch of the Government. They have conducted it through many perils, and generally with great success. Yet, with all this scope for precedent, I now enter upon the same task for the brief constitutional term of four years, under great and peculiar difficulty. A disruption of the Federal Union, heretofore only menaced, is now formidably attempted.

I hold that, in contemplation of universal law, and of the Constitution, *the Union of these States is perpetual.* Perpetuity is implied, if not expressed, in the fundamental law of all national governments. It is safe to assert that no government proper ever had a provision in its organic law for its own termination. Continue to execute all the express provisions of our national Constitution, and the Union will endure forever—it being impossible to destroy it, except by some action not provided for in the instrument itself.

Again, if the United States be not a government proper, but an association of States in the nature of contract merely, can it, as a contract, be peaceably unmade by less than all the parties who made it? One party to a contract may violate it—break it, so to speak; but does it not require all to lawfully rescind it?

Descending from these general principles, we find the proposition that, in legal contemplation, the Union is perpetual, confirmed by the history of the Union itself. The Union is much older than the Constitution. It was formed, in fact, by the Articles of Association in 1774. It was matured and continued by the Declaration of Independence in 1776. It was further matured, and the faith of all the then Thirteen States expressly plighted and engaged that it should be perpetual, by the Articles of Confederation in 1778. And, finally, in 1787, one of the declared objects for ordaining and establishing the Constitution was " to form a more perfect union."

But if destruction of the Union, by one, or by a part only, of the States be lawfully possible, the Union is less perfect than before, the Constitution having lost the vital element of perpetuity.

It follows, from these views, that no State, upon its own mere motion, can lawfully get out of the Union; that resolves and ordinances to that effect are legally void; and that acts of violence within any State or States, against the authority of the United States, are insurrectionary or revolutionary, according to circumstances.

I, therefore, consider that, in view of the Constitution and the laws, the Union is unbroken, and to the extent of my ability I shall take care, as the Constitution itself expressly enjoins upon me, that the laws of the Union be faithfully executed in all the States. Doing this I deem to be only a simple duty on my part; and I shall perform it, so far as practicable, unless my rightful masters, the American people, shall withhold the requisite means, or, in some authoritative manner, direct the contrary. I trust this will not be regarded as a menace, but only as the declared purpose of the Union that it will constitutionally defend and maintain itself.

In doing this there need be no bloodshed or violence; and there shall be none, unless it be forced upon the national authority. The power confided to me will be used to hold, occupy, and possess the property and places belonging to the Government, and to collect the duties and imposts; but beyond what may be but necessary for these objects, there will be no invasion, no using of force against or among the people anywhere. Where hostility to the United States, in any interior locality, shall be so great and universal as to prevent competent resident citizens from holding the Federal offices, there will be no attempt to force obnoxious strangers among the people for that object. Where the strict legal right may exist in the Government to enforce the exercise of these offices, the attempt to do so would be so irritating, and so nearly impracticable withal, I deem it better to forego, for the time, the uses of such offices.

The mails, unless repelled, will continue to be furnished in all parts of the Union. So far as possible the people everywhere shall have that sense of perfect security which is most favorable to calm thought and reflection. The course here indicated will be followed, unless current events and experience shall show a modification or change to be proper, and in every case and exigency my best discretion will be exercised, according to circumstances actually existing, and with a view and a hope of a peaceful solution of the national troubles, and the restoration of fraternal sympathies and affections.

That there are persons in one section or another who seek to destroy the Union at all events, and are glad of any pretext to do it, I will neither affirm nor deny; but if there be such, I need address no word to them. To those, however, who really love the Union, may I not speak?

Before entering upon so grave a matter as the destruction of our national fabric, with all its benefits, its memories, and its hopes, would it not be wise to ascertain precisely why we do it? Will you hazard so desperate a step while there is any possibility that any portion of the ills you fly from have no real existence? Will you while the certain ills you fly to are greater than all the real ones you fly from—will you risk the commission of so fearful a mistake?

All profess to be content in the Union, if all constitutional rights can be maintained. Is it true, then, that any right, plainly written in the Constitution, has been denied? I think not. Happily the human mind is so constituted that no party can reach to the audacity of doing this. Think, if you can, of a single instance in which a plainly written provision of the Constitution has ever been denied. If, by the mere force of numbers, a majority should deprive a minority of any clearly written constitutional right, it might, in a moral point of view justify revolution,—certainly would if such right were a vital one. But such is not our case. All the vital rights of minorities and of individuals are so plainly assured to them by affirmations and negations, guarantees and prohibitions in the Constitution, that controversies never arise concerning them. But no organic law can ever be framed with a provision specifically applicable to every question which may occur in practical administration. No foresight can anticipate, nor any document of reasonable length contain, express provisions for all possible questions. Shall fugitives from labor be surrendered by National or by State authority? The Constitution does not expressly say. May Congress prohibit slavery in the Territories? The Constitution does not expressly say. Must Congress protect slavery in the Territories? The Constitution does not expressly say.

From questions of this class spring all our constitutional controversies, and we divide upon them into majorities and minorities. If the minority will not acquiesce the majority must, or the Government must cease. There is no other alternative; for continuing the Government is acquiescence on one side or the other. If a minority in such case will secede rather than acquiesce, they make a precedent which, in turn, will divide and ruin them; for a minority of their own will secede from them whenever a majority refuses to be controlled by such minority. For instance, why may not any portion of a new Confederacy, a year or two hence, arbitrarily secede again, precisely as portions of the present Union now claim to secede from it? All who cherish disunion sentiments are now being educated to the exact temper of doing this.

Is there such perfect identity of interests among the States to compose a new Union, as to produce harmony only, and prevent renewed secession?

Plainly, the central idea of secession is the essence of anarchy. A majority held in restraint by constitutional checks and limitations, and always changing easily with deliberate changes of popular opinions and sentiments, is the only true sovereign of a free people. Whoever rejects it, does, of necessity, fly to anarchy or to despotism. Unanimity is impossible; the rule of a minority, as a permanent arrangement, is wholly inadmissible; so that, rejecting the majority principle, anarchy or despotism in some form is all that is left.

I do not forget the position assumed by some, that constitutional questions are to be decided by the Supreme Court; nor do I deny that such decisions must be binding, in any case, upon the parties to a suit as to the object of that suit, while they are also entitled to a very high respect and consideration, in all parallel cases, by all other departments of the Government. And while it is obviously possible that such decisions may be erroneous in any given case, still the evil effect following it being limited to that particular case, with the chance that it may be overruled, and never become a precedent for other cases, can better be borne than could the evils of a different practice. At the same time the candid citizen must confess that if the policy of the Government upon vital questions affecting the whole people, is to be irrevocably fixed by decisions of the Supreme Court, the instant they are made in ordinary litigation between parties in personal actions, the people will have ceased to be their own rulers, having to that extent practically resigned their Government into the hands of that eminent tribunal.

Nor is there in this view any assault upon the Court of the

Judges. It is a duty from which they may not shrink to decide cases properly brought before them, and it is no fault of theirs if others seek to turn their decisions to political purposes. One section of our country believes slavery is right, and ought to be extended, while the other believes it is wrong, and ought not to be extended. This is the only substantial dispute. The fugitive slave clause of the Constitution, and the law for the suppression of the foreign slave-trade, are each as well enforced, perhaps, as any law can ever be in a community where the moral sense of the people imperfectly support the law itself The great body of the people abide by the dry legal obligation in both cases, and a few break over in each. This, I think, cannot be perfectly cured ; and it would be worse in both cases after the separation of the sections than before. The foreign slave-trade, now imperfectly suppressed, would be ultimately revived without restriction in one section ; while fugitive slaves, now only partially surrendered, would not be surrendered at all by the other.

Physically speaking, we cannot separate. We cannot remove our respective sections from each other, nor build an impassable wall between them. A husband and wife may be divorced, and go out of the presence and beyond the reach of each other ; but the different parts of our country cannot do this. They cannot but remain face to face; and intercourse, either amicable or hostile, must continue between them. It is impossible, then, to make that intercourse more advantagous or more satisfactory after separation than before. Can aliens make treaties easier than friends can make laws? Can treaties be more faithfully enforced between aliens than laws can among friends? Suppose you go to war, you cannot fight always; and when, after much loss on both sides, and no gain on either, you cease fighting, the identical old questions as to terms of intercourse, are again upon you.

This country, with its institutions, belongs to the people who inhabit it. Whenever they shall grow weary of the existing Government, they can exercise their constitutional right of amending it, or their revolutionary right to dismember or overthrow it. I cannot be ignorant of the fact that many worthy and patriotic citizens are desirous of having the national Constitution amended. While I make no recommendation of amendments, I fully recognize the rightful authority of the people over the whole subject, to be exercised in either of the modes prescribed in the instrument itself; and I should, under existing circumstances, favor rather than oppose a fair opportunity being afforded the people to act upon it. I will venture to add, that to me the convention mode seems preferable, in that it allows amendments to originate with the people themselves, instead of only permitting them to take or reject propositions originated by others not especially chosen for the purpose, and which might not be precisely such as they would wish to either accept or refuse. I understand a proposed amendment to the Constitution—which amendment, however, I have not seen—has passed Congress, to the effect that the Federal Government shall never interfere with the domestic institutions of the States, including that of persons held to service. To avoid misconstruction of what I have said, I depart from my purpose not to speak of particular amendments so far as to say that, holding such a provision now to be implied constitutional law, I have no objections to its being made express and irrevocable.

The Chief Magistrate derives all his authority from the people, and they have conferred none upon him to fix terms for the separation of the States. The people themselves can do this also if they choose; but the Executive, as such, has nothing to do with it. His duty is to administer the present Government as it came to his hands, and to transmit it, unimpaired by him, to his successor.

Why should there not be a patient confidence in the ultimate justice of the people? Is there any better or equal hope in the world? In our present differences, is either party without faith of being in the right? If the Almighty Ruler of Nations, with his eternal truth and justice, be on your side of the North, or on yours of the South, that truth and that justice will surely prevail, by the judgment of this great tribunal of the American people.

By the frame of the Government under which we live, the same people have wisely given their public servants but little power for mischief; and have, with equal wisdom, provided for the return of that little to their own hands at very short intervals. While the people retain their virtue and vigilance, no Administration, by any extreme of wickedness or folly, can very seriously injure the Government in the short space of four years.

My countrymen, one and all, think calmly and well upon this whole subject. Nothing valuable can be lost, by taking time. If there be an object to hurry any of you in hot haste to a step which you would never take deliberately, that object will be frustrated by taking time, but no good object can be frustrated by it. Such of you as are now dissatisfied still have the old Constitution unimpaired, and, on the sensitive point, the laws of your own framing under it; while the new Administration will have no immediate power, if it would, to change either. If it were admitted that you who are dissatisfied hold the right side in the dispute, there still is no single good reason for precipitate action. Intelligence, patriotism, Christianity and a firm reliance on Him who has never yet forsaken this favored land, are still competent to adjust, in the best way, all our present difficulty.

In your hands, my dissatisfied fellow-countrymen, and not in mine, is the momentous issue of civil war. The Government will not assail you.

You can have no conflict without being yourselves the aggressors. You have no oath registered in heaven to destroy the Government; while I shall have the most solemn one to "preserve, protect, and defend" it.

I am loth to close. We are not enemies, but friends. We must not be enemies. Though passion may have strained, it must not break our bonds of affection.

The mystic chord of memory, stretching from every battle-field and patriot grave to every living heart and hearthstone all over this broad land, will yet swell the chorus of the Union, when again touched, as surely they will be, by the better angels of our nature.   ABRAHAM LINCOLN.

President Lincoln's views and announcement of his

policy in this address met general approval throughout the Free States; but in the Border Slave States it was at first a mere bone of contention between the Union men and the secessionists. The State Convention of Virginia, a decided majority of which was against secession, sent a committee of three to the President to ask him to define his position toward the South more clearly. He replied by the following letter which was presented to the Convention by the Committee, on the 13th of April:

REPLY TO THE COMMITTEE OF THE VIRGINIA CONVENTION.

To Hon. Messrs. Preston, Stuart, and Randolph:

GENTLEMEN: As a committee of the Virginia Convention, now in session, you present me a preamble and resolution in these words:

Whereas, In the opinion of this Convention, the uncertainty which prevails in the public mind as to the policy which the Federal Executive intends to pursue towards the seceded States, is extremely injurious to the industrial and commercial interests of the country, tends to keep up an excitement which is unfavorable to the adjustment of the pending difficulties, and threatens a disturbance of the public peace; therefore,

Resolved, That a committee of three delegates be appointed to await on the President of the United States, present to him this preamble, and respectfully ask him to communicate to this Convention the policy which the Federal Executive intends to pursue in regard to the Confederate States.

In answer I have to say, that having, at the beginning of my official term, expressed my intended policy as plainly as I was able, it is with deep regret and mortification I now learn there is great and injurious uncertainty in the public mind as to what that policy is, and what course I intend to pursue. Not having as yet seen occasion to change, it is now my purpose to pursue the course marked out in the Inaugural Address. I commend a careful consideration of the whole document as the best expression I can give to my purposes. As I then and therein said, I now repeat, "The power confided in me will be used to hold, occupy, and possess property and places belonging to the Government, and to collect the duties and imposts; but beyond what is necessary for these objects there will be no invasion, no using of force against or among the people anywhere." By the words "property and places belonging to the Government," I chiefly allude to the military posts and property which were in possession of the Government when it came into my hands. But if, as now appears to be true, in pursuit of a purpose to drive the United States authority from these places, an unprovoked assault has been made upon Fort Sumter, I shall hold myself at liberty to repossess it, if I can, like places which had been seized before the Government was devolved upon me; and in any event I shall, to the best of my ability, repel force by force. In case it proves true that Fort Sumter has been assaulted, as is reported, I shall perhaps, cause the United States mails to be withdrawn from all the States which claim to have seceded, believing that the commencement of actual war against the Government, justifies and possibly demands it. I scarcely need to say that I consider the military posts and property situated within the States which claim to have seceded, as yet belonging to the Government of the United States as much as they did before the supposed secession. Whatever else I may do for the purpose, I shall not attempt to collect the duties and imposts by any armed invasion of any part of the country; not meaning by this, however, that I may not land a force deemed necessary to relieve a fort upon the border of the country. From the fact that I have quoted a part of the Inaugural Address, it must not be inferred that I repudiate any other part, the whole of which I reaffirm, except so far as what I now say of the mails may be regarded as a modification.   ABRAHAM LINCOLN.

The leading secessionists felt sure that if they could bring about a collision between what they called the South and the Government, the immediate effect would be such an aroused spirit of resistance among all the leading men and "fire-eaters" in the Slave States as would immediately enable the secessionists to seize power in the Border States.   This collision they sought at Charleston, where, during the unavoidable inaction of the Government, they had at first planned the seizure of Fort Moultrie, under command of Major Anderson, and after his retirement with his little garrison to Fort Sumter, had surrounded the latter work with powerful shore batteries and a force of many thousand men.   When Mr. Lincoln took office it was already impossible to send reinforcements to the garrison before their provisions would be exhausted; and upon it being made known that provisions were about to be sent, General Beauregard, by command of Mr. Jefferson Davis, who had been elected "Provisional President" of a temporary Confederacy with headquarters at Montgomery, Alabama, opened his batteries upon Major Anderson, and after two days' bombardment set the fort on fire, and made it untenable.   It was evacuated on the 14th of April, amid the profoundest excitement throughout the country, and on the 15th Mr. Lincoln issued the following

PROCLAMATION.

Whereas, the laws of the United States have been for some time past and now are opposed, and the execution thereof obstructed, in the States of South Carolina, Georgia, Alabama, Florida, Mississippi, Louisiana, and Texas, by combinations too powerful to be suppressed by the ordinary course of judicial proceedings, or by the powers vested in the marshals by law; now, therefore, I Abraham Lincoln, President of the United States, in virtue of the power in me vested by the Constitution and the laws, have thought fit to call forth, and hereby do call forth, the militia of the several States of the Union to the aggregate number of 75,000, in order to suppress said combinations, and to cause the laws to be duly executed.

The details for this object will be immediately communicated to the State authorities through the War Department. I appeal to all loyal citizens to favor, facilitate, and aid this effort to maintain the honor, the integrity, and existence of our national Union, and the perpetuity of popular government, and to redress wrongs already long enough endured. I deem it proper to say that the first service assigned to the forces hereby called forth, will probably be to repossess the forts, places, and property which have been seized from the Union; and in every event the utmost care will be observed, consistently with the objects aforesaid, to avoid any devastation, any destruction of, or interference with, property, or any disturbance of peaceful citizens of any part of the country; and I hereby command the persons composing the combinations aforesaid, to disperse and retire peaceably to their respective abodes, within twenty days from this date.

Deeming that the present condition of public affairs presents an extraordinary occasion, I do hereby, in virtue of the power in me vested by the Constitution, convene both houses of Congress. The Senators and Representatives are, therefore, summoned to assemble at their respective chambers at twelve o'clock, noon, on Thursday, the fourth day of July next, then and there to consider and determine such measures as, in their wisdom, the pulbic safety and interest may seem to demand.

In witness whereof, I have hereunto set my hand, and caused the seal of the United States to be affixed.

Done at the City of Washington, this fifteenth day of April, in the year of our Lord one thousand eight hundred and sixty-one, and of the independence of the United States the eighty-fifth.

By the President,   ABRAHAM LINCOLN.

WILLIAM H. SEWARD, *Secretary of State.*

There can be no question that the President issued the foregoing Proclamation with some doubt as to the manner in which it would be received by the country. He must have been somewhat surprised as well as overjoyed at finding that it was the occasion of an instant and overwhelming outburst of loyalty and devotion to the flag. If instead of asking for 75,000 men he had asked for 750,000, they would have been forthcoming. As the confederated insurgents had issued proposals for letters of marque against the commerce of the United States, the President, to meet them on this point, issued the following:

PROCLAMATION.

Whereas, an insurrection against the Government of the United States has broken out in the States of South Carolina, Georgia, Alabama, Florida, Mississippi, Louisiana, and Texas, and the laws of the United States for the collection of the revenue cannot be efficiently executed therein conformable to that provision of the Constitution which requires duties to be uniform throughout the United States:

And *whereas* a combination of persons, engaged in such insurrection, have threatened to grant pretended letters of marque to authorize the bearers thereof to commit assaults on the lives, vessels, and property of the good citizens of the country, lawfully engaged in commerce on the high seas, and in waters of the United States:

And *whereas* an Executive Proclamation has been already issued, requiring the persons engaged in these disorderly proceedings to desist therefrom, calling out a militia force for the purpose of repressing the same, and convening Congress in extraordinary session to deliberate and determine thereon:

Now, therefore, I, Abraham Lincoln, President of the United States, with a view to the same purposes before mentioned, and to the protection of the public peace, and the lives and property of quiet and orderly citizens pursuing their lawful occupations, until Congress shall have assembled and deliberated on the said unlawful proceedings, or until the same shall have ceased, have further deemed it advisable to set on foot a blockade of the ports within the States aforesaid, in pursuance of the laws of the United States and of the laws of nations in such cases provided. For this purpose, a competent force will be posted so as to prevent entrance and exit of vessels from the ports aforesaid. If, therefore, with a view to violate such blockade, a vessel shall approach, or shall attempt to leave any of the said ports, she will be duly warned by the commander of one of the blockading vessels, who will endorse on her register the fact and date of such warning; and if the same vessel shall again attempt to leave or enter the blockaded port, she will be captured and sent to the nearest convenient port, for such proceedings against her and her cargo as prize, as may be deemed advisable.

And I hereby proclaim and declare, that if any person, under the pretended authority of such States, or under any other pretence, shall molest a vessel of the United States, or the persons or cargo on board of her, such persons will be held amenable to the laws of the United States for the prevention and punishment of piracy.

By the President, ABRAHAM LINCOLN.

WILLIAM H. SEWARD, *Secretary of State.*

WASHINGTON, *April* 19, 1861.

The consequences of the attack upon Fort Sumter were in the Slave States just what the insurgent leaders expected. Virginia was thrown immediately (on the 17th of April) into the hands of the insurgents. Tennessee soon followed, her Union majority being for the moment overborne by the audacity of the secessionists. But Maryland, Kentucky, and Missouri, although profoundly agitated, were kept within the pale of the Union. It is needless here to recount the exciting scenes which took place in the first of these States, and especially in Baltimore, immediately after the issuing of the Proclamation of April 15th, or the manner in which, by the wisdom and forbearance of Mr. Lincoln, and the sagacity and energetic action of General Butler, Maryland was prevented from falling into the hands of the audacious minority who wished to side with the insurgents. The Governor of this State in his perplexity at the novel condition of public affairs, so far forgot himself as to propose to Mr. Lincoln that the dispute between the Government and the rebels should be referred to the British Minister for arbitration. To this the following reply was made for Mr. Lincoln by Mr. Seward :

If eighty years could have obliterated all the other noble sentiments of that age [1776] in Maryland, the President would be hopeful, nevertheless, that there is one that would forever remain there and everywhere. That sentiment is, that no domestic contention whatever that may arise among the parties of this republic, ought in any case to be referred to any foreign arbitrament, least of all to the arbitrament of a European monarchy.

And here may be properly introduced the following extract of a despatch from Mr. Seward to Mr. Adams, dated April 10th, 1865, in which the bold and comprehensive policy of Mr. Lincoln's administration in regard to our foreign relations, which was maintained without swerving throughout the war, is clearly set forth.

POSITION ASSUMED TOWARDS FOREIGN GOVERNMENTS.

Before considering the arguments you are to use, it is important to indicate those which you are not to employ in executing that mission :

First. The President has noticed, as the whole American people have, with much emotion, the expressions of good-will and friendship toward the United States, and of concern for their present embarrassments, which have been made on apt occasions, by her Majesty and her ministers. You will make due acknowledgments for these manifestations, but at the same time you will not rely on any mere sympathies or national kindness. You will make no admissions of weakness in our Constitution, or of apprehension on the part of the Government. You will rather prove, as you easily can, by comparing the history of our country with that of other States, that its Constitution and Government are really the strongest and surest which have ever been erected for the safety of any people. You will in no case listen to any suggestion of compromise by this Government, under foreign auspices, with its discontented citizens. If, as the President does not at all apprehend, you shall unhappily find her Majesty's Government tolerating the application of the so-called seceding States, or wavering about it, you will not leave them to suppose for a moment that they can grant that application and remain the friends of the United States. You may even assure them promptly, in that case, that if they determine to recognize, they may at once prepare to enter into an alliance with the enemies of this republic. You alone will represent your country at London, and you will represent the whole of it there. When you are asked to divide that duty with others, diplomatic relations between the Government of Great Britain and this Government will be suspended, and will remain so until it shall be seen which of the two is most strongly intrenched in the confidence of their respective nations and of mankind.

You will not be allowed, however, even if you were disposed, as the President is sure you will not be, to rest your opposition to the application of the Confederate States on the ground of any favor this Administration, or the party which chiefly called it into existence, proposes to show to Great Britain, or claims that Great Britain ought to show them. You will not consent to draw into debate before the British Government any opposing moral principles which may be supposed to lie at the foundation of the controversy between those States and the Federal Union.

You will indulge in no expressions of harshness or disrespect, or even impatience, concerning the seceding States, their agents, or their people. But you will, on the contrary, all the while remember that those States are now, as they always heretofore have been, and, notwithstanding their temporary self-delusion, they must always continue to be, equal and honored members of this Federal Union, and that their citizens throughout all political misunderstandings and alienations still are and always must be our kindred and countrymen. In short, all your arguments must belong to one of three classes, namely: *First*. Arguments drawn from the principles of public law and natural justice, which regulate the intercourse of equal States. *Secondly*. Arguments which concern equally the honor, welfare, and happiness of the discontented States, and the honor, welfare, and happiness of the whole Union. *Thirdly*. Arguments which are equally conservative of the rights and interests, and even sentiments of the United States, and just in their bearing upon the rights, interests, and sentiments of Great Britain and all other nations.

That paper purports to contain a decision at which the British Government has arrived, to the effect that this country is divided into two belligerent parties, of which this Government represents one, and that Great Britain assumes the attitude of a neutral between them.

This Government could not, consistently with a just regard for the sovereignty of the United States, permit itself to debate these novel and extraordinary positions with the Government of her Britannic Majesty; much less can we consent that that Government shall announce to us a decision derogating from that sovereignty, at which it has arrived without previously conferring with us upon the question. The United States are still solely and exclusively sovereign within the territories they have lawfully acquired and long possessed, as they have always been. They are at peace with all the world, as, with unimportant exceptions, they have always been. They are living under the obligations of the law of nations, and of treaties with Great Britain, just the same now as heretofore; they are, of course, the friends of Great Britain, and they insist that Great Britain shall remain their friends now, just as she has hitherto been. Great Britain, by virtue of these relations, is a stranger to parties and sections in this country, whether they are loyal to the United States or not, and Great Britain can neither rightfully qualify the sovereignty of the United States, nor concede, nor recognize any rights, or interests, or power of any party, State, or section, in contravention to the unbroken sovereignty of the Federal Union. What is now seen in this country is the occurrence, by no means peculiar, but frequent in all countries, more frequent even in Great Britain than here, of an armed insurrection engaged in attempting to overthrow the regularly constituted and established Government. There is, of course, the employment of force by the Government to suppress the insurrection, as every other government necessarily employs force in such cases. But these incidents by no means constitute a state of war impairing the sovereignty of the Government, creating belligerent sections, and entitling foreign States to intervene, or to act as neutrals between them, or in any other way to cast off their lawful obligations to the nation thus for the moment disturbed. Any other principle than this would be to resolve government everywhere into a thing of accident and caprice, and ultimately all human society into a state of perpetual war.

We do not go into any argument of fact or of law in support of the position we have thus assumed. They are simply the suggestions of the instinct of self-defence, the primary law of human action—not more the law of individual than of national life.

The same proclamation which called for a volunteer army summoned an extra session of Congress, to take such measures as were required by the extraordinary state of the country. Congress assembled on the 4th of July, and received from the President the following Message, in which he set forth in detail the events which had made it necessary for him to call the Houses together. The document is remarkable not only for the calm, judicial tone which the writer preserved in it in the midst of such a period of excitement, but for the clearness with which it sets forth those views of the constitutional questions involved in the struggle just begun, which were sustained in the end by the soundest intellect in the country as well as by the whole mass of the people.

MESSAGE TO THE SPECIAL SESSION OF CONGRESS, JULY 4TH, 1861.

Fellow-Citizens of the Senate and House of Representatives—
Having been convened on an extraordinary occasion, as authorized by the constitution, your attention is not called to any ordinary subject of legislation.

At the beginning of the present presidential term, four months ago, the functions of the Federal Government were found to be generally suspended within the several States of South Carolina, Georgia, Alabama, Mississippi, Louisiana, and Florida, excepting only those of the Post-Office Department.

Within these States all the forts, arsenals, dock-yards, custom-houses and the like, including the movable and stationary property in and about them, had been seized, and were held in open hostility to this Government, excepting only Forts Pickens, Taylor, and Jefferson, on and near the Florida coast, and Fort Sumter, in Charleston harbor, South Carolina. The forts thus seized had been put in improved condition, new ones had been built, and armed forces had been organized and were organizing, all avowedly for the same hostile purpose.

The forts remaining in the possession of the Federal Government in and near these States were either besieged or menaced by warlike preparations, and especially Fort Sumter was nearly surrounded by well-protected hostile batteries, with guns equal in quality to the best of its own, and outnumbering the latter as perhaps ten to one. A disproportionate share of the Federal muskets and rifles had somehow found their way into these States, and had been seized to be used against the Government. Accumulations of the public revenue, lying within them, had been seized for the same object. The Navy was scattered in distant seas, leaving but a very small part of it within the immediate reach of the Government. Officers of the Federal Army and Navy had resigned in great numbers; and of those resigning, a large proportion had taken up arms against the Government. Simultaneously, and in connection with all this, the purpose to sever the Federal Union was openly avowed. In accordance with this purpose, an ordinance had been adopted in each of these States, declaring the States, respectively, to be separated from the National Union. A formula for instituting a combined government of these States had been promulgated; and this illegal organization, in the character of Confederate States, was already invoking recognition, aid, and intervention from foreign Powers.

Finding this condition of things, and believing it to be an imperative duty upon the incoming Executive to prevent, if possible, the consummation of such attempt to destroy the Federal Union, a choice of means to that end became indispensable. This choice was made, and was declared in the Inaugural Address. The policy chosen looked to the exhaustion of all peaceful measures before a resort to any stronger ones. It sought only to hold the public places and property not already wrested from the Government, and to collect the revenue, relying for the rest on time, discussion, and the ballot-box. It promised a continuance of the mails, at Government expense, to the very people who were resisting the Government; and it gave repeated pledges against any disturbance to any of the people, or any their rights. Of all that which a President might constitutionally and justifiably do in such a case, everything was forborne, without which it was believed possible to keep the Government on foot.

On the 5th of March (the present incumbent's first full day in office,) a letter of Major Anderson, commanding at Fort Sumter, written on the 28th of February, and received at the War Department on the 4th of March, was by that Department placed in his hands. This letter expressed the professional opinion of the writer, that reinforcements could not be thrown into that fort within the time for his relief, rendered necessary by the limited supply of provisions, and with a view of holding possession of the same, with a force of less than twenty thousand good and well-disciplined men. This opinion was concurred in by all the officers of his command, and their *memoranda* on the subject were made enclosures of Major Anderson's letter. The whole was immediately laid before Lieutenant-General Scott, who at once concurred with Major Anderson in opinion. On reflection, however, he took full time, consulting with other officers, both of the army and the navy; and at the end of four days came reluctantly, but decidedly, to the same conclusion as before. He also stated at the same time that no such sufficient force was then at the control of the Government, or could be raised and brought to the ground within the time when the provisions in the fort would be exhausted. In a purely military point of view, this reduced the duty of the Administration in the case to the mere matter of getting the garrison out of the fort.

It was believed, however, that to so abandon that position, under the circumstances, would be utterly ruinous; that the necessity under which it was to be done would not be fully understood; that by many it would be construed as a part of a voluntary policy; that at home it would discourage the friends of the Union, embolden its adversaries, and go far to insure to the latter a recognition abroad; that in fact, it would be our national destruction consummated. This could not be allowed. Starvation was not yet upon the garrison; and ere it would be reached Fort Pickens might be reinforced. This would be a clear indication of policy, and would better enable the country to accept the evacuation of Fort Sumter as a military necessity. An order was at once directed to be sent for the landing of the troops from the steamship Brooklyn into Fort Pickens. This order could not go by land, but must take the longer and slower route by sea. The first return news from the order was received just one week before the fall of Fort Sumter. The news itself was that the officer commanding the Sabine, to which vessel the troops had been transferred from the Brooklyn, acting upon some *quasi* armistice of the late Administration (and of the existence of which the present Administration, up to the time the order was despatched, had only too vague and uncertain rumors to fix attention), had refused to land the troops.

To now reinforce Fort Pickens before a crisis would be reached at Fort Sumter was impossible—rendered so by the near exhaustion of provisions in the latter-named fort. . In precaution against such a conjuncture, the Government had a few days before commenced preparing an expedition, as well adapted as might be, to relieve Fort Sumter, which expedition was intended to be ultimately used or not, according to circumstances. The strongest anticipated case for using it was now presented, and it was resolved to send it forward. As had been intended in this contingency, it was also resolved to notify the Governor of South Carolina, that he might expect an attempt would be made to provision the fort; and that, if the attempt should not be resisted, there would be no effort to throw in men, arms, or ammunition, without further notice, or in case of an attack upon the fort. This notice was accordingly given; whereupon the fort was attacked and bombarded to its fall, without even awaiting the arrival of the provisioning expedition.

It is thus seen that the assault upon and reduction of Fort Sumter was in no sense a matter of self-defence upon the part of the assailants. They well knew that the garrison in the fort could by no possibility commit aggression upon them. They knew—they were expressly notified—that the giving of bread to the few brave and hungry men of the garrison was all which would on that occasion be attempted, unless themselves, by resisting so much, should provoke more. They knew that this Government desired to keep the garrison in the fort, not to assail them, but to maintain visible possession, and thus to preserve the Union from actual and immediate dissolution—trusting, as hereinbefore stated, to time, discussion, and the ballot-box for final adjustment; and they assailed and reduced the fort for precisely the reverse object—to drive out the visible authority of the Federal Union, and thus force it to immediate dissolution. That this was their object the Executive well understood; and having said to them in the Inaugural Address, "You can have no conflict without being yourselves the aggressors," he took pains not only to keep this declaration good, but also to keep the case so free from the power of ingenious sophistry that the world should not be able to misunderstand it. By the affair at Fort Sumter, with its surrounding circumstances, that point was reached. Then and thereby the assailants of the Government began the conflict of arms, without a gun in sight, or in expectancy to return their fire, save only the few in the fort, sent to that harbor years before for their own protection, and still ready to give that protection in whatever was lawful. In this act, discarding all else, they have forced upon the country the distinct issue, "immediate dissolution or blood."

And this issue embraces more than the fate of these United States. It presents to the whole family of man the question, whether a constitutional republic or democracy—a government of the people by the same people—can or cannot maintain its territorial integrity against its own domestic foes. It presents the question, whether discontented individuals, too few in numbers to control administration, according to organic law, in any case, can always, upon the pretences made in this case or on any other pretences, or arbitrarily, without any pretence, break up their Government, and thus practically put an end to free government upon the earth. It forces us to ask, "Is there, in all republics, this inherent and fatal weakness?" "Must a government, of necessity, be too strong for the liberties of its own people, or too weak to maintain its own existence?"

So viewing the issue, no choice was left but to call out the war power of the Government; and so, to resist force employed for its destruction by force for its preservation.

The call was made, and the response of the country was most gratifying, surpassing in unanimity and spirit the most sanguine expectation. Yet none of the States commonly called Slave States, except Delaware, gave a regiment through regular State organization. A few regiments have been organized within some others of those States by individual enterprise, and received into the Government service. Of course, the seceded States, so called (and to which Texas had been joined about the time of the inauguration), gave no troops to the cause of the Union. The Border States, so called, were not uniform in their action, some of them being almost for the Union, while in others —as Virginia, North Carolina, Tennessee, and Arkansas—the Union sentiment was nearly repressed and silenced. The course taken in Virgina was the most remarkable—perhaps the most important.   A convention, elected by the people of that State to consider this very question of disrupting the Federal Union, was in session at the capital of Virginia when Fort Sumter fell. To this body the people had chosen a large majority of professed Union men.   Almost immediately after the fall of Sumter many members of that majority went over to the original disunion minority, and with them adopted an ordinance for withdrawing the State from the Union.   Whether this change was wrought by their great approval of the assault upon Sumter, or their great resentment at the Government's resistance to that assault is not definitely known.   Although they submitted the ordinance for ratification to a vote of the people, to be taken on a day then somewhat more than a month distant, the Convention and the Legislature (which was also in session at the same time and place), with leading men of the State not members of either, immediately commenced acting as if the State were already out of the Union.   They pushed military preparations vigorously forward all over the State.   They seized the United States armory at Harper's Ferry, and the navy-yard at Gosport, near Norfolk.   They received—perhaps invited—into their State large bodies of troops, with their warlike appointments from the so-called seceded States.   They formally entered into a treaty of temporary alliance and co-operation with the so-called " Confederate States," and sent members to their Congress at Montgomery; and, finally, they permitted the insurrectionary government to be transferred to their capital at Richmond.

The people of Virginia have thus allowed this giant insurrection to make its nest within her borders; and this Government has no choice left but to deal with it where it finds it.   And it has the less regret, as loyal citizens have in due form claimed its protection.   Those loyal citizens this Government is bound to recognize and protect as being Virginia.

In the Border States, so-called—in fact, the Middle States— there are those who favor a policy which they call " armed neutrality"—that is, an arming of those States to prevent the Union forces passing one way, or the disunion the other, over their soil.   This would be disunion completed.   Figuratively speaking, it would be the building of an impassable wall along the line of separation—and yet not quite an impassable one, for, under the guise of neutrality, it would tie the hands of Union men, and freely pass supplies from among them to the insurrectionists, which it could not do as an open enemy. At a stroke it would take all the trouble off the hands of secession, except only what proceeds from the external blockade. It would do for the disunionists that which of all things they most desire—feed them well, and give them disunion without a struggle of their own. It recognizes no fidelity to the Constitution, no obligation to maintain the Union; and while very many who have favored it are doubtless loyal citizens, it is, nevertheless, very injurious in effect.

Recurring to the action of the Government, it may be stated that at first a call was made for seventy-five thousand militia; and rapidly following this, a proclamation was issued for closing the ports of the insurrectionary districts by proceedings in the nature of a blockade. So far all was believed to be strictly legal. At this point the insurrectionists announced their purpose to enter upon the practice of privateering.

Other calls were made for volunteers to serve for three years unless sooner discharged, and also for large additions to the regular army and navy. These measures, whether strictly legal or not, were ventured upon under what appeared to be a popular demand and a public necessity; trusting then, as now, that Congress would readily ratify them. It is believed that nothing has been done beyond the constitutional competency of Congress.

Soon after the first call for militia, it was considered a duty to authorize the Commanding-General, in proper cases, according to his discretion, to suspend the privilege of the writ of habeas corpus, or, in other words, to arrest and detain, without resort to the ordinary processes and forms of law, such individuals as he might deem dangerous to the public safety. This authority has purposely been exercised but very sparingly. Nevertheless, the legality and propriety of what has been done under it are questioned, and the attention of the country has been called to the proposition, that one who has sworn to "take care that the laws be faithfully executed," should not himself violate them. Of course, some consideration was given to the question of power and propriety before this matter was acted upon. The whole of the laws which were required to be faithfully executed were being resisted, and failing of execution in nearly one-third of the States. Must they be allowed to finally fail of execution, even had it been perfectly clear that by the use of the means necessary to their execution some single law, made in such extreme tenderness of the citizen's liberty that practically it relieves more of the guilty than of the innocent, should to a very limited extent be violated? To state the question more directly: Are all the laws but one to go unexecuted, and the Government itself go to pieces, lest that one be violated? Even in such a case, would not the official oath be broken if the Government should be overthrown, when it was believed that disregarding the single law would tend to preserve it? But it was not believed that this question was presented. It was not believed that any law was violated. The provision of the Constitution that "the privilege of the writ of habeas corpus shall not be suspended unless, when, in cases of rebellion or invasion, the public safety may require it," is equivalent to a provision—is a provision—that such privilege may be suspended when, in case of rebellion or invasion, the public safety does require it. It was decided that we have a case of rebellion, and that the public safety does require the qualified suspension of the privilege of the writ, which was authorized to be made. Now, it is insisted that Congress, and not the Executive, is vested with this power. But the Constitution itself is silent as to which or who is to exercise the power; and as the provision was plainly made for a dangerous emergency, it cannot be believed the framers of the instrument intended that in every case the danger should run its course until Congress could be called together, the very assembling of which might be prevented, as was intended in this case, by the rebellion.

No more extended argument is now offered, as an opinion, at some length, will probably be presented by the Attorney-General. Whether there shall be any legislation on the subject and, if any, what, is submitted entirely to the better judgment of Congress.

The forbearance of this Government has been so extraordinary, and so long continued, as to lead some foreign nations to shape their action as if they supposed the early destruction of our national Union was probable. While this, on discovery, gave the Executive some concern, he is now happy to say that the sovereignty and rights of the United States are now everywhere practically respected by foreign powers; and a general sympathy with the country is manifested throughout the world.

The reports of the Secretaries of the Treasury, War, and the Navy, will give the information in detail deemed necessary and convenient for your deliberation and action; while the Executive and all the Departments will stand ready to supply omissions, or to communicate new facts considered important for you to know.

It is now recommended that you give the legal means for making this contest a short and decisive one; that you place at the control of the Government, for the work, at least four hundred thousand men and $400,000,000. That number of men is about one-tenth of those of proper ages within the regions where, apparently, all are willing to engage; and the sum is less than a twenty-third part of the money value owned by the men who seem ready to devote the whole. A debt of $600,000,000 now, is a less sum per head than was the debt of our Revolution when we came out of that struggle; and the money value in the country now bears even a greater proportion to what it was then, than does the population. Surely each man has as strong a motive now to preserve our liberties as each had then to establish them.

A right result, at this time, will be worth more to the world than ten times the men and ten times the money. The evidence reaching us from the country leaves no doubt that the material for the work is abundant, and that it needs only the hand of legislation to give it legal sanction, and the hand of the Executive to give it practical shape and efficiency. One of the greatest perplexities of the Government is to avoid receiving troops faster than it can provide for them. In a word, the people will save their Government, if the Government itself will do its part only indifferently well.

It might seem, at first thought, to be of little difference whether the present movement at the South be called "secession," or "rebellion." The movers, however, will understand the difference. At the beginning, they knew they could never raise their treason to any respectable magnitude by any name which implies violation of law. They knew their people possessed as much of moral sense, as much of devotion to law and order, and as much pride in, and reverence for the history and Government of their common country, as any other civilized and patriotic people. They knew they could make no advancement directly in the teeth of these strong and noble sentiments. Accordingly, they commenced by an insidious debauching of the public mind. They invented an ingenious sophism, which, if conceded, was followed by perfectly logical steps, through all the incidents, to the complete destruction of the Union. The sophism itself is, that any State of the Union may, consistently with the national Constitution, and therefore lawfully and peacefully, withdraw from the Union without the consent of the Union, or of any other State. The little disguise that the supposed right is to be exercised only for just cause, themselves to be the sole judges of its justice, is too thin to merit any notice.

With rebellion thus sugar-coated they have been drugging the public mind of their section for more than thirty years, and until at length they have brought many good men to a willingness to take up arms against the Government the day after some assemblage of men have enacted the farcical pretence of taking their State out of the Union, who could have been brought to no such thing the day before.

This sophism derives much, perhaps the whole, of its currency from the assumption that there is some omnipotent and sacred supremacy pertaining to a State—to each State of our Federal Union. Our States have neither more nor less power than that reserved to them in the Union by the Constitution—no one of them ever having been a State out of the Union. The original ones passed into the Union even before they cast off their British colonial dependence; and the new ones each came into the Union directly from a condition of dependence, excepting Texas. And even Texas, in its temporary independence, was never designated a State. The new ones only took the designation of States on coming into the Union, while that name was first adopted by the old ones in and by the Declaration of Independence. Therein the "United Colonies" were declared to be "free and independent States;" but, even then, the object plainly was not to declare their independence of one another, or of the Union, but directly the contrary; as their mutual pledge and their mutual action before, at the time, and afterwards, abundantly show. The express plighting of faith by each and all of the original thirteen in the Articles of Confederation, two years later, that the Union shall be perpetual, is most conclusive. Having never been States, either in substance or in name, outside of the Union, whence this magical omnipotence of "State rights," asserting a claim of power to lawfully destroy the Union itself? Much is said about the "sovereignty" of the States; but the word even is not in the national Constitution; nor, as is believed, in any of the State constitutions. What is "sovereignty" in the political sense of the term? Would it be far wrong to define it "a political community without a political superior?" Tested by this, no one of our States, except Texas, ever was a sovereignty. And even Texas gave up the character on coming into the Union; by which act she acknowledged the Constitution of the United States and the laws and treaties of the United States made in pursuance of the Constitution, to be for her the supreme law of the land. The States have their *status* in the Union, and they have no other legal *status*. If they break from this, they can only do so against law and by revolution. The Union, and not themselves, separately, procured their independence and their liberty. By conquest or purchase the Union gave each of them whatever of independence or liberty it has. The Union is older than any of the States, and, in fact, it created them as States. Originally some dependent colonies made the Union, and, in turn, the Union threw off their old dependence for them, and made them States, such as they are. Not one of them ever had a State constitution independent of the Union. Of course, it is not forgotten that all the new States framed their constitutions before they entered the Union; nevertheless dependent upon, and preparatory to, coming into the Union.

Unquestionably the States have the powers and rights reserved to them in and by the national Constitution; but among these, surely, are not included all conceivable powers, however mischievous or destructive; but, at most, such only as were known in the world, at the time, as governmental powers; and, certainly, a power to destroy the Government itself had never been known as a governmental—as a merely administrative power. This relative matter of national power and State rights, as a principle, is no other than the principle of generality and locality. Whatever concerns the whole should be confided to the whole—to the General Government; while whatever concerns only the State should be left exclusively to the State. This is all there is of original principle about it. Whether the national Constitution in defining boundaries between the two has applied the principle with exact accuracy, is not to be questioned. We are all bound by that defining, without question.

What is now combated, is the position that secession is consistent with the Constitution—is lawful and peaceful. It is not contended that there is any express law for it; and nothing should ever be implied as law which leads to unjust or absurd consequences. The nation purchased with money the countries out of which several of these States were formed; is it just that they shall go off without leave and without refunding? The nation paid very large sums (in the aggregate, I believe, nearly a hundred millions) to relieve Florida of the aboriginal tribes; is it just that she shall now be off without consent, or without making any return? The nation is now in debt for money applied to the benefit of these so-called seceding States in common with the rest; is it just either that creditors shall go unpaid, or the remaining States pay the whole? A part of the present national debt was contracted to pay the old debts of Texas; is it just that she shall leave and pay no part of this herself?

Again, if one State may secede, so may another; and when

all shall have seceded, none is left to pay the debts. Is this quite just to creditors? Did we notify them of this sage view of ours when we borrowed their money? If we now recognize this doctrine by allowing the seceders to go in peace, it is difficult to see what we can do if others choose to go, or to extort terms upon which they will promise to remain.

The seceders insist that our constitution admits of secession. They have assumed to make a national constitution of their own, in which, of necessity, they have either discarded or retained the right of secession, as they insist it exists in ours. If they have discarded it, they thereby admit that, on principle, it ought not to exist in ours. If they have retained it, by their own construction of ours, they show that to be consistent they must secede from one another whenever they shall find it the easiest way of settling their debts, or effecting any other selfish or unjust object. The principle itself is one of disintegration, and upon which no government can possibly endure.

If all the States save one should assert the power to drive that one out of the Union, it is presumed the whole class of seceder politicians would at once deny the power, and denounce the act as the greatest outrage upon State rights. But suppose that precisely the same act, instead of being called "driving the one out," should be called "the seceding of the others from that one," it would be exactly what the seceders claim to do; unless, indeed, they make the point that the one, because it is a minority, may rightfully do what the others, because they are a majority, may not rightfully do. These politicians are subtile and profound on the rights of minorities. They are not partial to that power which made the Constitution, and speaks from the preamble, calling itself "We, the People."

It may well be questioned whether there is to-day a majority of the legally qualified voters of any State, except, perhaps, South Carolina, in favor of disunion. There is much reason to believe that the Union men are the majority in many, if not in every other one, of the so-called seceded States. The contrary has not been demonstrated in any one of them. It is ventured to affirm this even of Virginia and Tennessee; for the result of an election held in military camps, where the bayonets are all on one side of the question voted upon, can scarcely be considered as demonstrating popular sentiment. At such an election, all that large class who are at once for the Union and against coercion would be coerced to vote against the Union.

It may be affirmed without extravagance, that the free institutions we enjoy have developed the powers and improved the condition of our whole people beyond any example in the world. Of this we now have a striking and impressive illustration. So large an army as the Government has now on foot was never before known without a soldier in it but who had taken his place there of his own free choice. But more than this; there are many single regiments whose members, one and another, possess full practical knowledge of all the arts, sciences, professions, and whatever else, whether useful or elegant, is known in the world; and there is scarcely one from which there could not be selected a President, a Cabinet, a Congress, and perhaps a court, abundantly competent to administer the Government itself. Nor do I say this is not true also in the army of our late friends, now adversaries in this contest; but if it is, so much better the reason why the Government which has conferred such benefits on both them and us, should not be broken up. Whoever, in any section, proposes to abandon such a Government, would do well to consider in deference to what principle it is that he does it; what better he is likely to get in its stead; whether the substitute will give, or be intended to give, so much of good to the people? There are some foreshadowings on this subject. Our adversaries have adopted some declarations of independence, in which, unlike the good old one, penned by Jefferson, they omit the words, "all men are created equal." Why? They have adopted a temporary national constitution, in the preamble of which, unlike our good old one, signed by Washington, they omit " We, the people," and substitute " We, the deputies of the sovereign and independent States." Why? Why this deliberate pressing out of view the rights of men and the authority of the people?

This is essentially a people's contest. On the side of the Union it is a struggle for maintaining in the world that form and substance of government whose leading object is to elevate the condition of men; to lift artificial weights from all shoulders; to clear the paths of laudable pursuits for all; to afford all an unfettered start and a fair chance in the race of life. Yielding to partial and temporary departures, from necessity, this is the leading object of the Government for whose existence we contend.

I am most happy to believe that the plain people understand and appreciate this. It is worthy of note, that while in this the Government's hour of trial, large numbers of those in the army and navy who have been favored with the offices have resigned and proved false to the hand which had pampered them, not one common soldier or common sailor is known to have deserted his flag.

Great honor is due to those officers who remained true, despite the example of their treacherous associates; but the greatest honor, and most important fact of all, is the unanimous firmness of the common soldiers and common sailors. To the last man, so far as known, they have successfully resisted the traitorous efforts of those whose commands but an hour before they obeyed as absolute law. This is the patriotic instinct of plain people. They understand, without an argument, that the destroying the Government which was made by Washington means no good to them.

Our popular Government has often been called an experiment. Two points in it our people have already settled—the successful establishing and the successful administering of it. One still remains—its successful maintenance against a formidable internal attempt to overthrow it. It is now for them to demonstrate to the world that those who can fairly carry an election can also suppress a rebellion; that ballots are the rightful and peaceful successors of bullets; and that when ballots have fairly and constitutionally decided, there can be no successful appeal back to bullets; that there can be no successful appeal, except to ballots themselves, at succeeding elections. Such will be a great lesson of peace; teaching men that what they can not take by an election, neither can they take by a war; teaching all the folly of being the beginners of a war.

Lest there be some uneasiness in the minds of candid men as

to what is to be the course of the Government toward the Southern States after the rebellion shall have been suppressed, the Executive deems it proper to say, it will be his purpose then, as ever, to be guided by the Constitution and the laws; and that he probably will have no different understanding of the powers and duties of the Federal Government relatively to the rights of the States and the people under the Constitution than that expressed in the inaugural address.

He desired to preserve the Government, that it may be administered for all, as it was administered by the men who made it. Loyal citizens everywhere have the right to claim this of their Government, and the Government has no right to withhold or neglect it. It is not perceived that in giving it there is any coercion, any conquest, or any subjugation, in any just sense of those terms.

The Constitution provides, and all the States have accepted the provision, that "the United States shall guarantee to every State in this Union a republican form of Government." But if a State may lawfully go out of the Union, having done so it may also discard the republican form of Government; so that to prevent its going out is an indispensable means to the end of maintaining the guarantee mentioned; and when an end is lawful and obligatory, the indispensable means to it are also lawful and obligatory.

It was with the deepest regret that the Executive found the duty of employing the war power in defence of the Government forced upon him. He could but perform this duty or surrender the existence of the Government. No compromise by public servants could in this case be a cure; not that compromises are not often proper, but that no popular Government can long survive a marked precedent that those who carry an election can only save the Government from immediate destruction by giving up the main point upon which the people gave the election. The people themselves, and not their servants, can safely reverse their own deliberate decisions.

As a private citizen the Executive could not have consented that these institutions shall perish; much less could he, in betrayal of so vast and so sacred a trust as these free people have confided to him. He felt that he had no moral right to shrink, or even to count the chances of his own life, in what might follow. In full view of his great responsibility he has so far done what he has deemed his duty. You will now, according to your own judgment, perform yours. He sincerely hopes that your views and your action may so accord with his as to assure all faithful citizens who have been disturbed in their rights of a certain and speedy restoration to them, under the Constitution and the laws.

And having thus chosen our course, without guile and with pure purpose, let us renew our trust in God, and go forward without fear and with manly hearts.

July 4, 1861.   ABRAHAM LINCOLN.

BORDER STATE POLICY.

As one of the first and most important tasks of the Government was to prevent the Border States from being placed in the power of the secessionists, so one of Mr. Lincoln's severest trials in the first year of his Administration was so to meet and check the moves of the leading men in those States, who were at heart with Jefferson Davis, that he would not irritate the sullen, or excite the lukewarm to open opposition. The following letter which explains itself fully, is a good example of the quiet manner in which he showed these men that he understood, and would withstand them.

REPLY TO GOVERNOR MAGOFFIN, OF KENTUCKY.

WASHINGTON, D. C., *August* 24, 1861.

To His Excellency B. MAGOFFIN, *Governor of the State of Kentucky*—Sir:—Your letter of the 19th inst., in which you " urge ' the removal from the limits of Kentucky of the military force now organized and in camp within that State," is received.

I may not possess full and precisely accurate knowledge upon this subject, but I believe it is true that there is a military force in camp within Kentucky, acting by authority of the United States, which force is not very large, and is not now being augmented. I also believe that some arms have been furnished to this force by the United States.

I also believe that this force consists exclusively of Kentuckians, having their camp in the immediate vicinity of their own homes, and not assailing or menacing any of the good people of Kentucky.

In all I have done in the premises, I have acted upon the urgent solicitation of many Kentuckians, and in accordance with what I believed, and still believe, to be the wish of a majority of all the Union loving people of Kentucky.

While I have conversed on the subject with many eminent men of Kentucky, including a large majority of her members of Congress, I do not remember that any one of them, or any other person, except your Excellency and the bearers of your Excellency's letter, has urged me to remove the military force from Kentucky or to disband it. One other very worthy citizen of Kentucky did solicit me to have the augmenting of the force suspended for a time.

Taking all the means within my reach to form a judgment, I do not believe it is the popular wish of Kentucky that the force shall be removed beyond her limits; and, with this impression, I must respectfully decline to remove it.

I most cordially sympathize with your Excellency in the wish to preserve the peace of my own native State, Kentucky, but it is with regret I search for and cannot find, in your not very short letter, any declaration or intimation that you entertain any desire for the preservation of the Federal Union.

ABRAHAM LINCOLN.

GENERAL FREMONT'S EMANCIPATION ORDER.

But Mr. Lincoln's perplexities were not all caused by the malignity of the slavery propagandists. Not a few were created for him by the unwise impetuosity of those who seemed to think that there was only one question to be considered in the war, or rather that the war was to be successfully prosecuted by attacking slavery without regard to law, or even to circumstances. Prominent among these was General Fremont, who assumed the responsibility of declaring the slaves of all active participants in the rebellion, free. This act Mr. Lincoln thought both ill-timed and an unwarrantable arrogation of power; and he annulled it in the following letter.

Washington, D. C., *September* 11, 1861.

*Major-General John C. Fremont—Sir—*Yours of the 8th, in answer to mine of the 2nd inst., is just received. Assured that you upon the ground could better judge of the necessities of your position than I could at this distance, on seeing your proclamation of August 30, I perceived no general objection to it; the particular clause, however, in relation to the confiscation of property and the liberation of slaves appeared to me to be objectionable in its non-conformity to the act of Congress, passed the 6th of last August, upon the same subjects, and hence I wrote you expressing my wish that that clause should be modified accordingly. Your answer just received expresses the preference on your part that I should make an open order for the modification, which I very cheerfully do. It is therefore ordered that the said clause of said proclamation be so modified, held and construed as to confirm with, and not to transcend, the provisions on the same subject contained in the act of Congress entitled " An Act to confiscate property used for insurrectionary purposes," approved August 6, 1861, and the said act be published at length with this order. Your obedient servant.

ABRAHAM LINCOLN.

Gen. Fremont was relieved in November, of his command in the Department of the West, which devolved upon General David Hunter. Mr. Lincoln always modestly disclaimed any military ability; but the following letter, addressed to that General on the occasion of his taking command, was justified in all its military views by the subsequent course of events in that Department throughout the war:

LETTER TO GENERAL HUNTER.

WASHINGTON, *October* 24, 1861.

Sir—The command of the Department of the West having devolved upon you, I propose to offer you a few *suggestions*, knowing how hazardous it is to bind down a distant commander in the field to specific lines of operation, as so much always depends on the knowledge of localities and passing events. It is intended, therefore, to leave considerable margin for the exercise of your judgment and discretion.

The main rebel army (Price's) west of the Mississippi is believed to have passed Dade County in full retreat upon Northwestern Arkansas, leaving Missouri almost free from the enemy, excepting in the southeast part of the State. Assuming this basis of fact, it seems desirable—as you are not likely to overtake Price, and are in danger of making too long a line from your own base of supplies and reinforcements—that you should give up the pursuit, halt your main army, divide it into two corps of observation, one occupying Sedalia and the other Rolla, the present termini of railroads, then recruit the condition of both corps by re-establishing and improving their discipline and instruction, perfecting their clothing and equipments, and providing less uncomfortable quarters. Of course, both railroads must be guarded and kept open, judiciously employing just so much force as is necessary for this. From these two two points, Sedalia and Rolla, and especially in judicious co-operation with Lane on the Kansas border, it would be very easy to concentrate, and repel any army of the enemy returning on Missouri on the Southwest. As it is not probable any such attempt to return will be made before or during the approaching cold weather, before spring the people of Missouri will be in no favorable mood for renewing for next year the troubles which have so much afflicted and impoverished them during this.

If you take this line of policy, and if, as I anticipate, you will see no enemy in great force approaching, you will have a surplus force which you can withdraw from those points, and direct to others, as may be needed—the railroads furnishing ready means of reinforcing those main points, if occasion requires.

Doubtless local uprisings for a time will continue to occur, but those can be met by detachments of local forces of our own, and will ere long tire out of themselves.

While, as stated at the beginning of this letter, a large discretion must be and is left with yourself, I feel sure that an indefinite pursuit of Price, or an attempt by this long and circuitous route to reach Memphis, will be exhaustive beyond endurance, and will end in the loss of the whole force engaged in it.

Your obedient servant,
A. LINCOLN.

The Commander of the Department of the West.

THE CONGRESSIONAL SESSION OF 1861–2.

Congress met for the second time after Mr. Lincoln's inauguration, on the 2d of December, 1861. The— so nearly a victory, closing in so shameful a panic— first battle of Manassas Plains, or Bull Run, which took place during the extra session of July, caused great exultation at the South, and was followed, as the reader will remember, by an adhesion of all the time-servers and waiters upon Providence south of Mason and Dixon's line to the cause of the insurgents, by the consolidation of the so-called Confederate Government, and the casting of the whole weight of the influence of the governing classes in Europe against the government of our Republic. It was followed also by greater preparations on the part of our Government, and excited, after the first day or two of depression, only a more fixed determination on the part of loyal people. Under these circumstances, Mr. Lincoln sent in his second Message.

MESSAGE.

Fellow-Citizens of the Senate and House of Representatives—In the midst of unprecedented political troubles, we have cause of great gratitude to God for unusual good health, and most abundant harvests.

You will not be surprised to learn that, in the peculiar exigencies of the times, our intercourse with foreign nations has been attended with profound solicitude, chiefly turning upon our own domestic affairs. A disloyal portion of the American people have, during the whole year, been engaged in an attempt to divide and destroy the Union. A nation which endures factious domestic division, is exposed to disrespect abroad; and one party, if not both, is sure, sooner or later, to invoke foreign intervention. Nations thus tempted to interfere are not always able to resist the counsels of seeming expediency and ungenerous ambition, although measures adopted under such influences seldom fail to be unfortunate and injurious to those adopting them.

The disloyal citizens of the United States who have offered the ruin of our country, in return for the aid and comfort which they have invoked abroad, have received less patronage and encouragement than they probably expected. If it were just to suppose, as the insurgents have seemed to assume, that foreign nations, in this case, discarding all moral, social, and treaty obligations, would act solely and selfishly for the most speedy restoration of commerce, including especially the acquisition of cotton, those nations appear, as yet, not to have seen their way to their object more directly, or clearly, through the destruction, than through the preservation, of the Union. If we could dare to believe that foreign nations are actuated by no higher principle than this, I am quite sure a sound argument could be made to show them that they can reach their aim more readily and easily by aiding to crush this rebellion, than by giving encouragement to it.

The principal lever relied on by the insurgents for exciting foreign nations to hostility against us, as already intimated, is the embarrassment of commerce. Those nations, however, not improbably, saw from the first that it was the Union which made, as well our foreign as our domestic commerce. They can scarcely have failed to perceive that the effort for disunion produced the existing difficulty; and that one strong nation promises more durable peace, and a more extensive, valuable, and reliable commerce, than can the same nation broken into hostile fragments.

It is not my purpose to review our discussions with foreign States; because whatever might be their wishes or dispositions, the integrity of our country and the stability of our Government mainly depend, not upon them, but on the loyalty, virtue, patriotism, and intelligence of the American people. The correspondence itself, with the usual reservations, is herewith submitted.

I venture to hope it will appear that we have practiced prudence and liberality towards foreign powers, averting causes of irritation ; and with firmness maintaining our own rights and honor.

Since, however, it is apparent that here, as in every other State, foreign dangers necessarily attend domestic difficulties, I recommend that adequate and ample measures be adopted for maintaining the public defences on every side. While, under this general recommendation, provision for defending our seacoast line readily occurs to the mind, I also, in the same connection, ask the attention of Congress to our great lakes and rivers. It is believed that some fortifications and depots of arms and munitions, with harbor and navigation improvements, all at well-selected points upon these, would be of great importance to the national defence and preservation. I ask attention to the views of the Secretary of War, expressed in his report upon the same general subject.

I deem it of importance that the loyal regions of East Tennessee and Western North Carolina should be connected with Kentucky and other faithful parts of the Union by railroad. I, therefore, recommend, as a military measure, that Congress provide for the construction of such road as speedily as possible.

Kentucky will no doubt co-operate, and, through her Legislature, make the most judicious selection of a line. The northern terminus must connect with some existing railroad, and whether the route shall be from Lexington or Nicholasville to the Cumberland Gap, or from Lebanon to the Tennessee line, in the direction of Knoxville, or on some still different line, can easily be determined. Kentucky and the General Government co-operating, the work can be completed in a very short time, and when done it will be not only of vast present usefulness, but also a valuable permanent improvement worth its cost in all the future.

Some treaties, designed chiefly for the interests of commerce, and having no grave political importance, have been negotiated, and will be submitted to the Senate for their consideration. Although we have failed to induce some of the commercial Powers to adopt a desirable melioration of the rigor of maritime war, we have removed all obstructions from the way of this humane reform, except such as are merely of temporary and accidental occurrence.

I invite your attention to the correspondence between her Britannic Majesty's Minister, accredited to this Government, and the Secretary of State, relative to the detention of the British ship *Perthshire* in June last by the United States Steamer *Massachusetts*, for a supposed breach of the blockade. As this detention was occasioned by an obvious misapprehension of the facts, and as justice requires that we should commit no belligerent act not founded in strict right as sanctioned by public law, I recommend that an appropriation be made to satisfy the reasonable demand of the owners of the vessel for her detention.

*   *   *   *   *   *   *   *

If any good reason exists why we should persevere longer in withholding our recognition of the independence and sovereignty of Hayti and Liberia, I am unable to discern it. Unwilling, however, to inaugurate a novel policy in regard to them without the approbation of Congress, I submit for your consideration the expediency of an appropriation for maintaining a *Chargé d'Affaires* near each of those new States. It does not admit of doubt that important commercial advantages might be secured by favorable treaties with them.

The operations of the Treasury during the period which has elapsed since your adjournment has been conducted with signal success. The patriotism of the people has placed at the disposal of the Government the large means demanded by the public exigencies. Much of the national loan has been taken by citizens of the industrial classes, whose confidence in their country's faith, and zeal for their country's deliverance from its present peril, have induced them to contribute to the support of the Government the whole of their limited acquisitions. This fact imposes peculiar obligations to economy and disbursement and energy in action. The revenue from all sources, including loans for the financial year ending on the 30th of June, 1861, was $86,835,900 27; and the expenditures for the same period, including payments on account of the public debt, were $84,578,034 47, leaving a balance in the treasury, on the 1st of July, of $2,257,065 80 for the first quarter of the financial year ending on September 30, 1861. The receipts from all sources, including the balance of July 1, were $102,532,509 27, and the expenses $98,239,733 09, leaving a balance, on the 1st of October, 1861, of $4,292,776 18.

Estimates for the remaining three-quarters of the year and for the financial year of 1863, together with his views of the ways and means for meeting the demands contemplated by them, will be submitted to Congress by the Secretary of the Treasury. It is gratifying to know that the expenses made necessary by the rebellion are not beyond the resources of the loyal people, and to believe that the same patriotism which has thus far sustained the Government will continue to sustain it till peace and union shall again bless the land. I respectfully refer to the report of the Secretary of War for information respecting the numerical strength of the army, and for recommendations having in view an increase of its efficiency, and the well-being of the various branches of the service intrusted to his care. It is gratifying to know that the patriotism of the people has proved equal to the occasion, and that the number of troops tendered greatly exceed the force which Congress authorized me to call into the field. I refer with pleasure to those portions of his report which make allusion to the creditable degree of discipline already attained by our troops, and to the excellent sanitary condition of the entire army. The recommendation of the Secretary for an organization of the militia upon a uniform basis is a subject of vital importance to the future safety of the country, and is commended to the serious attention of Congress. The large addition to the regular army, in connection with the defection that has so considerably diminished the number of its officers, gives peculiar importance to his recommendation for increasing the corps of cadets to the greatest capacity of the Military Academy.

By mere omission, I presume, Congress has failed to provide chaplains for the hospitals occupied by the volunteers. This subject was brought to my notice, and I was induced to draw up the form of a letter, one copy of which, properly addressed, has been delivered to each of the persons, and at the dates respectively named and stated in a schedule, containing, also, the form of the letter marked A, and herewith transmitted. These gentlemen, I understand, entered upon the duties designated at the times respectfully stated in the schedule, and have labored faithfully therein ever since. I therefore recommend that they be compensated at the same rate as chaplains in the army. I further suggest that general provision be made for chaplains to serve at hospitals, as well as with regiments.

The report of the Secretary of the Navy presents, in detail, the operations of that branch of the service, the activity and energy which have characterized its administration, and the results of measures to increase its efficiency and power. Such have been the additions, by construction and purchase, that it may almost be said a navy has been created and brought into service since our difficulties commenced.

Besides blockading our extensive coast, squadrons larger than ever before assembled under our flag have been put afloat, and performed deeds which have increased our naval renown.

I would invite special attention to the recommendation of the Secretary for a more perfect organization of the navy, by introducing additional grades in the service.

The present organization is defective and unsatisfactory, and the suggestions submitted by the department will, it is believed, if adopted, obviate the difficulties alluded to, promote harmony, and increase the efficiency of the navy.

There are three vacancies on the bench of the Supreme Court —two by the decease of Justices Daniel and McLean, and one by the resignation of Justice Campbell. I have so far forborne making nominations to fill these vacancies for reasons which I will now state. Two of the out-going judges resided within the States now overrun by revolt; so that if successors were appointed in the same localities, they could not now serve upon their circuits; and many of the most competent men there probably would not take the personal hazard of accepting to serve, even here, upon the supreme bench. I have been unwilling to throw all the appointments northward, thus disabling myself from doing justice to the South on the return of peace; although I may remark that to transfer to the North one which has heretofore been in the South, would rfot, with reference to territory and population, be unjust.

During the long and brilliant judicial career of Judge McLean, his circuit grew into an empire—altogether too large for any one judge to give the courts therein more than a nominal attendance—rising in population from one million four hundred and seventy thousand and eighteen, in 1830, to six million one hundred and fifty-one thousand four hundred and five, in 1860.

Besides this, the country generally has outgrown our present judicial system. If uniformity was at all intended, the system requires that all the States shall be accommodated with Circuit Courts, attended by supreme judges, while, in fact, Wisconsin, Minnesota, Iowa, Kansas, Florida, Texas, California and Oregon, have never had any such courts. Nor can this well be remedied without a change of the system; because the adding of judges to the Supreme Court, enough for the accommodation of all parts of the country with Circuit Courts, would create a court altogether too numerous for a judicial body of any sort. And the evil, if it be one, will increase as new States come into the Union. Circuit Courts are useful, or they are not useful. If useful, no State should be denied them, if not useful no State should have them. Let them be provided for all, or abolished as to all.

Three modifications occur to me, either of which, I think, would be an improvement upon our present system. Let the Supreme Court be of convenient number in every event. Then, first, let the whole country be divided into circuits of convenient size, the supreme judges to serve in a number of them corresponding to their own number, and independent circuit judges provided for all the rest. Or, secondly, let the supreme judges be relieved from circuit duties, and circuit judges provided for all the circuits. Or, thirdly, dispense with circuit courts altogether, leaving the judicial functions wholly to the district courts and an independent Supreme Court.

I respectfully recommend to the consideration of Congress the present condition of the statute laws, with the hope that Congress will be able to find an easy remedy for many of the inconveniences and evils which constantly embarrass those engaged in the practical administration of them. Since the organization of the Government, Congress has enacted some five thousand acts and joint resolutions, which fill more than six thousand closely-printed pages, and are scattered through many volumes. Many of these acts have been drawn in haste and without sufficient caution, so that their provisions are often obscure in themselves, or in conflict with each other, or at least so doubtful as to render it very difficult for even the best-informed persons to ascertain precisely what the statute law really is.

It seems to me very important that the statute laws should be made as plain and intelligible as possible, and be reduced to as small a compass as may consist with the fulness and precision of the will of the legislature and the perspicuity of its language. This, well done, would, I think, greatly facilitate the labors of those whose duty it is to assist in the administration of the laws, and would be a lasting benefit to the people, by placing before them, in a more accessible and intelligible form, the laws which so deeply concern their interests and their duties.

I am informed by some whose opinions I respect, that all the acts of Congress now in force, and of a permanent and general nature, might be revised and re-written, so as to be embraced in one volume (or, at most, two volumes) of ordinary and convenient size. And I respectfully recommend to Congress to consider of the subject, and if my suggestion be approved, to devise such plan as to their wisdom shall seem most proper for the attainment of the end proposed.

One of the unavoidable consequences of the present insurrection is the entire suppression, in many places, of all the ordinary means of administering civil justice by the officers, and in the forms of existing law. This is the case, in whole or in part in all the insurgent States; and as our armies advance upon and take possession of parts of those States, the practical evil becomes more apparent. There are no courts nor officers to whom the citizens of other States may apply for the enforcement of their lawful claims against citizens of the insurgent States; and there is a vast amount of debt constituting such claims. Some have estimated it as high as two hundred million dollars, due, in large part, from insurgents in open rebellion to loyal citizens who are, even now, making great sacrifices in the discharge of their patriotic duty to support the Government.

Under these circumstances, I have been urgently solicited to establish, by military power, courts to administer summary justice in such cases. I have thus far declined to do it, not because I had any doubt that the end proposed—the collection of the debts—was just and right in itself, but because I have been unwilling to go beyond the pressure of necessity in the unusual exercise of power. But the powers of Congress, I suppose, are equal to the anomalous occasion, and therefore I refer the whole matter to Congress, with the hope that a plan may be devised for the administration of justice in all such parts of the insurgent States and Territories as may be under the control of this Government, whether by a voluntary return to allegiance and order, or by the power of our arms; this, however, not to be a permanent institution, but a temporary substitute, and to cease as soon as the ordinary courts can be re-established in peace.

It is important that some more convenient means should be provided, if possible, for the adjustment of claims against the Government, especially in view of their increased number by reason of the war. It is as much the duty of Government to render prompt justice against itself, in favor of citizens, as it is to administer the same between private individuals. The investigation and adjudication of claims, in their nature belong to the judicial department; besides, it is apparent that the attention of Congress will be more than usually engaged, for some time to come, with great national questions. It is intended, by the organization of the Court of Claims, mainly to remove this branch of business from the halls of Congress; but while the court has proved to be an effective and valuable means of investigation, it in great degree fails to effect the object of its creation, for want of power to make its judgments final.

Fully aware of the delicacy, not to say the danger, of the subject, I commend to your careful consideration whether this power of making judgments final may not properly be given to the court, reserving the right of appeal on questions of law to the Supreme Court, with such other provisions as experience may have shown to be necessary.

* * * * * * * *

The present insurrection shows, I think, that the extension of this district across the Potomac River, at the time of establish-lishing the Capital here, was eminently wise, and consequently that the relinquishment of that portion of it which lies within the State of Virginia was unwise and dangerous. I submit for your consideration the expediency of regaining that part of the district, and the restoration of the original boundaries thereof, through negotiations with the State of Virginia.

The report of the Secretary of the Interior, with the accompanying documents, exhibits the condition of the several branches of the public business pertaining to that department. The depressing influences of the insurrection have been especially felt in the operations of the Patent and General Land Offices. The cash receipts from the sales of public lands during the past year have exceeded the expenses of our land system only about two hundred thousand dollars. The sales have been entirely suspended in the Southern States, while the interruptions to the business of the country, and the diversion of large numbers of men from labor to military service, have obstructed settlements in the new States and Territories of the Northwest.

* * * * * * * *

The demands upon the Pension Office will be largely increased by the insurrection. Numerous applications for pensions, based upon the casualties of the existing war, have already been made. There is reason to believe that many who are now upon the pension rolls, and in receipt of the bounty of the Government, are in the ranks of the insurgent army or giving them aid and comfort. The Secretary of the Interior has directed a suspension of the payment of the pensions of such persons upon proof of their disloyalty. I recommend that Congress authorize that officer to cause the names of such persons to be stricken from the pension rolls.

The relations of the Government with the Indian tribes have been greatly disturbed by the insurrection, especially in the southern superintendency and in that of New Mexico. The Indian country south of Kansas is in the possession of the insurgents from Texas and Arkansas. The agents of the United States appointed since the 4th of March for this superintendency have been unable to reach their posts, while the most of those who were in the office before that time have espoused the insurrectionary cause, and assume to exercise the power of agents by virtue of commissions from the insurrectionists. It has been stated in the public press that a portion of those Indians have been organized as a military force, and are attached to the army of the insurgents. Although the Government has no official information upon this subject, letters have been written to the Commissioner of Indian Affairs by several prominent chiefs, giving assurance of their loyalty to the United States, and expressing a wish for the presence of Federal troops to protect them. It is believed that upon the repossession of the country by the Federal forces, the Indians will readily cease all hostile demonstrations, and resume their former relations to the Government.

Agriculture, confessedly the largest interest in the nation, has not a department, nor a bureau, but a clerkship only, assigned to it in the Government. While it is fortunate that this great interest is so independent in its nature as to not have demanded and extorted more from the Government, I respectfully ask Congress to consider whether something more can not be given voluntarily with general advantage.

Annual reports exhibiting the condition of our agriculture, commerce, and manufactures, would present a fund of information of great practical value to the country. While I make no suggestion as to details, I venture the opinion that an agricultural and statistical bureau might profitably be organized.

The execution of the laws for the suppression of the African slave-trade has been confided to the Department of the Interior. It is a subject of gratulation that the efforts which have been made for the suppression of this inhuman traffic have been recently attended with unusual success. Five vessels being fitted out for the slave-trade have been seized and condemned. Two mates of vessels engaged in the trade, and one person in equipping a vessel as a slaver, have been convicted and subjected to the penalty of fine and imprisonment, and one captain taken with a cargo of Africans on board his vessel, has been convicted of the highest grade of offence under our laws, the punishment of which is death.

   *   *   *   *   *   *   *   *

Under and by virtue of the act of Congress entitled "An act to confiscate property used for insurrectionary purposes," approved August 6, 1861, the legal claims of certain persons to the labor and service of certain other persons have become forfeited; and numbers of the latter, thus liberated, are already dependent on the United States, and must be provided for in some way. Besides this, it is not impossible that some of the States will pass similar enactments for their own benefit respectively, and by operation of which persons of the same class will be thrown upon them for disposal. In such case I recommend that Congress provide for accepting such persons from such States, according to some mode of valuation, in lieu, *pro tanto*, of direct taxes, or upon some other plan to be agreed on with such States respectively; that such persons, on such acceptance by the General Government, be at once deemed free; and that, in any event, steps be taken for colonizing both classes (or the one first mentioned, if the other shall not be brought into existence) at some place or places in a climate congenial to them. It might be well to consider, too, whether the free colored people already in the United States could not, so far as individuals may desire, be included in such colonization.

To carry out the plan of colonization may involve the acquiring of territory, and also the appropriation of money beyond that to be expended in the territorial acquisition. Having practiced the acquisition of territory for nearly sixty years, the question of constitutional power to do so is no longer an open one with us. The power was questioned at first by Mr. Jefferson, who, however, in the purchase of Louisiana, yielded his scruples on the plea of great expediency. If it be said that the only legitimate object of acquiring territory is to furnish homes for white men, this measure effects that object; for the emigration of colored men leaves additional room for white men remaining or coming here. Mr. Jefferson, however, placed the importance of procuring Louisiana more on political and commercial grounds than on providing room for population.

On this whole proposition, including the appropriation of money with the acquisition of territory, does not the expediency amount to absolute necessity—that, without which the Government itself can not be perpetuated?

The war continues. In considering the policy to be adopted for suppressing the insurrection, I have been anxious and careful that the inevitable conflict for this purpose shall not degenerate into a violent and remorseless revolutionary struggle.

In the exercise of my best discretion I have adhered to the blockade of the ports held by the insurgents, instead of putting in force by proclamation the law of Congress enacted at the late session for closing those ports.

So, also, obeying the dictates of prudence, as well as the obligations of law, instead of transcending I have adhered to the act of Congress to confiscate property used for insurrectionary purposes. If a new law upon the same subject shall be proposed, its propriety will be duly considered. The Union must be preserved; and hence all the indispensable means must be employed. We should not be in haste to determine that radical and extreme measures, which may reach the loyal as well as the disloyal are indispensable.

The inaugural address at the beginning of the Administration, and the message to Congress at the late special session, were both mainly devoted to the domestic controversy out of which the insurrection and consequent war have sprung. Nothing now occurs to add or subtract to or from the principles or general purposes stated and expressed in those documents.

The last ray of hope for preserving the Union peaceably expired at the assault upon Fort Sumter; and a general review of what has occurred since may not be unprofitable. What was painfully uncertain then is much better defined and more distinct now; and the progress of events is plainly in the right direction. The insurgents confidently claimed a strong support from north of Mason and Dixon's line; and the friends of the Union were not free from apprehension on the point. This, however, was soon settled definitely, and on the right side. South of the line, noble little Delaware led off right from the first. Maryland was made to seem against the Union. Our soldiers were assaulted, bridges were burned, and railroads torn up within her limits; and we were many days, at one time, without the ability to bring a single regiment over her soil to the capital. Now her bridges and railroads are repaired and open to the Government; she already gives seven regiments to the cause of the Union, and none to the enemy; and her people, at a regular election, have sustained the Union by a larger majority and a larger aggregate vote than they ever before gave to any candidate or any question. Kentucky, too, for some time in doubt, is now decidedly and, I think, unchangeably ranged on the side of the Union. Missouri is comparatively quiet, and, I believe, can not again be overrun by the insurrectionists. These three States of Maryland, Kentucky, and Missouri, neither of which would promise a single soldier at first, have now an aggregate of not less than forty thousand in the field for the Union; while of their citizens, certainly not more than a third of that number, and they of doubtful whereabouts and doubtful existence, are in arms against it. After a somewhat bloody struggle of months, winter closes on the Union people of Western Virginia, leaving them masters of their own country.

An insurgent force of about fifteen hundred, for months dominating the narrow peninsular region constituting the counties of Accomac and Northampton, and known as the Eastern Shore of Virginia, together with some contiguous parts of Maryland, have laid down their arms; and the people there have renewed their allegiance to, and accepted the protection of the old flag. This leaves no armed insurrectionist north of the Potomac, or east of the Chesapeake.

Also, we have obtained a footing at each of the isolated points on the Southern coast, of Hatteras, Port Royal, Tybee Island, near Savannah, and Ship Island; and we likewise have some general accounts of popular movements in behalf of the Union in North Carolina and Tennessee.

These things demonstrate that the cause of the Union is advancing steadily and certainly southward.

Since your last adjournment Lieutenant-General Scott has retired from the head of the army. During his long life the nation has not been unmindful of his merit; yet, on calling to mind how faithfully, ably, and brilliantly he has served the country, from a time far back in our history, when few of the now living had been born, and thenceforward continually, I can not but think we are still his debtors. I submit, therefore, for your consideration what further mark of recognition is due to him, and to ourselves as a grateful people.

With the retirement of General Scott came the executive duty of appointing in his stead a general-in-chief of the army. It is a fortunate circumstance that neither in council nor country was there, so far as I know, any difference of opinion as to the proper person to be selected. The retiring chief repeatedly expressed his judgment in favor of General McClellan for the position; and in this the nation seemed to give a unanimous concurrence. The designation of General McClellan is, therefore, in considerable degree, the selection of the country as well as of the Executive; and hence there is better reason to hope there will be given him the confidence and cordial support thus, by fair implication promised, and without which he can not, with so full efficiency, serve the country.

It has been said that one bad general is better than two good ones: and the saying is true, if taken to mean no more than that an army is better directed by a single mind, though inferior, than by two superior ones at variance and cross-purposes with each other.

And the same is true in all joint operations wherein those engaged can have none but a common end in view, and can differ only as to the choice of means. In a storm at sea, no one on board can wish the ship to sink; and yet not unfrequently all go down together, because too many will direct, and no single mind can be allowed to control.

It continues to develop that the insurrection is largely, if not exclusively a war upon the first principle of popular government—the rights of the people. Conclusive evidence of this is found in the most grave and maturely-considered public documents, as well as in the general tone of the insurgents. In those documents we find the abridgment of the existing right of suffrage, and the denial to the people of all right to participate in the selection of public officers, except the legislative, boldly advocated, with labored arguments to prove that large control of the people in government is the source of all political evil. Monarchy itself is sometimes hinted at as a possible refuge from the power of the people.

In my present position, I could scarcely be justified were I to omit raising a warning voice against this approach of returning despotism.

It is not needed, nor fitting here, that a general argument should be made in favor of popular institutions; but there is one point, with its connections, not so hackneyed as most others, to which I ask a brief attention. It is the effort to place capital on an equal footing with, if not above, labor, in the structure of Government. It is assumed that labor is available only in connection with capital; that nobody labors unless somebody else, owning capital, somehow by the use of it induces him to labor. This assumed, it is next considered whether it is best that capital shall hire laborers, and thus induce them to work by their own consent, or buy them, and drive them to it without their consent. Having proceeded so far, it is naturally concluded that all laborers are either hired laborers, or what we call slaves. And further, it is assumed that whoever is once a hired laborer is fixed in that condition for life.

Now, there is no such relation between capital and labor as assumed; nor is there any such thing as a free man being fixed for life in the condition of a hired laborer. Both these assumptions are false, and all inferences from them are groundless.

Labor is prior to and independent of capital. Capital is only the fruit of labor, and could never have existed if labor had not first existed. Labor is the superior of capital, and deserves much the higher consideration. Capital has its rights, which are as worthy of protection as any other rights. Nor is it denied that there is, and probably always will be, a relation between labor and capital, producing mutual benefits. The error is in assuming that the whole labor of community exists within that relation. A few men own capital, and those few avoid labor themselves, and, with their capital, hire or buy another few to labor for them. A large majority belong to neither class —neither work for others, nor have others working for them. In most of the Southern States, a majority of the whole people of all colors are neither slaves nor masters; while in the Northern, a large majority are neither hirers nor hired. Men, with their families—wives, sons, and daughters—work for themselves, on their farms, in their houses, and in their shops, taking the whole product to themselves, and asking no favors of capital on the one hand, nor of hired laborers or slaves on the other. It is not forgotten that a considerable number of persons mingle their own labor with capital—that is, they labor with their own hands, and also buy or hire others to labor for them; but this is only a mixed, and not a distinct class. No principle stated is disturbed by the existence of this mixed class.

Again: as has already been said, there is not of necessity any such thing as the free hired laborer being fixed to that condition for life. Many independent men everywhere in these States, a few years back in their lives, were hired laborers. The prudent, penniless beginner in the world labors for wages awhile, saves a surplus with which to buy tools or land for himself, then labors on his own account another while, and at length hires another new beginner to help him. This is the just, and generous, and prosperous system, which opens the way to all, gives hope to all, and consequent energy, and progress, and improvement of condition to all. No men living are more worthy to be trusted than those who toil up from poverty— none less inclined to take or touch aught which they have not honestly earned. Let them beware of surrendering a political power which they already possess, and which, if surrendered, will surely be used to close the door of advancement against such as they, and to fix new disabilities and burdens upon them, till all of liberty shall be lost.

From the first taking of our national census to the last are seventy years; and we find our population, at the end of the period, eight times as great as it was at the beginning. The increase of those other things which men deem desirable has been even greater. We thus have, at one view, what the popular principle applied to the Government through the machinery of the States and the Union, has produced in a given time; and also what, if firmly maintained, it promises for the future. There are already among us those who, if the Union be preserved, will live to see it contain two hundred and fifty millions. The struggle of to-day is not altogether for to-day; it is for a vast future also. With a reliance on Providence, all the more firm and earnest, let us proceed in the great task which events have devolved upon us.   ABRAHAM LINCOLN.

GENERAL M'CLELLAN.

The appointment of General McClellan to the command of the Army of the Potomac after the battle of Bull Run, was received with satisfaction in military circles, and by the public generally. We all remember the hearty confidence which all loyal people gave him, and the high hopes we all based upon the general estimate of his abilities. We all remember, too, how, accomplished military man and capable organizer as he was, he yet tried the nation's soul by his delay and his hesitating strategy. Of our impatience the following Orders were the first public official expression:

ARMY ORDER.

EXECUTIVE MANSION, WASHINGTON, *January* 27, 1862.

Ordered, That the twenty-second day of February, 1862, be the day for a general movement of the land and naval forces of the United States against the insurgent forces. That especially the army at and about Fortress Monroe, the army of the Potomac, the army of Western Virginia, the army near Munfords-ville, Kentucky, the army and flotilla at Cairo, and a naval force in the Gulf of Mexico, be ready to move on that day.

That all other forces, both land and naval, with their respective commanders, obey existing orders for the time, and be ready to obey additional orders when duly given.

That the heads of departments, and especially the Secretaries of War and of the Navy, with all their subordinates, and the General-in-Chief, with all other commanders and subordinates of land and naval forces, will severally be held to their strict and full responsibilities for prompt execution of this order.

ABRAHAM LINCOLN.

ARMY ORDER.

EXECUTIVE MANSION, WASHINGTON, *January* 31, 1862.

Ordered, That all the disposable force of the Army of the Potomac, after providing safely for the defence of Washington, be formed into an expedition for the immediate object of seizing and occupying a point upon the railroad southwest of what is known as Manassas Junction, all details to be in the discretion of the Commander-in-Chief, and the expedition to move before or on the twenty-second day of February next.

ABRAHAM LINCOLN.

The following letter from Mr. Lincoln to General McClellan is one of the earliest manifestations of a radical discrepancy of views between the General and the Administration, which became the source of great embarrasment, out of which the soldier did not extricate himself or his country by success, and in the course of which the civilian showed at least the ability always to touch with his pen the right point.

TO GENERAL M'CLELLAN ON THE PLAN OF THE CAMPAIGN AGAINST RICHMOND.

EXECUTIVE MANSION, WASHINGTON, *February* 3, 1862.

My Dear Sir—You and I have distinct and different plans for a movement of the Army of the Potomac ; yours to be done by the Chesapeake, up the Rappahannock to Urbana, and across land to the terminus of the railroad on the York River; mine to move directly to a point on the railroad southwest of Manassas.

If you will give satisfactory answers to the following questions, I shall gladly yield my plan to yours:

1st. Does not your plan involve a greatly larger expenditure of *time* and *money* than mine?

2d. Wherein is a victory *more certain* by your plan than mine?

8d. Wherein is a victory *more valuable* by your plan than mine?

4th. In fact, would it not be *less* valuable in this: that it would break no great line of the enemy's communication, while mine would?

6th. In case of disaster, would not a retreat be more difficult by your plan than mine?

Yours, truly,   ABRAHAM LINCOLN.

Major-General McClellan.

"ARBITRARY" ARRESTS.

At the outbreak of the rebellion, emissaries of the rebels, and their active sympathizers, hardly less dangerous, were scattered over the country. Mr. Lincoln, following in this matter the example of Washington, ordered the summary arrest and imprisonment of some of these persons, and in this manner, without a doubt, neutralized many efforts that could have been met in no other way. Maryland was the scene of many of these arrests as to which Mr. Lincoln spoke frankly thus:

"The public safety renders it necessary that the grounds of these arrests should at present be withheld, but at the proper time they will be made public. Of one thing the people of Maryland may rest assured, that no arrest has been made, or will be made, not based on substantial and unmistakable complicity with those in armed rebellion against the Government of the United States. In no case has an arrest been made on mere suspicion, or through personal or partisan animosity, but in all cases the Government is in possession of tangible and unmistakable evidence, which will, when made public, be satisfactory to every loyal citizen."

These arrests were made at first under the authority of the State Department, but on the 14th of February, 1862, this matter was transferred to the War Department, which transfer was made the occasion of the following State paper upon the subject, in which the reasons for these "arbitrary arrests" are fully set forth. After the appearance of this order there was little complaint heard upon this subject, except from those journals and individuals who were well known as sympathizers with the rebellion.

EXECUTIVE ORDERS IN RELATION TO STATE PRISONERS.

WAR DEPARTMENT, WASHINGTON, *Feb.* 14, 1862.

The breaking out of a formidable insurrection, based on a conflict of political ideas, being an event without precedent in the United States, was necessarily attended by great confusion and perplexity of the public mind. Disloyalty, before unsuspected, suddenly became bold, and treason astonished the world by bringing at once into the field military forces superior in numbers to the standing army of the United States.

Every department of the Government was paralyzed by treason. Defection appeared in the Senate, in the House of Representatives, in the Cabinet, in the Federal Courts; Ministers and Consuls returned from foreign countries to enter the insurrectionary councils, or land or naval forces; commanding and other officers of the army and in the navy betrayed the counsels or deserted their posts for commands in the insurgent forces. Treason was flagrant in the revenue and in the post-office service, as well as in the territorial governments and in the Indian reserves.

Not only Governors, Judges, Legislators, and ministerial officers in the States, but even whole States, rushed, one after another, with apparent unanimity, into rebellion. The capital was besieged and its connection with all the States cut off.

Even in the portions of the country which were most loyal, political combinations and secret societies were formed further_ing the work of disunion, while, from motives of disloyalty or cupidity, or from excited passions or perverted sympathies, individuals were found furnishing men, money, and materials of war and supplies to the insurgents' military and naval forces. Armies, ships, fortifications, navy yards, arsenals, military posts and garrisons, one after another, were betrayed or abandoned to the insurgents.

Congress had not anticipated and so had not provided for the emergency. The municipal authorities were powerless and inactive. The judicial machinery seemed as if it had been designed not to sustain the Government, but to embarrass and betray it.

Foreign intervention, openly invited and industriously instigated by the abettors of the insurrection, became imminent, and has only been prevented by the practice of strict and impartial justice with the most perfect moderation in our intercourse with nations.

The public mind was alarmed and apprehensive, though fortunately not distracted or disheartened. It seemed to be doubtful whether the Federal Government, which one year before had been thought a model worthy of universal acceptance, had indeed the ability to defend and maintain itself.

Some reverses, which perhaps were unavoidable, suffered by newly levied and inefficient forces, discouraged the loyal, and gave new hopes to the insurgents. Voluntary enlistments seemed about to cease, and desertions commenced. Parties speculated upon the questions whether conscriptions had not become necessary to fill up the armies of the United States.

In this emergency the President felt it his duty to employ with energy the extraordinary powers which the Constitution confides to him in cases of insurrection. He called into the field such military and naval forces, unauthorized by the existing laws, as seemed necessary. He directed measures to prevent the use of the post-office for treasonable correspondence. He subjected passengers to and from foreign countries to new passport regulations, and he instituted a blockade, suspended the writ of *habeas corpus* in various places, and caused persons who were represented to him as being engaged or about to engage in disloyal and treasonable practices to be arrested by special civil as well as military agencies, and detained in military custody, when necessary, to prevent them and deter others from such practices. Examinations of such cases were instituted, and some of the persons so arrested have been discharged from time to time, under circumstances or upon conditions compatible, as was thought, with the public safety.

Meantime a favorable change of public opinion has occurred. The line between loyalty and disloyalty is plainly defined; the whole structure of the Government is firm and stable; appre-prehensions of public danger and facilities for treasonable practices have diminished with the passions which prompted heedless persons to adopt them. The insurrection is believed to have culminated and to be declining.

The President, in view of these facts, and anxious to favor a return to the normal course of the Administration, as far as regard for the public welfare will allow, directs that all political prisoners or State prisoners now held in military custody, be released, on their subscribing to a parole engaging them to render no aid or comfort to the enemies in hostility to the United States.

The Secretary of War will, however, at his discretion, except from the effect of this order any persons detained as spies in the service of the insurgents, or others whose release at the present moment may be deemed incompatible with the public safety.

To all persons who shall be so released, and who shall keep their parole, the President grants an amnesty for any past offences of treason or disloyalty which they may have committed.

Extraordinary arrests will hereafter be made under the direction of the military authorities alone.

By order of the President:

EDWIN M. STANTON, Secretary of War.

THE QUESTION OF SLAVERY.

The public mind had now been brought to a point by the resistance and the spirit of the insurgents, at which

Mr. Lincoln thought it prudent to bring before Congress the question of the abolition of slavery. This he did in the following Message, whereby he proposed only, it will be seen, such a co-operation of Congress with the people of the Slave States, as might provide for the gradual extinction of the institution which in three years was to be utterly destroyed.

MESSAGE PROPOSING AID FOR THE GRADUAL ABOLITION OF SLAVERY.

WASHINGTON, *March* 6, 1862.

Fellow-Citizens of the Senate and House of Representatives—I recommend the adoption of a joint resolution by your honorable body, which shall be, substantially, as follows:

Resolved, That the United States, in order to co-operate with any State which may adopt gradual abolition of slavery, give to such State pecuniary aid, to be used by such State, in its discretion, to compensate it for the inconvenience, public and private, produced by such change of system.

If the proposition contained in the resolution does not meet the approval of Congress and the country, there is an end of it. But if it does command such approval, I deem it of importance that the States and people immediately interested should be at once distinctly notified of the fact, so that they may begin to consider whether to accept or reject it.

The Federal Government would find its highest interest in such a measure as one of the most important means of self-preservation. The leaders of the existing rebellion entertain the hope that this Government will ultimately be forced to acknowledge the independence of some part of the disaffected region, and that all the Slave States north of such part will then say, "The Union for which we have struggled being already gone, we now choose to go with the Southern section." To deprive them of this hope substantially ends the rebellion; and the initiation of emancipation deprives them of it, and of all the States initiating it.

The point is not that all the States tolerating slavery would very soon, if at all, initiate emancipation; but while the offer is equally made to all, the more Northern shall, by such initiation, make it certain to the more Southern that in no event will the former ever join the latter in their proposed Confederacy. I say initiation, because, in my judgment, gradual and not sudden emancipation is better for all.

In the mere financial or pecuniary view, any member of Congress with the census or an abstract of the Treasury report before him, can, readily see for himself how very soon the current expenditures of this war would purchase, at a fair valuation, all the slaves in any named State.

Such a proposition on the part of the General Government sets up no claim of a right by the Federal authority to interfere with slavery within State limits—referring as it does the absolute control of the subject, in each case, to the State and the people immediately interested. It is proposed as a matter of perfectly free choice to them.

In the annual message, last December, I thought fit to say "the Union must be preserved, and hence all indispensable means must be employed." I said this, not hastily but deliberately. War has been made, and continues to be an indispensable means to this end. A practical reacknowledgment of the national authority would render the war unnecessary, and it would at once cease. But resistance continues, and the war must also continue; and it is impossible to foresee all the incidents which may attend, and all the ruin which may follow it. Such as may seem indispensable, or may obviously promise great efficiency towards ending the struggle, must and will come.

The proposition now made (though an offer only) I hope it may be esteemed no offence to ask whether the pecuniary consideration tendered would not be of more value to the States and private persons concerned than would be the institution and property in it, in the present aspect of affairs. While it is true that the adoption of the proposed resolution would be merely initiatory, and not within itself a practical measure, it is recommended in the hope that it would lead to important practical results.

In full view of my great responsibility to my God and my country, I earnestly beg the attention of Congress and the people to the subject. ABRAHAM LINCOLN.

GENERAL M'CLELLAN.

The McClellan trouble grew day by day. We see in this brief letter how tenderly Mr. Lincoln dealt with his touchy commander.

EXECUTIVE MANSION,
WASHINGTON, *March* 31, 1862.

My Dear Sir—This morning I felt constrained to order Blenker's division to Fremont, and I write this to assure you that I did so with great pain, understanding that you would wish it otherwise. If you could know the full pressure of the case I am confident that you would justify it, even beyond a mere acknowledgment that the Commander-in-Chief may order what he pleases.

Yours, very truly, A. LINCOLN.

Major-General McCLELLAN.

In this longer communication there is the same kindness, the same consideration; and although it is pervaded by a tone of authority, that authority seems almost paternal in its expression.

WASHINGTON, *April* 9, 1862.

My Dear Sir—Your dispatches, complaining that you are not properly sustained, while they do not offend me, do pain me very much.

Blenker's division was withdrawn from you before you left here, and you know the pressure under which I did it, and, as I thought, acquiesced in it—certainly not without reluctance.

After you left, I ascertained that less than twenty thousand unorganized men, without a single field battery, were all you designed to be left for the defence of Washington and Manassas Junction, and part of this even was to go to General Hooker's old position. General Banks's corps, once designed for Manassas

Junction, was diverted and tied up on the line of Winchester and Strasburg, and could not leave it without again exposing the upper Potomac and the Baltimore and Ohio Railroad. This presented, or would present, when McDowell and Sumner should be gone, a great temptation to the enemy to turn back from the Rappahannock and sack Washington. My implicit order that Washington should, by the judgment of all the commanders of army corps, be left entirely secure, had been neglected. It was precisely this that drove me to detain McDowell.

I do not forget that I was satisfied with your arrangement to leave Banks at Manassas Junction: but when that arrangement was broken up, and nothing was substituted for it, of course I was constrained to substitute something for it myself. And allow me to ask, do you really think I should permit the line from Richmond, *via* Manassas Junction, to this city, to be entirely open, except what resistance could be presented by less than twenty thousand unorganized troops? This is a question which the country will not allow me to evade.

There is a curious mystery about the number of troops now with you. When I telegraphed you on the sixth, saying you had over a hundred thousand with you, I had just obtained from the Secretary of War a statement taken, as he said, from your own returns, making one hundred and eight thousand then with you and *en route* to you. You now say you will have but eighty five thousand when all *en route* to you shall have reached you. How can the discrepancy of twenty-three thousand be accounted for?

As to General Wool's command, I understand it is doing for you precisely what a like number of your own would have to do if that command was away.

I suppose the whole force which has gone forward for you is with you by this time. And if so, I think it is the precise time for you to strike a blow. By delay, the enemy will relatively gain upon you—that is, he will gain faster by fortifications and reinforcements than you can by reinforcements alone. And once more let me tell you, it is indispensable to you that you strike a blow. I am powerless to help this. You will do me the justice to remember I always insisted that going down the bay in search of a field, instead of fighting at or near Manassas, was only shifting, and not surmounting a difficulty; that we would find the same enemy, and the same or equal intrench- ment, at either place. The country will not fail to note, is now noting, that the present hesitation to move upon an intrenched enemy is but the story of Manassas repeated.

I beg to assure you that I have never written to you or spoken to you in greater kindness of feeling than now, nor with a fuller purpose to sustain you, so far as, in my most anxious judgment, I consistently can. But you must act.

Yours, very truly,   A. LINCOLN.

Major-General McClellan.

But it was only in the movement upon Richmond that there was delay and defeat, if not disaster, in the field. In all other quarters, and under all other generals, the National armies achieved victory, and attained substantial success. Grant had captured Fort Donelson and the army by which it was defended, Missouri had been cleared of rebels, Fort Pulaski had fallen. Island No. 10, Memphis and Nashville had been taken, and the signal victory of Pittsburg Landing had been won. Upon occasion of the latter success, Mr. Lincoln issued the following (his first) almost meek and humble

PROCLAMATION OF THANKSGIVING.

It has pleased Almighty God to vouchsafe signal victories to the land and naval forces engaged in suppressing an internal rebellion, and at the same time to avert from our country the dangers of foreign intervention and invasion.

It is therefore recommended to the people of the United States, that at their next weekly assemblages in their accustomed places of public worship, which shall occur after the notice of this Proclamation shall have been received, they especially acknowledge and render thanks to our Heavenly Father for these inestimable blessings; that they then and there implore spiritual consolation in behalf of all those who have been brought into affliction by the casualties and calamities of sedition and civil war; and that they reverently invoke the Divine guidance for our national counsels, to the end that they may speedily result in the restoration of peace, harmony, and unity throughout our borders, and hasten the establishment of fraternal relations among all the countries of the earth.

In witness whereof I have hereunto set my hand and caused the seal of the United States to be affixed.

Done at the city of Washington, this tenth day of April, in the year of our Lord one thousand eight hundred and sixty-[L. S.] two, and of the independence of the United States the eighty-sixth.　　　　ABRAHAM LINCOLN.

By the President:

WM. H. SEWARD, *Secretary of State.*

ABOLITION OF SLAVERY IN THE DISTRICT OF COLUMBIA.

The first step toward the abolition of slavery elicited from Mr. Lincoln the following:

MESSAGE.

April 16, 1862.

Fellow-Citizens of the Senate and House of Representatives—The act entitled "An act for the release of certain persons held to service or labor in this District of Columbia," has this day been approved and signed.

I have never doubted the constitutional authority of Congress to abolish slavery in this District; and I have ever desired to see the national capital freed from the institution in some satisfactory way. Hence there has never been in my mind any question upon the subject except the one of expediency, arising in view of all the circumstances. If there be matters within and about this act which might have taken a course or shape more satisfactory to my judgment, I do not attempt to specify them. I am gratified that the two principles of compensation and colonization are both recognized and practically applied in the act.

In the matter of compensation, it is provided that claims may be presented within ninety days from the passage of the act, "but not thereafter;" and there is no saving for minors, *femmes covert*, insane, or absent persons. I presume this is an omission by mere oversight, and I recommend that it be supplied by an amendatory or supplemental act.   ABRAHAM LINCOLN.

GENERAL HUNTER'S DECLARATION OF FREEDOM.

On the 9th of May, 1862, General Hunter, in command of the Department of the South, issued another of those precipitate and unauthorized orders upon the subject of slavery, which embarrassed Mr. Lincoln so much in the early part of his administration. He boldly declared that order null, thereby provoking the censure of the extreme abolitionists, in the following

PROCLAMATION.

Whereas, There appears in the public prints what purports to be a proclamation of Major-General Hunter, in the words and figures following:

HEADQUARTERS DEPARTMENT OF THE SOUTH,
HILTON HEAD, S. C., May 9, 1862. }

General Order, No. 11.

The three States of Georgia, Florida, and South Carolina, comprising the Military Department of the South, having deliberately declared themselves no longer under the United States of America, and having taken up arms against the United States, it becomes a military necessity to declare them under martial law.

This was accordingly done on the 25th day of April, 1862. Slavery and martial law in a free country are altogether incompatible. The persons in these States—Georgia, Florida, and South Carolina—heretofore held as slaves, are therefore declared forever free.

Signed,   DAVID HUNTER,

[OFFICIAL.]   Major-General Commanding.

ED. W. SMITH, *Acting Assistant Adjutant-General.*

And, whereas, the same is producing some excitement and misunderstanding, therefore I, Abraham Lincoln, President of the United States, proclaim and declare that the Government of the United States had no knowledge or belief of an intention on the part of General Hunter to issue such proclamation, nor has it yet any authentic information that the document is genuine; and, further, that neither General Hunter nor any other commander or person has been authorized by the Government of the United States to make proclamation declaring the slaves of any State free, and that the supposed proclamation now in question, whether genuine or false, is altogether void so far as respects such declaration. I further make known that, whether it be competent for me, as Commander-in-Chief of the Army and Navy, to declare the slaves of any State or States free; and whether at any time, or in any case, it shall have become a necessity indispensable to the maintenance of the Government to exercise such supposed power, are questions which, under my responsibility, I reserve to myself, and which I cannot feel justified in leaving to the decision of commanders in the field.

These are totally different questions from those of police regulations in armies or in camps.

On the sixth day of March last, by a special Message, I recommended to Congress the adoption of a joint resolution, to be substantially as follows:

Resolved, That the United States ought to co-operate with any State which may adopt a gradual abolishment of slavery, giving to such State earnest expression to compensate for its inconveniences, public and private, produced by such change of system.

The resolution in the language above quoted was adopted by large majorities in both branches of Congress, and now stands an authentic, definite, and solem proposal of the Nation to the States and people most interested in the subject matter. To the people of these States now, I mostly appeal. I do not argue —I beseech you to make the arguments for yourselves. You cannot, if you would, be blind to the signs of the times.

I beg of you a calm and enlarged consideration of them, ranging, if it may be, far above partisan and personal politics.

This proposal makes common cause for a common object, casting no reproaches upon any. It acts not the Pharisee. The changes it contemplates would come gently as the dews of Heaven, not rending or wrecking anything. Will you not embrace it? So much good has not been done by one effort in all past time, as in the Providence of God it is now your high privilege to do. May the vast future not have to lament that you have neglected it.

In witness whereof, I have hereunto set my hand and caused the seal of the United States to be hereunto affixed.

Done at the city of Washington, this 19th day of May, in the year of our Lord one thousand eight hundred and sixty-two, and of the independence of the United States the eighty-sixth.

Signed,   ABRAHAM LINCOLN.

By the President:

WILLIAM H. SEWARD, *Secretary of State.*

THE M'CLELLAN AFFAIR.

Chief among the President's sources of personal annoyance, as well as of grave concern, were the difficulties constantly occurring between General McClellan and the War Department, and between the Commander-in-Chief and his Generals of Corps and Division; all occurring, too, while the failure of General McClellan to make any effective movement made the country sick at heart. The following letters on this subject, like most of Mr. Lincoln's writings, fully explain themselves.

The first refers to General McClellan's complaints as to the re-organization of the army into corps, and to his favoritism, which excited much ill-feeling.

FORTRESS MONROE, *May* 9, 1865.

MY DEAR SIR:—I have just assisted the Secretary of War in forming the part of a dispatch to you, relating to army corps, which dispatch, of course, will have reached you long before this will. I wish to say a few words to you privately on this subject. I ordered the army corps organization not only on the unanimous opinion of the twelve generals of division, but also on the unanimous opinion of every *military man* I could get an opinion from, and every modern military book, yourself only excepted. Of course I did not on my own judgment pretend to understand the subject. I now think it indispensable for you to know how your struggle against it is received in quarters which we can not entirely disregard. It is looked upon as merely an effort to pamper one or two pets, and to persecute and degrade their supposed rivals. I have had no word from Sumner, Heintzelman and Keyes. The commanders of these corps are of course the three highest officers with you, but I am constantly told that you have no consultation or communication with them, that you consult and communicate with nobody but Fitz John Porter, and perhaps General Franklin. I do not say these complaints are true or just; but, at all events, it is proper you should know of their existence. Do the commanders of corps disobey your orders in anything?

When you relieved General Hamilton of his command the other day, you thereby lost the confidence of at least one of your best friends in the Senate. And here let me say, not as applicable to you personally, that Senators and Representatives speak of me in their places as they please without question ; and that officers of the army must cease addressing insulting letters to them for taking no greater liberty with them. But to return, are you strong enough, even with my help, to set your foot upon the neck of Sumner, Heintzelman and Keyes, all at once? This is a practical and very serious question to you.

Yours truly,   A. LINCOLN.

Major-General G. B. McCLELLAN.

The following letter was elicited by General McClellan's complaints that he feared he had not men enough to meet the overwhelming force of the rebels, and that General McDowell, who had been ordered to co-operate with him, was not sufficiently under his orders.

WASHINGTON, *May* 24, 1865.

I left General McDowell's camp at dark last evening. Shields' command is there, but it is so worn that he can not move before Monday morning, the 26th. We have so thinned our line to get troops for other places, that it was broken yesterday at Front Royal, with a probable loss to us of one regiment infantry, two companies cavalry, putting General Banks in some peril.

The enemy's forces, under General Anderson, now opposing General McDowell's advance, have, as their line of supply and retreat, the road to Richmond.

If, in conjunction with McDowell's movement against Anderson, you could send a force from your right to cut off the enemy's supplies from Richmond, preserve the railroad bridge across the two forks of the Pamunky, and intercept the enemy's retreat, you will prevent the army now opposing you from receiving an accession of numbers of nearly 15,000 men ; and if you succeed in saving the bridges, you will secure a line of railroad for supplies in addition to the one you now have. Can you not do this almost as well as not, while you are building the Chickahominy bridges? McDowell and Shields both say they can, and positively will, move Monday morning. I wish you to move cautiously and safely.

You will have command of McDowell, after he joins you, precisely as you indicated in your long dispatch to us of the 21st.

A. LINCOLN, *President.*

Major-General McCLELLAN.

The peril in which General Banks was placed by Stonewall Jackson's march up the Shenandoah made it necessary to send General McDowell to his support. Against this General McClellan remonstrated, and received in answer the following letter from the President:

WASHINGTON, *May* 25, 1865.

Your dispatch received. General Banks was at Strasburg with about 6,000 men, Shields having been taken from him to swell a column for McDowell to aid you at Richmond, and the rest of his force scattered at various places. On the 23d, a force of 7,000 to 10,000 fell upon one regiment and two companies guarding the bridge at Port Royal, destroying it entirely; crossed the Shenandoah, and on the 24th, yesterday, pushed on to get north of Banks on the road to Winchester. General Banks ran a race with them, beating them into Winchester yesterday evening. This morning a battle ensued between the two forces, in which General Banks was beaten back into full retreat toward Martinsburg, and probably is broken up into a total rout. Geary, on the Manassas Gap Railroad, just now reports that Jackson is now near Front Royal with 10,000 troops, following up and supporting, as I understand, the force now pursuing Banks. Also, that another force of ten thousand is near Orleans, following on in the same direction. Stripped bare, as we are here, I will do all we can to prevent them crossing the Potomac at Harper's Ferry or above. McDowell has about twenty thousand of his forces moving back to the vicinity of Port Royal, and Fremont, who was at Franklin, is moving to Harrisonburg, both these movements intended to get in the enemy's rear.

One more of McDowell's brigades is ordered through here to Harper's Ferry; the rest of his forces remain for the present at Fredericksburg. We are sending such regiments and dribs from here and Baltimore as we can spare to Harper's Ferry, supplying their places in some sort, calling in militia from the adjacent States. We also have eighteen cannon on the road to Harper's Ferry, of which arm there is not one at that point. This is now our situation.

If McDowell's force was now beyond our reach, we should be entirely helpless. Apprehensions of something like this, and no unwillingness to sustain you, has always been my reason for withholding McDowell's forces from you.

Please understand this and do the best you can with the forces you have.

A. LINCOLN, President.

Major-General McCLELLAN.

The following dispatch, sent within a few hours of the former, probably convinced General McClellan that Mr.

Lincoln had some reason on his side, as the whole country soon discovered.

WASHINGTON, May 25, 1862—2 P. M.

The enemy is moving north in sufficient force to drive General Banks before him; precisely in what force we cannot tell. He is also threatening Leesburg and Geary on the Manasses Gap Railroad, from both north and south; in precisely what force we cannot tell. I think the movement is a general and concerted one. Such as would not be if he was acting upon the purpose of a very desperate defence of Richmond. I think the time is near when you must either attack Richmond or give up the job, and come to the defence of Washington. Let me hear from you instantly.

A. LINCOLN.

One little exhibition of promptitude, followed by success, is to be credited to General McClellan about this time. He sent General Fitz John Porter to operate against a part of the rebel force which threatened General McDowell near Hanover Court House. Porter drove the enemy from his position. Of this creditable but comparatively small affair General McClellan made so much as to elicit the following somewhat ironical expression of gratitude from the long-suffering, good-natured President.

WASHINGTON, May 28, 1862.

I am very glad of General F. J. Porter's victory; still, if it was a total rout of the enemy, I am puzzled to know why the Richmond and Fredericksburg Railroad was not seized again, as you say you have all the railroads but the Richmond and Fredericksburg. I am puzzled to see how, lacking that, you can have any, except the scrap from Richmond to West Point. The scrap of the Virginia Central, from Richmond to Hanover Junction, without more, is simply nothing. That the whole of the enemy is concentrating on Richmond, I think, cannot be certainly known to you or me. Saxton, at Harper's Ferry, informs us that large forces, supposed to be Jackson's and Ewell's, forced his advance from Charlestown to-day. General King telegraphs us from Fredericksburg that contrabands give certain information that fifteen hundred left Hanover Junction Monday morning to reinforce Jackson. I am painfully impressed with the importance of the struggle before you, and shall aid you all I can consistently with my view of the due regard to all points.

A. LINCOLN.

Major-General McClellan.

THE CAMERON AND CUMMINGS AFFAIR.

On the 30th of April, 1862, the House of Representatives passed a vote of censure upon Simon Cameron, Mr. Lincoln's first Secretary of War, (who had then been succeeded by Mr. Stanton,) for employing a Mr. Alexander Cummings of Philadelphia, then residing in New York, to purchase with public money placed at his unrestrained disposal, supplies for troops and armed vessels. The action of the House brought out the following very interesting and honorable Message from Mr. Lincoln. Mr. Cummings was much blamed and ridiculed in connection with this affair, but very unjustly. It proved that he committed no error whatever, except some trifling mistakes due to inexperience; and the President assumed the responsibility of the whole affair.

To the Senate and House of Representatives,—The insurrection which is yet existing in the United States, and aims at the overthrow of the Federal Constitution and the Union, was clandestinely prepared during the winter of 1860 and 1861, and assumed an open organization in the form of a treasonable provisional government at Montgomery, Alabama, on the eighteenth day of February, 1861. On the twelfth day of

April, 1861, the insurgents committed the flagrant act of civil war by the bombardment and capture of Fort Sumter, which cut off the hope of immediate conciliation. Immediately afterwards all the roads and avenues to this city were obstructed, and the capital was put into the condition of a siege. The mails in every direction were stopped and the lines of telegraph cut off by the insurgents, and military and naval forces which had been called out by the Government for the defence of Washington were prevented from reaching the city by organized and combined treasonable resistance in the State of Maryland. There was no adequate and effective organization for the public defence. Congress had indefinitely adjourned. There was no time to convene them. It became necessary for me to choose whether, using only the existing means, agencies, and processes which Congress had provided, I should let the government fall into ruin, or whether, availing myself of the broader powers conferred by the Constitution in cases of insurrection, I would make an effort to save it, with all its blessings, for the present age and for posterity. I thereupon summoned my constitutional advisers, the heads of all the departments, to meet on Sunday, the twentieth day of April, 1861, at the office of the Navy Department, and then and there, with their unanimous concurrence, I directed that and armed revenue cutter should proceed to sea to afford protection to the commercial marine, especially to the California treasure-ships, then on their way to this coast. I also directed the Commandant of the Navy Yard at Boston to purchase or charter, and arm, as quickly as possible, five steamships for purposes of public defence. I directed the the Commandant of the Navy Yard at Philadelphia to purchase or charter and arm an equal number for the same purpose. I directed the Commandant at New York to purchase or charter, and arm an equal number. I directed Commander Gillis to purchase or charter, and arm and put to sea two other vessels. Similar directions were given to Commodore Dupont, with a view to the opening of passages by water to and from the capital. I directed the several officers to take the advice and obtain the efficient services in the matter of his Excellency Edwin D. Morgan, the Governor of New York, or, in his absence,

George D. Morgan, Wm. M. Evarts, R. M. Blatchford, and Moses H. Grinnell, who were, by my directions, especially empowered by the Secretary of the Navy to act for his department in that crisis, in matters pertaining to the forwarding of troops and supplies for the public defence.

On the same occasion I directed that Governor Morgan and Alexander Cummings, of the city of New York, should be authorized by the Secretary of War, Simon Cameron, to make all necessary arrangements for the transportation of troops and munitions of war in aid and assistance of the officers of the army of the United States, until communication by mails and telegraph should be completely re-established between the cities of Washington and New York. No security was required to be given by them, and either of them was authorized to act in case of inability to consult with the other. On the same occasion I authorized and directed the Secretary of the Treasury to advance, without requiring security, two millions of dollars of public money to John A. Dix, George Opdyke, and Richard M. Blatchford, of New York, to be used by them in meeting such requisitions as should be directly consequent upon the military and naval measures for the defence and support of the Government, requiring them only to act without compensation, and to report their transactions when duly called upon. The several departments of the Government at that time contained so large a number of disloyal persons that it would have been impossible to provide safely through official agents only, for the performance of the duties thus confided to citizens favorably known for their ability, loyalty, and patriotism. The several orders issued upon these occurrences were transmitted by private messengers, who pursued a circuitous way to the seaboard cities, inland across the States of Pennsylvania and Ohio, and the northern lakes. I believe that by these and other similar measures taken in *that* crisis, some of which were without any authority of law, the Government was saved from overthrow. I am not aware that a dollar of the public funds thus confided without authority of law, to unofficial persons, was either lost or wasted, although apprehensions of such misdirections occurred to me as objections to these extraordinary proceedings, and were necessarily overruled. I recall these transactions now because my attention has been directed to a resolution which was passed by the House of Representatives on the thirtieth of last month, which is in these words:

"*Resolved*, That Simon Cameron, late Secretary of War, by intrusting Alexander Cummings with the control of large sums of the public money, and authority to purchase military supplies without restriction, without requiring from him any guarantee for the faithful performance of his duties, while the services of competent public officers were available, and by involving the Government in a vast number of contracts with persons not legitimately engaged in the business pertaining to the subject matter of such contracts, especially in the purchase of arms for future delivery, has adopted a policy highly injurious to the public service, and deserves the censure of the House."

Congress will see that I should be wanting in candor and in justice if I should leave the censure expressed in this resolution to rest exclusively or chiefly upon Mr. Cameron. The same sentiment is unanimously entertained by the heads of the departments, who participated in the proceedings which the House of Representatives has censured. It is due to Mr. Cameron to say that although he fully approved the proceedings, they were not moved nor suggested by himself, and that not only the President, but all the other heads of departments were at least equally responsible with him for whatever error, wrong or fault was committed in the premises.   ABRAHAM LINCOLN.

GENERAL M'CLELLAN'S CHANGE OF BASE.

About the 25th of June, the rebels, apparently weary of waiting for General McClellan to attack them, made up their minds to attack him. This he discovered, and the War Department had discovered it before him. They concentrated an overwhelming force upon his right wing, just as he was about to withdraw it from Gaines' Mill, drove it back, and followed it across the peninsula in that dreadful series of battles ending with a complete defeat for them at Malvern Hill, which the country remembers so well under the name of the Seven Days' Battles. The following four letters addressed to General McClellan, tell the story of that movement almost as well as a detailed description :

WASHINGTON, *June* 26, 1862.

Your three dispatches of yesterday in relation to the advance of your picket lines, ending with the statement that you completely succeeded in making your point, are very gratifying. The later one, suggesting the probability of your being overwhelmed by 200,000 men, and talking of to whom the responsibility will belong, pains me very much. I give you all I can, and act on the presumption that you will do the best you can with what you have; while you continue, ungenerously I think, to assume that I could give you more if I would. I have omitted—I shall omit—no opportunity to send you reinforcements whenever I can. A. LINCOLN.

WASHINGTON, *June* 28, 1862.

Save your army at all events. Will send reinforcements as fast as we can. Of course they cannot reach you to-day, to-morrow, or next day. I have not said you were ungenerous for saying you needed reinforcements; I thought you were ungenerous in assuming that I did not send them as fast as I could. I feel any misfortune to you and your army quite as keenly as you feel it yourself. If you have had a drawn battle or a repulse, it is the price we pay for the enemy not being in Washington. We protected Washington, and the enemy concentrated on you. Had we stripped Washington, he would have been upon us before the troops sent could have got to you. Less than a week ago you notified us that reinforcements were leaving Richmond to come in front of us. It is the nature of the case, and neither you nor the Government is to blame. A. LINCOLN.

WASHINGTON, *July* 1, 1862,—3.30 P. M.

It is impossible to reinforce you for your present emergency. If we had a million of men we could not get them to you in time. We have not the men to send. If you are not strong enough to face the enemy, you must find a place of security, and wait, rest, and repair. Maintain your ground if you can, but save the army at all events, even if you fall back to Fort Monroe. We still have strength enough in the country, and will bring it out.   A. LINCOLN.

Major-General G. B. McCLELLAN.

WASHINGTON, *July* 2, 1862.

Your despatch of yesterday induces me to hope that your army is having some rest. In this hope, allow me to reason with you for a moment. When you ask for 50,000 men to be promptly sent you, you surely labor under some gross mistake of fact. Recently you sent papers showing your disposal of forces made last spring for the defence of Washington, and advising a return to that plan. I find it included in and about Washington 75,000 men. Now, please be assured that I have not men enough to fill that very plan by 15,000. All of General Fremont's in the Valley, all of General Banks's, all of General McDowell's not with you, and all in Washington taken together, do not exceed, if they reach, 60,000. With General Wool and General Dix added to those mentioned, I have not outside of your army, 75,000 men east of the mountains. Thus, the idea of sending you 50,000, or any other considerable forces promptly, is simply absurd. If in your frequent mention of responsibility you have the impression that I blame you for not doing more than you can, please be relieved of such impression. I only beg, that in like manner, you will not ask impossibilities of me. If you think you are not strong enough to take Richmond just now, I do not ask you to try just now. Save the army, material, and *personnel*, and I will strengthen it for the offensive again as fast as I can. The governors of eighteen States offer me a new levy of 300,000, which I accept.

       A. LINCOLN.

WAR DEPARTMENT, WASHINGTON CITY, *July* 4, 1862.

I understand your position as stated in your letter, and by General Marcy. To reinforce you so as to enable you to resume the offensive within a month, or even six weeks, is impossible. In addition to that arrived and now arriving from the Potomac (about ten thousand men, I suppose), and about ten thousand, I hope, you will have from Burnside very soon, and about five thousand from Hunter a little later, I do not see how I can send you another man within a month. Under these circumstances, the defensive, for the present, must be your only care. Save the army, first, where you are, if you *can*; and secondly, by removal, if you must. You, on the ground, must be the judge as to which you will attempt, and of the means for effecting it. I but give it as my opinion, that with the aid of the gunboats and the reinforcements mentioned above, you can hold your present position; provided, and so long as you can keep the James River open below you. If you are not tolerably confident you can keep the James River open, you had better remove as soon as possible. I do not remember that you have expressed any apprehension as to the danger of having your communication cut on the river below you, yet I do not suppose it can have escaped your attention. A. LINCOLN.

P. S.—If at any time you feel able to take the offensive, you are not restrained from doing so. A. L.

SLAVERY IN THE BORDER STATES.

Mr. Lincoln's message advocating the gradual emancipation of slaves, with compensation to the owners, elicited no response from the leading men of the Border Slave States. Impressed with the importance of this subject, he therefore asked the Members of Congress from those States to meet him at the White House, on the 12th of July, and delivered to them the following

ADDRESS.

Gentlemen—After the adjournment of Congress, now near, I shall have no opportunity of seeing you for several months. Believing that you of the Border States hold more power for good than any other equal number of members, I feel it a duty which I cannot justifiably waive, to make this appeal to you.

I intend no reproach or complaint when I assure you that, in my opinion, if you all had voted for the resolution in the gradual emancipation Message of last March the war would now be substantially ended. And the plan therein proposed is yet one of the most potent and swift means of ending it. Let the States which are in rebellion see definitely and certainly that in no event will the States you represent ever join their proposed Confederacy, and they cannot much longer maintain the contest. But you cannot divest them of their hope to ultimately have you with them as long as you show a determination to perpetuate the institution within your own States. Beat them at elections, as you have overwhelmingly done, and, nothing daunted, they still claim you as their own. You and I know what the lever of their power is. Break that lever before their faces, and they can shake you no more forever.

Most of you have treated me with kindness and consideration, and I trust you will not now think I improperly touch what is exclusively your own, when, for the sake of the whole country, I ask, Can you, for your States, do better than to take the course I urge? Discarding *punctilio* and maxims adapted to more manageable times, and looking only to the unprecedently stern facts of our case, can you do better in any possible event? You prefer that the constitutional relation of the States to the nation shall be practically restored without disturbance of the institution : and if this were done, my whole duty, in this respect, under the Constitution and my oath of office, would be performed. But it is not done, and we are trying to accomplish it by war. The incidents of the war cannot be avoided. If the war continues long, as it must if the object be not sooner attained, the institution in your States will be extinguished by mere friction and abrasion—by the mere incidents of the war. It will be gone, and you will have nothing valuable in lieu of it. Much of its value is gone already. How much better for you and for your people to take the step which at once shortens the war, and secures substantial compensation for that which is sure to be wholly lost in any other event! How much better to thus save the money which else we sink forever in the war! How much better to do it while we can, lest the war ere long render us pecuniarily unable to do it! How much better for you, as seller, and the nation, as buyer, to sell out and buy out that without which the war never could have been, than to sink both the thing to be sold and the price of it in cutting one another's throats!

I do not speak of emancipation at once, but of a decision at once to emancipate gradually. Room in South America for colonization can be obtained cheaply, and in abundance, and when numbers shall be large enough to be company and encouragement for one another, the freed people will not be so reluctant to go.

I am pressed with a difficulty not yet mentioned—one which threatens division among those who, united, are none too strong. An instance of it is known to you. General Hunter is an honest man. He was, and I hope still is, my friend. I valued him none the less for his agreeing with me in the general wish that all men everywhere could be free. He proclaimed all men free within certain States, and I repudiated the proclamation. He expected more good and less harm from the measure than I could believe would follow. Yet, in repudiating it, I gave dissatisfaction, if not offence, to many whose support the country can not afford to lose. And this is not the end of it. The pressure in this direction is still upon me, and is increasing. By conceding what I now ask you can relieve me, and much more, can relieve the country in this important point.

Upon these considerations I have again begged your attention to the Message of March last. Before leaving the Capital, consider and discuss it among yourselves. You are patriots and statesmen, and as such I pray you consider this proposition; and at the least commend it to the consideration of your States and people. As you would perpetuate popular government for the best people in the world, I beseech you that you do in nowise omit this. Our common country is in great peril, demanding the loftiest views and boldest action to bring a speedy relief. Once relieved, its form of government is saved to the world; its beloved history and cherished memories are vindicated, and its happy future fully assured and rendered inconceivably grand. To you, more than to any others, the privilege is given to assure that happiness and swell that grandeur and to link your own names therewith forever.

THE CONFISCATION BILL.

On the same day of the delivery of the foregoing address Mr. Lincoln sent the following Message to the House of Representatives approving the Confiscation Bill which had been passed by that body, except in one point, to which he objected as being unconstitutional.

Fellow-Citizens of the Senate and House of Representatives—Considering the bill for " An act to suppress insurrection, to punish treason and rebellion, to seize and confiscate the property of rebels, and for other purposes," and the joint resolution explanatory of said act as being substantially one, I have approved and signed both.

Before I was informed of the resolution, I had prepared the draft of a message, stating objections to the bill becoming a law, a copy of which draft is herewith submitted.

ABRAHAM LINCOLN.

July 12, 1862.

[Copy.]

Fellow-Citizens of the House of Representatives—I herewith return to the honorable body, in which it originated, the bill for an act entitled "An act to suppress treason and rebellion, to seize and confiscate the property of rebels, and for other purposes," together with my objections to its becoming a law.

There is much in the bill to which I perceive no objection. It is wholly prospective; and it touches neither person nor property of any loyal citizen, in which particular it is just and proper.

The first and second sections provide for the conviction and punishment of persons who shall be guilty of treason, and persons who shall " incite, set on foot, assist, or engage in any rebellion or insurrection against the authority of the United States, or the laws thereof, or shall give aid or comfort thereto, or shall engage in or give aid and comfort to any such existing rebellion or insurrection." By fair construction, persons within those sections are not punished without regular trials in duly constituted courts, under the forms and all the substantial provisions of law and the Constitution applicable to their several cases. To this I perceive no objection; especially as such persons would be within the general pardoning power, and also the special provision for pardon and amnesty contained in this act.

It is also provided that the slaves of persons convicted under these sections shall be free. I think there is an unfortunate form of expression, rather than a substantial objection, in this. It is startling to say that Congress can free a slave within a State, and yet, if it were said the ownership of a slave had first been transferred to the nation, and Congress had then liberated him, the difficulty would at once vanish. And this is the real case. The traitor against the General Government forfeits his slave at least as justly as he does any other property; and he forfeits both to the Government against which he offends. The Government, so far as there can be ownership, thus owns the forfeited slaves, and the question for Congress in regard to them is, "Shall they be made free or sold to new masters?" I perceive no objection to Congress deciding in advance that they shall be free. To the high honor of Kentucky, as I am informed, she is the owner of some slaves by *escheat*, and has sold none, but liberated all. I hope the same is true of some other States. Indeed, I do not believe it will be physically possible for the General Government to return persons so circumstanced to actual slavery. I believe there would be physical resistance to it, which could neither be turned aside by argument nor driven away by force. In this view I have no objection to this feature of the bill. Another matter involved in these two sections, and running through other parts of the act will be noticed hereafter.

I perceive no objections to the third or fourth sections.

So far as I wish to notice the fifth and sixth sections, they may be considered together. That the enforcement of these sections would do no injustice to the persons embraced within them is clear. That those who make a causeless war should be compelled to pay the cost of it is too obviously just to be called in question. To give governmental protection to the property of persons who have abandoned it, and gone on a crusade to overthrow the same Government, is absurd, if considered in the mere light of justice. The severest justice may not always be the best policy. The principle of seizing and appropriating the property of the person embraced within these sections is certainly not very objectionable, but a justly discriminating application of it would be very difficult, and, to a great extent, impossible. And would it not be wise to place a power of remission somewhere, so that these persons may know they have something to loose by persisting and something to gain by desisting? I am not sure whether such power of remission is or is not in section thirteen. Without any special act of Congress, I think our military commanders, when, in military phrase, "they are within the enemy's country," should, in orderly manner, seize and use whatever of real or personal property may be necessary or convenient for their commands; at the same time preserving, in some way, the evidence of what they do.

What I have said in regard to slaves, while commenting on the first and second sections, is applicable to the ninth, with the difference that no provision is made in the whole act for determining whether a particular individual slave does or does not fall within the classes defined in that section. He is to be free upon certain conditions; but whether those conditions do or do not pertain to him, no mode of ascertaining is provided. This could be easily supplied.

To the tenth section I make no objection. The oath therein required seems to be proper, and the remainder of the section is substantially identical with a law already existing.

The eleventh section simply assumes to confer discretionary power upon the Executive. Without the law, I have no hesitation to go as far in the direction indicated as I may at any time deem expedient. And I am ready to say now, I think it is proper for our military commanders to employ, as laborers, as many persons of African descent as can be used to advantage.

The twelfth and thirteenth sections are something better than unobjectionable; and the fourteenth is entirely proper, if all other parts of the act shall stand.

That to which I chiefly object pervades most part of the Act, but more distinctly appears in the first, second, seventh and eighth sections. It is the sum of those provisions which results in the divesting of title forever.

For the causes of treason and ingredients of treason, not amounting to the full crime, it declares forfeiture extending beyond the lives of the guilty parties; whereas the Constitution of the United States declares that "no attainder of treason shall work corruption of blood or forfeiture except during the life of the person attainted." True, there is to be no formal attainder in this case; still, I think, the greater punishment cannot be constitutionally inflicted, in a different form, for the same offence.

With great respect I am constrained to say I think this feature of the Act is unconstitutional. It would not be difficult to modify it.

I may remark that the provision of the Constitution, put in language borrowed from Great Britain, applies only in this country, as I understand, to real or landed estate.

Again, this act, *in rem*, forfeits property for the ingredients of treason without a conviction of the supposed criminal, or a personal hearing given him in any proceeding. That we may not touch property lying within our reach, because we cannot give personal notice to an owner who is absent endeavoring to destroy the Government, is certainly satisfactory. Still, the owner may not be thus engaged; and I think a reasonable time should be provided for such parties to appear and have personal hearings. Similar provisions are not uncommon in connection with proceedings *in rem*.

For the reasons stated, I return the Bill to the House in which it originated.

GENERAL M'CLELLAN AGAIN.

Here we have another of those gentle, but firm reproofs, which Mr. Lincoln was continually called upon to administer to General McClellan.

EXECUTIVE MANSION, WASHINGTON, *July* 13, 1862.

My Dear Sir—I am told that over 160,000 men have gone with your army on the Peninsula. When I was with you the other day, we made out 86,000 remaining, leaving 73,500 to be accounted for. I believe 3,500 will cover all the killed, wounded, missing, in all your battless and skirmishes, leaving 50,000 who have left otherwise. Not more than 5,000 of these have died, leaving 45,000 of your army still alive, and not with it. I believe half or two-thirds of them are fit for duty to-day. Have you any more perfect knowledge of this than I have? If I am right, and you had these men with you, you could go into Richmond in the next three days. How can they be got to you, and how can they be prevented from getting away in such numbers for the future?　　　　　　　　　　A. LINCOLN.

COLONIZATION.

It was yet uncertain whether one result of the war would be the setting free of all the slaves in the country; but it was plain enough that the number of free negroes in the South would be enormously increased thereby. The question as to the disposition to be made of these emancipated slaves was one of much difficulty. Mr. Lincoln bearing in mind the dislike of his own race to mingle with the negro race socially and politically, favored the project of a vast scheme of colonization. This he broached in an address to a deputation of negroes whom he received at the White House on the 14th of August, 1862.

ADDRESS.

Having all been seated, the President, after a few preliminary observations, informed them that a sum of money had been appropriated by Congress, and placed at his disposition, for the purpose of aiding the colonization in some country, of the people, or a portion of them, of African descent, thereby making it his duty, as it had for a long time been his inclination, to favor that cause; and why, he asked, should the people of your race be colonized, and where? Why should they leave this country? This is, perhaps, the first question for proper consideration. You and we are different races. We have between us a broader difference than exists between almost any other two races. Whether it is right or wrong I need not discuss; but this physical difference is a great disadvantage to us both, as I think. Your race suffer very greatly, many of them by living among us, while ours suffer from your presence. In a word we suffer on each side. If this is admitted, it affords a reason, at least, why we should be separated. You here are freemen, I suppose.

A voice—Yes, Sir.

The President—Perhaps you have long been free, or all your lives. Your race are suffering, in my judgment, the greatest wrong inflicted on any people. But even when you cease to be slaves, you are yet far removed from being placed on an equality with the white race. You are cut off from many of the advantages which the other race enjoys. The aspiration of men is to enjoy equality with the best when free, but on this broad continent not a single man of your race is made the equal of a single man of ours. Go where you are treated the best, and the ban is still upon you. I do not propose to discuss this, but to present it as a fact, with which we have to deal. I cannot alter it if I would. It is a fact about which we all think and feel alike, I and you. We look to our condition. Owing to the existence of the two races on this continent, I need not recount to you the effects upon white men, growing out of the institution of slavery. I believe in its general evil on the white race. See our present condition—the country engaged in war! our white men cutting one another's throats—none knowing how far it will extend—and then consider what we know to be the truth. But for your race among us there could not be war, although many men engaged on either side do not care for you one way or the other. Nevertheless, I repeat, without the institution of slavery, and the colored race as a basis, the war could not have an existence. It is better for us both, therefore, to be separated. I know that there are free men among you who, even if they could better their condition, are not as much inclined to go out of the country as those who, being slaves, could obtain their freedom on this condition. I suppose one of the principal difficulties in the way of colonization is that the free colored man cannot see that his comfort would be advanced by it. You may believe that you can live in Washington, or elsewhere in the United States, the remainder of your life; perhaps more so than you can in any foreign country, and hence you may come to the conclusion that you have nothing to do with the idea of going to a foreign country. This (I speak in no unkind sense) is an extremely selfish view of the case. But you ought to do something to help those who are not so fortunate as yourselves. There is an unwillingness on the part of our people, harsh as it may be, for you free colored people to remain with us. Now if you could give a start to the white people you would open a wide door for many to be made free. If we deal with those who are not free at the beginning, and whose intellects are clouded by slavery, we have very poor material to start with. If intelligent colored men, such as are before me, would move in this matter, much might be accomplished. It is exceedingly important that we have men at the beginning capable of thinking as white men, and not those who have been systematically oppressed. There is much to encourage you. For the sake of your race you should sacrifice something of your present comfort for the purpose of being as grand in that respect as the white people. It is a cheering thought throughout life, that something can be done to ameliorate the condition of those who have been subject to the hard usages of the world. It is difficult to make a man miserable while he feels he is worthy of himself and claims kindred to the great God who made him. In the American Revolutionary War sacrifices were made by men engaged in it, but they were cheered by the future. General Washington himself endured greater physical hardships than if he had remained a British subject, yet he was a happy man because he was engaged in benefiting his race; in doing something for the children of his neighbors, having none of his own.

The colony of Liberia has been in existence a long time. In a certain sense, it is a success. The old President of Liberia,

Roberts, has just been with me for the first time I ever saw him. He says they have within the bounds of that colony between three and four hundred thousand people, or more than in some of our old States, such as Rhode Island or Delaware, or in some of our newer States, and less than in some of our larger ones. They are not all American colonists or their descendants. Something less than 12,000 have been sent thither from this country. Many of the original settlers have died, yet, like people elsewhere, their offspring outnumber those deceased. The question is, if the colored people are persuaded to go anywhere, why not there? One reason for unwillingness to do so is, that some of you would rather remain within reach of the country of your nativity. I do not know how much attachment you may have toward our race. It does not strike me that you have the greatest reason to love them. But still you are attached to them at all events. The place I am thinking about having for a colony is in Central America. It is nearer to us than Liberia—not much more than one-fourth as far as Liberia, and within seven days' run by steamers. Unlike Liberia it is a great line of travel—it is a highway. The country is a very excellent one for any people, and with great natural resources and advantages, and especially because of the similarity of climate with your native soil, thus being suited to your physical condition. The particular place I have in view, is to be a great highway from the Atlantic or Caribbean Sea to the Pacific Ocean, and this particular place has all the advantages for a colony. On both sides there are harbors among the finest in the world. Again, there is evidence of very rich coal mines. A certain amount of coal is valuable in any country, and there may be more than enough for the wants of any country. Why I attach so much importance to coal is, it will afford an opportunity to the inhabitants for immediate employment till they get ready to settle permanently in their homes. If you take colonists where there is no good landing, there is a bad show; and so where there is nothing to cultivate, and of which to make a farm. But if something is started so that you can get your daily bread as soon as you reach there, it is a great advantage. Coal land is the best thing I know of with which to com-

6*

mence an enterprise. To return—you have been talked to upon this subject, and told that a speculation is intended by gentlemen who have an interest in the country, including the coal mines. We have been mistaken all our lives if we do not know whites, as well as blacks, look to their self-interest. Unless among those deficient of intellect, everybody you trade with makes something. You meet with these things here and everywhere. If such persons have what will be an advantage to them, the question is, whether it can be made of advantage to you? You are intelligent and know that success does not as much depend on external help as on self-reliance. Much, therefore, depends upon yourselves. As to the coal mines, I think I see the means available for your self-reliance. I shall, if I get a sufficient number of you engaged, have provision made that you shall not be wronged. If you will engage in the enterprise I will spend some of the money intrusted to me. I am not sure you will succeed. The Government may lose the money, but we can not succeed unless we try; but we think with care we can succeed. The political affairs in Central America are not in quite as satisfactory condition as I wish. There are contending factions in that quarter; but it is true, all the factions are agreed alike on the subject of colonization, and want it, and are more generous than we are here. To your colored race they have no objection. Besides, I would endeavor to have you made equals, and have the best assurance that you should be the equals of the best. The practical thing I want to ascertain is, whether I can get a number of able-bodied men, with their wives and children, who are willing to go when I present evidence of encouragement and protection. Could I get a hundred tolerably intelligent men, with their wives and children, and able to "cut their own fodder," so to speak? Can I have fifty? If I could find twenty-five able-bodied men, with a mixture of women and children—good things in the family relation, I think—I could make a successful commencement. I want you to let me know whether this can be done or not. This is the practical part of my wish to see you. These are subjects of very great importance—worthy of a month's study of a speech delivered in an hour. I ask you, then, to consider seriously, not pertaining to yourselves merely, nor for your race and ours for the present time, but as one of the things, if successfully managed, for the good of mankind—not confined to the present generation, but as

> "From age to age descends the lay
> To millions yet to be,
> Till far its echoes roll away
> Into eternity."

The above is merely given as the substance of the President's remarks.

The chairman of the delegation briefly replied, that "they would hold a consultation, and in a short time give an answer." The President said, "Take your full time—no hurry at all."

The delegation then withdrew.

THE CLAMORS FOR EMANCIPATION.

There were some persons who seemed to think that Mr. Lincoln was elected not constitutional President of the United States, but President of an enormous Anti-Slavery Society. Prominent among these was the eminent and estimable philanthropist who had made the *New York Tribune* a power in the land, through the columns of which journal he addressed a letter to the President, on the 19th of August, 1862, urging upon him with great earnestness, and with all his wonted vigor of style, a policy of unreserved emancipation. To that letter Mr. Lincoln made the following clear and calm reply:

EXECUTIVE MANSION, WASHINGTON, *August* 22, 1862.

Hon. Horace Greeley—Dear Sir—I have just read yours of the 19th instant, addressed to myself through the New York *Tribune.*

If there be in it any statements or assumptions of fact which I may know to be erroneous, I do not now and here controvert them.

If there be any inferences which I may believe to be falsely drawn, I do not now and here argue against them.

If there be perceptible in it an impatient and dictatorial tone, I waive it in deference to an old friend whose heart I have always supposed to be right.

As to the policy I "seem to be pursuing," as you say, I have not meant to leave any one in doubt. I would save the Union. I would save it in the shortest way under the Constitution.

The sooner the national authority can be restored the nearer the Union will be—the Union as it was.

If there be those who would not save the Union unless they could at the same time save slavery, I do not agree with them.

If there be those who would not save the Union unless they could at the same time destroy slavery, I do not agree with them.

My paramount object is to save the Union, and not either to save or destroy slavery.

If I could save the Union without freeing any slave, I would do it—if I could save it by freeing all the slaves, I would do it —and if I could do it by freeing some and leaving others alone, I would also do that.

What I do about slavery and the colored race, I do because I believe it helps to save this Union, and what I forbear, I forbear because I do not believe it would help to save the Union.

I shall do less whenever I shall believe what I am doing hurts the cause, and I shall do more whenever I believe doing more will help the cause.

I shall try to correct errors when shown to be errors, and I shall adopt new views so fast as they shall appear to be true views.

I have here stated my purpose according to my views of official duty, and I intend no modification of my oft-expressed personal wish that all men everywhere could be free.

Yours,   A. LINCOLN.

Such appeals as that to which Mr. Lincoln replied in the foregoing letter, became more frequent, taking in some instances almost the shape of demands; and on the 13th of September, the President formally received a deputation from the various religious denominations of

Chicago, who presented a memorial asking immediate and unconditional emancipation, to which he made the following response:

The subject presented in the memorial is one upon which I have thought much for weeks past, and I may even say for months. I am approached with the most opposite opinions and advice, and that by religious men, who are equally certain that they represent the Divine will. I am sure that either the one or the other class is mistaken in that belief, and perhaps in some respects both. I hope it will not be irreverent for me to say that if it is probable that God would reveal his will to others, on 'a point so connected with my duty, it might be supposed he would reveal it directly to me; for, unless I am more deceived in myself than I often am, it is my earnest desire to know the will of Providence in this matter. And if I can learn what it is I will do it! These are not, however, the days of miracles, and I suppose it will be granted that I am not to expect a direct revelation. I must study the plain physical facts of the case, ascertain what is possible, and learn what appears to be wise and right.

The subject is difficult, and good men do not agree. For instance, the other day, four gentlemen of standing and intelligence from New York called as a delegation on business connected with the war; but before leaving two of them earnestly besought me to proclaim general emancipation, upon which the other two at once attacked them. You know, also, that the last session of Congress had a decided majority of anti-slavery men, yet they could not unite on this policy. And the same is true of the religious people. Why, the rebel soldiers are praying with a great deal more earnestness, I fear, than our own troops, and expecting God to favor their side: for one of our soldiers, who had been taken prisoner, told Senator Wilson a few days since, that he met nothing so discouraging as the evident sincerity of those he was among, in their prayers. But we will talk over the merits of the case.

What good would a proclamation of emancipation from me do, especially as we are now situated? I do not want to issue a document that the whole world will see must necessarily be inoperative, 'like the Pope's bull against the comet! Would my word free the slaves, when I cannot even enforce the Constitution in the rebel States? Is there a single court, or magistrate, or individual that would be influenced by it there? And what reason is there to think it would have any greater effect upon the slaves than the late law of Congress, which I approved, and which offers protection and freedom to the slaves of rebel masters who come within our lines? Yet I cannot learn that the law has caused a single slave to come over to us. And suppose they could be induced by a proclamation of freedom from me to throw themselves upon us, what should we do with them? How can we feed and care for such a multitude? General Butler wrote me a few days since that he was issuing more rations to the slaves who have rushed to him than to all the white troops under his command. They eat, and that is all; though it is true General Butler is feeding the whites also by the thousand; for it nearly amounts to a famine there. If, now, the pressure of the war should call off our forces from New Orleans to defend some other point, what is to prevent the masters from reducing the blacks to slavery again; for I am told that whenever the rebels take any black prisoners, free or slave, they immediately auction them off! They did so with those they took from a boat that was aground in the Tennessee river a few days ago. And then I am very ungenerously attacked for it! For instance, when, after the late battles at and near Bull Run, an expedition went out from Washington, under a flag of truce, to bury the dead and bring in the wounded, and the rebels seized the blacks who went along to help, and sent them into slavery, Horace Greeley said in his paper that the Government would probably do nothing about it. What could I do?

Now, then, tell me, if you please, what possible result of good would follow the issuing of such a proclamation as you desire? Understand, I raise no objections against it on legal or constitutional grounds, for, as commander-in-chief of the army and navy, in time of war I suppose I have a right to take any measure which may best subdue the enemy, nor do I urge objections of a moral nature, in view of possible consequences of insurrection and massacre at the South. I view this matter as a practical war measure, to be decided on according to the advantages or disadvantages it may offer to the suppression of the rebellion.

I admit that slavery is at the root of the rebellion, or at least its *sine qua non*. The ambition of politicians may have instigated them to act, but they would have been impotent without slavery as their instrument. I will also concede that emancipation would help us in Europe, and convince them that we are incited by something more than ambition. I grant, further, that it would help somewhat at the North, though not so much, I fear, as you and those you represent imagine. Still, some additional strength would be added in that way to the war, and then, unquestionably, it would weaken the rebels by drawing off their laborers, which is of great importance; but I am not so sure we could do much with the blacks. If we were to arm them, I fear that in a few weeks the arms would be in the hands of the rebels; and, indeed, thus far, we have not had arms enough to equip our white troops. I will mention another thing, though it meet only your scorn and contempt. There are 50,000 bayonets in the Union army from the border slave States. It would be a serious matter if, in consequence of a proclamation such as you desire, they should go over to the rebels. I do not think they all would—not so many, indeed, as a year ago, or as six months ago—not so many to-day as yesterday. Every day increases their Union feeling. They are also getting their pride enlisted, and want to beat the rebels. Let me say one thing more: I think you should admit that we already have an important principle to rally and unite the people, in the fact that constitutional government is at stake. This is a fundamental idea going down about as deep as any thing.

Do not misunderstand me because I have mentioned these objections. They indicate the difficulties that have thus far prevented my action in some such way as you desire. I have not decided against a proclamation of liberty to the slaves, but hold the matter under advisement. And I can assure you that the subject is on my mind, by day and night, more than any other. Whatever shall appear to be God's will I will do. I trust that in the freedom with which I have canvassed your views I have not in any respect injured your feelings.

EMANCIPATION DECIDED UPON.

Being convinced that a policy of emancipation was right in itself and that the time had arrived when it would receive that degree of public approval without which, right or wrong, it would have been in vain, the President issued on the 22d of September the following

PRELIMINARY PROCLAMATION OF EMANCIPATION.

I, ABRAHAM LINCOLN, President of the United States of America and Commander-in-Chief of the army and navy thereof, do hereby proclaim and declare that hereafter, as heretofore, the war will be prosecuted for the object of practically restoring the constitutional relation between the United States and each of the States, and the people thereof, in which States that relation is or may be suspended or disturbed.

That it is my purpose, upon the next meeting of Congress, to again recommend the adoption of a practical measure tendering pecuniary aid to the free acceptance or rejection of all Slave States so-called, the people whereof may not then be in rebellion against the United States, and which States may then have voluntarily adopted, or thereafter may voluntarily adopt, immediate or gradual abolishment of slavery within their respective limits; and that the effort to colonize persons of African descent, with their consent, upon this continent or elsewhere, with the previously obtained consent of the governments existing there, will be continued.

That on the first day of January, in the year of our Lord one thousand eight hundred and sixty-three, all persons held as slaves within any State, or designated part of a State, the people whereof shall then be in rebellion against the United States, shall be then, thenceforward, and forever free; and the Executive Government of the United States, including the military and naval authority thereof, will recognize and maintain the freedom of such persons, and will do no act or acts to repress such persons, or any of them, in any efforts they may make for their actual freedom.

That the Executive will, on the first day of January aforesaid, by proclamation, designate the States and parts of States, if any, in which the people thereof respectively shall then be in rebellion against the United States; and the fact that any State, or the people thereof, shall on that day be in good faith represented in the Congress of the United States, by members chosen thereto at elections wherein a majority of the qualified voters of such State shall have participated, shall, in the absence of strong countervailing testimony, be deemed conclusive evidence that such State, and the people thereof, are not then in rebellion against the United States.

That attention is hereby called to an act of Congress entitled "An Act to make an additional Article of War," approved March 13th, 1862, and which act as is in the words and figures following:

Be it enacted by the Senate and House of Representatives of the United States of America in Congress assembled, That hereafter the following shall be promulgated as an additional article of war for the government of the army of the United States, and shall be obeyed and observed as such:

ARTICLE.—All officers or persons in the military or naval service of the United States are prohibited from employing any of the forces under their respective commands for the purpose of returning fugitives from service or labor who may have escaped from any persons to whom such service or labor is claimed to be due; and any officer who shall be found guilty by a court-martial of violating this article shall be dismissed from the service.

SEC. 2. *And be it further enacted*, That this act shall take effect from and after its passage.

Also, to the ninth and tenth sections of an act entitled "An Act to suppress Insurrection, to punish Treason and Rebellion, to seize and confiscate Property of Rebels, and for other purposes," approved July 16, 1862, and which sections are in the words and figures following:

SEC. 9. *And be it further enacted*, That all slaves of persons who shall hereafter be engaged in rebellion against the Government of the United States, or who shall in any way give aid or comfort thereto, escaping from such persons and taking refuge within the lines of the army; and all slaves captured from such persons, or deserted by them and coming under the control of the Government of the United States; and all slaves of such persons found *on* [or] being within any place occupied by rebel forces and afterwards occupied by forces of the United States, shall be deemed captives of war, and shall be forever free of their servitude, and not again held as slaves.

SEC. 10. *And be it further enacted*, That no slave escaping into any State, Territory, or the District of Columbia, from any other State, shall be delivered up, or in any way impeded or hindered of his liberty, except for crime, or some offence against the laws, unless the person claiming said fugitive shall first make oath that the person to whom the labor or service of such fugitive is alleged to be due is his lawful owner, and has not borne arms against the United States in the present rebellion, nor in any way given aid and comfort thereto; and no person engaged in the military or naval service of the United States shall, under any pretence whatever, assume to decide on the validity of the claim of any person to the service or labor of any other person, or surrender up any such person to the claimant, on pain of being dismissed from the service.

And I do hereby enjoin upon and order all persons engaged in the military and naval service of the United States to observe, obey, and enforce, within their respective spheres of service, the act and sections above recited.

And the Executive will in due time recommend that all citizens of the United States who shall have remained loyal thereto throughout the rebellion, shall (upon the restoration of the constitutional relation between the United States and their respective States and people, if that relation shall have been suspended or disturbed) be compensated for all losses by acts of the United States, including the loss of slaves.

In witness whereof I have hereunto set my hand and caused the seal of the United States to be affixed.

Done at the city of Washington, this tenth day of April, in the
year of our Lord one thousand eight hundred and sixty-
[L. S.] two, and of the independence of the United States the
eighty-seventh.   ABRAHAM LINCOLN.
By the President:
WM. II. SEWARD, *Secretary of State.*

This proclamation caused a very profound sensation
throughout the country. On the evening of the 24th
of September a large body of people assembled before
the White House with music. The President came out
to them and made the following speech. It is manifest,
even more than by words, how great was his sense of
responsibility in taking this step, and with what anxiety
he watched for its effect upon the country.

Fellow-Citizens—I appear before you to do little more than to
acknowledge the courtesy you pay me, and to thank you for it.
I have not been distinctly informed why it is that on this occasion you appear to do me this honor, though I suppose it is
because of the Proclamation. What I did, I did after a very
full deliberation, and under a very heavy and solemn sense of
responsibility. I can only trust in God I have made no mistake. I shall make no attempt on this occasion to sustain what
I have done or said by any comment. It is now for the country
and the world to pass judgment, and, may be, take action upon
it. I will say no more upon this subject. In my position I am
environed with difficulties. Yet they are scarcely so great as
the difficulties of those who, upon the battle-field, are endeavoring to purchase with their blood and their lives, the future
happiness and prosperity of this country. Let us never forget
them. On the 14th and 17th days of this present month, there
have been battles bravely, skillfully, and successfully fought.
We do not yet know the particulars. Let us be sure that,
in giving praise to certain individuals, we do no injustice to
others. I only ask you at the conclusion of these few remarks,
to give three hearty cheers to all good and brave officers and
men who fought those successful battles.

SUSPENSION OF THE WRIT OF HABEAS CORPUS.

Early in the rebellion it had been found necessary by the President, in pursuance of the clause in the Constitution providing for such action, to suspend the privalege of the writ of *habeas corpus* in a few isolated instances, by orders issued to military officers. But the following is the first proclamation ordering such suspension in regard to all persons in military custody :

PROCLAMATION.

Whereas, it has been necessary to call into service, not only volunteers, but also portions of the militia of the States by draft, in order to suppress the insurrection existing in the United States, and disloyal persons are not adequately restrained by the ordinary processes of law from hindering this measure, and from giving aid and comfort in various ways to the insurrection,

Now, therefore, be it ordered—

First, That during the existing insurrection, and as a necessary measure for suppressing the same, all rebels and insurgents, their aiders and abettors, within the United States, and all persons discouraging volunteer enlistments, resisting military drafts, or guilty of any disloyal practice affording aid and comfort to the rebels against the authority of the United States, shall be subject to martial law, and liable to trial and punishment by court-martial or military commission.

Second, That the writ of *habeas corpus* is suspended in respect to all persons arrested, or who are now, or hereafter during the rebellion shall be, imprisoned in any fort, camp, arsenal, military prison, or other place of confinement, by any military authority, or by the sentence of any court-martial or military commission.

In witness whereof I have hereunto set my hand and seal, and caused the seal of the United States to be affixed.

Done at the city of Washington, this twenty-fourth day of
September, in the year of our Lord one thousand
[L. S.] eight hundred and sixty-two, and of the independ-
ence of the United States the eighty-seventh.

ABRAHAM LINCOLN.

By the President:

WILLIAM H. SEWARD, *Secretary of State.*

GENERAL M'CLELLAN AGAIN.

On the 6th of October, after a visit made by the President to the Army of the Potomac, General McClellan
received an order through General Halleck, then general-in-chief, to cross the Potomac immediately and give
battle or drive the enemy southward. But the commander was not yet ready and went into correspondence
about supplies and reinforcements. Meantime the rebel
General of cavalry, Stuart, rode round and round him,
going into Pennsylvania, and setting him openly at
naught. Upon this, Mr. Lincoln addressed him the following letter, which elicited only replies, the nature of
which is clearly enough shown by the President's brief
dispatches which are appended to it.

EXECUTIVE MANSION, WASHINGTON, *Oct.* 13, 1862.

My Dear Sir—You remember my speaking to you of what I
called your overcautiousness. Are you not overcautious when
you assume that you can not do what the enemy is constantly
doing? Should you not claim to be at least his equal in prowess,
and act upon the claim?

As I understand, you telegraphed General Halleck that you
can not subsist your army at Winchester, unless the railroad
from Harper's Ferry to that point be put in working order.
But the enemy does now subsist his army at Winchester, at a
distance nearly twice as great from railroad transportation as
you would have to do without the railroad last named. He

now wagons from Culpepper Court-House, which is just about twice as far as you would have to do from Harper's Ferry. He is certainly not more than half as well provided with wagons as you are. I certainly should be pleased for you to have the advantage of the railroad from Harper's Ferry to Winchester; but it wastes all the remainder of autumn to give it to you, and, in fact, ignores the question of *time*, which can not and must not be ignored.

Again, one of the standard maxims of war, as you know, is, "to operate upon the enemy's communications as much as possible without exposing your own." You seem to act as if this applies *against* you, but can not apply in your *favor*. Change positions with the enemy, and think you not he would break your communication with Richmond within the next twenty-four hours? You dread his going into Pennsylvania. But if he does so in full force, he gives up his communications to you absolutely, and you have nothing to do but to follow and ruin him; if he does so with less than full force, fall upon and beat what is left behind all the easier.

Exclusive of the water line, you are now nearer Richmond than the enemy is by the route that you *can* and he *must* take. Why can you not reach there before him, unless you admit that he is more than your equal on a march? His route is the arc of a circle, while yours is the chord. The roads are as good on yours as on his.

You know I desired, but did not order you, to cross the Potomac below instead of above the Shenandoah and Blue Ridge. My idea was, that this would at once menace the enemy's communications, which I would seize if he would permit. If he should move northward, I would follow him closely, holding his communications. If he should prevent our seizing his communications, and move toward Richmond, I would press closely to him, fight him if a favorable opportunity should present, and at least try to beat him to Richmond on the inside track. I say "try;" if we never try, we shall never succeed. If he make a stand at Winchester, moving neither north nor south, I would fight him there, on the idea that if we cannot beat him when he bears the wastage of coming to us, we never can when we bear the wastage of going to him. This proposition is a simple truth, and is too important to be lost sight of for a moment. In coming to us, he tenders us an advantage which we should not waive. We should not so operate as to merely drive him away. As we must beat him somewhere, or fail finally, we can do it, if at all, easier near to us than far away. If we cannot beat the enemy where he now is, we never can, he again being within the intrenchments of Richmond. Recurring to the idea of going to Richmond on the inside track, the facility of supplying from the side away from the enemy is remarkable, as it were, by the different spokes of a wheel, extending from the hub toward the rim, and this whether you move directly by the chord, or on the inside arc, hugging the Blue Ridge more closely. The chord-line, as you see, carries you by Aldie, Haymarket, and Fredericksburg, and you see how turnpikes, railroads, and finally the Potomac by Aquia Creek, meet you at all points from Washington. The same, only the lines lengthened a little, if you press closer to the Blue Ridge part of the way. The gaps through the Blue Ridge I understand to be about the following distances from Harper's Ferry, to wit; Vestal's, five miles; Gregory's, thirteen; Snicker's, eighteen; Ashby's, twenty-eight; Manassas, thirty-eight; Chester, forty-five; and Thornton's, fifty-three. I should think it preferable to take the route nearest the enemy, disabling him to make an important move without your knowledge, and compelling him to keep his forces together for dread of you. The gaps would enable you to attack if you should wish. For a great part of the way you would be practically between the enemy and both Washington and Richmond, enabling us to spare you the greatest number of troops from here. When, at length, running to Richmond ahead of him enables him to move this way, if he does so, turn and attack him in the rear. But I think he should be engaged long before such point is reached. It is all easy if our troops march as well as the enemy, and it is unmanly to say they cannot do it. This letter is in no sense an order.

Yours, truly,
ABRAHAM LINCOLN.

Major-General McClellan.

War Department, Washington, *Oct.* 25, 1862.

I have just read your dispatch about sore-tongue and fatigued horses. Will you pardon me for asking what the horses of your army have done since the battle of Antictam that fatigues anything? ABRAHAM LINCOLN.

Executive Mansion,
Washington, *Oct.* 26, 1862.

Yours in reply to mine about horses received. Of course you know the facts better than I. Still, two considerations remain: Stuart's cavalry outmarched ours, having certainly done more marked service on the Peninsula and everywhere since. Secondly: will not a movement of our army be a relief to the cavalry, compelling the enemy to concentrate instead of "foraging" in squads everywhere? But I am so rejoiced to learn from your dispatch to General Halleck that you began crossing the river this morning. ABRAHAM LINCOLN.

Executive Mansion,
Washington, *Oct.* 26, 1862.

Yours of yesterday received. Most certainly I intend no injustice to any, and if I have done any I deeply regret it. To be told, after more than five weeks' total inaction of the army, and during which period we had sent to that army every fresh horse we possibly could, amounting in the whole to 7,918, that the cavalry horses were too much fatigued to move, presented a very cheerless, almost hopeless, prospect for the future, and it may have forced something of impatience into my dispatches. If not recruited and rested then, when could they ever be? I suppose the river is rising, and I am glad to believe you are crossing. A. LINCOLN.

Executive Mansion,
Washington, *Oct.* 27, 1862.

Your dispatch of 3 P.M. to-day, in regard to filling up old regiments with drafted men, is received, and the request therein shall be complied with as far as practicable. And now I ask a distinct answer to the question, "Is it your purpose not to go into *action* again till the men now being drafted in the States are incorporated in the old regiments?" A. LINCOLN.

DEFENCE OF GENERAL M'CLELLAN.

Sorely tried as President Lincoln was by General McClellan, he yet sustained him to the best of his ability and with great magnanimity as long as he was kept in command. On the 6th of August a war meeting was held in Washington, at which Mr. Lincoln was present, and delivered the following brief address. It was just after General M'Clellan's retreat across the Peninsula, when popular feeling was turning strongly against him. Whoever will bear in mind the correspondence which took place about that time, and which was not published until long after will find no trace of it in this generous defence.

Fellow-Citizens—I believe there is no precedent for my appearing before you on this occasion, but it is also true that there is no precedent for your being here yourselves, and I offer, in justification of myself and of you, that, upon examination, I have found nothing in the Constitution against it. I, however, . have an impression that there are younger gentlemen who will entertain you better, and better address your understanding than I will or could, and therefore I propose but to detain you a moment longer.

I am very little inclined on any occasion to say anything unless I hope to produce some good by it. The only thing I think of just now not likely to be better said by some one else, is a matter in which we have heard some other persons blamed for what I did myself. There has been a very wide-spread attempt to have a quarrel between General McClellan and the Secretary of War. Now, I occupy a position that enables me to observe, that these two gentlemen are not nearly so deep in the quarrel as some pretending to be their friends. General McClellan's attitude is such that, in the very selfishness of his nature, he cannot but wish to be successful, and I hope he will —and the Secretary of War is in precisely the same situation. If the military commanders in the field cannot be successful, not only the Secretary of War, but myself, for the time being the master of them both, cannot but be failures. I know General McClellan wishes to be successful, and I know he does not wish it any more than the Secretary of War for him, and both of them together no more than I wish it. Sometimes we have a dispute about how many men General McClellan has had, and those who would disparage him say that he had a very large number, and those who would disparage the Secretary of War insist that General McClellan has had a very small number, The basis for this is, there is always a wide difference, and on this occasion, perhaps a wider one than usual, between the grand total on McClellan's rolls and the men actually fit for duty; and those who would disparage him talk of the grand total on paper, and those who would disparage the Secretary of War talk of those at present fit for duty. General McClellan has sometimes asked for things that the Secretary of War did not give him. General McClellan is not to blame for asking what he wanted and needed, and the Secretary of War is not to blame for not giving when he had none to give. And I say here, as far as I know, the Secretary of War has withheld no one thing at any time in my power to give him. I have no accusation against him. I believe he is a brave and able man, and I stand here, as justice requires me to do, to take upon myself what has been charged on the Secretary of War, as withholding from him.

I have talked longer than I expected to do, and now I avail myself of my privilege of saying no more.

OBSERVANCE OF SUNDAY.

A needless amount of labor on the one hand, and of noisy hilarity upon the other, upon Sunday, having been noticed in the army, Mr. Lincoln issued the following circular-letter upon that subject:

EXECUTIVE MANSION, WASHINGTON, *November* 16, 1862.

The President, commander-in-chief of the army and navy, desires and enjoins the orderly observance of the Sabbath by the officers and men in the military and naval service. The importance for man and beast of the prescribed weekly rest, the sacred rights of Christian soldiers and sailors, a becoming deference to the best sentiment of a Christian people, and a due regard for the Divine will, demand that Sunday labor in the army and navy be reduced to the measure of strict necessity.

The discipline and character of the national forces should not suffer, nor the cause they defend be imperiled by the profanation of the day or name of the Most High. "At this time of public distress," adopting the words of Washington in 1776, "men may find enough to do in the service of God and their country, without abandoning themselves to vice and immorality." The first general order issued by the Father of his Country, after the Declaration of Independence, indicates the spirit in which our institutions were founded, and should ever be defended. "The general hopes and trusts that every officer and man will endeavor to live and act as becomes a Christian soldier defending the dearest rights and liberties of his country."

A. LINCOLN.

ELECTIONS IN LOUISIANA.

About this time there was an effort making to get up some sort of make-shift representation of Louisiana ·in Congress. How wrongful was the often repeated charge that Mr. Lincoln endeavored to secure support for his administration and a reëlection for himself by irregular and violent means of conducting elections, and how opposed he was in feeling, as well as in policy to any such methods, are strikingly shown in the following letter:

EXECUTIVE MANSION, WASHINGTON, *November* 21, 1862.
Dear Sir—Dr. Kennedy, bearer of this, has some apprehension that Federal officers, not citizens of Louisiana, may be set up as candidates for Congress in that State. In my view there could be no possible object in such an election. We do not particularly need members of Congress from those States to en-

able us to get along with legislation here. What we do want is the conclusive evidence that respectable citizens of Louisiana are willing to be members of Congress and to swear support to the Constitution, and that other respectable citizens there are willing to vote for them and send them. To send a parcel of Northern men here as representatives, elected as would be understood (and perhaps really so), at the point of the bayonet, would be disgraceful and outrageous; and were I a member of Congress here, I would vote against admitting any such man to a seat.   Yours, very truly,   A. LINCOLN.

Hon. G. F. SHEPLEY.

MESSAGE TO CONGRESS, DEC. 1st, 1862.

What had been the recent experience of the country, and what was its internal condition and its relations with foreign powers, are very fully and lucidly set forth in Mr. Lincoln's Message to Congress at the opening of its session of 1862–3, which follows:

Fellow-Citizens of the Senate and House of Representatives—Since your last annual assembling, another year of health and bountiful harvests has passed, and while it has not pleased the Almighty to bless us with a return of peace, we can but press on, guided by the best light He gives us, trusting that, in his own good time and wise way, all will be well.

The correspondence, touching foreign affairs, which has taken place during the last year, is herewith submitted, in virtual compliance with a request to that effect made by the House of Representatives near the close of the last session of Congress. If the condition of our relations with other nations is less gratifying than it has usually been at former periods, it is certainly more satisfactory than a nation so unhappily distracted as we are might reasonably have apprehended. In the month of June last there were some grounds to expect that the maritime Powers which, at the beginning of our domestic difficulties, so unwisely and so unnecessarily, as we think, recognized the insurgents as a belligerent, would soon recede from that position, which has proved only less injurious to themselves than to our country. But the temporary reverses which afterward befell the National arms, and which were exaggerated by our own disloyal citizens abroad, have hitherto delayed that act of simple justice.

The civil war which has so radically changed for the moment the occupations and habits of the American people, has necessarily disturbed the social condition, and affected very deeply the prosperity of the nations with which we have carried on a commerce that has been steadily increasing throughout a period of half a century. It has, at the same time, excited political ambitions and apprehensions which have produced a profound agitation throughout the civilized world. In this unusual agitation we have forborne from taking part in any controversy between foreign states, and between parties or factions in such states. We have attempted no propagandism, and acknowledged no revolution. But we have left to every nation the exclusive conduct and management of its own affairs. Our struggle has been, of course, contemplated by foreign nations with reference less to its own merits, than to its supposed and often exaggerated effects and consequences resulting to those nations themselves. Nevertheless, complaint on the part of this Government, even if it were just, would certainly be unwise.

The treaty with Great Britain for the suppression of the slave trade has been put into operation with a good prospect of complete success. It is an occasion of special pleasure to acknowledge that the execution of it on the part of Her Majesty's Government, has been marked with a jealous respect for the authority of the United States and the rights of their moral and loyal citizens.

The convention with Hanover for the abolition of the stade dues has been carried into full effect, under the act of Congress for that purpose.

A blockade of three thousand miles of seacoast could not be established and vigorously enforced, in a season of great commercial activity like the present, without committing occasional mistakes, and inflicting unintentional injuries upon foreign nations and their subjects.

A civil war occurring in a country where foreigners reside and carry on trade under treaty stipulations, is necessarily fruitful of complaints of the violation of neutral rights. All such collisions tend to excite misapprehensions, and possibly to produce mutual reclamations between nations which have a common interest in preserving peace and friendship. In clear cases of these kinds I have, so far as possible, heard and redressed complaints which have been presented by friendly Powers. There is still, however, a large and augmenting number of doubtful cases, upon which the Government is unable to agree with the Governments whose protection is demanded by the claimants. There are, moreover, many cases in which the United States, or their citizens, suffer wrongs from the naval or military authorities of foreign nations, which the Governments of these states are not at once prepared to redress. I have proposed to some of the foreign states thus interested, mutual conventions to examine and adjust such complaints. This proposition has been made especially to Great Britain, to France, to Spain, and to Prussia. In each case it has been kindly received, but has not yet been formally adopted.

I deem it my duty to recommend an appropriation in behalf of the owners of the Norwegian bark Admiral P. Tordenskiold, which vessel was, in May, 1861, prevented by the commander of the blockading force off Charleston from leaving that port with cargo, notwithstanding a similar privilege had, shortly before, been granted to an English vessel. I have directed the Secretary of State to cause the papers in the case to be communicated to the proper committees.

Applications have been made to me by many free Americans of African descent to favor their emigration, with a view to such colonization as was contemplated in recent acts of Congress. Other parties, at home and abroad—some from interested motives, others upon patriotic considerations, and still others influenced by philanthropic sentiments—have suggested similar measures; while, on the other hand, several of the Spanish-American Republics have protested against the sending of such colonies to their respective territories. Under these circumstances I have declined to move any such colony to any state without first obtaining the consent of its Government, with an agreement on its part to receive and protect such emigrants in all the rights of freemen; and I have at the same time offered to the several states situated within the tropics, or having colonies there, to negotiate with them, subject to the advice and consent of the Senate, to favor the voluntary emigration of persons of that class to their respective territories, upon conditions that shall be equal, just, and humane. Liberia and Hayti are, as yet, the only countries to which colonists of African descent from here could go with certainty of being received and adopted as citizens; and I regret to say such persons, contemplating colonization, do not seem so willing to migrate to those countries as to some others, nor so willing as I think their interest demands. I believe, however, opinion among them in this respect is improving; and that ere long there will be an augmented and considerable migration to both these countries from the United States.

The new commercial treaty between the United States and the Sultan of Turkey has been carried into execution.

A commercial and consular treaty has been negotiated, subject to the Senate's consent, with Liberia; and a similar negotiation is now pending with the Republic of Hayti. A considerable improvement of the national commerce is expected to result from these measures.

Our relations with Great Britain, France, Spain, Portugal, Russia, Prussia, Denmark, Sweden, Austria, the Netherlands, Italy, Rome, and the other European states, remain undisturbed. Very favorable relations also continue to be maintained with Turkey, Morocco, China, and Japan.

During the last year there has not only been no change of our previous relations with the Independent States of our own continent, but more friendly sentiments than have heretofore existed are believed to be entertained by these neighbors, whose safety and progress are so intimately connected with our own. This statement especially applies to Mexico, Nicaragua, Costa Rica, Honduras, Peru, and Chili.

The commission under the convention with the Republic of New Grenada closed its session without having audited and passed upon all the claims which were submitted to it. A proposition is pending to revive the convention, that it be able to do more complete justice. The joint commission between the United States and the Republic of Costa Rica has completed its labors and submitted its report.

I have favored the project for connecting the United States with Europe by an Atlantic telegraph, and a similar project to extend the telegraph from San Francisco to connect by a Pacific telegraph with the line which is being extended across the Russian Empire.

The Territories of the United States, with unimportant exceptions, have remained undisturbed by the civil war; and they are exhibiting such evidence of prosperity as justifies an expectation that some of them will soon be in a condition to be organized as States, and be constitutionally admitted into the Federal Union.

The immense mineral resources of some of those Territories ought to be developed as rapidly as possible. Every step in that direction would have a tendency to improve the revenues of the Government and diminish the burdens of the people. It is worthy of your serious consideration whether some extraordinary measures to promote that end cannot be adopted. The means which suggests itself as most likely to be effective, is a scientific exploration of the mineral regions in those Territories, with a view to the publication of its results at home and in foreign countries—results which cannot fail to be auspicious.

The condition of the finances will claim your most diligent consideration. The vast expenditures incident to the military and naval operations required for the suppression of the rebellion have been hitherto met with a promptitude and certainty unusual in similar circumstances; and the public credit has been fully maintained. The continuance of the war, however, and the increased disbursements made necessary by the augmented forces now in the field, demand your best reflections as to the best modes of providing the necessary revenue, without injury to business, and with the least possible burdens upon labor.

The suspension of specie payments by the banks, soon after

the commencement of your last session, made large issues of United States notes unavoidable. In no other way could the payment of the troops and the satisfaction of other just demands, be so economically or so well provided for. The judicious legislation of Congress, securing the receivability of these notes for loans and internal duties, and making them a legal tender for other debts, has made them a universal currency, and has satisfied, partially at least, and for the time, the long felt want of an uniform circulating medium, saving thereby to the people immense sums in discounts and exchanges.

A return to specie payments, however, at the earliest period compatible with due regard to all interests concerned, should ever be kept in view. Fluctuations in the value of currency are always injurious, and to reduce these fluctuations to the lowest possible point will always be a leading purpose in wise legislation. Convertibility, prompt and certain convertibility into coin, is generally acknowledged to be the best and surest safeguard against them; and it is extremely doubtful whether a circulation of United States notes, payable in coin, and sufficiently large for the wants of the people, can be permanently, usefully, and safely maintained.

Is there, then, any other mode in which the necessary provision for the public wants can be made, and the great advantages of a safe and uniform currency secured?

I know of none which promises so certain results, and is at the same time so unobjectionable as the organization of banking associations, under a general act of Congress, well guarded in its provisions. To such associations the Government might furnish circulating notes, on the security of United States bonds deposited in the Treasury. These notes, prepared under the supervision of proper officers, being uniform in appearance and security, and convertible always into coin, would at once protect labor against the evils of a vicious currency, and facilitate commerce by cheap and safe exchanges.

A moderate reservation from the interest on the bonds would compensate the United States for the preparation and distribution of the notes, and a general supervision of the system, and would lighten the burden of that part of the public debt employed as securities.   The public credit, moreover, would be greatly improved, and the negotiation of new loans greatly facil- itated by the steady market demand for Government bonds which the adoption of the proposed system would create.

It is an additional recommendation of the measure, of con- siderable weight, in my judgment, that it would reconcile as far as possible all existing interests, by the opportunity offered to existing institutions to reorganize under the act, substitut- ing only the secured uniform national circulation for the local and various circulation, secured and unsecured, now issued by them.

The receipts into the Treasury, from all sources, including loans, and balance from the preceding year, for the fiscal year ending on the 30th of June, 1862, were $583,885,247 60, of which sum $49,056,397 62 were derived from customs; $1,795,- 331 73 from the direct tax; from public lands, $152,203 77; from miscellaneous sources, $931,787 64; from loans in all forms, $529,692,460 50.   The remainder, $2,257,065 80, was the bal- ance from last year.

The disbursements during the same period were for Congres- sional, Executive, and Judicial purposes, $5,939,009 29; for for- eign intercourse, $1,339,710 35; for miscellaneous expenses, including the mints, loans, post-office deficiencies, collection of revenue, and other like charges, $14,129,771 50; for expenses under the Interior Department, $3,102,985 52; under the War Department, $394,368,407 36; under the Navy Department, $42,674,569 69; for interest on the public debt, $13,190,324 45; and for payment of public debt, including reimbursement of temporary loan, and redemptions, $96,096,922 09; making an aggregate of $570,841,700 25, and leaving a balance in the Treasury on the 1st day of July, 1862, of $13,043,546 81.

It should be observed that the sum of $96,096,922 09, ex- pended for reimbursements and redemption of public debt, being included also in the loans made, may be properly de- ducted, both from receipts and expenditures, leaving the actual receipts for the year, $487,788,324 97, and the expenditures, $474,744,778.16.

Other information on the subject of the finances will be found in the report of the Secretary of the Treasury, to whose statements and views I invite your most candid and considerate attention.

The reports of the Secretaries of War and of the Navy are herewith transmitted. These reports, though lengthy, are scarcely more than brief abstracts of the very numerous and extensive transactions and operations conducted through those Departments. Nor could I give a summary of them here, upon any principle which would admit of its being much shorter than the reports themselves. I therefore content myself with laying the reports before you, and asking your attention to them.

It gives me pleasure to report a decided improvement in the financial condition of the Post-Office Department, as compared with several preceding years. The receipts for the fiscal year 1861 amounted to $8,349,296 40, which embraced the revenue from all the States of the Union for three-quarters of that year. Notwithstanding the cessation of revenue from the so-called seceded States during the last fiscal year, the increase of the correspondence of the loyal States has been sufficient to produce a revenue during the same year of $8,299,820 90, being only $50,000 less than was derived from all the States of the Union during the previous year. The expenditures show a still more favorable result. The amount expended in 1861 was $13,606,759 11. For the last year the amount has been reduced to $11,125,364 13, showing a decrease of about $2,481,000 in the expenditures as compared with the preceding year, and about $3,750,000 as compared with the fiscal year 1860. The deficiency in the Department for the previous year was $4,551,-966 98. For the last fiscal year it was reduced to $2,112,814 57. These favorable results are in part owing to the cessation of mail service in the insurrectionary States, and in part to a careful review of all expenditures in that Department in the interest of economy. The efficiency of the postal service, it is believed, has also been much improved. The Postmaster-General has also opened a correspondence, through the Department of State, with foreign governments, proposing a convention of postal representatives for the purpose of simplifying the rates of foreign postage, and to expedite the foreign mails. This proposition, equally important to our adopted citizens and to the commercial interests of this country, has been favorably entertained and agreed to by all the governments from whom replies have been received.

I ask the attention of Congress to the suggestions of the Post-master-General in his report respecting the further legislation required, in his opinion, for the benefit of the postal service.

. The Secretary of the Interior reports as follows in regard to the public lands:

"The public lands have ceased to be a source of revenue. From the 1st July, 1861, to the 30th September, 1862, the entire cash receipts from the sale of lands were $137,476 26—a sum much less than the expenses of our land system during the same period. The homestead law, which will take effect on the 1st of January next, offers such inducements to settlers that sales for cash cannot be expected, to an extent sufficient to meet the expense of the General Land Office, and the cost of surveying and bringing the land into market."

The discrepancy between the sum here stated as arising from the sales of the public lands, and the sum derived from the same source as reported from the Treasury Department, arises, I understand, from the fact that the periods of time, though apparently, were not really coincident at the beginning-point—the Treasury report including a considerable sum now which had previously been reported from the Interior—sufficiently large to greatly overreach the sum derived from the three months now reported upon by the Interior, and not by the Treasury.

The Indian tribes upon our frontiers have, during the past year, manifested a spirit of insubordination, and, at several points, have engaged in open hostilities against the white settlements in their vicinity. The tribes occupying the Indian country south of Kansas renounced their allegiance to the United States, and entered into treaties with the insurgents. Those who remained loyal to the United States were driven from the country. The chief of the Cherokees has visited this city for the purpose of restoring the former relations of the tribe with the United States. He alleges that they were constrained, by superior force, to enter into treaties with the insurgents, and that the United States neglected to furnish the protection which their treaty stipulations required.

In the month of August last, the Sioux Indians in Minnesota, attacked the settlements in their vicinity with extreme ferocity, killing, indiscriminately, men, women, and children. This attack was wholly unexpected, and therefore no means of defence had been provided. It is estimated that not less than eight hundred persons were killed by the Indians, and a large amount of property was destroyed. How this outbreak was induced is not definitely known, and suspicions, which may be unjust, need not to be stated. Information was received by the Indian Bureau, from different sources, about the time hostilities were commenced, that a simultaneous attack was to be made upon the white settlements by all the tribes between the Mississippi River and the Rocky Mountains. The State of Minnesota has suffered great injury from this Indian war. A large portion of her territory has been depopulated, and a severe loss has been sustained by the destruction of property. The people of that State manifest much anxiety for the removal of the tribes beyond the limits of the State, as a guarantee against future hostilities. The Commissioner of Indian Affairs will furnish full details. I submit for your especial consideration, whether our Indian system shall not be remodeled. Many wise and good men have impressed me with the belief that this can be profitably done.

I submit a statement of the proceedings of commissioners, which shows the progress that has been made in the enterprise of constructing the Pacific railroad. And this suggests the earliest completion of this road, and also the favorable action of Congress upon the projects now pending before them for enlarging the capacities of the great canals in New York and Illinois, as being of vital and rapidly increasing importance to the whole nation, and especially to the vast interior region hereinafter to be noticed at some greater length. I purpose having prepared and laid before you at an early day some interesting and valuable statistical information upon this subject. The military and commercial importance of enlarging the Illinois and Michigan canal, and improving the Illinois River, is presented in the report of Col. Webster to the Secretary of War, and now transmitted to Congress. I respectfully ask attention to it.

To carry out the provisions of the act of Congress of the 15th of May last, I have caused the Department of Agriculture of the United States to be organized.

The commissioner informs me that within the period of a few months this department has established an extensive system of correspondence and exchanges, both at home and abroad, which promises to effect highly beneficial results 'in the development of a correct knowledge of recent improvements in agriculture, in the introduction of new products, and in the collection of the agricultural statistics of the different States. Also that it will soon be prepared to distribute largely seeds, cercals, plants and cuttings, and has already published and liberally diffused much valuable information in anticipation of a more elaborate report, which will in due time be furnished, embracing some valuable tests in chemical science now in progress in the laboratory.

The creation of this department was for the more immediate benefit of a large class of our most valuable fellow-citizens; and I trust that the liberal basis upon which it has been organized will not only meet your approbation, but that it will realize, at no distant day, all the fondest anticipations of its most sanguine friends, and become the fruitful source of advantage to all our people.

On the 22d day of September last, a proclamation was issued by the Executive, a copy of which is herewith submitted.

In accordance with the purpose expressed in the second paragraph of that paper, I now respectfully call your attention to what may be called "compensated emancipation."

A nation may be said to consist of its territory, its people, and its laws. The territory is the only part which is of certain durability. "One generation passeth away, and another generation cometh, but the earth abideth forever." It is of the first importance to duly consider and estimate this ever-enduring part. That portion of the earth's surface which is owned and inhabited by the people of the United States, is well adapted to the home of one national family; and it is not well adapted for two or more. Its vast extent, and its variety of climate and productions, are of advantage in this age for one people, whatever they might have been in former ages. Steam, telegraphs, and intelligence have brought these to be an advantageous combination for one united people.

In the Inaugural Address I briefly pointed out the total inadequacy of disunion as a remedy for the differenes between the people of the two sections. I did so in language which I can not improve, and which, therefore, I beg to repeat:

"One section of our country believes slavery is right, and ought to be extended, while the other believes it is wrong, and ought not to be extended. This is the only substantial dispute. The fugitive slave-clause of the Constitution, and the law for the suppression of the foreign slave-trade, are each as well enforced, perhaps, as any law can ever be in a community where the moral sense of the people imperfectly supports the law itself. The great body of the people abide by the dry legal obligation in both cases, and a few break over in each. This, I think, can not be perfectly cured; and it would be worse, in both cases, after the separation of the sections than before. The foreign slave-trade, now imperfectly suppressed, would be ultimately revived without restriction in one section; while fugitive slaves, now only partially surrendered, would not be surrendered at all by the other.

"Physically speaking, we can not separate. We can not remove our respective sections from each other, nor build an impassable wall between them. A husband and wife may be divorced, and go out of the presence and beyond the reach of each other; but the different parts of our country can not do this. They can not but remain face to face; and intercourse, either amicable or hostile, must continue between them. Is it possible, then, to make that intercourse more advantageous or more satisfactory after separation than before? Can aliens make treaties easier than friends can make laws? Can treaties be more faithfully enforced between aliens than laws can among friends? Suppose you go to war, you can not fight always; and when, after much loss on both sides, and no gain on either, you cease fighting, the identical old questions, as to terms of intercourse, are again upon you."

There is no line, straight or crooked, suitable for a national boundary, upon which to divide. Trace through, from east to west, upon the line between the free and slave country, and we shall find a little more than one-third of its length are rivers, easy to be crossed, and populated, or soon to be populated, thickly upon both sides; while nearly all its remaining length are merely surveyors' lines, over which people may walk back and forth without any consciousness of their presence. No part of this line can be made any more difficult to pass by writing it down on paper or parchment as a national boundary. The fact of separation, if it comes, gives up, on the part of the seceding sections, the fugitive-slave clause, along with all other constitutional obligations upon the section seceded from, while I should expect no treaty stipulation would ever be made to take its place.

But there is another difficulty. The great interior region, bounded east by the Alleghanies, north by the British dominions, west by the Rocky Mountains, and south by the line along which the culture of corn and cotton meets, and which includes part of Virginia, part of Tennessee, all of Kentucky, Ohio, Indiana, Michigan, Wisconsin, Illinois, Missouri, Kansas, Iowa, Minnesota, and the Territories of Dakota, Nebraska, and part of Colorado, already has above ten millions of people, and will have fifty millions within fifty years if not prevented by any political folly or mistake. It contains more than one-third of the country owned by the United States—certainly more than one million of square miles. Once half as populous as Massachusetts already is, it would have more than seventy-five millions of people. A glance at the map shows that, territorially speaking, it is the great body of the Republic. The other parts are but marginal borders to it, the magnificent region sloping west from the Rocky Mountains to the Pacific being the deepest, and also the richest in undeveloped resources. In the production of provisions, grains, grasses, and all which proceed from them, this great interior region is naturally one of the most important of the world. Ascertain from the statistics the small propor-

tion of the region which has as yet been brought into cultivation, and also the large and rapidly increasing amount of its
products, and we shall be overwhelmed with the magnitude of
the prospect presented. And yet this region has no seacoast—
touches no ocean anywhere. As part of one nation, its people
now find, and may forever find, their way to Europe by New
York, to South America and Africa by New Orleans, and to Asia
by San Francisco. But separate our common country into two
nations, as designed by the present rebellion, and every man of
this great interior region is thereby cut off from some one or
more of these outlets, not perhaps by a physical barrier, but by
embarrassing and onerous trade regulations.

And this is true, wherever a dividing or boundary line may
be fixed. Place it between the now free and slave country, or
place it south of Kentucky, or north of Ohio, and still the
truth remains that none south of it can trade to any port or
place north of it, and none north of it can trade to any port or
place south of it except upon terms dictated by a government
foreign to them. These outlets, east, west, and south, are
indispensable to the well-being of the people inhabiting and to
inhabit this vast interior region. Which of the three may be
the best is no proper question. All are better than either, and
all of right belong to that people and to their successors forever.
True to themselves, they will not ask where a line of separation shall be, but will vow rather that there shall be no such
line. Nor are the marginal regions less interested in these
communications to and through them to the great outside
world. They too, and each of them, must have access to this
Egypt of the West, without paying toll at the crossing of any
national boundary.

Our national strife springs not from our permanent part; not
from the land we inhabit; not from our national homestead.
There is no possible severing of this but would multiply and
not mitigate evils among us. In all its adaptations and apti-
tudes it demands union and abhors separation. In fact, it
would ere long force reunion, however much of blood and
treasure the separation might have cost.

Our strife pertains to ourselves—to the passing generations

of men ; and it can, without convulsion, be hushed forever with the passing of one generation.

In this view, I recommend the adoption of the following resolution and articles amendatory to the Constitution of the United States :

Resolved by the Senate and House of Representatives of the United States of America in Congress assembled (two-thirds of both Houses concurring), That the following articles be proposed to the Legislatures (or Conventions) of the several States, as amendments to the Constitution of the United States, all or any of which articles, when ratified by three-fourths of the said Legislatures (or Conventions), to be valid as part or parts of the said Constitution, viz:

ARTICLE.—Every State, wherein Slavery now exists, which shall abolish the same therein at any time or times before the first day of January, in the year of our Lord one thousand and nine hundred, shall receive compensation from the United States as follows, to wit:

The President of the United States shall deliver to every such State bonds of the United States, bearing interest at the rate of —— per cent. per annum, to an amount equal to the aggregate sum of —— for each slave shown to have been therein by the eighth census of the United States, said bonds to be delivered to such State by installments, or in one parcel, at the completion of the abolishment, accordingly as the same shall have been gradual, or at one time, within such State; and interest shall begin to run upon any such bond only from the proper time of its delivery as aforesaid. Any State having received bonds as aforesaid, and afterwards reintroducing or tolerating slavery therein, shall refund to the United States the bonds so received, or the value thereof, and all interest paid thereon.

ARTICLE.—All slaves who shall have enjoyed actual freedom by the chances of the war, at any time before the end of the rebellion, shall be forever free; but all owners of such who shall not have been disloyal shall be compensated for them at the same rates as is provided for States adopting abolishment of slavery, but in such way that no slave shall be twice accounted for.

ARTICLE.—Congress may appropriate money, and otherwise provide for colonizing free colored persons, with their own consent, at any place or places without the United States.

I beg indulgence to discuss these proposed articles at some length. Without slavery the rebellion could never have existed; without slavery it could not continue.

Among the friends of the Union there is great diversity of sentiment and of policy in regard to slavery, and the African race amongst us. Some would perpetuate slavery; some would abolish it suddenly, and without compensation; some would abolish it gradually, and with compensation; some would remove the freed people from us, and some would retain them with us: and there are yet other minor diversities. Because of these diversities we waste much strength among ourselves. By mutual concession we should harmonize and act together. This would be compromise; but it would be compromise among the friends and not the enemies of the Union. These articles are intended to embody a plan of such mutual concessions. If the plan shall be adopted, it is assumed that emancipation will follow in at least several of the States.

As to the first article, the main points are: first, the emancipation, secondly, the length of time for consummating it—thirty-seven years; and, thirdly, the compensation.

The emancipation will be unsatisfactory to the advocates of perpetual slavery; but the length of time should greatly mitigate their dissatisfaction. The time spares both races from the evils of sudden derangement—in fact, from the necessity of any derangement; while most of those whose habitual course of thought will be disturbed by the measure will have passed away before its consummation. They will never see it. Another class will hail the prospect of emancipation, but will deprecate the length of time. They will feel that it gives too little to the now living slaves. But it really gives them much. It saves them from the vagrant destitution which must largely attend immediate emancipation in localities where their numbers are very great; and it gives the inspiring assurance that their posterity shall be free forever. The plan leaves to each State choosing to act under it, to abolish slavery now, or at the end of the century, or at any intermediate time, or by degrees, extending over the whole or any part of the period; and it obliges no two States to proceed alike. It also provides for compensation, and generally the mode of making it. This, it would seem, must further mitigate the dissatisfaction of those who favor perpetual slavery, and especially of those who are to receive the compensation. Doubless some of those who are to pay and not receive will object. Yet the measure is both just and economical. In a certain sense the liberation of slaves is the destruction of property—property acquired by descent or by purchase, the same as any other property. It is no less true for having been often said, that the people of the South are not more responsible for the original introduction of this property than are the people of the North; and when it is remembered how unhesitatingly we all use cotton and sugar, and share the profits of dealing in them, it may not be quite safe to say that the South has been more responsible than the North for its continuance. If, then, for a common object this property is to be sacrificed, is it not just that it be done at a common charge?

And if with less money, or money more easily paid, we can preserve the benefits of the Union by this means than we can by the war alone, is it not also economical to do it? Let us consider it, then. Let us ascertain the sum we have expended in the war since compensated emancipation was proposed last March, and consider whether, if that measure had been promptly accepted by even some of the Slave States, the same sum would not have done more to close the war than has been otherwise done. If so, the measure would save money, and, in that view, would be a prudent and economical measure. Certainly it is not so easy to pay something as it is to pay nothing; but it is easier to pay a large sum than it is to pay a larger one. And it is easier to pay any sum when we are able than it is to pay it before we are able. The war requires large sums, and requires them at once. The aggregate sum necessary for compensated emancipation of course would be large. But it would require no ready cash, nor the bonds even, any faster than emancipation progresses. This might not, and probably would not, close before the end of the thirty-seven years. At that time we shall probably have a hundred millions of people to share the burden, instead of thirty-one millions, as now. And not only so, but the increase of our population may be expected to continue for a long time after that period as rapidly as before; because our territory will not have become full. I do not state this inconsiderately.

At the same ratio of increase which we have maintained, on an average, from our first national census, in 1790, until that of 1860, we should, in 1900, have a population of 103,208,415. And why may we not continue that ratio—far beyond that period? Our abundant room—our broad national homestead is our ample resource. Were our territory as limited as are the British Isles, very certainly our population could not expand as stated. Instead of receiving the foreign born as now, we should be compelled to send part of the native born away. But such is not our condition. We have two millions nine hundred and sixty-three thousand square miles. Europe has three millions and eight hundred thousand, with a population averaging seventy-three and one-third persons to the square mile. Why may not our country at some time average as many? Is it less fertile? Has it more waste surface, by mountains, rivers, lakes, deserts, or other causes? Is it inferior to Europe in any natural advantage? If then we are, at some time, to be as populous as Europe, how soon? As to when this may be, we can judge by the past and the present; as to when it will be, if ever, depends much on whether we maintain the Union. Several of our States are already above the average of Europe—seventy-three and a third to the square mile. Massachusetts 157; Rhode Island 133; Connecticut 99; New York and New Jersey, each 80. Also two other great States, Pennsylvania and Ohio, are not far below, the former having 63 and the latter 59. The States already above the European average, except New York, have increased in as rapid a ratio, since passing that point, as ever before; while no one of them is equal to some other parts of our country in natural capacity for sustaining a dense population.

Taking the nation in the aggregate, and we find its population and ratio of increase, for the several decennial periods, to be as follows:

```
1799....  3,929,827
1800....  5,305,937   35.02 per cent. ratio of increase.
1810....  7,239,814   86.45  "        "        "
1820....  9,638,131   33.13  "        "        "
1830.... 12,866,020   83.49  "        "        "
1840.... 17,069,453   32.67  "        "        "
1850.... 23,191,876   35.87  "        "        "
1860.... 31,443,790   35.58  "        "        "
```

This shows an average decennial increase in 84.60 per cent. in population through the seventy years, from our first to our last census yet taken. It is seen that the ratio of increase, at no one of these two periods, is either two per cent. below or two per cent. above the average; thus showing how inflexible, and consequently how reliable, the law of increase in our case is. Assuming that it will continue, it gives the following results·

```
1870 ....................................  42,323,341
1880 ....................................  56,966,216
1890 ....................................  76,677,872
1900 .................................... 103,208,415
1910 .................................... 138,918,526
1920 .................................... 186,984,335
1930 .................................... 251,680,914
```

These figures show that our country may be as populous as Europe now is at some point between 1920 and 1930—say about 1925—our territory, at seventy-three and a third persons to the square mile, being of capacity to contain 217,186,000.

And we will reach this, too, if we do not ourselves relinquish the chance, by the folly and evils of disunion, or by long and exhausting wars springing from the only great element of national discord among us. While it cannot be foreseen exactly how much one huge example of secession, breeding lesser ones indefinitely, would retard population, civilization, and prosperity, no one can doubt that the extent of it would be very great and injurious.

The proposed emancipation would shorten the war, perpetuate peace, insure this increase of population, and proportionately the wealth of the country. With these we should pay all the emancipation would cost, together with our other debt, easier than we should pay our other debt without it. If we had allowed our old national debt to run at six per cent. per annum, simple interest, from the end of our Revolutionary struggle until to-day, without paying anything on either principal or interest, each man of us would owe less upon that debt now than each man owed upon it then; and this because our increase of men, through the whole period, has been greater than six per cent.; has run faster than the interest upon the debt. Thus, time alone relieves a debtor nation, so long as its population increases faster than unpaid interest accumulates on its debt.

This fact would be no excuse for delaying payment of what is justly due; but it shows the great importance of time in this connection—the great advantage of a policy by which we shall not have to pay until we number a hundred millions, what, by a different policy, we would have to pay now, when we number but thirty-one millions. In a word, it shows that a dollar will be much harder to pay for the war than will be a dollar for the emancipation on the proposed plan. And then the latter will cost no blood, no precious life. It will be a saving of both.

As to the second article, I think it would be impracticable to return to bondage the class of persons therein contemplated. Some of them, doubtless, in the property sense, belong to loyal owners; and hence provision is made in this article for compensating such.

The third article relates to the future of the freed people. It does not oblige, but merely authorizes Congress to aid in colonizing such as may consent. This ought not to be regarded as objectionable on the one hand or on the other, in so much as it comes to nothing unless by the mutual consent of the people to be deported, and the American voters through their representatives in Congress.

I can not make it better known than it already is that I strongly favor colonization. And yet I wish to say there is an objection urged against free colored persons remaining in the country which is largely imaginary, if not sometimes malicious.

It is insisted that their presence would injure and displace white labor and white laborers. If there ever could be a proper time for mere catch arguments, that time surely is not now. In times like the present men should utter nothing for which they would not willingly be responsible through time and in eternity. Is it true, then, that colored people can displace any more white labor by being free than by remaining slaves? If they stay in their old places they jostle no white laborers; if they leave their old places they leave them open to white laborers. Logically there is neither more nor less of it. Emancipation even without deportation, would probably enhance the wages of white labor, and, very surely, would not reduce them. Thus the customary amount of labor would still have to be performed —the freed people would surely not do more than their old proportion of it, and very probably for a time would do less, leaving an increased part to white laborers, bringing their labor into greater demand, and consequently enhancing the wages of it. With deportation, even to a limited extent, enhanced wages to white labor is mathematically certain. Labor is like any other commodity in the market—increase the demand for it and you increase the price of it. Reduce the supply of black labor, by colonizing the black laborer out of the country, and by precisely so much you increase the demand for and wages of white labor.

But it is dreaded that the freed people will swarm forth and cover the whole land! Are they not already in the land? Will liberation make them any more numerous? Equally distributed among the whites of the whole country, there would be but one colored to seven whites. Could the one, in any way, greatly disturb the seven? There are many communities now having more than one free colored person to seven whites; and this, without any apparent consciousness of evil from it. The District of Columbia and the States of Maryland and Delaware are all in this condition. The District has more than one free colored to six whites; and yet, in its frequent petitions to Congress, I believe it has never presented the presence of free colored persons as one of its grievances. But why should emancipation South send the freed people North? People of any color seldom run unless there be something to run from. Heretofore colored people, to some extent, have fled North from bondage; and now, perhaps, from bondage and destitution. But if gradual emancipation and deportation be adopted they will have neither to flee from. Their old masters will give them wages, at least until new laborers can be procured, and the freed men in turn will gladly give their labor for the wages till new homes can be found for them in congenial climes, and with people of their own blood and race. This proposition can be trusted on the mutual interests involved. And in any event, can not the North decide for itself whether to receive them?

Again, as practice proves more than theory, in any case, has there been any irruption of colored people northward because of the abolishment of slavery in this District last spring?

What I have said of the proportion of free colored persons to the whites in the District is from the census of 1860, having no reference to persons called contrabands, nor to those made free by the act of Congress, abolishing slavery here.

The plan consisting of these articles is recommended, not but that a restoration of national authority would be accepted without its adoption.

Nor will the war, nor proceedings under the proclamation of September 22, 1862, be stayed because of the recommendation of this plan. Its timely adoption, I doubt not, would bring restoration, and thereby stay both.

And, notwithstanding this plan, the recommendation that Congress provide by law for compensating any State which may adopt emancipation before this plan shall have been acted upon, is hereby earnestly renewed. Such would be only an advanced part of the plan, and the same arguments apply to both.

This plan is recommended as a means not in exclusion of, but additional to, all others for restoring and preserving the national authority throughout the Union. The subject is presented exclusively in its economical aspect. The plan would, I am confident, secure peace more speedily, and maintain it more permanently, than can be done by force alone; while all it would cost, considering amounts, and manner of payment, and times of payment, would be easier paid than will be the additional cost of the war, if we solely rely upon force. It is much—very much—that it would cost no blood at all.

The plan is proposed as permanent constitutional law. It can not become such, without the concurrence of, first, two-thirds of Congress, and afterward three-fourths of the States. The requisite three-fourths of the States will necessarily include seven of the Slave States. Their concurrence, if obtained, will give assurance of their severally adopting emancipation, at no very distant day, upon the new constitutional terms. This assurance would end the struggle now, and save the Union forever.

I do not forget the gravity which should characterize a paper addressed to the Congress of the nation by the Chief Magistrate of the nation. Nor do I forget that some of you are my seniors; nor that many of you have more experience than I in the conduct of public affairs. Yet I trust that, in view of the great responsibility resting upon me, you will perceive no want of respect to yourselves in any undue earnestness I may seem to display.

Is it doubted, then, that the plan I propose, if adopted, would shorten the war, and thus lessen its expenditure of money and of blood? Is it doubted that it would restore the national authority and national prosperity, and perpetuate both indefinitely? Is it doubted that we here—Congress and Executive—can secure its adoption? Will not the good people respond to a united and earnest appeal from us? Can we, can they, by any other means, so certainly or so speedily assure these vital objects? We can succeed only by concert. It is not "can any of us imagine better?" but "can we all do better?"

Object whatsoever is possible, still the question recurs, " can we do better?" The dogmas of the quiet past are inadequate to the stormy present. The occasion is piled high with difficulty, and we must rise with the occasion. As our case is new, so we must think anew, and act anew. We must disenthrall ourselves, and then we shall save our country.

Fellow-citizens, we cannot escape history. We of this Congress and this Administration will be remembered in spite of ourselves. No personal significance or insignificance can spare one or another of us. The fiery trial through which we pass will light us down in honor or dishonor to the latest generation. We say that we are for the Union. The world will not forget that we say this. We know how to save the Union. The world knows we do know how to save it. We—even we here—hold the power and bear the responsibility. In giving freedom to the slave we assure freedom to the free—honorable alike in what we give and what we preserve. We shall nobly save or meanly lose the last best hope of earth. Other means may succeed; this could not, cannot fail. The way is plain, peaceful, generous, just—a way, which, if followed, the world will forever applaud and God must forever bless.   ABRAHAM LINCOLN.
December 1, 1862.

TO FERNANDO WOOD ON THE WAR.

Prominent among the apostles of Peace and the advocates of a cessation of the war upon the rebels by the Government, was Mr. Fernando Wood, formerly Mayor of New York. To one of his letters, urging his views on that subject, the President made the following conclusive reply. History, to which Mr. Lincoln was willing to leave his treatment of this question, has already justified it :

EXECUTIVE MANSION, WASHINGTON, *December* 12, 1862.

*Hon. Fernando Wood—My Dear Sir—*Your letter of the 8th, with the accompanying note of same date, was received yesterday.

The most important paragraph in the letter, as I consider, is in these words : "On the 25th of November last I was advised by an authority which I deemed likely to be well informed, as well as reliable and truthful, that the Southern States would send representatives to the next Congress, provided that a full and general amnesty should permit them to do so. No guarantee or terms were asked for other than the amnesty referred to."

I strongly suspect your information will prove to be groundless ; nevertheless, I thank you for communicating it to me. Understanding the phrase in the paragraph above quoted—"the Southern States would send representatives to the next Congress"—to be substantially the same as that "the people of the Southern States would cease resistance, and would reinaugurate, submit to, and maintain the national authority within the limits of such States, under the Constitution of the United States," I say that in such case the war would cease on the part of the United States ; and that if within a reasonable time "a full and general amnesty" were necessary to such end, it would not be withheld.

I do not think it would be proper now to communicate this, formally, or informally, to the people of the Southern States. My belief is that they already know it ; and when they choose, if ever, they can communicate with me unequivocally. Nor do I think it proper now to suspend military operations to try any experiment of negotiation.

I should nevertheless receive, with great pleasure, the exact information you now have, and also such other as you may in any way obtain. Such information might be more valuable before the 1st of January than afterward.

While there is nothing in this letter which I shall dread to see in history, it is, perhaps, better for the present that its existence should not become public. I therefore have to request that you will regard it as confidential.

Your obedient servant,   A. LINCOLN.

MESSAGE ON THE FINANCES.

One of the most important measures of this session of Congress was the passage of an act authorizing the issue of $100,000,000, in Treasury notes, the main purpose of which was the payment of the army and navy. President Lincoln promptly affixed his signature to the bill; but he returned it accompanied by the following message, in which he set forth views of the financial condition of the country, the wisdom of which after-experience fully sustained:

MESSAGE.

To the Senate and House of Representatives:

I have signed the joint resolution to provide for the immediate payment of the army and navy of the United States, passed by the House of Representatives on the 14th, and by the Senate on the 15th inst. The joint resolution is a simple authority, amounting, however, under the existing circumstances, to a direction to the Secretary of the Treasury to make an additional issue of $100,000,000 in United States notes, if so much money is needed, for the payment of the army and navy. My approval is given in order that every possible facility may be afforded for the prompt discharge of all arrears of pay due to our soldiers and our sailors.

While giving this approval, however, I think it my duty to express my sincere regret that it has been found necessary to authorize so large an additional issue of United States notes, when this circulation, and that of the suspended banks together, have become already so redundant as to increase prices beyond real values, thereby augmenting the cost of living, to the injury of labor, and the cost of supplies, to the injury of the whole country. It seems very plain that continued issues of United States notes, without any check to the issues of suspended banks, and without adequate provision for the raising of money by loans, and for funding the issues, so as to keep them within due limits, must soon produce disastrous consequences; and this matter appears to me so important that I feel bound to avail myself of this occasion to ask the special attention of Congress to it.

That Congress has power to regulate the currency of the country can hardly admit of doubt, and that a judicious measure to prevent the deterioration of this currency, by a reasonable taxation of bank circulation, or otherwise, is needed, seems equally clear. Independently of this general consideration, it would be unjust to the people at large to exempt banks enjoying the special privilege of circulation, from their just proportion of the public burdens.

In order to raise money by way of loans most easily and cheaply, it is clearly necessary to give every possible support to the public credit. To that end, a uniform currency, in which taxes, subscriptions, loans, and all other ordinary public dues may be paid, is almost if not quite indispensable. Such a currency can be furnished by banking associations authorized under a general act of Congress, as suggested in my message at the beginning of the present session. The securing of this circulation by the pledge of the United States bonds, as herein suggested, would still further facilitate loans, by increasing the present and causing a future demand for such bonds.

In view of the actual financial embarrassments of the Government, and of the greater embarrassment sure to come if the necessary means of relief be not afforded, I feel that I should not perform my duty by a simple announcement of my approval of the joint resolution, which proposes relief only by increasing the circulation, without expressing my earnest desire that measures, such in substance as that I have just referred to, may receive the early sanction of Congress. By such measures, in my opinion, will payment be most certainly secured, not only to the army and navy, but to all honest creditors of the Government, and satisfactory provisions made for future demands on the Treasury. ABRAHAM LINCOLN.

PROCLAMATION OF EMANCIPATION.

The first day of the year 1863 was signalized by the issuing of a Proclamation of Emancipation according to the President's promise in his preliminary proclamation. It not only declared the persons mentioned in it free, but announced that they would be received into the service of the Government.

PROCLAMATION.

Whereas, on the 22d day of September, in the year of our Lord one thousand eight hundred and sixty-two, a proclamation was issued by the President of the United States, containing, among other things, the following, to wit:

That on the first day of January, in the year of our Lord one thousand eight hundred and sixty-three, all persons held as slaves within any States or designated part of a State, the people whereof shall then be in rebellion against the United States, shall be then, thenceforward, and forever free; and the Executive Government of the United States, including the military and naval authority thereof, will recognize and maintain the freedom of such persons, and will do no act or acts to repress such persons, or any of them, in any efforts they may make for their actual freedom.

That the Executive will, on the first day of January aforesaid, by proclamation, designate the States and parts of States, if any, in which the people thereof respectively shall then be in rebellion against the United States; and the fact that any State, or the people thereof shall on that day be in good faith represented in the Congress of the United States, by members chosen thereto at elections wherein a majority of the qualified voters of such State shall have participated, shall, in the absence of strong countervailing testimony, be deemed conclusive evidence that such State, and the people thereof, are not then in rebellion against the United States.

Now, therefore, I ABRAHAM LINCOLN, President of the United States, by virtue of the power in me vested as Commander-in-Chief of the Army and Navy of the United States in time of actual armed rebellion against the authority and Government of the United States, and as a fit and necessary war measure for suppressing said rebellion, do, on this first day of January, in the year of our Lord one thousand eight hundred and sixty-three, and in accordance with my purpose so to do, publicly proclaimed for the full period of one hundred days, from the day first above mentioned, order and designate, as the States and parts of States wherein the people thereof respectively are this day in rebellion against the United States, the following, to wit:

Arkansas, Texas, Louisiana (except the parishes of St. Bernard, Plaquemines, Jefferson, St. John, St. Charles, St. James, Ascension, Assumption, Terre Bonne, Lafourche, St. Marie, St. Martin and Orleans, including the city of New Orleans), Mississippi, Alabama, Florida, Georgia, South Carolina, North Carolina, and Virginia (except the forty-eight counties designated as West Virginia, and also the counties of Berkely, Accomac, Northampton, Elizabeth City, York, Princess Anne, and Norfolk, including the cities of Norfolk and Portsmouth), and which excepted parts are for the present left precisely as if this proclamation were not issued.

And by virtue of the power and for the purpose aforesaid, I do order and declare that all persons held as slaves within said designated States and parts of States are and henceforward shall be free; and that the Executive Government of the United States, including the military and naval authorities thereof, will recognize and maintain the freedom of said persons.

And I hereby enjoin upon the people so declared to be free to abstain from all violence, unless in necessary self-defence; and I recommend to them that, in all cases when allowed, they labor faithfully for reasonable wages.

And I further declare and make known that such persons, of suitable condition, will be received into the armed service of the United States to garrison forts, positions, stations, and other places, and to man vessels of all sorts in said service.

And upon this act, sincerely believed to be an act of justice warranted by the Constitution upon military necessity, I invoke the considerate judgment of mankind, and the gracious favor of Almighty God.

In testimony whereof, I have hereunto set my name, and caused the seal of the United States to be affixed.

Done at the city of Washington, this first day of January, in the
      year of our Lord one thousand eight hundred and sixty-
[L. S.] three, and of the independence of the United States the
      eighty-seventh.   ABRAHAM LINCOLN.

    By the President:
WM. H. SEWARD, *Secretary of State.*

LETTERS TO BRITISH WORKINGMEN.

The workingmen in some of the large cities of Great
Britain showed themselves almost from the beginning of
the rebellion friendly to the cause of the Republic, although they suffered from the consequences of the war.
In two of these cities—Manchester and London—at large
meetings they adopted addresses which were sent to Mr.
Lincoln, and to these he made the following replies :

EXECUTIVE MANSION, WASHINGTON, *Jan.* 19, 1863.

To the Workingmen of Manchester :—I have the honor to acknowledge the receipt of the address and resolutions which
you sent me on the eve of the new year. When I came on the
4th of March, 1861, through a free and constitutional election,
to preside in the Government of the United States, the country
was found at the verge of civil war. Whatever might have
been the cause, or whosesoever the fault, one duty, paramount
to all others, was before me, namely, to maintain and preserve
at once the Constitution and the integrity of the Federal
Republic. A conscientious purpose to perform this duty, is
the key to all the measures of administration which have been,
and to all which will hereafter be pursued. Under our frame
of government and my official oath, I could not depart from
this purpose if I would. It is not always in the power of governments to enlarge or restrict the scope of moral results which
follow the policies that they may deem it necessary, for the
public safety, from time to time to adopt.

    I have understood well that the duty of self-preservation rests
solely with the American people. But I have at the same time

been aware that favor or disfavor of foreign nations might have a material influence in enlarging or prolonging the struggle with disloyal men in which the country is engaged. A fair examination of history has served to authorize a belief that the past actions and influences of the United States, were generally regarded as having been beneficial toward mankind. I have, therefore, reckoned upon the forbearance of nations. Circumstances—to some of which you kindly allude—induced me especially to expect that if justice and good faith should be practised by the United States, they would encounter no hostile influence on the part of Great Britain. It is now a pleasant duty to acknowledge the demonstration you have given of your desire that a spirit of amity and peace toward this country may prevail in the councils of your Queen, who is respected and esteemed in your own country only more than she is by the kindred nation which has its home on this side of the Atlantic.

I know, and deeply deplore the sufferings which the working-men at Manchester, and in all Europe, are called to endure in this crisis. It has been often and studiously represented that the attempt to overthrow this Government, which was built upon the foundation of human rights, and to substitute for it one which should rest exclusively on the basis of human slavery, was likely to obtain the favor of Europe. Through the action of our disloyal citizens, the workingmen of Europe have been subjected to severe trials, for the purpose of forcing their sanction to that attempt. Under the circumstances, I cannot but regard your decisive utterances upon the question as an instance of sublime Christian heroism, which has not been surpassed in any age or in any country. It is indeed an energetic and reinspiring assurance of the inherent power of truth, and of the ultimate and universal triumph of justice, humanity, and freedom. I do not doubt that the sentiments you have expressed will be sustained by your great nation, and on the other hand, I have no hesitation in assuring you that they will excite admiration, esteem, and the most reciprocal feelings of friendship among the American people. I hail this interchange of sentiment, therefore, as an augury that whatever else may happen, whatever misfortune may befall your country or my own, the peace and friendship which now exist between the two nations will be, as it shall be my desire to make them, perpetual.

ABRAHAM LINCOLN.

EXECUTIVE MANSION, WASHINGTON, *Feb.* 2, 1863.

To the Workingmen of London:—I have received the New Year's Address which you have sent me, with a sincere appreciation of the exalted and humane sentiments by which it was inspired.

As these sentiments are manifestly the enduring support of the free institutions of England, so I am sure also that they constitute the only reliable basis for free institutions throughout the world.

The resources, advantages, and powers of the American people are very great, and they have consequently succeeded to equally great responsibilities. It seems to have devolved upon them to test whether a government established on the principles of human freedom, can be maintained against an effort to build one upon the exclusive foundation of human bondage. They will rejoice with me in the new evidences which your proceedings furnish, that the magnanimity they are exhibiting is justly estimated by the true friends of freedom and humanity in foreign countries.

Accept my best wishes for your individual welfare, and for the welfare and happiness of the whole British people.

ABRAHAM LINCOLN.

THE CHRISTIAN COMMISSION

received from the President the following characteristic approval of its benevolent organization:

EXECUTIVE MANSION, WASHINGTON, *February* 22, 1863.

*Rev. Alexander Reed—My Dear Sir—*Your note, by which you, as General Superintendent of the U. S. Christian Commission, invite me to preside at a meeting to be held this day, at the hall of the House of Representatives in this city, is received.

While, for reasons which I deem sufficient, I must decline to preside, I cannot withhold my approval of the meeting, and its worthy objects. Whatever shall be, sincerely and in God's name, devised for the good of the soldiers and seamen in their hard spheres of duty, can scarcely fail to be blessed. And whatever shall tend to turn our thoughts from the unreasoning and uncharitable passions, prejudices, and jealousies incident to a great national trouble such as ours, and to fix them on the vast and long-enduring consequences, for weal or for woe, which are to result from the struggle, and especially to strengthen our reliance on the Supreme Being for the final triumph of the right, cannot but be well for us all.

The birthday of Washington and the Christian Sabbath coinciding this year, and suggesting together the highest interests of this life and of that to come, is most propitious for the meeting proposed.

Your obedient servant,   A. LINCOLN.

HALF-MADE CITIZENS OF FOREIGN BIRTH.

The endeavor of many aliens who wished to obtain the advantage of citizenship of the Republic without incurring its responsibilities, were met by Mr. Lincoln in the following

PROCLAMATION.

WASHINGTON, May 8, 1863.

By the President of the United States of America, a Proclamation—Whereas, The Congress of the United States, at its last session, enacted a law, entitled "An act for enrolling and calling out the national forces, and for other purposes," which was approved on the 3d day of March last; and

Whereas, It is recited in the said act that there now exists in the United States an insurrection and rebellion against the authority thereof, and it is, under the Constitution of the United States, the duty of the Government to suppress insubordination and rebellion, to guarantee to each State a republican form of government, and to preserve the public tranquillity; and

Whereas, For these high purposes, a military force is indispensable, to raise and support which all persons ought willingly to contribute; and

Whereas, No service can be more praiseworthy and honorable than that which is rendered for the maintenance of the Constitution and the Union, and the consequent preservation of free government; and

Whereas, For the reasons thus recited it was enacted by the said statute that all able-bodied male citizens of the United States, and persons of foreign birth who shall have declared on oath their intentions to become citizens under and in pursuance of the laws thereof, between the ages of twenty and forty-five years, with certain exemptions not necessary to be here mentioned, are declared to constitute the national forces, and shall be liable to perform military duty in the service of the United States, when called out by the President for that purpose; and

Whereas, It is claimed, on and in behalf of persons of foreign birth, within the ages specified in said act, who have heretofore declared on oath their intention to become citizens under and in pursuance to the laws of the United States, and who have not exercised the right of suffrage or any other political franchise under the laws of the United States, or of any of the States thereof, that they are not absolutely precluded by their aforesaid declaration of intention from renouncing their purpose to become citizens; and that, on the contrary, such persons, under treaties and the law of nations, retain a right to renounce that purpose, and to forego the privilege of citizenship and residence within the United States, under the obligations imposed by the aforesaid act of Congress:

Now, therefore, to avoid all misapprehensions concerning the liability of persons concerned to perform the service required by such enactment, and to give it full effect, I do hereby order and proclaim that no plea of alienage will be received, or allowed to exempt from the obligations imposed by the aforesaid act of Congress any person of foreign birth who shall have declared on oath his intention to become a citizen of the United States under the laws thereof, and who shall be found within the Uni ted States at any time during the continuance of the present insurrection and rebellion, at or after the expiration of the period of sixty-five days from the date of this proclamation; nor shall any such plea of alienage be allowed in favor of any such person who has so, as aforesaid, declared his intention to become a citizen of the United States, and shall have exercised at any time the right of suffrage, or any other political franchise within the United States, under the laws thereof, or under the laws of any of the several States.

In witness whereof, I have hereunto set my hand, and caused the seal of the United States to be affixed.

Done at the city of Washington this 8th day of May, in the [L. S.]   year of our Lord 1863, and of the independence of the United States the eighty-seventh.

By the President: ABRAHAM LINCOLN.
WM. H. SEWARD, *Secretary of State.*

THE UNCONDITIONAL EMANCIPATIONISTS IN MISSOURI.

In Missouri there was a division of opinion among the loyal men upon the subject of slavery. One party was for doing it away instantly and completely, and without regard to consequences; the other for gradual emancipation. Gen. Curtis, in command of that district, was of the former party; and Governor Gamble, being of the latter, would not turn over the militia of the State to General Curtis. This state of things produced a disgraceful feud, which disgusted the country and worried the President for a long time. He finally, in May of this year, removed General Curtis, and to a remonstrance thereupon, sent the following reply, which showed how he could "put down his foot" when occasion required:

Your dispatch of to-day is just received. It is very painful to me that you, in Missouri, cannot, or will not, settle your factional quarrel among yourselves. I have been tormented with

it beyond endurance, for months, by both sides. Neither side
pays the least respect to my appeals to your reason. I am now
compelled to take hold of the case.   A. LINCOLN.

General Curtis was superseded by General Schofield,
to whom Mr. Lincoln addressed the following letter:

EXECUTIVE MANSION, WASHINGTON, *May* 27, 1863.

General J. M. Schofield—Dear Sir—Having removed General
Curtis and assigned you to the command of the Department of
the Missouri, I think it may be of some advantage to me to state
to you why I did it. I did not remove General Curtis because
of my full conviction that he had done wrong by commission or
omission. I did it because of a conviction in my mind that the
Union men of Missouri, constituting, when united, a vast majority of the people, have entered into a pestilent, factious
quarrel, among themselves, General Curtis, perhaps not of
choice, being the head of one faction, and Governor Gamble that
of the other. After months of labor to reconcile the difficulty, it
seemed to grow worse and worse, until I felt it my duty to break
it up somehow, and as I could not remove Governor Gamble I had
to remove General Curtis. Now that you are in the position, I
wish you to undo nothing merely because General Curtis or
Governor Gamble did it, but to exercise your own judgment,
and do right for the public interest. Let your military measures
be strong enough to repel the invaders and keep the peace, and
not so strong as to unnecessarily harass and persecute the people. It is a difficult *role*, and so much greater will be the honor
if you perform it well. If both factions or neither shall abuse
you, you will probably be about right. Beware of being assailed
by one and praised by the other.

Yours truly,   A. LINCOLN.

At this action the Germans of St. Louis thought proper
to take umbrage; and they also thought it proper to de-
pute one of their number to wait upon the President
with their remonstrances, not only against his course in
this matter, but in many others, demanding. among other

things, some changes in the Cabinet and the removal of General Halleck from his position of commander-in-chief. What sort of reception these foreign gentlemen met with from Mr. Lincoln, is very vividly set forth in the following report of the interview of the President with their deputy, made by himself:

Messrs. Emile Pretorious, Theodore Olshausen, R. E. Rombaur, etc.—Gentlemen—During a professional visit to Washington city, I presented to the President of the United States, in compliance with your instructions, a copy of the resolutions adopted in mass meeting at St. Louis, on the 10th of May, 1863, and I requested a reply to the suggestions therein contained. The President, after a careful and loud reading of the whole report of proceedings, saw proper to enter into a conversation of two hours' duration, in the course of which most of the topics embraced in the resolutions and other subjects were discussed.

As my share in the conversation is of secondary importance, I propose to omit it entirely in this report, and, avoiding details, to communicate to you the substance of noteworthy remarks made by the President.

1. The President said that it may be a misfortune for the nation that he was elected President. But, having been elected by the people, he meant to be President, and perform his duty according to *his* best understanding, if he had to die for it. No General will be removed, nor will any change in the Cabinet be made, to suit the views or wishes of any particular party, faction, or set of men. General Halleck is not guilty of the charges made against him, most of which arise from misapprehension or ignorance of those who prefer them.

2. The President said that it was a mistake to suppose that Generals John C. Fremont, B. F. Butler, and F. Sigel are " systematically kept out of command," as stated in the fourth resolution; that, on the contrary, he fully appreciated the merits of the gentlemen named; that by their own actions they had placed themselves in the positions which they occupied; that he was not only willing, but anxious to place them again in com-

mand as soon as he could find spheres of action for them, without doing injustice to others, but that at present he "had more pegs than holes to put them in."

3. As to the want of unity, the President, without admitting such to be the case, intimated that each member of the Cabinet was responsible mainly for the manner of conducting the affairs of his particular department; that there was no centralization of responsibility for the action of the Cabinet anywhere, except in the President himself.

4. The dissensions between Union men in Missouri are due solely to a factious spirit which is exceedingly reprehensible. The two parties "ought to have their heads knocked together." "Either would rather see the defeat of their adversary than that of Jefferson Davis." To this spirit of faction is to be ascribed the failure of the Legislature to elect Senators and the defeat of the Missouri Aid Bill in Congress, the passage of which the President strongly desired.

The President said that the Union men in Missouri who are in favor of *gradual emancipation* represented his views better than those who are in favor of *immediate emancipation.* In explanation of his views on this subject, the President said that in his speeches he had frequently used as an illustration the case of a man who had an excrescence on the back of his neck, the removal of which, *in one operation,* would result in the death of the patient, while "tinkering it off by degrees" would preserve life. Although sorely tempted, I did not reply with the illustration of the dog whose tail was amputated by inches, but confined myself to arguments. *The President announced clearly that, as far as he was at present advised, the Radicals in Missouri had no right to consider themselves the exponents of his views on the subject of emancipation in that State.*

5. General Curtis was not relieved on account of any wrong act or great mistake committed by him. The System of Provost-Marshals, established by him throughout the State, gave rise to violent complaint. That the President had thought at one time to appoint General Fremont in his place; that at another time he thought of appointing General McDowell, whom he characterised as a good and loyal though very unfor-

tunate soldier; and that, at last, General Schofield was appointed, with a view, if possible, to reconcile and satisfy the two factions in Missouri. He has instructions not to interfere with either party, but to confine himself to his military duties. I assure you, gentlemen, that our side was as fully presented as the occasion permitted. At the close of the conversation, the President remarked that there was evidently a "serious misunderstanding" springing up between him and the Germans of St. Louis, which he would like to see removed. Observing to him that the difference of opinion related to facts, men, and measures, I withdrew.　　　　　　　　I am, very respectfully, etc.,

JAMES TAUSSIG.

THE VALLANDIGHAM CASE.

Among the most active supporters that the rebellion found in the Free States, was the Hon. C. C. Vallandigham, Member of the House from Ohio, who opposed all measures for the prosecution of the war, denounced Mr. Lincoln's Government as endeavoring to establish a despotism, and advocated the calling in of a foreign government to settle the dispute between the rebels and the National Government. Finally—it was at a public meeting at Mount Vernon, Ohio—he proclaimed his intention of disobeying an order issued by General Burnside, in command of the Department, and called upon the people to set it at naught and resist its execution. For this he was arrested by General Burnside, and, after vain applications to the Circuit Court for a writ of *habeas corpus*, tried by a military commission, found guilty, and sentenced to close confinement in Fort Warren. This sentence the President commuted to banishment within the rebel lines, which was immediately carried into effect.

These occurrences were seized upon by the sympathisers with the rebels, who held meetings at various places over the country to denounce what one of the most distinguished of their number, Governor Seymour, of New York, called the establishment of military despotism. These words he used in a letter addressed to the organizers of one of the meetings in question, which was held in Albany, on the 16th of May. The resolutions of this meeting were transmitted to the President by Mr. Erastus Corning, the chairman, to whom Mr. Lincoln sent the following reply :

EXECUTIVE MANSION, WASHINGTON, *June* 13, 1863.

HON. ERASTUS CORNING AND OTHERS :

Gentlemen—Your letter of May 19, inclosing the resolutions of a public meeting held at Albany, N. Y., on the 16th of the same month, was received several days ago.

The resolutions, as I understand them, are resolvable into two propositions—first, the expression of a purpose to sustain the cause of the Union, to secure peace through victory, and to support the Administration in every constitutional and lawful measure to suppress the rebellion; and, secondly, a declaration of censure upon the Administration for supposed unconstitutional action, such as the making of military arrests. And from the two propositions a third is deduced, which is, that the gentlemen composing the meeting are resolved on doing their part to maintain our common Government and country, despite the folly or wickedness, as they may conceive, of any Administration. This position is eminently patriotic, and as such I thank the meeting and congratulate the nation for it. My own purpose is the same, so that the meeting and myself have a common object, and can have no difference, except in the choice of means or measures for effecting that object.

And here I ought to close this paper, and would close it, if there were no apprehensions that more injurious consequences than any merely personal to myself might follow the censures systematically cast upon me for doing what, in my view of duty,

I could not forbear. The resolutions promise to support me in every constitutional and lawful measure to suppress the rebellion, and I have not knowingly employed, nor shall knowingly employ, any other. But the meeting, by their resolutions, assert and argue that certain military arrests, and proceedings following them, for which I am ultimately responsible, are unconstitutional. I think they are not. The resolutions quote from the Constitution the definition of treason, and also the limiting safeguards and guarantees therein provided for the citizen on trial for treason, and on his being held to answer for capital or otherwise infamous crime, and, in criminal prosecutions, his right to a speedy and public trial by an impartial jury. They proceed to resolve, " that these safeguards of the rights of the citizen against the pretensions of arbitrary power were intended more *especially* for his protection in times of civil commotion."

And, apparently to demonstrate the proposition, the resolutions proceed : " They were secured substantially to the English people *after* years of protracted civil war, and were adopted into our Constitution at the *close* of the Revolution." Would not the demonstration have been better if it could have been truly said that these safeguards had been adopted and applied *during* the civil wars and *during* our Revolution, instead of *after* the one and at the *close* of the other ? I, too, am devotedly for them *after* civil war, and *before* civil war, and at all times, " except when, in cases of rebellion or invasion, the public safety may require" their suspension. The resolutions proceed to tell us that these safeguards " have stood the test of seventy-six years of trial, under our republican system, under circumstances which show that, while they constitute the foundation of all free government, they are the elements of the enduring stability of the Republic." No one denies that they have so stood the test up to the beginning of the present rebellion, if we except a certain occurrence at New Orleans ; nor does any one question that they will stand the same test much longer after the rebellion closes. But these provisions of the Constitution have no application to the case we have in hand, because the arrests complained of were not made for treason—that is, not for *the* treason defined in the Constitution, and upon conviction of which the punishment is death—nor yet were they made to hold persons to answer for any capital or otherwise infamous crimes; nor were the proceedings following, in any constitutional or legal sense, "criminal prosecutions." The arrests were made on totally different grounds, and the proceedings following accorded with the grounds of the arrest. Let us consider the real case with which we are dealing, and apply to it the parts of the Constitution plainly made for such cases.

Prior to my installation here, it had been inculcated that any State had a lawful right to secede from the national Union, and that it would be expedient to exercise the right whenever the devotees of the doctrine should fail to elect a President to their own liking. I was elected contrary to their liking, and accordingly, so far as it was legally possible, they had taken seven States out of the Union, had seized many of the United States forts, and fired upon the United States flag, all before I was inaugurated, and, of course, before I had done any official act whatever. The rebellion thus began soon ran into the present civil war; and, in certain respects, it began on very unequal terms between the parties. The insurgents had been preparing for it for more than thirty years, while the Government had taken no steps to resist them. The former had carefully considered all the means which could be turned to their account. It undoubtedly was a well-pondered reliance with them that, in their own unrestricted efforts to destroy Union, Constitution, and law altogether, the Government would, in great degree, be restrained by the same Constitution and law from arresting their progress. Their sympathizers pervaded all departments of the Government, and nearly all communities of the people. From this material, under cover of "liberty of speech," "liberty of the press," and "habeas corpus," they hoped to keep on foot among us a most efficient corps of spies, informers, suppliers, and aiders and abettors of their cause in a thousand ways. They knew that in times such as they were inaugurating, by the Constitution itself, the "habeas corpus" might be suspended; but they also knew they had friends who would make a question as to *who* was to suspend it; meanwhile, their spies and others might remain at large to help on their cause. Or if, as has happened, the Executive should suspend the writ, without ruinous waste of time, instances of arresting innocent persons might occur, as are always likely to occur in such cases, and then a clamor could be raised in regard to this which might be, at least, of some service to the insurgent cause. It needed no very keen perception to discover this part of the enemy's programme, so soon as, by open hostilities, their machinery was put fairly in motion. Yet, thoroughly imbued with a reverence for the guaranteed rights of individuals, I was slow to adopt the strong measures which by degrees I have been forced to regard as being within the exceptions of the Constitution, and as indispensable to the public safety. Nothing is better known to history than that courts of justice are utterly incompetent in such cases. Civil courts are organized chiefly for trials of individuals, or, at most, a few individuals acting in concert, and this in quiet times, and on charges of crimes well defined in the law. Even in times of peace, bands of horse-thieves and robbers frequently grow too numerous and powerful for the ordinary courts of justice. But what comparison, in numbers, have such bands ever borne to the insurgent sympathizers even in many of the loyal States? Again, a jury too frequently has at least one member more ready to hang the panel than to hang the traitor. And yet, again, he who dissuades one man from volunteering, or induces one soldier to desert, weakens the Union cause as much as he who kills a Union soldier in battle. Yet this dissuasion or inducement may be so conducted as to be no defined crime of which any civil court would take cognizance.

Ours is a case of rebellion—so called by the resolution before me—in fact, a clear, flagrant, and gigantic case of rebellion; and the provision of the Constitution that "the privilege of the writ of *habeas corpus* shall not be suspended unless when, in cases of rebellion or invasion, the public safety may require it," is *the* provision which specially applies to our present case. This provision plainly attests the understanding of those who made the Constitution, that ordinary courts of justice are inadequate to "cases of rebellion"—attests their purpose that, in such cases, men may be held in custody whom the courts, acting on ordinary rules, would discharge. *Habeas corpus* does not discharge men who are proved to be guilty of defined crime; and its suspension is allowed by the Constitution on purpose that men may be arrested and held who cannot be proved to be guilty of defined crime, "when, in cases of rebellion or invasion, the public safety may require it." This is precisely our present case—a case of rebellion, wherein the public safety *does* require the suspension. Indeed, arrests by process of courts, and arrests in cases of rebellion, do not proceed altogether upon the same basis. The former is directed at the small percentage of ordinary and continuous perpetration of crime; while the latter is directed at sudden and extensive uprisings against the government, which at most will succeed or fail in no great length of time. In the latter case arrests are made, not so much for what has been done as for what probably would be done. The latter is more for the preventive and less for the vindictive than the former. In such cases the purposes of men are much more easily understood than in cases of ordinary crime. The man who stands by and says nothing when the peril of his government is discussed, cannot be misunderstood. If not hindered, he is sure to help the enemy; much more, if he talks ambiguously—talks for his country with "buts," and "ifs" and "ands." Of how little value the constitutional provisions I have quoted will be rendered, if arrests shall never be made until defined crimes shall have been committed, may be illustrated by a few notable examples. Gen. John C. Breckinridge, Gen. Robert E. Lee, Gen. Joseph E. Johnston, Gen. John B. Magruder, Gen. Wm. B. Preston, Gen. Simon B. Buckner, and Commodore Franklin Buchanan, now occupying the very highest places in the rebel war service, were all within the power of the Government since the rebellion began, and were nearly as well known to be traitors then as now. Unquestionably, if we had seized and held them, the insurgent cause would be much weaker. But no one of them had then committed any crime defined in the law. Every one of them, if arrested, would have been discharged on *habeas corpus*, were the writ allowed to operate. In view of these and similar cases, I think the time not unlikely to come when I shall be blamed for having made too few arrests rather than too many.

By the third resolution, the meeting indicate their opinion that military arrests may be constitutional in localities where rebellion actually exists, but that such arrests are unconstitutional in localities where rebellion or insurrection does *not* actually exist. They insist that such arrests shall not be made "outside of the lines of necessary military occupation and the scenes of insurrection." Inasmuch, however, as the Constitution itself makes no such distinction, I am unable to believe that there *is* any such constitutional distinction. I concede that the class of arrests complained of can be constitutional only when, in cases of rebellion or invasion, the public safety may require them: and I insist that in such cases they are constitutional *wherever* the public safety does require them; as well in places to which they may prevent the rebellion extending as in those where it may be already prevailing; as well where they may restrain mischievous interference with the raising and supplying of armies to suppress the rebellion, as where the rebellion may actually be; as well where they may restrain the enticing men out of the army, as where they would prevent mutiny in the army; equally constitutional at all places where they will conduce to the public safety, as against the dangers of rebellion or invasion. Take the particular case mentioned by the meeting. It is asserted, in substance, that Mr. Vallandigham was, by a military commander, seized and tried "for no other reason than words addressed to a public meeting, in criticism of the course of the Administration, and in condemnation of the military orders of the general." Now, if there be no mistake about this; if this assertion is the truth and the whole truth; if there was no other reason for the arrest, then I concede that the arrest was wrong. But the arrest, as I understand, was made for a very different reason. Mr. Vallandigham avows his hostility to the war on the part of the Union; and his arrest was made because he was laboring, with some effect, to prevent the raising of troops; to encourage desertions from the army; and to leave the rebellion without an adequate military force to suppress it. He was not arrested because he was damaging the political prospects of the Administration, or the personal interests of the commanding general, but because he was damaging the army, upon

the existence and vigor of which the life of the nation depends.
He was warring upon the military, and this gave the military
constitutional jurisdiction to lay hands upon him. If Mr. Vallandigham was not damaging the military power of the country,
then this arrest was made on mistake of fact, which I would be
glad to correct on reasonably satisfactory evidence.

I understand the meeting, whose resolutions I am considering, to be in favor of suppressing the rebellion by military force
by armies. Long experience has shown that armies cannot be
maintained unless desertions shall be punished by the severe
penalty of death. The case requires, and the law and the Constitution sanctions, this punishment. Must I shoot a simple-
minded soldier boy who deserts, while I must not touch a hair of
a wily agitator who induces him to desert ? This is none the
less injurious when effected by getting a father, or brother, or
friend, into a public meeting, and there working upon his feelings till he is persuaded to write the soldier boy that he is
fighting in a bad cause, for a wicked Administration of a con-
temptible Government, too weak to arrest and punish him if he
shall desert. I think that in such a case to silence the agitator
and save the boy is not only constitutional, but withal a great
mercy.

If I be wrong on this question of constitutional power, my
error lies in believing that certain proceedings are constitutional
when, in cases of rebellion or invasion, the public safety requires
them, which would not be constitutional when, in the absence
of rebellion or invasion, the public safety does *not* require them ;
in other words, that the Constitution is not, in its application,
in all respects the same, in cases of rebellion or invasion involving the public safety, as it is in time of profound peace and
public security. The Constitution itself makes the distinction ;
and I can no more be persuaded that the Government can constitutionally take no strong measures in time of rebellion,
because it can be shown that the same could not be lawfully
taken in time of peace, than I can be persuaded that a particular drug is not good medicine for a sick man, because it can be
shown not to be good food for a well one. Nor am I able to
appreciate the danger apprehended by the meeting that the

American people will, by means of military arrests during the rebellion, lose the right of public discussion, the liberty of speech and the press, the law of evidence, trial by jury, and *habeas corpus*, throughout the indefinite peaceful future, which I trust lies before them, any more than I am able to believe that a man could contract so strong an appetite for emetics during temporary illness as to persist in feeding upon them during the remainder of his healthful life.

In giving the resolutions that earnest consideration which you request of me, I cannot overlook the fact that the meeting speak as "Democrats." Nor can I, with full respect for their known intelligence, and the fairly presumed deliberation with which they prepared their resolutions, be permitted to suppose that this occurred by accident, or in any way other than that they preferred to designate themselves "Democrats" rather than "American citizens."

In this time of national peril, I would have preferred to meet you on a level one step higher than any party platform; because I am sure that, from such more elevated position, we could do better battle for the country we all love than we possibly can from those lower ones where, from the force of habit, the prejudices of the past, and selfish hopes of the future, we are sure to expend much of our ingenuity and strength in finding fault with and aiming blows at each other. But, since you have denied me this, I will yet be thankful, for the country's sake, that not all Democrats have done so. He on whose discretionary judgment Mr. Vallandigham was arrested and tried is a Democrat, having no old party affinity with me; and the judge who rejected the constitutional view expressed in these resolutions, by refusing to discharge Mr. Vallandigham on *habeas corpus*, is a Democrat of better days than these, having received his judicial mantle at the hands of President Jackson. And still more, of all those Democrats who are nobly exposing their lives and shedding their blood on the battle-field, I have learned that many approve the course taken with Mr. Vallandigham, while I have not heard of a single one condemning it. I cannot assert that there are none such. And the name of Jackson recalls an incident of pertinent history: After the battle of New Orleans, and while the fact that the treaty of peace had been concluded was well known in the city, but before official knowledge of it had arrived, General Jackson still maintained martial or military law. Now that it could be said the war was over, the clamor against martial law, which had existed from the first, grew more furious. Among other things, a Mr. Louiallier published a denunciatory newspaper article. General Jackson arrested him. A lawyer by the name of Morrel procured the United States Judge Hall to issue a writ of *habeas corpus* to relieve Mr. Louiallier. General Jackson arrested both the lawyer and the judge. A Mr. Hollander ventured to say of some part of the matter that "it was a dirty trick." General Jackson arrested him. When the officer undertook to serve the writ of *habeas corpus*, General Jackson took it from him, and sent him away with a copy. Holding the judge in custody a few days, the General sent him beyond the limits of his encampment, and set him at liberty, with an order to remain till the ratification of peace should be regularly announced, or until the British should have left the Southern coast. A day or two more elapsed, the ratification of a treaty of peace was regularly announced, and the judge and others were fully liberated. A few days more, and the judge called General Jackson into court and fined him $1,000 for having arrested him and the others named. The General paid the fine, and there the matter rested for nearly thirty years, when Congress refunded principal and interest. The late Senator Douglas, then in the House of Representatives, took a leading part in the debates, in which the constitutional question was much discussed. I am not prepared to say whom the journals would show to have voted for the measure.

It may be remarked: First, that we had the same Constitution then as now; secondly, that we then had a case of invasion, and now we have a case of rebellion; and, thirdly, that the permanent right of the people to public discussion, the liberty of speech and of the press, the trial by jury, the law of evidence, and the *habeas corpus*, suffered no detriment whatever by that conduct of General Jackson, or its subsequent approval by the American Congress.

And yet, let me say that, in my own discretion, I do not know whether I would have ordered the arrest of Mr. Vallandigham. While I cannot shift the responsibility from myself, I hold that, as a general rule, the commander in the field is the better judge of the necessity in any particular case. Of course I must practise a general directory and revisory power in the matter.

One of the resolutions expresses the opinion of the meeting that arbitrary arrests will have the effect to divide and distract those who should be united in suppressing the rebellion, and I am specifically called on to discharge Mr. Vallandigham. I regard this as, at least, a fair appeal to me on the expediency of exercising a constitutional power which I think exists. In response to such appeal, I have to say, it gave me pain when I learned that Mr. Vallandigham had been arrested—that is, I was pained that there should have seemed to be a necessity for arresting him—and that it will afford me great pleasure to discharge him so soon as I can, by any means, believe the public safety will not suffer by it. I further say that, as the war progresses, it appears to me, opinion and action, which were in great confusion at first, take shape and fall into more regular channels, so that the necessity for strong dealing with them gradually decreases. I have every reason to desire that it should cease altogether; and far from the least is my regard for the opinions and wishes of those who, like the meeting at Albany, declare their purpose to sustain the Government in every constitutional and lawful measure to suppress the rebellion. Still, I must continue to do so much as may seem to be required by the public safety.   A. LINCOLN.

Erroneously supposing that the people of Ohio sympathized with Mr. Vallandigham, and wishing to take advantage of his eclat as a political martyr, the Democratic Convention held at Columbus, June 11, 1863, nominated him as Governor of the State, and sent a committee to Washington to wait on the President, present the resolutions of the Convention, and demand the immediate recall of Mr. Vallandigham. To this committee Mr. Lincoln addressed the following letter:

WASHINGTON, D. C., June 29. 1863.

*Messrs. M. Burchard, David A. Houck, George Bliss, T. W. Bart-
ley, W. J. Gordon, John O'Neill, C. A. White, W. E. Fink,
Alexander Long, J. W. White, George H. Pendleton, George L.
Converse, Hanzo P. Noble, James R. Morris, W. A. Hutchins,
Abner L. Backus, J. F. McKinney, P. C. De Blond, Louis
Schaefer.*

Gentlemen—The resolutions of the Ohio Democratic State
Convention, which you present me, together with your intro-
ductory and closing remarks, being in position and argument
mainly the same as the resolutions of the Democratic meeting at
Albany, New York, I refer you to my response to the latter as
meeting most of the points in the former.

This response you evidently used in preparing your remarks,
and I desire no more than that it be used with accuracy.
In a single reading of your remarks, I only discover one
inaccuracy in matter which I suppose you took from that
paper. It is where you say, "The undersigned are unable to
agree with you in the opinion you have expressed that the Constitution is different in time of insurrection or invasion from what
it is in time of peace and public security."

A recurrence to the paper will show you that I have not
expressed the opinion you suppose. I expressed the opinion
that the Constitution is different *in its application* in cases of
rebellion or invasion, involving the public safety, from what it
is in times of profound peace and public security; and this
opinion I adhere to, simply because by the Constitution itself
things may be done in the one case which may not be done in
the other.

I dislike to waste a word on a merely personal point, but I
must respectfully assure you that you will find yourselves at
fault should you ever seek for evidence to prove your assumption that I "opposed in discussions before the people the policy
of the Mexican war."

You say: "Expunge from the Constitution this limitation
upon the power of Congress to suspend the writ of *habeas corpus*, and yet the other guarantees of personal liberty would
remain unchanged." Doubtless, if this clause of the Constitu-

tion, improperly called, as I think, a limitation upon the power of Congress, were expunged, the other guarantees would remain the same; but the question is, not how those guarantees would stand with that clause *out* of the Constitution, but how they stand with that clause remaining in it, in case of rebellion or invasion, involving the public safety. If the liberty could be indulged in expunging that clause, letter and spirit, I really think the constitutional argument would be with you.

My general view on this question was stated in the Albany response, and hence I do not state it now. I only add that, as seems to me, the benefit of the writ of *habeas corpus* is the great means through which the guarantees of personal liberty are conserved and made available in the last resort; and corroborative of this view is the fact that Mr. Vallandigham, in the very case in question, under the advice of able lawyers, saw not where else to go but to the *habeas corpus.* But by the Constitution the benefit of the writ of *habeas corpus* itself may be suspended, when, in case of rebellion or invasion, the public safety may require it.

You ask, in substance, whether I really claim that I may override all the guaranteed rights of individuals, on the plea of conserving the public safety—when I may choose to say the public safety requires it. This question divested of the phraseology calculated to represent me as struggling for an arbitrary personal prerogative, is either simply a question *who* shall decide, or an affirmation that *nobody* shall decide, what the public safety does require in cases of rebellion or invasion. The Constitution contemplates the question as likely to occur for decision, but it does not expressly declare who is to decide it. By necessary implication, when rebellion or invasion comes, the decision is to be made from time to time; and I think the man whom, for the time, the people have, under the Constitution, made the commander-in-chief of their army and navy, is the man who holds the power and bears the responsibility of making it. If he uses the power justly, the same people will probably justify him; if he abuses it, he is in their hands to be dealt with by all the modes they have reserved to themselves in the Constitution.

The earnestness with which you insist that persons can only, in times of rebellion, be lawfully dealt with in accordance with the rules for criminal trials and punishments in times of peace, induce me to add a word to what I said on that point in the Albany response. You claim that men may, if they choose, embarrass those whose duty it is to combat a giant rebellion, and then be dealt with only in turn as if there were no rebellion. The Constitution itself rejects this view. The military arrests and detentions which have been made, including those of Mr. Vallandigham, which are not different in principle from the other, have been for *prevention*, and not for *punishment*—as injunctions to stay injury, as proceedings to keep the peace—and hence, like proceedings in such cases, and for like reasons, they have not been accompanied with indictments, or trial by juries, nor in a single case by any punishment whatever beyond what is purely incidental to the prevention. The original sentence of imprisonment in Mr. Vallandigham's case was to prevent injury to the military service only, and the modification of it was made as a less disagreable mode to him of securing the same prevention.

I am unable to perceive an insult to Ohio in the case of Mr. Vallandigham. Quite surely nothing of this sort was or is intended. I was wholly unaware that Mr. Vallandigham was, at the time of his arrest, a candidate for the Democratic nomination of governor, until so informed by your reading to me the resolutions of the convention. I am grateful to the State of Ohio for many things, especially for the brave soldiers and officers she has given in the present national trial to the armies of the Union.

You claim, as I understand, that according to my own position in the Albany response, Mr. Vallandigham should be released; and this because, as you claim, he has not damaged the military service by discouraging enlistments, encouraging desertions, or otherwise; and that if he had, he should have been turned over to the civil authorities under the recent acts of Congress. I certainly do not *know* that Mr. Vallandigham has specifically and by direct language advised against enlistments and in favor of desertions, and resistance to drafting.

We all know that combinations, armed in some instances, to resist the arrest of deserters, began several months ago; that more recently the like has appeared in resistance to the enrolment preparatory to a draft; and that quite a number of assassinations have occurred from the same animus. These had to be met by military force, and this again has led to bloodshed and death. And now, under a sense of responsibility more weighty and enduring than any which is merely official, I solemnly declare my belief that this hindrance to the military, including the maiming and murder, is due to the cause in which Mr. Vallandigham has been engaged, in a greater degree than to any other cause; and it is due to him personally in a greater degree than to any other man.

These things have been notorious, known to all, and of course known to Mr. Vallandigham. Perhaps I would not be wrong to say they originated with his especial friends and adherents. With perfect knowledge of them he has frequently, if not constantly, made speeches in Congress and before popular assemblies; and if it can be shown that, with these things staring him in the face he has ever uttered a word of rebuke or counsel against them, it will be a fact greatly in his favor with me, and of which, as yet, I am totally ignorant. When it is known that the whole burden of his speeches has been to stir up men against the prosecution of the war, and that in the midst of resistance to it he has not been known in any instance to counsel against such resistance, it is next to impossible to repel the inference that he has counseled directly in favor of it.

With all this before their eyes the convention you represent have nominated Mr. Vallandigham for governor of Ohio, and both they and you have declared the purpose to sustain the national Union by all constitutional means, but, of course, they and you, in common, reserve to yourselves to decide what are constitutional means, and, unlike the Albany meeting, you omit to state or intimate that, in your opinion, an army is a constitutional means of saving the Union against a rebellion, or even to intimate that you are conscious of an existing rebellion being in progress with the avowed object of destroying that very Union. At the same time, your nominee for governor, in whose behalf you appeal, is known to you, and to the world, to declare against the use of an army to suppress the rebellion. Your own attitude, therefore, encourages desertion, resistance to the draft, and the like, because it teaches those who incline to desert and to escape the draft to believe it is your purpose to protect them, and to hope that you will become strong enough to do so.

After a short personal intercourse with you, gentlemen of the committee, I cannot say I think you desire this effect to follow your attitude ; but I assure you that both friends and enemies of the Union look upon it in this light. It is a substantial hope, and by consequence, a real strength to the enemy. If it is a false hope, and one which you would willingly dispel, I will make the way exceedingly easy. I send you duplicates of this letter, in order that you, or a majority, may, if you choose, endorse your names upon one of them, and return it, thus endorsed, to me, with the understanding that those signing are thereby committed to the following propositions, and to nothing else :

1. That there is now rebellion in the United States, the object and tendency of which is to destroy the national Union ; and that, in your opinion, an army and navy are constitutional means for suppressing that rebellion.

2. That no one of you will do anything which, in his own judgment, will tend to hinder the increase, or favor the decrease, or lessen the efficiency of the army and navy, while engaged in the effort to suppress that rebellion ; and—

3. That each of you will, in his sphere, do all he can to have the officers, soldiers, and seamen of the army and navy, while engaged in the effort to suppress the rebellion, paid, fed, clad, and otherwise well provided for and supported.

And with the further understanding that upon receiving the letter and names thus endorsed, I will cause them to be published, which publication shall be, within itself, a revocation of the order in relation to Mr. Vallandigham.

It will not escape observation that I consent to the release of Mr. Vallandigham upon terms not embracing any pledge from him or from others as to what he will or will not do. I do this because he is not present to speak for himself, or to authorize others to speak for him; and hence I shall expect that, on returning, he would not put himself practically in antagonism with the position of his friends. But I do it chiefly because I thereby prevail on other influential gentlemen of Ohio to so define their position as to be of immense value to the army—thus more than compensating for the consequences of any mistake in allowing Mr. Vallandigham to return, so that, on the whole, the public safety will not have suffered by it. Still, in regard to Mr. Vallandigham and all others, I must hereafter, as heretofore, do so much as the public service may seem to require.

I have the honor to be respectfully, yours, etc.,

A. LINCOLN.

The reader need hardly be reminded that the President was heartily sustained in his action in this matter, not only by the country at large, but especially by Ohio, where Mr. Vallandigham, in spite of his "martyrdom," was defeated by an overwhelming majority.

GETTYSBURG AND VICKSBURG.

The important defeat of the rebels, under General Lee, by General Meade at Gettysburg on July 2d and 3d, of this year, and the hardly less important capture of Vicksburg, with General Pemberton's army, on the 4th, did much to sustain and cheer the country in its trials. On the 7th, the President was waited on, at the White House, by a large crowd of people, with music, and made to them the following speech :

Fellow-Citizens—I am very glad indeed to see you to-night, and yet I will not say I thank you for this call, but I do most sincerely thank Almighty God for the occasion on which you have called. (Cheers.) How long ago is it—eighty odd years—since on the 4th of July, for the first time in the history of the world, a nation, by its representatives, assembled and declared, as a self-evident truth, that "all men are created equal?" (Cheers.) That was the birthday of the United States of America. Since then the 4th of July has had several very peculiar recognitions. The two most distinguished men in the framing and support of the Declaration were Thomas Jefferson and John Adams—the one having penned it, and the other sustained it the most forcibly in debate—the only two of the fifty-five who sustained it being elected President of the United States. Precisely fifty years after they put their hands to the paper, it pleased Almighty God to take both from this stage of action. This was, indeed, an extraordinary and remarkable event in our history. Another President, five years after, was called from this stage of existence on the same day and month of the year; and now, in this last 4th of July just passed, when we have a gigantic rebellion, at the bottom of which is an effort to overthrow the principles that all men were created equal, we have the surrender of a most powerful position and army on that very day. (Cheers.) And not only so, but in a succession of battles in Pennsylvania, near to us, through three days, so rapidly fought that they might be called one great battle on the 1st, 2d, and 3d of the month of July; and on the 4th, the cohorts of those who opposed the declaration that all men are created equal, "turned tail" and ran. (Long continued cheers.) Gentlemen, this is a glorious theme, and the occasion for a speech; but I am not prepared to make one worthy of the occasion. I would like to speak in terms of praise, due to the many brave officers and soldiers who have fought in the cause of the Union and liberties of their country from the beginning of the war. There are trying occasions not only in success, but for the want of success. I dislike to mention the name of one single officer, lest I might do wrong to those I might forget. Recent events bring up glorious names and particularly prominent ones; but these I will not mention. Having said this much, I will now take the music.

Mr. Lincoln did not, however, confine his acknowledgments of the great services then rendered to the country to public speeches or formal communications. He wrote kind personal letters to the commanders.   The following, which he addressed to General Grant, contains a frank confession of erroneous judgment on the part of the President:

EXECUTIVE MANSION, WASHINGTON, *July* 13, 1863.

*Major-General Grant—My Dear General—*I do not remember that you and I ever met personally.   I write this now as a grateful acknowledgment for the almost inestimable services you have done the country.   I write to say a word further.   When you first reached the vicinity of Vicksburg, I thought you should do what you finally did—march the troops across the neck, run the batteries with the transports, and thus go below; and I never had any faith, except a general hope that you knew better than I, that the Yazoo Pass expedition, and the like, could succeed.   When you got below, and took Port Gibson, Grand Gulf, and vicinity, I thought you should go down the river, and join General Banks, and when you turned northward, east of the Big Black, I feared it was a mistake.   I now wish to make the personal acknowledgment, that you were right and I was wrong.   Yours, truly,   A. LINCOLN.

The proclamation which the President issued upon occasion of these victories is worthy of perusal on account of the truly grateful spirit with which it is imbued, and the appearance of that tenderness of heart and forgiving disposition which were such marked traits in Mr. Lincoln's character.

PROCLAMATION.

It has pleased Almighty God to hearken to the supplications and prayers of an afflicted people, and to vouchsafe to the Army and the Navy of the United States, on the land and on the sea, victories so signal and so effective as to furnish reasonable grounds for augmented confidence that the Union of these States will be maintained, their Constitution preserved, and their peace and prosperity permanently secured; but these vic tories have been accorded, not without sacrifice of life, limb, and liberty, incurred by brave, patriotic, and loyal citizens. Domestic affliction, in every part of the country, follows in the train of these fearful bereavements. It is meet and right to recognize and confess the presence of the Almighty Father, and the power of his hand equally in these triumphs and these sorrows.

Now, therefore, be it known, that I do set apart Thursday, the sixth day of August next, to be observed as a day for National Thanksgiving, praise, and prayer; and I invite the people of the United States to assemble on that occasion in their customary places of worship, and in the form approved by their own conscience, render the homage due to the Divine Majesty, for the wonderful things He has done in the nation's behalf, and invoke the influence of His Holy Spirit, to subdue the anger which has produced, and so long sustained a needless and cruel rebellion; to change the hearts of the insurgents; to guide the counsels of the Government with wisdom adequate to so great a national emergency, and to visit with tender care, and consolation, throughout the length and breadth of our land, all those who, through the vicissitudes of marches, voyages, battles, and sieges, have been brought to suffer in mind, body, or estate, and finally, to lead the whole nation through paths of repentance and submission to the Divine will, back to the perfect enjoyment of union and fraternal peace.

In witness whereof, I have hereunto set my hand, and caused the seal of the United States to be affixed.

Done at the City of Washington, this 15th day of July, in the year of our Lord one thousand eight hundred and [L. S.] sixty-three, and of the independence of the United States of America the eighty-eighth.

ABRAHAM LINCOLN.

By the President:

WILLIAM H. SEWARD, *Secretary of State.*

PROTECTION TO NEGRO SOLDIERS.

Although the rebels had from the beginning of the war made such use of their slaves in their armies as seemed good to them, they became furious when the Government proposed to put negroes actually into the ranks. They denounced this as a savage attempt to excite a servile insurrection, and they declared that negro soldiers, if taken prisoners, should not be regarded as ordinary prisoners of war, but be handed over to the local authorities of the State in which they were captured. This was only another way of saying that they should be put to death under the "black laws" of the Slave States. They carried out this threat in many instances; and in many more they slaughtered upon the field negro soldiers who had surrendered. Slow to anger, and shrinking with horror from bloody retaliation, President Lincoln, however, at last was driven to issue upon this subject the following order:

WAR DEPARTMENT, ADJUTANT-GENERAL'S OFFICE,
WASHINGTON, July 31, 1863.

General Order No. 252.—The following order of the President is published for the information and government of all concerned:

EXECUTIVE MANSION,
WASHINGTON, July 30.

It is the duty of every Government to give protection to its citizens, of whatever class, color or condition, and especially those who are duly organized as soldiers in the public service. The law of nations and the usages and customs of war, as carried on by civilized powers, permit no distinction as to color in the treatment of prisoners of war as public enemies. To sell or enslave any captured person on account of his color, and for no offence against the laws of war, is a relapse into barbarism and a crime against the civilization of the age. The Government of the United States will give the same protection to all its soldiers, and if the enemy shall sell or enslave any one because of his color, the offence shall be punished by retaliation upon the enemy's prisoners in our possession. It is, therefore, ordered that for every soldier of the United States killed in violation of the laws of war, a rebel soldier shall be executed, and for every one enslaved by the enemy or sold into slavery, a rebel soldier shall be placed at hard labor on the public works, and continued at such labor until the other shall be released and receive the treatment due to a prisoner of war.

ABRAHAM LINCOLN.

By order of the Secretary of War.

E. D. TOWNSEND, *Assistant Adjutant-General.*

THE ANTI-DRAFT RIOTS—GOVERNOR SEYMOUR.

A law was passed by Congress providing that the ranks of the army should be filled by a draft. This was in accordance with a suggestion made by General McClellan, August 20th, 1861, when he was in command of the Army of the Potomac. The unscrupulous among the opponents of Mr. Lincoln's Administration, and the defenders of the rebellion generally in the Free States endeavored for months to stir up the people in resistance to this law. A provision of the law by which any drafted man might be furnished at his choice with a substitute by paying $300 to the Government, was particularly used as a means of exciting animosity, on the ground that it was directed against the poor who could not command that sum, while it favored the rich who could. *The World*, a daily journal of New York, which, according to evidence produced in a court of law, had been offered for sale, with the services of its editor, Mr. M. Marble, both to the supporters of the war and to its opponents, and which, having been purchased by the latter, was chiefly known by its active encouragement of the rebellion, having even gone so far as to declare that it had "always maintained" that the President "had no right to complain of the action of the Slave States," and that the people of New York "no more lived under the Constitution than the people now in Georgia," and having counseled its readers to provide themselves with arms, and keep in

" every family" a " good rifled musket, a few pounds of powder, and a hundred or so of shot," to " defend their homes and personal liberties from invasion from *any* quarter"—meaning, of course, from Canada — distinguished itself by its efforts to provoke active ill-feeling upon this subject. These efforts, directed by the malignant, and inflaming the thoughtless and the ignorant, were followed by events equally disastrous and significant. It would be superfluous to mention more in detail the Irish Anti-Draft Riots of July, 1863, in which New York, in the absence of its militia regiments, was for three days disgraced by scenes of blood, arson, and plunder. The riots were subdued by the vigorous action of the Metropolitan Police force, aided by a few troops brought up from the forts in the harbor, and order was secured by the arrival of some regiments from the army in the field, and the return of some of the militia. The draft, of course, was ordered to go on as soon as tranquillity was restored, all the more in consequence of the riots. But Horatio Seymour, then Governor of New York, who on more than one occasion seemed to be regarded by the rioters as their particular friend, thought, it would appear, that this assertion of its authority and this execution of an Act of Congress in the face of threatened violence was unbecoming, or at least impolitic, and he applied by letter to the President to have the draft postponed until the constitutionality of the law could be decided by the judicial tribunals. To this the President replied by the following letter.

EXECUTIVE MANSION, WASHINGTON, *August* 7, 1863.

His Excellency Horatio Seymour, Governor of New York, Albany, N. Y.—Your communication of the 3d inst. has been received and attentively considered. I can not consent to suspend the draft in New York, as you request, because, among other reasons, TIME is too important. By the figures you send, which I presume are correct, the twelve districts represented fall in two classes of eight and four respectively.

The disparity of the quotas for the draft in these two classes is certainly very striking, being the difference between an average of 2,200 in one class, and 4,864 in the other. Assuming that the districts are equal, one to another, in entire population, as required by the plan on which they were made, this disparity is such as to require attention. Much of it, however, I suppose will be accounted for by the fact that so many more persons fit for soldiers are in the city than in the country, who have too recently arrived from other parts of the United States and from Europe to be either included in the census of 1860, or to have voted in 1862. Still, making due allowance for this, I am yet unwilling to stand upon it as an entirely sufficient explanation of the great disparity. I shall direct the draft to proceed in all the districts, drawing, however, at first, from each of the four districts—to wit, the Second, Fourth, Sixth and Eighth—only 2,200, being the average quota of the other class. After this drawing, these four districts, and also the Seventeenth and Twenty-ninth, shall be carefully reënrolled; and, if you please, agents of yours may witness every step of the process. Any deficiency which may appear by the new enrolment will be supplied by a special draft for that object, allowing due credit for volunteers who may be obtained from these districts respectively during the interval; and at all points, so far as consistent with practical convenience, due credits shall be given for volunteers, and your excellency shall be notified of the time fixed for commencing a draft in each district.

I do not object to abide a decision of the United States Supreme Court, or of the judges thereof, on the constitutionality of the draft law. In fact I should be willing to facilitate the obtaining of it. But I can not consent to lose the time while it is being obtained. We are contending with an enemy who, as I understand, drives every able-bodied man he can reach into his ranks, very much as a butcher drives bullocks into a slaughter-pen. No time is wasted, no argument is used. This produces an army which will soon turn upon our now victorious soldiers already in the field, if they shall not be sustained by recruits as they should be. It produces an army with a rapidity not to be matched on our side, if we first waste time to reëxperiment with the volunteer system, already deemed by Congress, and palpably, in fact, so far exhausted as to be inadequate; and then more time to obtain a court decision as to whether a law is constitutional which requires a part of those not now in the service to go to the aid of those who are already in it; and still more time to determine with absolute certainty that we get those who are to go in the precisely legal proportion to those who are not to go. My purpose is to be in my action just and constitutional, and yet practical, in performing the important duty with which I am charged, of maintaining the unity and the free principles of our common country. Your obedient servant,   A. LINCOLN.

Governor Seymour returned to the charge in another letter, reasserting the injustice of the law, and supporting his position by an opinion prepared by Nelson J. Waterbury, then Judge Advocate of New York. To this letter Mr. Lincoln replied as follows:

EXECUTIVE MANSION, WASHINGTON, *August* 11, 1863.

His Excellency Horatio Seymour, Governor of New York:— Yours of the 8th, with Judge-Advocate General Waterbury's report, was received to-day.

Asking you to remember that I consider time as being very important, both to the general cause of the country and to the soldiers in the field, I beg to remind you that I waited, at your request, from the 1st until the 6th inst. to receive your commucation dated the 3d. In view of its great length, and the known time and apparent care taken in its preparation, I did not doubt that it contained your full case as you desired to present it. It contained the figures for twelve districts, omitting the other nineteen, as I supposed, because you found nothing to complain of as to them. I answered accordingly. In doing so I laid down the principle to which I purpose adhering, which is to proceed with the draft, at the same time employing infallible means to avoid any great wrong. With the communication received to-day you send figures for twenty-eight districts, including the twelve sent before, and still omitting three, for which I suppose the enrolments are not yet received. In looking over the fuller list of twenty-eight districts, I find that the quotas for sixteen of them are above 2,000 and below 2,700, while of the rest, six are above 2,700, and six are below 2,000. Applying the principle to these new facts, the Fifth and Seventh Districts must be added to the four in which the quotas have already been reduced to 2,200 for the first draft; and with these four others must be added to those to be reënrolled. The correct case will then stand : the quotas of the Second, Fourth, Fifth, Sixth, Seventh and Eighth Districts fixed at 2,200 for the first draft. The Provost-Marshal General informs me that the drawing is already completed in the Sixteenth, Seventeenth, Eighteenth, Twenty-second, Twenty-fourth, Twenty-sixth, Twenty-seventh, Twenty-Eighth, Twenty-ninth, and Thirtieth Districts. In the others, except the three outstanding, the drawing will be made upon the quotas as now fixed. After the first draft, the Second, Fourth, Fifth, Sixth, Seventh, Eighth, Sixteenth, Seventeenth, Twenty-first, Twenty-fifth, Twenty-ninth, and Thirty-first will be enrolled for the purpose and in the manner stated in my letter of the 7th inst. The same principle will be applied to the now outstanding districts when they shall come in. No part of my former letter is repudiated by reason of not being restated in this, or for any other cause.

Your obedient servant,

A. LINCOLN.

The draft was resumed on the 19th of August, and completed without further opposition.

"UNCONDITIONAL UNION MEN."

About the beginning of the second year of the rebellion certain men, hearty supporters of the war for its suppression, and hitherto of the policy of the Administration, began to talk of "unconditional loyalty," and to style themselves "Unconditional Union Men." Mr. Lincoln thought that he discovered that their unconditional loyalty meant loyalty on condition that slavery was immediately and entirely abolished, and the ranks of the army recruited from the negroes; and although his hatred of slavery was no less than theirs, he thought that their purposes were unwise, and their professions somewhat inconsistent with their demands. In August they held a Convention at Springfield, Illinois, and invited the President to be present. He declined the invitation in the following letter:

EXECUTIVE MANSION, WASHINGTON, *August* 26, 1863.

*Hon. James M. Conkling—Dear Sir—*Your letter inviting me to attend a mass meeting of the Unconditional Union men, to be held at the capital of Illinois, on the 3d day of September, has been received. It would be very agreeable for me thus to meet my old friends at my own home; but I cannot just now be absent from here so long as a visit there would require.

The meeting is to be of all those who maintain unconditional devotion to the Union; and I am sure that my old political friends will thank me for tendering, as I do, the nation's gratitude to those other noble men whom no partisan malice or partisan hope can make false to the nation's life.

There are those who are dissatisfied with me. To such I would say: you desire peace, and you blame me that we do not have it. But how can we attain it? There are but three conceivable ways: First—to suppress the Rebellion by force of arms. This I am trying to do. Are you for it? If you are, so far we are agreed. If you are not for it, a *second* way is to give up the Union. I am against this. Are you for it? If you are you should say so plainly. If you are not for *force*, nor yet for *dissolution*, there only remains some imaginable *compromise*.

I do not believe that any compromise embracing the maintenance of the Union is now possible. All that I learn leads to a directly opposite belief. The strength of the Rebellion is its military, its army. That army dominates all the country, and all the people within its range. Any offer of terms made by any man or men within that range, in opposition to that army, is simply nothing for the present; because such man or men have no power whatever to enforce their side of a compromise, if one were made with them.

To illustrate: Suppose refugees from the South and peace men from the North get together in convention, and frame and proclaim a compromise embracing a restoration of the Union. In what way can that compromise be used to keep Lee's army out of Pennsylvania? Meade's army can keep Lee's army out of Pennsylvania, and, I think, can ultimately drive it out of existence. But no paper compromise to which the controllers of Lee's army are not agreed can at all affect that army. In an effort at such compromise we would waste time, which the enemy would improve to our disadvantage; and that would be all.

A compromise, to be effective, must be made either with those who control the rebel army, or with the people, first liberated from the domination of that army by the success of our own army. Now, allow me to assure you that no word or intimation from that rebel army, or from any of the men controlling it, in relation to any peace compromise, has ever come to my knowledge or belief. All charges and insinuations to the contrary are deceptive and groundless. And I promise you that if any such proposition shall hereafter come, it shall not be rejected and kept a secret from you. I freely acknowledge myself to be the servant of the people, according to the bond of service, the United States Constitution; and that, as such, I am responsible to them.

But, to be plain. You are dissatisfied with me about the negro. Quite likely there is a difference of opinion between you and myself upon that subject. I certainly wish that all men could be free, while you, I suppose, do not. Yet, I have neither adopted nor proposed any measure which is not consistent with even your views, provided that you are for the Union. I suggested compensated emancipation; to which you replied you wished not be taxed to buy negroes. But I had not asked you to be taxed to buy negroes, except in such way as to save you from greater taxation to save the Union, exclusively by other means.

You dislike the Emancipation Proclamation, and perhaps would have it retracted. You say it is unconstitutional. I think differently. I think the Constitution invests its Commander-in-Chief with the law of war in time of war. The most that can be said, if so much, is, that slaves are property. Is there, has there ever been, any question that by the law of war, property, both of enemies and friends, may be taken when needed? And is it not needed whenever it helps us and hurts the enemy? Armies, the world over, destroy enemies property when they cannot use it; and even destroy their own to keep it from the enemy. Civilized belligerents do all in their power to help themselves or hurt the enemy, except a few things regarded as barbarous or cruel. Among the exceptions are the massacre of vanquished foes and non-combatants, male and female.

But the Proclamation, as law, either is valid, or is not valid. If it is not valid it needs no retraction. If it is valid it cannot be retracted, any more than the dead can be brought to life. Some of you profess to think its retraction would operate favorably for the Union. Why better *after* the retraction than *before* the issue? There was more than a year and a half of trial to suppress the Rebellion before the Proclamation was issued, the last one hundred days of which passed under an explicit notice that it was coming, unless averted by those in revolt returning to their allegiance. The war has certainly progressed as favorably for us since the issue of the Proclamation as before.

I know, as fully as one can know the opinions of others, that some of the commanders of our armies in the field, who have given us our most important victories, believe the emancipation policy and the use of colored troops constitute the heaviest blows yet dealt to the Rebellion, and that at least one of those important successes could not have been achieved when it was but for the aid of black soldiers.

Among the commanders who hold these views are some who have never had any affinity with what is called "Abolitionism," or with "Republican party politics," but who hold them purely as military opinions. I submit their opinions as entitled to some weight against the objections often urged that emancipation and arming the blacks are unwise as military measures, and were not adopted as such in good faith.

You say that you will not fight to free negroes. Some of them seem willing to fight for you; but no matter. Fight you, then, exclusively to save the Union. I issued the Proclamation on purpose to aid you in saving the Union. Whenever you shall have conquered all resistance to the Union, if I shall urge you to continue fighting, it will be an apt time then for you to declare you will not fight to free negroes. I thought that in your struggle for the Union, to whatever extent the negroes should cease helping the enemy, to that extent it weakened the enemy in his resistance to you. Do you think differently? I thought that whatever negroes can be got to do as soldiers, leaves just so much less for white soldiers to do in saving the Union. Does it appear otherwise to you? But negroes, like other people, act upon motives. Why should they do anything for us if we will do nothing for them? If they stake their lives for us they must be prompted by the strongest motive, even the promise of freedom. And the promise, being made, must be kept.

The signs look better. The Father of Waters again goes unvexed to the sea. Thanks to the great Northwest for it; nor yet wholly to them. Three hundred miles up they met New England, Empire, Keystone, and Jersey, hewing their way right and left. The sunny South, too, in more colors than one, also lent a helping hand. On the spot, their part of the history was jotted down in black and white. The job was a great national one, and let none be slighted who bore an honorable part in it. And while those who have cleared the great river may well be proud, even that is not all. It is hard to say that anything has been more bravely and well done than at Antietam, Murfreesboro, Gettysburg, and on many fields of less note. Nor must Uncle Sam's web feet be forgotten. At all the watery margins they have been present, not only on the deep sea, the broad bay, and the rapid river, but also up the narrow, muddy bayou, and wherever the ground was a little damp they have been and made their tracks. Thanks to all. For the great Republic—for the principle it lives by and keeps alive—for man's vast future—thanks to all.

Peace does not appear so distant as it did. I hope it will come soon and come to stay; and so come as to be worth the keeping in all future time. It will then have been proved that among freemen there can be no successful appeal from the ballot to the bullet, and that they who take such appeal are sure to lose their case and pay the cost. And there will be some black men who can remember that with silent tongue, and clinched teeth, and steady eye, and well-poised bayonet, they have helped mankind on to this great consummation, while I fear there will be some white ones unable to forget that with malignant heart and deceitful speech they have striven to hinder it.

Still, let us not be over-sanguine of a speedy, final triumph. Let us be quite sober. Let us diligently apply the means, never doubting that a just God, in His own good time, will give us the rightful result.   Yours, very truly,   A. LINCOLN.

HABEAS CORPUS.

It was pretended by those who wished to embarrass the Government that although Congress had authorized the suspension of the privilege of the writ of *habeas corpus*, that suspension could only take place legally in those military districts in which it had been formally proclaimed. To meet these cavils Mr. Lincoln issued the following proclamation that the privilege in question was suspended throughout the United States in all cases effected by the existing rebellion.

PROCLAMATION.

Whereas, The Constitution of the United States has ordained that " The privilege of the writ of *habeas corpus* shall not be suspended, unless, when in cases of rebellion or invasion, the public safety may require it; and, whereas, a rebellion was existing on the 3d day of March, 1863, which rebellion is still existing; and, whereas, by a statute which was approved on that day, it was enacted by the Senate and House of Representatives of the United States, in Congress assembled, that during the present insurrection the President of the United States, whenever, in his judgment, the public safety may require, is authorized to suspend the privilege of the writ of *habeas corpus* in any case throughout the United States, or any part thereof; and, whereas, in the judgment of the President the public safety does require that the privilege of the said writ shall now be suspended throughout the United States in cases where, by the authority of the President of the United States, military, naval and civil officers of the United States, or any of them, hold persons under their command or in their custody, either as prisoners of war, spies, or aiders or abettors of the enemy, or officers, soldiers, or seamen enrolled, drafted or mustered, or enlisted in, or belonging to the land or naval forces of the United States, or as deserters therefrom, or otherwise amenable to military law, or to the rules and articles of war, or the rules and regulations prescribed for the military or naval services by the authority of the President of the United States, or for resisting the draft, or for any other offence against the military or naval service; now, therefore, I, ABRAHAM LINCOLN, President of the United States, do hereby proclaim and make known to all whom it may concern, that the privilege of the writ of *habeas corpus* is suspended throughout the United States, in the several cases before mentioned, and that this suspension will continue throughout the duration of the said rebellion, or until this Proclamation shall, by a subsequent one, to be issued by the President of the United States, be modified and revoked. And I do hereby require all magistrates, attorneys, and other civil officers within the United States, and all officers and others in the military and naval services of the United States, to take distinct notice of this suspension and give it full effect, and all citizens of the United States to conduct and govern themselves accordingly, and in conformity with the Constitution of the United States, and the laws of Congress in such cases made and provided.

In testimony whereof, I have hereunto set my hand and caused the seal of the United States to be affixed, this fifteenth day of September, in the year of our Lord one thousand eight hundred and sixty-three, and of the independence of the United States of America the eighty-eighth.

ABRAHAM LINCOLN.

By the President:
WM. H. SEWARD, *Secretary of State.*

THANKSGIVING.

To observers not fully informed, or who saw only what they wished to see, the rebellion seemed as formidable as ever.   But very important progress had been made in its suppression, and the country north of the Potomac had begun to recover its prosperity, while the fear of foreign intervention had passed away.   In thankful acknowledgment of these blessings the President issued the following

PROCLAMATION.

The year that is drawing towards its close has been filled with the blessings of fruitful fields and healthful skies.   To these bounties, which are so constantly enjoyed that we are prone to forget the source from which they come, others have been added which are of so extraordinary a nature that they cannot fail to penetrate and soften even the heart which is habitually insensible to the ever watchful providence of Almighty God.   In the midst of a civil war of unequaled magnitude and severity, which has sometimes seemed to invite and provoke the aggressions of foreign states, peace has been preserved with all nations, order has been maintained, the laws have been respected and obeyed, and harmony has prevailed everywhere, except in the theatre of military conflict, while that theatre has been greatly contracted by the advancing armies and navies of the Union. The needful diversion of wealth and strength from the fields ot peaceful industry to the national defence, have not arrested the plough, the shuttle, or the ship. The axe has enlarged the borders of our settlements, and the mines as well of iron and coal as of the precious metals, have yielded even more abundantly than heretofore. Population has steadily increased, notwithstanding the waste that has been made in the camp, the siege, and the battlefield; and the country, rejoicing in the consciousness of augmented strength and vigor, is permitted to expect a continuance of years, with large increase of freedom.

No human counsel hath devised, nor hath any mortal hand worked out these great things. They are the gracious gifts of the Most High God, who, while dealing with us in anger for our sins, hath nevertheless remembered mercy.

It has seemed to me fit and proper that they should be solemnly, reverently, and gratefully acknowledged, as with one heart and voice, by the whole American people. I do, therefore, invite my fellow-citizens in every part of the United States, and also those who are at sea, and those who are sojourning in foreign lands, to set apart and observe the last Thursday ot November next, as a day of thanksgiving and prayer to our beneficent Father, who dwelleth in the heavens. And I recommend to them that, while offering up the ascriptions justly due to him for such singular deliverances and blessings, they do, also, with humble penitence for our national perverseness and disobedience, commend to his tender care all those who have become widows, orphans, mourners, or sufferers in the lamentable civil strife in which we are unavoidably engaged, and fervently implore the interposition of the Almighty hand to heal the wounds of the nation, and to restore it, as soon as may be consistent with the divine purposes, to the full enjoyment of peace, harmony, tranquillity, and union.

In testimony whereof, I have hereunto set my hand, and caused the seal of the United States to be affixed.

Done at the city of Washington, this third day of October, in
  [L. S.]   the year of our Lord, 1863, and of the independence
       of the United States the eighty-eighth.

ABRAHAM LINCOLN.

By the President:
WM. H. SEWARD, *Secretary of State.*

THE GETTYSBURG CEMETERY.

General Meade's victory at Gettysburg had done away
all fear of a serious invasion of the Free States. The
importance of the victory gained by those bloody three-
days' battles, made some commemoration of it highly
proper; and it was very fitly determined that a monument should be erected in a cemetery at Gettysburg, in
which all the soldiers who fell in those battles should be
interred. Mr. Lincoln was present at the dedication of
that cemetery on the 19th of November, 1863, and made
the following brief, but now world-renowned

SPEECH.

Four score and seven years ago our fathers brought forth upon
this continent a new nation, conceived in liberty, and dedicated
to the proposition that all men are created equal. Now we are
engaged in a great civil war, testing whether that nation, or any
nation so conceived and so dedicated can long endure. We are
met on a great battle-field of that war. We have come to
dedicate a portion of that field as a final resting-place for those
who here gave their lives that that nation might live. It is
altogether fitting and proper that we should do this. But in a
larger sense we cannot dedicate, we cannot consecrate, we cannot hallow this ground. The brave men, living and dead, who
struggled here, have consecrated it far above our power to add
or detract. The world will little note, nor long remember,
what we say here, but it can never forget what they did here.

It is for us, the living, rather to be dedicated here to the unfinished work which they who fought here have thus far so nobly advanced. It is rather for us to be here dedicated to the great task remaining before us, that from these honored dead we take increased devotion to that cause for which they gave the last full measure of devotion; that we here highly resolve that these dead shall not have died in vain; that this nation, under God, shall have a new birth of freedom, and that government of the people, by the people, and for the people, shall not perish from the earth.

THE VICTORY OF CHATTANOOGA.

The long struggle for the possession of East Tennessee, the key of the country southward, was brought to a close by General Grant's great victory at Chattanooga, after which the rebellion settled steadily downward to its final ruin. Of this victory the President made the following announcement, accompanied by a recommendation of thanksgiving:

EXECUTIVE MANSION, WASHINGTON, D. C., *December* 7, 1863.

Reliable information being received that the insurgent force is retreating from East Tennessee, under circumstances rendering it probable that the Union forces can not hereafter be dislodged from that important position; and esteeming this to be of high national consequence, I recommend that all loyal people do, on receipt of this information, assemble at their places of worship, and render special homage and gratitude to Almighty God for this great advancement of the national cause.

A. LINCOLN.

THE MISSOURI FEUD.

The conflict between the self-styled Unconditional Union party and those who really were loyal to the republic without condition, continued, and in fact became more and more bitter. The former party complained that General Schofield and Governor Gamble were really friends of the rebels in that district. How truly they were so, with the support of the Government, will appear from the following :

INSTRUCTONS TO GENERAL SCHOFIELD.

EXECUTIVE MANSION, WASHINGTON, D. C., *October* 1, 1863.

General John M. Schofield—There is no organized military force in avowed opposition to the General Government now in Missouri, and if any shall reappear, your duty in regard to it will be too plain to require any special instruction. Still, the condition of things, both there and elsewhere, is such as to render it indispensable to maintain, for a time, the United States military establishment in that State, as well as to rely upon it for a fair contribution of support to that establishment generally. Your immediate duty in regard to Missouri now is to advance the efficiency of that establishment, and to so use it, as far as practicable, to compel the excited people there to let one another alone.

Under your recent order, which I have approved, you will only arrest individuals, and suppress assemblies or newspapers, when they may be working *palpable* injury to the military in your charge; and in no other case will you interfere with the expression of opinion in any form, or allow it to be interfered with violently by others. In this you have a discretion to exercise with great caution, calmness, and forbearance.

With the matter of removing the inhabitants of certain counties *en masse*, and of removing certain individuals from time to time, who are supposed to be mischievous, I am not now interfering, but am leaving to your own discretion.

Nor am I interfering with what may still seem to you to be necessary restrictions upon trade and intercourse. I think proper, however, to enjoin upon you the following : Allow no part of the military under your command to be engaged in either returning fugitive slaves, or in forcing or enticing slaves from their homes; and, so far as practicable, enforce the same forbearance among the people.

Report to me your opinion upon the availability for good of the enrolled militia of the State. Allow no one to enlist colored troops, except upon orders from you, or from here through you.

Allow no one to assume the functions of confiscating property, under the law of Congress, or otherwise, except upon orders from here.

At elections see that those, and only those, are allowed to vote, who are entitled to do so by the laws of Missouri, including as those laws the restrictions laid by the Missouri Convention upon those who may have participated in the rebellion.

So far as practicable, you will, by means of your military force, expel guerrillas, marauders, and murderers, and all who are known to harbor, aid, or abet them. But in like manner you will repress assumptions of unauthorized individuals to perform the same service, because under pretence of doing this they become marauders and murderers themselves.

To now restore peace, let the military obey orders; and those not of the military leave each other alone, thus not breaking the peace themselves.

In giving the above directions, it is not intended to restrain you in other expedient and necessary matters not falling within their range. Your obedient servant,

A. LINCOLN.

The unconditional anti-slavery party, however, were not to be thus satisfied. They were formidable in numbers, and bold in action. They held a convention at the capital of the State, and sent a delegation consisting of one from each county of the State to make certain demands of the President. They also attempted with some success to organize a support of their views and measures throughout the Free States. To the address of the committee of delegates Mr. Lincoln made the following reply:

EXECUTIVE MANSION, WASHINGTON, *Oct.* 5, 1863.

*Hon. Charles Drake and others, Committee—Gentlemen—*Your original address, presented on the 30th ult., and the four supplementary ones presented on the 3d inst., have been carefully considered. I hope you will regard the other duties claiming my attention, together with the great length and importance of these documents, as constituting a sufficient apology for my not having responded sooner.

These papers, framed for a common object, consist of the things demanded, and the reasons for demanding them.

The things demanded are:

First—That General Schofield shall be relieved, and General Butler be appointed as Commander of the Military Department of Missouri;

Second—That the system of enrolled militia in Missouri may be broken up, and National forces be substituted for it; and

Third—That at elections, persons may be allowed to vote who are not entitled by law to do so.

Among the reasons given, enough of suffering and wrong to Union men, is certainly, and I suppose truly, stated. Yet the whole case, as presented, fails to convince me that General Schofield, or the enrolled militia, is responsible for that suffering and wrong. The whole can be explained on a more charitable, and, as I think, a more rational hypothesis.

We are in civil war. In such cases there always is a main question; but in this case that question is a perplexing compound—Union and Slavery. It thus becomes a question not of two sides merely, but of at least four sides, even among those who are for the Union, saying nothing of those who are against it. Thus, those who are for the Union *with,* but not *without slavery*—those for it *without* but not *with*—those for it *with or without,* but prefer it *with,* and those for it *with* or *without* but prefer it *without.*

Among these, again, is a subdivision of those who are for *gradual,* but not for *immediate,* and those who are for *immediate,* but not for *gradual* extinction of slavery.

It is easy to conceive that all these shades of opinion and even more, may be sincerely entertained by honest and truthful men. Yet, all being for the Union, by reason of these differences each will prefer a different way of sustaining the Union. At once, sincerity is questioned, and motives are assailed. Actual war coming, blood grows hot, and blood is spilled. Thought is forced from old channels into confusion. Deception breeds and thrives. Confidence dies, and universal suspicion reigns. Each man feels an impulse to kill his neighbor, lest he be killed by him. Revenge and retaliation follow. And all this, as before said, may be among honest men only. But this is not all. Every foul bird comes abroad, and every dirty reptile rises up. These add crime to confusion. Strong measures deemed indispensable but harsh at best, such men make worse by maladministration. Murders for old grudges, and murders for pelf proceed under any cloak that will best serve for the occasion.

These causes amply account for what has occurred in Missouri, without ascribing it to the weakness or wickedness of any general. The newspaper files, those chroniclers of current events, will show that the evils now complained of, were quite as prevalent under Fremont, Hunter, Halleck, and Curtis, as under Schofield. If the former had greater force opposed to them, they also had greater force with which to meet it. When the organized rebel army left the State, the main Federal force had to go also, leaving the Department commander at home, relatively no stronger than before. Without disparaging any, I affirm with confidence, that no commander of that Department has, in proportion to his means, done better than General Schofield.

The first specific charge against General Schofield is, that the enrolled militia was placed under his command, whereas it had not been placed under the command of General Curtis. The fact is, I believe, true; but you do not point out, nor can I conceive how that did, or could, injure loyal men or the Union cause.

You charge that General Curtis being superseded by General Schofield, Franklin A. Dick was superseded by James O. Broad head as Provost-Marshal General. No very specific showing is made as to how this did or could injure the Union cause. It recalls, however, the condition of things, as presented to me, which led to a change of commander of that Department.

To restrain contraband intelligence and trade, a system of searches, seizures, permits and passes, had been introduced, I think, by General Fremont. When General Halleck came, he found and continued the system, and added an order, applicable to some parts of the State, to levy and collect contributions from noted rebels, to compensate losses, and relieve destitution caused by the rebellion. The action of General Fremont and General Halleck, as stated, constituted a sort of system which General Curtis found in full operation when he took command of the Department. That there was a necessity for something of the sort was clear; but that it could only be justified by stern necessity, and that it was liable to great abuse in administration, was equally clear. Agents to execute it, contrary to the great prayer, were led into temptation. Some might, while others would not resist that temptation. It was not possible to hold any to a very strict accountability; and those yielding to the temptation, would sell permits and passes to those who would pay most, and most readily for them ; and would seize property and collect levies in the aptest way to fill their own pockets. Money being the object, the man having money, whether loyal or disloyal, would be a victim. This practice doubtless existed to some extent, and it was a real additional evil, that it could be, and was plausibly charged to exist in greater extent than it did.

When General Curtis took command of the Department, Mr. Dick, against whom I never knew anything to allege, had general charge of this system. A controversy in regard to it rapidly grew into almost unmanageable proportions. One side ignored the *necessity* and magnified the evils of the system, while the other ignored the evils and magnified the necessity ; and each bitterly assailed the other. I could not fail to see that the controversy enlarged in the same proportion as the professed Union men there distinctly took sides in two opposing political parties. I exhausted my wits, and very nearly my patience also, in efforts to convince both that the evils they charged on each other were inherent in the case, and could not be cured by giving either party a victory over the other.

Plainly, the irritating system was not to be perpetual; and it was plausibly urged that it could be modified at once with advantage. The case could scarcely be worse, and whether it could be made better could only be determined by a trial. In this view, and not to ban, or brand General Curtis, or to give a victory to any party, I made the change of commander for the Department. I now learn that soon after this change Mr. Dick was removed, and that Mr. Brodhead, a gentleman of no less good character, was put in the place. The mere fact of this change is more distinctly complained of than is any conduct of the new officer, or other consequence of the change.

I gave the new commander no instructions as to the administration of the system mentioned, beyond what is contained in the private letter afterward surreptitiously published, in which I directed him to act solely for the public good, and independently of both parties. Neither anything you have presented me, nor anything I have otherwise learned, has convinced me that he has been unfaithful to this charge.

Imbecility is urged as one cause for removing General Schofield, and the late massacre at Lawrence, Kansas, is pressed as evidence of that imbecility. To my mind that fact scarcely tends to prove the proposition. That massacre is only an example of what Grierson, John Morgan, and many others, might have repeatedly done on their respective raids, had they chosen to incur the personal hazard, and possessed the fiendish hearts to do it.

The charge is made that General Schofield, on purpose to protect the Lawrence murderers, would not allow them to be pursued into Missouri. While no punishment could be too sudden or too severe for those murderers, I am well satisfied that the preventing of the threatened remedial raid into Missouri was the only way to avoid an indiscriminate massacre there, including probably more innocent than guilty. Instead of condemning, I therefore approve what I understand General Schofield did in that respect.

The charge that General Schofield had purposely withheld protection from loyal people, and purposely facilitated the objects of the disloyal, are altogether beyond my power of belief. I do not arraign the veracity of gentlemen as to the facts complained of; but I do more than question the judgment which would infer that these facts occurred in accordance with the purposes of General Schofield.

With my present views, I must decline to remove General Schofield. In this I decide nothing against General Butler. I sincerely wish it were convenient to assign him a suitable command.

In order to meet some existing evils, I have addressed a letter of instruction to General Schofield, a copy of which I inclose to you. As to the "Enrolled Militia," I shall endeavor to ascertain, better than I now know, what is its exact value. Let me say now, however, that your proposal to substitute national force for the "Enrolled Militia," implies that, in your judgment, the latter is doing something which needs to be done; and if so, the proposition to throw that force away, and to supply its place by bringing other forces from the field where they are urgently needed, seems to me very extraordinary. Whence shall they come? Shall they be withdrawn from Banks, or Grant, or Steele, or Rosecrans?

Few things have been so grateful to my anxious feelings, as when, in June last, the local force in Missouri aided General Schofield to so promptly send a large general force to the relief of General Grant, then investing Vicksburg, and menaced from without by General Johnston. Was this all wrong? Should the "enrolled militia" then have been broken up, and General Heron kept from Grant to police Missouri? So far from finding cause to object, I confess to a sympathy for whatever relieves our general force in Missouri, and allows it to serve elsewhere.

I therefore, as at present advised, cannot attempt the destruction of the enrolled militia of Missouri. I may add, that the force being under the national military control, it is also within the proclamation with regard to the *habeas corpus*.

I concur in the propriety of your request in regard to elections, and have, as you see, directed General Schofield accordingly.

I do not feel justified to enter upon the broad field you present in regard to the political differences between Radicals and Conservatives. From time to time I have done and said what appeared to me proper to do and say. The public knows it well. It obliges nobody to follow me, and I trust it obliges me to follow nobody. The Radicals and Conservatives each agree with me in some things and disagree in others. I could wish both to agree with me in all things; for then they would agree with each other, and would be too strong for any foe from any quarter. They, however, choose to do otherwise, and I do not question their right. I, too, shall do what seems to be my duty. I hold whoever commands in Missouri or elsewhere responsible to me, and not to either Radicals or Conservatives. It is my duty to hear all; but, at last, I must, within my sphere, judge what to do and what to forbear.

Your obedient servant,   A. Lincoln.

THE CONGRESSIONAL SESSION OF 1863-4.

Congress assembled in regular session on the 7th of December, 1863, and received from the President the following

MESSAGE.

Fellow-Citizens of the Senate and House of Representatives:— Another year of health and of sufficiently abundant harvests has passed. For these, and especially for the improved condition of our national affairs, our renewed and - profoundest gratitude to God is due. We remain in peace and friendship with foreign Powers. The efforts of disloyal citizens of the United States to involve us in foreign wars to aid an inexcusable insurrection have been unavailing. Her Britannic Majesty's Government, as was justly expected, have exercised their authority to prevent the departure of new hostile expeditions from British ports.

The Emperor of France has, by a like proceeding, promptly vindicated the neutrality which he proclaimed at the beginning of the contest.

Questions of great intricacy and importance have arisen out of the blockade, and other belligerent operations between the Government and several of the maritime Powers, but they have been discussed, and, as far as was possible, accommodated in a spirit of frankness, justice, and mutual good-will.

It is especially gratifying that our prize courts, by the impartiality of their adjudications, have commanded the respect and confidence of maritime Powers.

The supplemental treaty between the United States and Great Britain for the suppression of the African Slave-trade, made on the 17th day of February last, has been duly ratified and carried into execution. It is believed that so far as American ports and American citizens are concerned, that inhuman and odious traffic has been brought to an end.

*   *   *   *   *   *   *   *

Incidents occurring in the progress of our civil war have forced upon my attention the uncertain state of international questions touching the rights of foreigners in this country and of United States citizens abroad.

In regard to some governments, these rights are at least partially defined by treaties. In no instance, however, is it expressly stipulated that in the event of civil war a foreigner residing in this country, within the lines of the insurgents, is to be exempted from the rule which classes him as a belligerent, in whose behalf the government of his country cannot expect any privileges or immunities distinct from that character. I regret to say, however, that such claims have been put forward, and, in some instances, in behalf of foreigners who have lived in the United States the greater part of their lives.

There is reason to believe that many persons born in foreign countries, who have declared their intention to become citizens, or who have been fully naturalized, have evaded the military duty required of them by denying the fact, and thereby throwing upon the Government the burden of proof. It has been found difficult or impracticable to obtain this proof, from the want of guides to the proper sources of information. These might be supplied by requiring Clerks of Courts, where declarations of intention may be made, or naturalizations effected, to send periodically lists of the names of the persons naturalized or declaring their intention to become citizens, to the Secretary of the Interior, in whose Department those names might be arranged and printed for general information. There is also reason to believe that foreigners frequently become citizens of the United States for the sole purpose of evading duties imposed by the laws of their native countries, to which, on becoming naturalized here, they at once repair, and though never returning to the United States, they still claim the interposition of this Government as citizens.

Many altercations and great prejudices have heretofore arisen out of this abuse. It is, therefore, submitted to your serious consideration. It might be advisable to fix a limit beyond which no citizen of the United States residing abroad may claim the interposition of his Government.

The right of suffrage has often been assumed and exercised by aliens under pretences of naturalization, which they have disavowed when drafted into the military service.

Our ministers abroad have been faithful in defending American rights. In protecting commercial interests, our consuls have necessarily had to encounter increased labors and responsibilities growing out of the war. These they have, for the most part, met and discharged with zeal and efficiency. This acknowledgment justly includes those consuls who, residing in Morocco, Egypt, Turkey, Japan, China, and other Oriental countries, are charged with complex functions and extraordinary powers.

The condition of the several organized territories is generally satisfactory, although Indian distubances in New Mexico have not been entirely suppressed.

The mineral resources of Colorado, Nevada, Idaho, New Mexico, and Arizona, are proving far richer than has been heretofore understood. I lay before you a communication on this subject from the Governor of New Mexico. I again submit to your consideration the expediency of establishing a system for the encouragement of emigration. Although this source of national wealth and strength is again flowing with greater freedom than for several years before the insurrection occurred, there is still a great deficiency of laborers in every field of industry, especially in agriculture and in our mines, as well of iron and coal as of the precious metals. While the demand for labor is thus increased here, tens of thousands of persons, destitute of remunerative occupation, are thronging our foreign consulates, and offering to emigrate to the United States, if essential, but very cheap assistance can be afforded them. It is easy to see that under the sharp discipline of civil war the nation is beginning a new life. This noble effort demands the aid, and ought to receive the attention and support of the Government.

Injuries unforeseen by the Government, and unintended, may in some cases have been inflicted on the subjects or citizens of foreign countries, both at sea and on land, by persons in the service of the United States. As this Government expects redress from other Powers when similar injuries are inflicted by persons in their service upon citizens of the United States, we must be prepared to do justice to foreigners. If the existing judicial tribunals are inadequate to this purpose, a special Court may be authorized, with power to hear and decide such claims of the character referred to as may have arisen under treaties and the public law. Conventions for adjusting the claims by joint commission have been proposed to some Governments, but no definite answer to the proposition has yet been received from any.

In the course of the session I shall probably have occasion to request you to provide indemnification to claimants where decrees of restitution have been rendered, and damages awarded by Admiralty Courts, and in other cases, where this Government may be acknowledged to be liable in principle, and where the amount of that liability has been ascertained by an informal arbitration, the proper officers of the Treasury have deemed themselves required by the law of the United States upon the subject, to demand a tax upon the incomes of foreign consuls in this country. While such a demand may not, in strictness, be in derogation of public law, or perhaps of any existing treaty between the United States and a foreign country, the expediency of so far modifying the act as to exempt from tax the income of such consuls as are not citizens of the United States, derived from the emoluments of their office, or from property not situate in the United States, is submitted to your serious consideration. I make this suggestion upon the ground that a comity which ought to be reciprocated exempts our consuls in all other countries from taxation to the extent thus indicated. The United States, I think, ought not to be exceptionally illiberal to international trade and commerce.

The operations of the treasury during the last year have been successfully conducted. The enactment by Congress of a National Banking Law has proved a valuable support of the public credit, and the general legislation in relation to loans has fully answered the expectation of its favorers. Some amendment may be required to perfect existing laws, but no change in their principles or general scope is believed to be needed. Since these measures have been in operation, all demands on the Treasury, including the pay of the Army and Navy, have been promptly met and fully satisfied. No considerable body of troops, it is believed, were ever more amply provided and more liberally and punctually paid; and, it may be added, that by no people were the burthens incident to a great war more cheerfully borne.

The receipts during the year, from all sources, including loans and the balance in the Treasury at its commencement, were $901,125,674 86, and the aggregate disbursements $895,- 796,630 65, leaving a balance on the 1st of July, 1863, of $5,329,- 044 21. Of the receipts, there were derived from Customs, $69,059,642 40; from Internal Revenue, $37,640,787 95; from direct tax, $1,485,103 61; from lands, $167,617 17; from miscellaneous sources, $3,046,615 35; and from loans, $776,682,- 361 57, making the aggregate, $901,125,674 86. Of the disbursements there were for the civil service, $23,253,922 08; for pensions and Indians, $4,216,520 79; for interest on public debt, $24,729,846 51; for the War Department, $599,298,600 83; for the Navy Department, $63,211,105 27; for payment of funded and temporary debt, $181,086,635 07, making the aggregate $895,796,630 65, and leaving the balance of $5,329,044 21.

But the payment of the funded and ·temporary debt, having

been made from moneys borrowed during the year, must be regarded as merely nominal payments, and the moneys borrowed to make them as merely nominal receipts; and their amount, $181,086,535 07, should therefore be deducted both from receipts and disbursements. This being done, there remains as actual receipts, $720,039,039 79, and the actual disbursements, $714,709,995 58, leaving the balance as already stated.

The actual receipts and disbursements for the first quarter, and the estimated receipts and disbursements for the remaining three quarters of the current fiscal year, 1864, will be shown in detail by the report of the Secretary of the Treasury, to which I invite your attention.

It is sufficient to say here, that it is not believed that actual results will exhibit a state of the finances less favorable to the country than the estimates of that officer heretofore submitted, while it is confidently expected that, at the close of the year, both disbursements and debt will be found very considerably less than has been anticipated.

The report of the Secretary of War is a document of great interest. It consists of:

First.—The military operations of the year detailed in the report of the General-in-Chief.

Second.—The organization of colored persons into the war service.

Third.—The exchange of prisoners fully set forth in the letter of General Hitchcock.

Fourth.—The operations under the act for enrolling and calling out the National forces, detailed in the report of the Provost-Marshal General.

Fifth.—The organization of the Invalid Corps. And—

Sixth.—The operations of the several departments of the Quartermaster-General, Commissary-General, Paymaster-General, Chief of Engineers, Chief of Ordnance, and Surgeon-General. It has appeared impossible to make a valuable summary of this report, except such as would be too extended for this place, and hence I content myself by asking your careful attention to the report itself. The duties devolving on the naval branch of the service during the year, and throughout the whole of this unhappy contest, have been discharged with fidelity and eminent success. The extensive blockade has been constantly increasing in efficiency, as the navy has expanded, yet on so long a line it has, so far, been impossible entirely to suppress illicit trade. From returns received at the Navy Department, it appears that more than one thousand vessels have been captured since the blockade was instituted, and that the value of prizes already sent in for adjudication, amounts to over thirteen millions of dollars.

The naval force of the United States consists at this time of five hundred and eighty-eight vessels completed and in course of completion, and of these seventy-five are iron-clad or armored steamers. The events of the war give an increased interest and importance to the navy, which will probably extend beyond the war itself. The armored vessels in our navy, completed and in service, or which are under contract and approaching completion, are believed to exceed in number those of any other Power; but while these may be relied upon for harbor defence and coast service, others of greater strength and capacity will be necessary for cruising purposes, and to maintain our rightful position on the ocean.

The change that has taken place in naval vessels and naval warfare since the introduction of steam as a motive power for ships of war, demands either a corresponding change in some of our existing navy-yards, or the establishment of new ones, for the construction and necessary repair of modern naval vessels. No inconsiderable embarrassment, delay, and public injury have been experienced from the want of such governmental establishments.

The necessity of such a navy-yard, so furnished, at some suitable place upon the Atlantic seaboard, has, on repeated occasions, been brought to the attention of Congress by the Navy Department, and is again presented in the report of the Secretary, which accompanies this communication. I think it my duty to invite your special attention to this subject, and also to that of establishing a yard and depot for naval purposes upon one of the western rivers. A naval force has been created upon these interior waters, and under many disadvantages, within a little more than two years, exceeding in number the whole naval force of the country at the commencement of the present Administration. Satisfactory and important as have been the performances of the heroic men of the navy at this interesting period, they are scarcely more wonderful than the success of our mechanics and artisans in the production of war-vessels, which has created a new form of naval power.

Our country has advantages superior to any other nation in our resources of iron and timber, with inexhaustible quantities of fuel in the immediate vicinity of both, and all available and in close proximity to navigable waters. Without the advantage of public works, the resources of the nation have been developed, and its power displayed, in the construction of a navy of such magnitude, which has at the very period of its creation rendered signal service to the Union.

The increase of the number of seamen in the public service from 7,500 men in the Spring of 1861, to about 34,000 at the present time, has been accomplished without special legislation or extraordinary bounties to promote that increase. It has been found, however, that the operation of the draft, with the high bounties paid for army recruits, is beginning to affect injuriously the naval service, and will, if not corrected, be likely to impair its efficiency by detaching seamen from their proper vocation, and inducing them to enter the army. I therefore respectfully suggest that Congress might aid both the army and naval service by a definite provision on this subject, which would at the same time be equitable to the communities more especially interested.

I commend to your consideration the suggestions of the Secretary of the Navy, in regard to the policy of fostering and training seamen, and also the education of officers and engineers for the naval service. The Naval Academy has rendered signal service in preparing midshipmen for the highly responsible duties which in after life they will be required to perform. In order that the country should not be deprived of the proper quota of educated officers, for which legal provision has been made at the naval school, the vacancies caused by the neglect or omission to make nominations from the States in insurrection, have been filled by the Secretary of the Navy. The, school is now more full and complete than at any former period, and in every respect entitled to the favorable consideration of Congress.

*   *   *   *   *   *   *   *

The quantity of land disposed of during the last, and first quarter of the present, fiscal years, was three millions, eight hundred and forty-one thousand, five hundred and forty-nine acres, of which one hundred and sixty-one thousand, nine hundred and eleven acres were sold for cash. One million, four hundred and fifty-six thousand, five hundred and fourteen acres, were taken up under the Homestead Law, and the residue disposed of under laws granting lands for military bounties, for railroad and other purposes. It also appears that the sale of public lands is largely on the increase.

It has long been a cherished opinion of some of our wisest statesmen that the people of the United States had a higher and more enduring interest in the early settlement and substantial cultivation of the public lands than in the amount of direct revenue to be derived from the sale of them. This opinion has had a controlling influence in shaping legislation upon the subject of our national domain. I may cite, as evidence of this, the liberal measures adopted in reference to actual settlers, the grant to the States of the overflowed lands within their limits, in order to their being reclaimed and rendered fit for cultivation, the grants to railroad companies of alternate sections of land upon the contemplated lines of their roads, which, when completed, will so largely multiply the facilities for reaching our distant possessions. This policy has received its most signal and beneficent illustration in the recent enactment granting homesteads to actual settlers. Since the first day of January last the before mentioned quantity of one million, four hundred and fifty-six thousand, five hundred and fourteen acres of land have been taken up under its provisions. This fact, and the amount of sales, furnish gratifying evidence of increasing settlement upon the public lands, notwithstanding the great struggle in which the energies of the nation have been engaged, and which has required so large

,a withdrawal of our citizens from their accustomed pursuits. I cordially concur in the recommendation of the Secretary of the Interior, suggesting a modification of the act in favor of those engaged in the military and naval service of the United States.

I doubt not that Congress will cheerfully adopt such measures as will, without essentially changing the general features of the system, secure to the greatest practical extent its benefits to those who have left their homes in defence of the country in this arduous crisis.

I invite your attention to the views of the Secretary as to the propriety of raising, by appropriate legislation, a revenue from the mineral lands of the United States. The measures provided at your last session for the removal of certain Indian tribes have been carried into effect. Sundry treaties have been negotiated, which will, in due time, be submitted for the constitutional action of the Senate. They contain stipulations for extinguishing the possessory rights of the Indians to large and valuable tracts of lands. It is hoped that the effect of these treaties will result in the establishment of permanent friendly relations with such of these tribes as have been brought into frequent and bloody collision with our outlying settlements and emigrants. Sound policy, and our imperative duty to these wards of the Government, demand our anxious and constant attention to their material well-being, to their progress in the arts of civilization, and above all, to that moral training which, under the blessing of Divine Providence, will confer upon them the elevated and sanctifying influences, the hopes and consolations of the Christian faith. I suggested, in my last Annual Message, the propriety of remodeling our Indian system. Subsequent events have satisfied me of its necessity. The details set forth in the report of the Secretary evince the urgent need for immediate legislative action.

I commend the benevolent institutions, established or patronized by the Government in this District, to your generous and fostering care.

The attention of Congress, during the last session, was engaged to some extent with a proposition for enlarging the water com munication between the Mississippi River and the northeastern seaboard, which proposition, however, failed for the time. Since then, upon a call of the greatest respectability, a Convention has been held at Chicago upon the same subject, a summary of whose views is contained in a memorial address to the President and Congress, and which I now have the honor to lay before you. That the interest is one which will ere long force its own way I do not entertain a doubt, while it is submitted entirely to your wisdom as to what can be done now. Augmented interest is given to this subject by the actual commencement of work upon the Pacific railroad, under auspices so favorable to rapid progress and completion. The enlarged navigation becomes a palpable need to the great road.

I transmit the second annual report of the Commissioners of the Department of Agriculture, asking your attention to the developments in that vital interest of the nation.

When Congress assembled a year ago, the war had already lasted nearly twenty months, and there had been many conflicts on both land and sea, with varying results; the rebellion had been pressed back into reduced limits; yet the tone of public feeling and opinion, at home and abroad, was not satisfactory. With other signs, the popular elections, then just past, indicated uneasiness among ourselves, while, amid much that was cold and menacing, the kindest words coming from Europe were uttered in accents of pity that we were too blind to surrender a hopeless cause. Our commerce was suffering greatly by a few vessels built upon and furnished from foreign shores, and we were threatened with such additions from the same quarters as would sweep our trade from the seas and raise our blockade. We had failed to elicit from European governments anything hopeful upon this subject.

The preliminary Emancipation Proclamation issued in September, was running its assigned period to the beginning of the new year. A month later, the final proclamation came, including the announcement that colored men of suitable condition would be received in the war service. The policy of emancipation and of employing black soldiers gave to the future a new aspect, about which hope, and fear, and doubt, contended in uncertain conflict. According to our political system, as a matter of civil administration, the Government had no lawful power to effect emancipation in any State, and for a long time it had been hoped that the rebellion could be suppressed without resorting to it as a military measure. It was all the while deemed possible that the necessity for it might come, and that if it should, the crisis of the contest would then be presented. It came, and, as was anticipated, was followed by dark and doubtful days.

Eleven months having now passed, we are permitted to take another view. The rebel borders are pressed still further back, and by the complete opening of the Mississippi, the country dominated by the rebellion is divided into distinct parts with no practical communication between them. Tennessee and Arkansas have been substantially cleared of insurgent control, and influential citizens in each—owners of slaves and advocates of slavery at the beginning of the rebellion—now declare openly for emancipation in their respective States. Of those States not included in the Emancipation Proclamation, Maryland and Missouri, neither of which, three years ago, would tolerate any restraint upon the extension of slavery into new Territories, only dispute now as to the best mode of removing it within their own limits.

Of those who were slaves at the beginning of the rebellion, full one hundred thousand are now in the United States military service, about one-half of which number actually bear arms in the ranks—thus giving the double advantage of taking so much labor from the insurgent cause and supplying the places which otherwise must be filled with so many white men. So far as tested, it is difficult to say they are not as good soldiers as any. No servile insurrection or tendency to violence or cruelty has marked the measures of emancipation and arming the blacks. These measures have been much discussed in foreign countries, and cotemporary with such discussion, the tone of public sentiment there is much improved. At home the same measures have been fully discussed, supported, criticised and denounced, and the annual elections following are highly encouraging to those whose official duty it is to bear the country through this great trial. Thus we have the new reckoning. The crisis which threatened to divide the friends of the Union is past..

Looking now to the present and future, and with a reference to a resumption of the national authority in the States wherein that authority has been suspended, I have thought fit to issue a proclamation—a copy of which is herewith transmitted. On examination of this proclamation, it will appear, as is believed, that nothing is attempted beyond what is amply justified by the Constitution. True, the form of an oath is given, but no man is coerced to take it. The man is only promised a pardon in case he voluntarily takes the oath. The Constitution authorizes the Executive to grant or withdraw the pardon at his own absolute discretion, and this includes the power to grant on terms, as is fully established by judicial and other authorities. It is also proffered that if in any of the States named, a State Government shall be in the mode prescribed set up, such government shall be recognized and guaranteed by the United States, and that under it the State shall, on the constitutional conditions, be protected against invasion and domestic violence.

The constitutional obligation of the United States to guarantee to every State in the Union a Republican form of Government, and to protect the State in the cases stated, is explicit and full. But why tender the benefits of this provision only to a State Government set up in this particular way? This section of the Constitution contemplates a case wherein the element within a State favorable to Republican government in the Union may be too feeble for an opposite and hostile element external to or even within the State, and such are precisely the cases with which we are now dealing.

An attempt to guarantee and protect a revived State Government, constructed in whole or in preponderating part from the very element against whose hostility and violence it is to be protected, is simply absurd. There must be a test by which to separate the opposing elements, so as to build only from the sound; and that test is a sufficiently liberal one which accepts as sound whoever will make a sworn recantation of his former unsoundness.

But if it be proper to require, as a test of admission to the political body, an oath of allegiance to the Constitution of the United States and to the Union under it, why also to the laws and proclamations in regard to slavery?

Those laws and proclamations were enacted and put forth for the purpose of aiding in the suppression of the rebellion. To give them their fullest effect there had to be a pledge for their maintenance. In my judgment they have aided and will further aid the cause for which they were intended.

To now abandon them would be not only to relinquish a lever of power, but would also be a cruel and an astounding breach of faith.

I may add, at this point, that while I remain in my present position, I shall not attempt to retract or modify the Emancipation Proclamation, nor shall I return to slavery any person who is free by the terms of that proclamation, or by any of the acts of Congress.

For these and other reasons, it is thought best that support of these measures shall be included in the oath, and it is believed that the Executive may lawfully claim it in return for pardon and restoration of forfeited rights, which he has a clear constitutional power to withhold altogether or grant upon the terms which he shall deem wisest for the public interest. It should be observed, also, that this part of the oath is subject to the modifying and abrogating power of legislation and supreme judicial decision.

The proposed acquiescence of the National Executive in any reasonable temporary State arrangement for the freed people, is made with the view of possibly modifying the confusion and destitution which must at best attend all classes by a total revolution of labor throughout whole States. It is hoped that the already deeply afflicted people in those States may be somewhat more ready to give up the cause of their affliction, if, to this extent, this vital matter be left to themselves, while no power of the National Executive to prevent an abuse is abridged by the proposition.

The suggestion in the proclamation as to maintaining the political frame-work of the States on what is called reconstruction, is made in the hope that it may do good, without danger of harm. It will save labor, and avoid great confusion. But why any proclamation now upon this subject? This question is beset with the conflicting views that the step might be delayed too long, or be taken too soon. In some States the elements for resumption seem ready for action but remain inactive, apparently for want of a rallying point—a plan of action. Why shall A adopt the plan of B, rather than B that of A? And if A and B should agree, how can they know but that the General Government here will reject their plan? By the proclamation a plan is presented which may be accepted by them as a rallying point—and which they are assured in advance will not be rejected here. This may bring them to act sooner than they otherwise would.

The objection to a premature presentation of a plan by the National Executive consists in the danger of committals on points which could be more safely left to further developments. Care has been taken to so shape the document as to avoid embarrassments from this source. Saying that on certain terms certain classes will be pardoned with rights restored, it is not said that other classes or other terms will never be included. Saying that reconstruction will be accepted if presented in a specified way, it is not said it will never be accepted in any other way. The movements by State action for emancipation in several of the States not included in the Emancipation Proclamation are matters of profound gratulation. And while I do not repeat in detail what I have heretofore so earnestly urged upon this subject, my general views and feelings remain unchanged; and I trust that Congress will omit no fair opportunity of aiding these important steps to the great consummation.

In the midst of other cares, however important, we must not lose sight of the fact that the war power is still our main reliance. To that power alone can we look for a time, to give confidence to the people in the contested regions, that the insurgent power will not again overrun them. Until that confidence shall be established, little can be done anywhere for what is called reconstruction. Hence our chiefest care must still be directed to the army and navy, who have thus far borne their harder part so nobly and well. And it may be esteemed fortunate that in giving the greatest efficiency to these indispensable arms, we do also honorably recognize the gallant men, from commander to sentinel, who compose them, and to whom, more than to others, the world must stand indebted for the home of freedom, disenthralled, regenerated, enlarged and perpetuated.

(Signed)   ABRAHAM LINCOLN.

December 8, 1863.

To the Message was appended the following

PROCLAMATION.

Whereas, In and by the Constitution of the United States, it is provided that the President shall have power to grant reprieves and pardons for offences against the United States, except in cases of impeachment—and, whereas, a rebellion now exists, whereby the loyal State Governments of several States have for a long time been subverted, and many persons have committed and are now guilty of treason against the United States; and

Whereas, With reference to said rebellion and treason, laws have been enacted by Congress, declaring forfeitures and confiscation of property and liberation of slaves, all upon terms and conditions therein stated, and also declaring that the President was thereby authorized at any time thereafter, by proclamation, to extend to persons who may have participated in the existing rebellion in any State or part thereof, pardon and amnesty, with such exceptions and at such times and on such conditions as he may deem expedient for the public welfare; and

Whereas, The Congressional declaration for limited and conditional pardon accords with the well established judicial exposition of the pardoning power; and

Whereas, With reference to the said rebellion, the President of the United States has issued several proclamations with provisions in regard to the liberation of slaves; and

Whereas, It is now desired by some persons heretofore engaged in said rebellion to resume their allegiance to the United States, and to reinaugurate loyal State Governments within and for their respective States; therefore

I, Abraham Lincoln, President of the United States, do proclaim, declare, and make known to all persons who have directly or by implication participated in the existing rebellion, except as herein after excepted, that a full pardon is hereby granted to them and each of them, with restoration of all rights of property, except as to slaves, and in property cases where rights of third parties shall have intervened, and upon the condition that every such person shall take and subscribe an oath and thenceforward keep and maintain said oath inviolate, an oath which shall be registered for permanent preservation, and shall be of the tenor and effect following, to wit:

"I, ——— ———, do solemnly swear, in the presence of Almighty God, that I will henceforth faithfully support, protect, and defend the Constitution of the United States and the Union of the States thereunder; and that I will in like manner abide by and faithfully support all acts of Congress passed during the existing rebellion with reference to slaves, so long and so far as not repealed, modified, or held void by Congress or by decisions of the Supreme Court; and that I will in like manner abide by and faithfully support all proclamations of the President made during the existing rebellion having reference to slaves, so long and so far as not modified or declared void by decision of the Supreme Court. So help me God."

The persons excepted from the benefits of the foregoing provisions are: All who are, or shall have been civil or diplomatic officers or agents of the so-called Confederate Government; all who have left judicial stations under the United States to aid the rebellion; all who are or shall have been military or naval officers of said so-called Confederate Government, above the rank of Colonel in the army, or of Lieutenant in the navy; all who left seats in the United States Congress to aid the rebellion; all who resigned commissions in the army or navy of the United States, and afterward aided the rebellion; and all who have engaged in any way in treating colored persons, or white persons in charge of such, otherwise than lawfully as prisoners of war, and which persons may have been found in the United States service as soldiers, seamen, or any other capacity; and I do further proclaim, declare, and make known that, whenever, in any of the States of Arkansas, Texas, Louisiana, Mississippi, Tennessee, Alabama, Georgia, Florida, South Carolina, and North Carolina, a number of persons not less than one-tenth in number of the votes cast in such States at the Presidential election of the year of our Lord one thousand eight hundred and sixty, each having taken the oath aforesaid, and not having since violated it, and being a qualified voter by the election law of the State existing immediately before the so-called act of Secession, and excluding all others, shall re-establish a State Government which shall be Republican, and in no wise contravening said oath, such shall be recognized as the true government of the State, and the State shall receive thereunder the benefits of the constitutional provision, which declares that

"The United States shall guarantee to every State in this Union a Republican form of government, and shall protect each of them against invasion, and on application of the Legislature, or the Executive, when the Legislature cannot be convened, against domestic violence."

And I do further proclaim, declare, and make known, that any provision which may be adopted by such State Government in relation to the freed people of such State, which shall recognize and declare their permanent freedom, provide for their education, and which may yet be consistent, as a temporary arrangement, with their present condition as a laboring, landless, and homeless class, will not be objected to by the National Executive.

And it is suggested as not improper, that, in constructing a loyal State Government in any State, the name of the State, the boundary, the subdivisions, the Constitution, and the general code of laws, as before the rebellion, be maintained, subject only to the modifications made necessary by the conditions herein before stated, and such others, if any, not contravening said conditions, and which may be deemed expedient by those framing the new State Government. To avoid misunderstanding, it may be proper to say that this proclamation, so far as it relates to State Government, has no reference to States wherein loyal State Governments have all the while been maintained; and for the same reason it may be proper to further say, that.

whether members sent to Congress from any State shall be admitted to seats, constitutionally rests exclusively with the respective Houses, and not to any extent with the Executive. And still further, that this proclamation is intended to present the people of the States wherein the national authority has been suspended, and loyal State Governments have been subverted, a mode in and by which the national authority and loyal State Governments may be re-established within said States, or in any of them. And, while the mode presented is the best the Executive can suggest with his present impressions, it must not be understood that no other possible mode would be acceptable.

Given under my hand at the city of Washington, the eighth day of December, A.D. one thousand eight hundred and sixty-three, and of the independence of the United States of America the eighty-eighth.

By the President: ABRAHAM LINCOLN.

WM. H. SEWARD, *Secretary of State.*

RESTRAINTS UPON THE CLERGY.

Clergymen and the representatives of clergymen, many on one side, and some on the other, complained of the restraints which, owing to the condition of the country, were placed upon them, sometimes by the Government, sometimes by the local authorities, and often by the very people to whom they sought to minister. The following letter, in reply to an appeal for the exercise of the President's authority to restore the Rev. Dr. McPheeters, of St. Louis, to the pulpit, from which he had been excluded by General Curtis for teaching disloyalty, shows that Mr. Lincoln insisted only that clergymen, like all other citizens, should not use their influence for the support of the rebellion and the consequent destruction of the Government.

EXECUTIVE MANSION, WASHINGTON, *Dec.* 28, 1863.

I have just looked over a petition signed by some three dozen citizens of St. Louis, and their accompanying letters, one by yourself, one by a Mr. Nathan Ranney, and one by a Mr. John D. Coalter, the whole relating to the Rev. Dr. McPheeters. The petition prays, in the name of justice and mercy, that I will restore Dr. McPheeters to all his ecclesiastical rights.

This gives no intimation as to what ecclesiastical rights are withdrawn. Your letter states that Provost-Marshal Dick, about a ago, ordered the arrest of Dr. McPheeters, Pastor of the Vine Street Church, prohibited him from officiating, and placed the management of affairs of the church out of the control of the chosen trustees; and near the close you state that a certain course "would insure his release." Mr. Ranney's letter says: "Dr. Samuel McPheeters is enjoying all the rights of a civilian, but cannot preach the gospel!" Mr. Coalter, in his letter, asks: "Is it not a strange illustration of the condition of things, that the question who shall be allowed to preach in a church in St. Louis shall be decided by the President of the United States?"

Now, all this sounds very strangely; and, withal, a little as if you gentlemen, making the application, do not understand the case alike; one affirming that his doctor is enjoying all the rights of a civilian, and another pointing out to me what will secure his *release!* On the 2d of January last, I wrote to General Curtis in relation to Mr. Dick's order upon Dr. McPheeters; and, as I suppose the doctor is enjoying all the rights of a civilian, I only quote that part of my letter which relates to the church. It was as follows: "But I must add that the United States Government must not, as by this order, undertake to run the churches. When an individual, in a church or out of it, becomes dangerous to the public interest, he must be checked; but the churches, as such, must take care of themselves. It will not do for the United States to appoint trustees, supervisors, or other agents for the churches."

This letter going to General Curtis, then in command, I supposed, of course, it was obeyed, especially as I heard no further complaint from Doctor McPheeters or his friends for nearly an entire year. I have never interferred, nor thought of interfering, as to who shall or shall not preach in any church; nor have I knowingly or believingly tolerated any one else to interfere by my authority. If any one is so interfering by color of my authority, I would like to have it specifically made known to me.

If, after all, what is now sought, is to have me put Doctor McPheeters back over the heads of a majority of his own congregation, that too, will be declined. I will not have control of any church or any side. A. LINCOLN.

EFFECT OF SO-CALLED SECESSION.

In the following letter addressed by Mr. Lincoln to the editors of the *North American Review* he gives his views upon the effect of secession ordinances upon State governments and individual citizens.

EXECUTIVE MANSION, WASHINGTON, *Jan.* 16, 1864.

*Messrs. Crosby & Nichols :—Gentlemen—*The number for this month and year of the *North American Review* was duly received, and for which please accept my thanks. Of course I am not the most impartial judge; yet, with due allowance for this, I venture to hope that the article entitled ' The President's Policy,' will be of value to the country. I fear I am not worthy of all which is therein kindly said of me personally.

" The sentence of twelve lines, commencing at the top of page 252, I could wish to be not exactly what it is. In what is there expressed the writer has not correctly understood me. I have never had a theory that secession could absolve States or people from their obligations. Precisely the contrary is asserted in the inaugural address; and it was because of my belief in the continuation of those *obligations* that I was puzzled for a time, as to denying the legal *rights* of those citizens who remained individually innocent of treason or rebellion. But I mean no more now than to merely call attention to this point.

Yours respectfully, A. LINCOLN."

11*

REORGANIZATION IN ARKANSAS.

In spite of the position of Arkansas, lying as it does west of the Mississippi and between Texas and Missouri, there was from the beginning not only a strong Union party in that State, but it was bolder and more outspoken and active than was the case under similar circumstances in the eastern Slave States. In the winter of 1863-4 efforts were made by the loyal men of the State to reorganize its government and bring it again under the national authority. These efforts elicited the following letters from Mr. Lincoln:

EXECUTIVE MANSION, WASHINGTON, *Jan.* 20, 1864.

Major-General Steele—Sundry citizens of the State of Arkansas petition me that an election may be held in that State, at which to elect a governor; that it be assumed at that election and thenceforward, that the Constitution and laws of the State, as before the rebellion, are in full force, except that the Consti-tution is so modified as to declare that there shall be neither slavery nor involuntary servitude, except in the punishment of crimes whereof the party shall have been duly convicted; that the General Assembly may make such provisions for the freed people as shall recognize and declare their permanent freedom, and provide for their education, and which may yet be con-strued as a temporary arrangement suitable to their condition as a laboring, landless, and homeless class; that said election shall be held on the 28th of March, 1864, at all the usual places of the State, or all such as voters may attend for that purpose; that the voters attending at 8 o'clock in the morning of said day may choose judges and clerks of election for such purpose; that all persons qualified by said Constitution and laws, and taking the oath presented in the President's proclamation of December 8, 1863, either before or at the election, and none others, may be voters; that each set of judges and clerks may make returns directly to you on or before the —th day of —— next; that in all other respects said election may be conducted according to said Constitution and laws; that on receipt of said returns, when, 5,406 votes shall have been cast, you can receive said votes and ascertain all who shall thereby appear to have been elected; that on the —th day of ——— next, all persons so appearing to have been elected, who shall appear before you at Little Rock, and take the oath, to be by you severally administered, to support the Constitution of the United States, and said modified Constitution of the State of Arkansas, may be declared by you qualified and empowered to immediately enter upon the duties of the offices to which they shall have been respectively elected.

You will please order an election to take place on the 28th of March, 1864, and returns to be made in fifteen days thereafter. A. LINCOLN.

To William Fishback.—When I fixed a plan for an election in Arkansas, I did it in ignorance that your convention was at the same work. Since I learned the latter fact, I have been constantly trying to yield my plan to theirs. I have sent two letters to General Steele, and three or four dispatches to you and others, saying that he (General Steele) must be master, but that it will probably be best for him to keep the convention on its own plan. Some single mind must be master, else there will be no agreement on anything; and General Steele, commanding the military and being on the ground, is the best man to be that master. Even now citizens are telegraphing me to postpone the election to a later day than either fixed by the convention or me. This discord must be silenced. A. LINCOLN.

THE SANITARY AND CHRISTIAN COMMISSIONS.

The following letters may well be grouped together here without regard to that chronological order which has been preserved elsewhere throughout this volume. They express the feelings with which Mr. Lincoln regarded the efforts made by those who were coöperating with the Sanitary and Christian Commissions.

AT THE FAIR IN WASHINGTON IN AID OF THE SANITARY COMMISSION, MARCH 16, 1864.

Ladies and Gentlemen:—I appear to say but a word. This extraordinary war in which we are engaged falls heavily upon all classes of people, but the most heavily upon the soldier. For it has been said, all that a man hath will he give for his life; and while all contribute of their substance, the soldier puts his life at stake, and often yields it up in his country's cause. The highest merit, then, is due to the soldier.

In this extraordinary war, extraordinary developments have manifested themselves, such as have not been seen in former wars; and among these manifestations nothing has been more remarkable than these fairs for the relief of suffering soldiers and their families. And the chief agents in these fairs are the women of America.

I am not accustomed to the use of language of eulogy; I have never studied the art of paying compliments to women; but I must say, that if all that has been said by orators and poets since the creation of the world in praise of women were applied to the women of America, it would not do them justice for their conduct during this war. I will close by saying, God bless the women of America!

AT THE FAIR IN BALTIMORE, IN AID OF THE SANITARY COMMISSION, APRIL 18, 1864.

Ladies and Gentlemen:—Calling to mind that we are in Baltimore, we cannot fail to note that the world moves. Looking upon these many people assembled here to serve, as they best may, the soldiers of the Union, it occurs at once that three years ago the same soldiers could not so much as pass through Baltimore. The change from then till now is both great and gratifying. Blessings on the brave men who have wrought the change, and the fair women who strive to reward them for it.

But Baltimore suggests more than could happen within Baltimore. The change within Baltimore is part only of a far wider change. When the war began, three years ago, neither party, nor any man, expected it would last till now. Each looked for the end, in some way, long ere to-day. Neither did any anticipate that domestic slavery would be much affected by the war. But here we are; the war has not ended, and slavery has been much affected—how much needs not now to be recounted. So true it is that man proposes and God disposes.

But we can see the past, though we may not claim to have directed it; and seeing it, in this case, we feel more hopeful and confident for the future.

The world has never had a good definition of the word liberty, and the American people, just now, are much in want of one. We all declare for liberty; but in using the same *word* we do not all mean the same *thing*. With some the word liberty may mean for each man to do as he pleases with himself, and the product of his labor; while with others the same word may mean for some men to do as they please with other men, and the product of other men's labor. Here are two, not only different, but incompatible things, called by the same name, liberty. And it follows that each of the things is, by the respective parties, called by two different and incompatible names—liberty and tyranny.

The shepherd drives the wolf from the sheep's throat, for which the sheep thanks the shepherd as a *liberator*, while the wolf denounces him for the same act, as the destroyer of liberty, especially as the sheep was a black one. Plainly, the sheep and the wolf are not agreed upon a definition of the word liberty; and precisely the same difference prevails to-day among us human creatures, even in the North, and all professing to love liberty. Hence we behold the process by which thousands are daily passing from under the yoke of bondage hailed by some as the advance of liberty, and bewailed by others as the destruction of all liberty. Recently, as it seems, the people of Maryland have been doing something to define liberty; and thanks to them that, in what they have done, the wolf's dictionary has been repudiated.

It is not very becoming for one in my position to make speeches at great length; but there is another subject upon which I feel that I ought to say a word. A painful rumor, true, I fear, has reached us of the massacre, by the rebel forces at Fort Pillow, in the west end of Tennessee, on the Mississipp' River, of some three hundred colored soldiers and white officers, who had just been overpowered by their assailants. There seems to be some anxiety in the public mind whether the Government is doing its duty to the colored soldier, and to the service at this point. At the beginning of the war, and for some time, the use of colored troops was not contemplated; and how the change of purpose was wrought I will not now take time to explain. Upon a clear conviction of duty, I resolved to turn that element of strength to account; and I am responsible for it to the American people, to the Christian world, to history, and on my final account to God. Having determined to use the negro as a soldier, there is no way but to give him all the protection given to any other soldier. The difficulty is not in stating the principle, but in practically applying it. It is a mistake to suppose the Government is indifferent to this matter, or is not doing the best it can in regard to it. We do not to-day *know* that a colored soldier, or white officer commanding colored soldiers has been massacred by the rebels when made a prisoner. We fear it, believe it, I may say, but we do not *know* it. To take the life of one of their prisoners on the assumption that they murder ours, when it is short of certainty that they do murder ours, might be too serious, too cruel a mistake. We are having the Fort Pillow affair thoroughly investigated; and such investigation will probably show conclusively how the truth is. If, after all that has been said, it shall turn out that there has been no massacre at Fort Pillow, it will be almost safe to say there has been none, and will be none elsewhere. If there has been the massacre of three hundred there, or even the tenth part of three hundred, it will be conclusively proven; and being so proven, the retribution shall as surely come. It will be a matter of grave consideration in what exact course to apply the retribution; but in the supposed case it must come.

THE WORKINGMEN'S ASSOCIATION OF NEW YORK.

This Association elected Mr. Lincoln one of its honorary members, and on the 21st of March, 1864, a committee of the Association presented to him an address setting forth the objects of the association, and requesting him to accept the membership. He replied as follows:

Gentlemen of the Committee—The honorary membership in your association, as generously tendered, is gratefully accepted.

You comprehend, as your address shows, that the existing rebellion means more and tends to do more than the perpetua-ation of African slavery—that it is, in fact, a war upon the rights of all working people. Partly to show that this view had not escaped my attention, and partly that I cannot better express myself, I read a passage from the message to Congress in December, 1861:

"It continues to develop that the insurrection is largely, if not exclusively, a war upon the first principle of popular government, the rights of the people. Conclusive evidence of this is found in the most grave and maturely considered public documents, as well as in the general tone of the insurgents. In those documents we find the abridgment of the existing right of suffrage, and the denial to the people of all right to participate in the selection of public officers, except the legislative, boldly advocated, with labored argument to prove that large control of the people in government is the source of all political evil. Monarchy itself is sometimes hinted at as a possible refuge from the power of the people.

"In my present position I could scarcely be justified were I to omit raising a warning voice against this approach of returning despotism.

"It is not needed, nor fitting here, that a general argument should be made in favor of popular institutions; but there is one point with its connections, not so hackneyed as most others, to which I ask a brief attention. It is the effort to place *capital* on an equal footing, if not above *labor*, in the structure of government. It is assumed that labor is available only in connection with capital; that nobody labors unless somebody else, owning capital, somehow by the use of it induces him to labor. This assumed, it is next considered whether it is best that capital shall *hire* laborers, and thus induce them to work by their own consent, or *buy* them, and drive them to it without their consent. Having proceeded so far, it is naturally concluded that all laborers are either *hired* laborers, or what we call slaves. And, further, it is assumed that whoever is once a hired laborer, is fixed in that condition for life. Now there is no such relation between capital and labor as assumed, nor is there any such thing as a free man being fixed for life in the condition of a hired laborer. Both these assumptions are false, and all inferences from them are groundless.

"Labor is prior to, and independent of, capital. Capital is only the fruit of labor, and could never have existed if labor had not first existed. Labor is the superior of capital, and deserves much the higher consideration. Capital has its rights, which are as worthy of protection as any other rights. Nor is it denied that there is, and probably always will be, a relation between capital and labor; producing mutual benefits. The error is in assuming that the whole labor of a community exists within that relation. A few men own capital, and that few avoid labor themselves, and, with their capital, hire or buy another few to labor for them. A large majority belong to neither class—neither work for others, nor have others working for them. In most of the Southern States a majority of the whole people of all colors are neither slaves nor masters; while in the Northern, a large majority are neither hirers nor hired. Men with their families—wives, sons, and daughters—work for themselves, on their farms, in their houses, and in their shops, taking the whole product to themselves, and asking no favors of capital on the one hand nor of hired laborers or slaves on the other. It is not forgotten that a considerable number of persons mingle their own labor with capital; that is, they labor with their own hands, and also buy or hire others to labor for them, but this is only a mixed and not a distinct class. No principle stated is disturbed by the existence of this mixed class.

"Again, as has already been said, there is not, of necessity, any such thing as the free hired laborer being fixed to that condition for life. Many independent men everywhere in these States, a few years back in their lives were hired laborers. The prudent penniless beginner in the world labors for wages awhile,

saves a surplus with which to buy tools or land for himself,
then labors on his own account another while, and at length
hires another new beginner to help him. This is the just and
generous and prosperous system which opens the way to all—
gives hope to all, and consequent energy and progress, and improvement of condition to all. No men living are more worthy
to be trusted than those who toil up from poverty—none less
inclined to touch or take aught which they have not honestly
earned. Let them beware of surrendering a political power
they already possess, and which, if surrendered, will surely be
used to close the door of advancement against such as they, and
to fix new disabilities and burdens upon them, till all of liberty
shall be lost."

The views then expressed remain unchanged, nor have I much
to add. None are so deeply interested to resist the present rebellion as the working people. Let them beware of prejudices,
working division and hostility among themselves. The most
notable feature of a disturbance in your city last summer was
the hanging of some working people by other working people.
It should never be so. The strongest bond of human sympathy,
outside of the family relation, should be one uniting all working
people, of all nations and tongues, and kindreds. Nor should
this lead to a war upon property or the owners of property.
Property is the fruit of labor; property is desirable; is a posi-
tive good in the world. That some should be rich shows that
others may become rich, and, hence, is just encouragement to
industry and enterprise. Let not him who is houseless pull
down the house of another, but let him labor diligently and
build one for himself, thus by example assuring that his own
shall be safe from violence when built.

DEFINING THE AMNESTY PROCLAMATION.

The Proclamation of Amnesty, issued in December,
1863, was scouted by the defenders and apologists of the
rebellion as adapted only to irritate the insurgents and
stimulate them to prolong resistance. But early in 1864

the waning of confidence in the so-called Confederacy began to be manifested on the part of prisoners taken by the national forces. Many of these claimed the benefits of the amnesty, and wished to return to their allegiance as a mode of relieving themselves of the consequences of capture. These unreasonable expectations called out the following

PROCLAMATION.

Whereas, it has become necessary to define the cases in which insurgent enemies are entitled to the benefits of the Proclamation of the President of the United States, which was made on the 8th day of December, 1863, and the manner in which they shall proceed to avail themselves of these benefits; and whereas the objects of that proclamation were to suppress the insurrection and to restore the authority of the United States; and whereas the amnesty therein proposed by the President was offered with reference to these objects alone;

Now, therefore, I, Abraham Lincoln, President of the United States, do hereby proclaim and declare that the said proclamation does not apply to the cases of persons who, at the time when they seek to obtain the benefits thereof by taking the oath thereby prescribed, are in military, naval or civil confinement or custody, or under bonds, or on parole of the civil, military or naval authorities or agents of the United States, as prisoners of war, or persons detained for offences of any kind, either before or after conviction; and that on the contrary it does apply only to those persons who, being yet at large, and free from any arrest, confinement, or duress, shall voluntarily come forward and take the said oath, with the purpose of restoring peace and establishing the national authority.

Persons excluded from the amnesty offered in the said proclamation may apply to the President for clemency, like all other offenders, and their application will receive due consideration.

I do further declare and proclaim that the oath presented in the aforesaid proclamation of the 8th of December, 1863, may be taken and subscribed before any commissioned officer, civil, military or naval, in the service of the United States, or any civil or military officer of a State or Territory not in insurrection, who, by the laws thereof, may be qualified for administering oaths.

All officers who receive such oaths are hereby authorized to give certificates thereof to the persons respectively by whom they are made, and such officers are hereby required to transmit the original records of such oaths at as early a day as may be convenient, to the Department of State, where they will be deposited, and remain in the archives of the Government.

The Secretary of State will keep a registry thereof, and will, on application, in proper cases, issue certificates of such records in the customary form of official certificates.

In testimony whereof, I have hereunto set my hand, and caused the seal of the United States to be affixed. Done at the City of Washington, this 26th day of March, in the [L. S.] year of our Lord one thousand eight hundred and sixty-three, and of the independence of the United States of America the eighty-eighth.

By the President: ABRAHAM LINCOLN.

WILLIAM H. SEWARD, *Secretary of State.*

POLICY WITH REGARD TO SLAVERY.

Mr. Lincoln, in various speeches and documents which are to be found in their places in this volume, set forth his views as to his duty, and his consequent policy, in regard to slavery. None of these, however, seem to be so complete an expression, both of his feeling and his purposes upon this subject, as that contained in the following letter. It was addressed to Mr. A. G. Hodges, who, in company with Governor Bramlette of Kentucky, and some other gentlemen from that State, had waited upon the President in regard to a modification of the draft. In the course of their interview, a conversation had taken place upon Mr. Lincoln's policy in regard to slavery, which he thought was misapprehended in Kentucky, and which he explained in the terms re-collected in this letter:

EXECUTIVE MANSION, WASHINGTON, *April* 4, 1864.

A. G. Hodges, Esq., Frankfort, Ky.—My Dear Sir—You ask me to put in writing the substance of what I verbally said the other day, in your presence, to Governor Bramlette and Senator Dixon. It was about as follows:

" I am naturally anti-slavery. If slavery is not wrong, nothing is wrong. I cannot remember when I did not so think and feel, and yet I have never understood that the Presidency conferred upon me an unrestricted right to act officially upon this judgment and feeling. It was in the oath I took, that I would, to the best of my ability, preserve, protect, and defend the Constitution of the United States. I could not take the office without taking the oath. Nor was it my view that I might take an oath to get power, and break the oath in using the power. I understood, too, that in ordinary civil administration this oath even forbade me to practically indulge my primary abstract judgment on the moral question of slavery. I had publicly declared this many times, and in many ways. And I aver that, to this day, I have done no official act in mere deference to my abstract judgment and feeling on slavery. I did understand, however, that my oath to preserve the Constitution to the best of my ability, imposed upon me the duty of preserving, by every indispensable means, that government—that nation, of which that Constitution was the organic law. Was it possible to lose the nation and yet preserve the Constitution? By general law, life *and* limb must be protected; yet often a limb must be amputated to save a life; but a life is never wisely given to save a limb. I felt that measures, otherwise unconstitutional, might become lawful by becoming indispensable to the preservation of the Constitution, through the preservation of the nation. Right or wrong, I assumed this ground, and now avow it. I could not feel that, to the best of my ability, I had even tried to preserve the Constitution, if, to save slavery, or any minor matter, I should permit the wreck of government, country, and Constitution, altogether. When, early in the war, General Fremont attempted military emancipation, I forbade it, because I did not then think it an indispensable necessity. When, a little later, General Cameron, then Secretary of War, suggested the arming of the blacks, I objected, because I did not yet think it an indispensable necessity. When, still later, General Hunter attempted military emancipation, I again forbade it, because I did not yet think the indispensable necessity had come. When, in March, and May, and July, 1862, I made earnest and successive appeals to the border States to favor compensated emancipation, I believed the indispensable necessity for military emancipation and arming the blacks would come, unless averted by that measure. They declined the proposition, and I was, in my best judgment, driven to the alternative of either surrendering the Union, and with it, the Constitution, or of laying strong hand upon the colored element. I chose the latter. In choosing it, I hoped for greater gain than loss, but of this I was not entirely confident. More than a year of trial now shows no loss by it in our foreign relations, none in our home popular sentiment, none in our white military force, no loss by it anyhow, or anywhere. On the contrary, it shows a gain of quite a hundred and thirty thousand soldiers, seamen, and laborers. These are palpable facts, about which, as facts, there can be no caviling. We have the men; and we could not have had them without the measure.

"And now let any Union man who complains of the measure, test himself by writing down in one line, that he is for subduing the rebellion by force of arms; and in the next, that he is for taking a hundred and thirty thousand men from the Union side, and placing them where they would be best for the measure he condemns. If he cannot face his case so stated, it is only because he cannot face the truth."

I add a word which was not in the verbal conversation. In telling this tale, I attempt no compliment to my own sagacity. I claim not to have controlled events, but confess plainly that events have controlled me. Now at the end of three years' struggle, the nation's condition is not what either party or any man devised, or expected. God alone can claim it. Whither it is tending seems plain. If God now wills the removal of a great wrong, and wills also that we of the North, as well as you of the South, shall pay fairly for our complicity in that wrong, impartial history will find therein new causes to attest and revere the justice and goodness of God.

Yours, truly,   A. LINCOLN.

GENERAL GRANT.

Mr. Lincoln expressed his high appreciation of General Grant, and his estimation of the difficulties he had before him, in the following letter addressed to the managers of a meeting in New York, held directly after that eminent soldier's opening of the long campaign which ended in the capture of Richmond and the crushing of the rebellion :

EXECUTIVE MANSION, WASHINGTON, June 3, 1864.

Hon. F. A. Conkling, and others—Gentlemen—Your letter inviting me to be present at a mass meeting of the loyal citizens, to be held at New York on the 4th inst., for the purpose of expressing gratitude to Lieutenant-General Grant for his signal services, was received yesterday. It is impossible for me to attend. I approve, nevertheless, whatever may tend to strengthen and sustain General Grant and the noble armies now under his direction. My previous high estimate of General Grant has been maintained and heightened by what has occurred in the remarkable campaign he is now conducting; while the magnitude and difficulty of the task before him does not prove less than I expected. He and his brave soldiers are now in the midst of their great trial, and I trust that, at your meeting, you will so shape your good words that they may turn to men and guns moving to his and their support.

Yours truly,   A. LINCOLN.

CONGRESSIONAL SESSION OF 1864-5.

Congress met in regular session on the 7th of December, 1864, and received from the President the following Message, in which the passages chiefly worthy of note are those referring to the Constitutional Amendment abolishing slavery, to the futility of any attempt to negotiate with " the insurgent leaders," and to the development of the resources and the increase in the power of the country in the midst of the vast and long continued civil war.

Fellow-Citizens of the Senate and House of Representatives—
Again the blessings of health and abundant harvests claim our profoundest gratitude to Almighty God.

The condition of our foreign affairs is reasonably satisfactory.

Mexico continues to be a theatre of civil war. While our political relations with that country have undergone no change, we have at the same time strictly maintained neutrality between the belligerents.

At the request of the States of Costa Rica and Nicaragua, a competent engineer has been authorized to make a survey of the River San Juan and the port of San Juan. It is a source of much satisfaction that the difficulties, which for a moment excited some political apprehension and caused a closing of the inter-oceanic transit route, have been amicably adjusted, and that there is a good prospect that the route will soon be re-opened, with an increase of capacity and adaptation. We could not exaggerate either the commercial or the political importance of that great improvement. It would be doing injustice to an important South American State, not to acknowl edge the directness, frankness, and cordiality with which the States of Colombia have entered into intimate relations with this Government. A claims-convention has been constituted to complete the unfinished work of the one which closed its session in 1861.

The new liberal Constitution of Venezuela having gone into effect with the universal acquiescence of the people, the government under it has been recognized, and diplomatic intercourse with it has been opened in a cordial and friendly spirit.

The long deferred Aves Island claim has been satisfactorily paid and discharged. Mutual payments have been made of the claims awarded by the late Joint Commission for the settlement of claims between the United States and Peru. An earnest and cordial friendship continues to exist between the two countries; and such efforts as were in my power have been used to remove misunderstanding and avert a threatened war between Peru and Spain. Our relations are of the most friendly nature with Chili, the Argentine Republic, Bolivia, Costa Rica, Paraguay, San Salvador and Hayti. During the past year no differences of any kind have arisen with any of these Republics. And, on the other hand, their sympathies with the United States are constantly expressed with cordiality and earnestness.

The claim arising from the seizure of the cargo of the brig Macedonian, in 1821, has been paid in full by the Government of Chili.

Civil war continues in the Spanish part of San Domingo, apparently without prospect of an early close.

Official correspondence has been freely opened with Liberia, and it gives us a pleasing view of social and political progress in that Republic. It may be expected to derive new vigor from American influence, improved by the rapid disappearance of slavery in the United States.

I solicit your authority to furnish to the Republic a gunboat at a moderate cost, to be reimbursed to the United States by installments. Such a vessel is needed for the safety of that State against the native African races, and in Liberian hands it would be more effective in arresting the African slave-trade, than a squadron in our own hands. The possession of the least organized naval force would stimulate a generous ambition in the Republic, and the confidence which we should manifest by furnishing it would win forbearance and favor toward the colony from all civilized nations.

The proposed overland telegraph between America and Europe by the way of Behring's Straits and Asiatic Russia, which was sanctioned by Congress at the last session, has been undertaken under very favorable circumstances by an association of American citizens, with the cordial good-will and support as well of this Government as of those of Great Britain and Russia. Assurances have been received from most of the South American States of their high appreciation of the enterprise and their readiness to co-operate in constructing lines tributary to that world-encircling communication.

I learn with much satisfaction that the noble design of a telegraphic communication between the Eastern Coast of America and Great Britain has been renewed, with full expectation of its early accomplishment. Thus it is hoped that with the return of domestic peace, the country will be able to resume with energy and advantage her former high career of commerce and civilization.

Our very popular and estimable representative in Egypt died in April last. An unpleasant altercation which arose between the temporary incumbent of the office and the Government of the Pacha, resulted in a suspension of intercourse. The evil was promptly corrected on the arrival of the successor in the consulate and our relations with Egypt, as well as our relations with the Barbary Powers, are entirely satisfactory.

The rebellion, which has so long been flagrant in China, has at last been suppressed, with the co-operating good offices of this Government, and of the other Western commercial States. The judicial consular establishment has become very difficult and onerous, and it will need legislative organization to adapt it to the extension of our commerce, and to the more intimate intercourse which has been instituted with the government and people of that vast empire. China seems to be accepting, with hearty good will, the conventional laws which regulate commerce and social intercourse among Western nations.

Owing to the peculiar situation of Japan and the anomalous form of its government, the action of that empire in performing treaty stipulations is inconstant and capricious. Nevertheless, good progress has been effected by the Western Powers, moving with enlightened concert. Our own pecuniary claims have been allowed, or put in course of settlement, and the inland sea has been reopened to commerce. There is reason also to believe that these proceedings have increased rather than diminished the friendship of Japan toward the United States.

The ports of Norfolk, Fernandina and Pensacola have been opened by proclamation. It is hoped that foreign merchants will now consider whether it is not safer and more profitable to themselves, as well as just to the United States, to resort to them and other open ports, than it is to pursue, through many hazards and at vast cost, a contraband trade with other ports which are closed, if not by actual military operation, at least by a lawful and effective blockade.

For myself, I have no doubt of the power and duty of the Executive, under the law of nations, to exclude enemies of the human race from an asylum in the United States. If Congress should think that proceedings in such cases lack the authority of law, or ought to be further regulated by it, I recommend that provision be made for effectually preventing foreign slave-traders from acquiring domicile and facilities for their criminal occupation in our country.

It is possible that if it were a new and open question, the Maritime Powers, with the light they now enjoy, would not concede the privileges of a naval belligerent to the insurgents of the United States, destitute as they are and always have been, equally of ships and of ports and harbors. Disloyal emissaries have been neither less assiduous nor more successful during the last year than they were before that time in their efforts, under favor of that privilege, to embroil our country in foreign wars. The desire and determination of the Maritime States to defeat that design are believed to be as sincere as, and cannot be more earnest than our own. Nevertheless unforeseen political difficulties have arisen, especially in Brazilian and British ports and on the Northern boundary of the United States, which have required and are likely to continue to require the practice of constant vigilance and a just and conciliatory spirit on the part of the United States, as well as of the nations concerned and their governments. Commissioners have been appointed under the treaty with Great Britain on the adjustment of the claims of the Hudson Bay and Puget's Sound Agricultural Companies in Oregon, and are now proceeding to the execution of the trust assigned to them.

In view of the insecurity of life in the region adjacent to the Canadian border, by recent assaults and depredations committed by inimical and desperate persons, who are harbored there, it has been thought proper to give notice that after the expiration of six months, the period conditionally stipulated in the existing arrangements with Great Britain, the United States must hold themselves at liberty to increase their naval armament upon the Lakes, if they shall find that proceeding necessary. The condition of the border will necessarily come into consideration in connection with the question of continuing or modifying the rights of transit from Canada through the United States, as well as the regulation of imports, which were temporarily established by the Reciprocity Treaty of the 5th June, 1854. I desire, however, to be understood while making this statement, that the colonial authorities are not deemed to be intentionally unjust or unfriendly toward the United States, but on the contrary, there is every reason to expect that with the approval of the Imperial Government they will take the necessary measure to prevent new incursions across the border.

The act passed at the last session for the encouragement of emigration has, as far as was possible, been put into operation. It seems to need amendment, which will enable the officers of the Government to prevent the practice of frauds against the immigrants while on their way, and on their arrival in the ports, so as to secure them here a free choice of avocations and places of settlement. A liberal disposition toward this great national policy is manifested by most of the European States, and ought to be reciprocated on our part, by giving the immigrants effective national protection. I regard our emigrants as one of the principal replenishing streams which are appointed by Providence to repair the ravages of internal war and its wastes of national strength and health. All that is necessary is to secure the flow of that stream in its present fulness, and to that end the Government must in every way make it manifest that it neither needs nor designs to impose involuntary military service upon those who come from other lands to cast their lot in our country.

The financial affairs of the Government have been successfully administered during the last year. The legislation of the last session of Congress has beneficially affected the revenue. Although sufficient time has not yet elapsed to experience the full effect of several of the provisions of the acts of Congress imposing increased taxation, the receipts during the year, from all sources, upon the basis of warrants signed by the Secretary of the Treasury, including loans, and the balance in the Treasury on the 1st day of July, 1863, were $1,394,796,007 62, and the aggregate disbursements upon the same basis, were $1,298,-056,101 89, leaving a balance in the Treasury, as shown by warrants, of $96,739,905 73. Deduct from these amounts the amount of the principal of the public debt redeemed and the amount of issues in substitution therefor, and the actual cash operations of the Treasury were: Receipts, $884,076,646 77; disbursements, $865,234,087 86, which leaves a cash balance in the Treasury of $18,842,558 71. Of the receipts, there were derived from customs, $102,316,152 99: from lands, $388,333 29; from direct taxes, $475,648 96; from internal revenue, $109,-741,134 10; from miscellaneous sources, $47,511,448 10; and from loans applied to actual expenditures, including former balance, $623,443,929 13. There were disbursed for the civil service, $27,505,599 46; for pensions and Indians, $7,517,930 97; for the War Department, $60,791,842 97; for the Navy Department, $85,733,292 79; for interest of the public debt, $53,685,-421 69, making an aggregate of $865,234,087 86, and leaving a balance in the Treasury of $18,842,558 71, as before stated.

For the actual receipts and disbursements for the first quarter, and the estimated receipts and disbursements for the three remaining quarters of the current fiscal year, and the general operations of the Treasury in detail, I refer you to the report of the Secretary of the Treasury. I concur with him in the opinion that the proportion of the moneys required to meet the expenses consequent upon the war, derived from taxation, should be still further increased; and I earnestly invite your attention to this subject to the end that there may be such additional legislation as shall be required to meet the just expectations of the Secretary. The public debt on the 1st day of July last, as appears by the books of the Treasury, amounted to one billion, seven hundred and forty thousand million, six hundred and ninety thousand, four hundred and eighty-nine dollars and forty-nine cents. Probably should the war continue for another year, that amount may be increased by not far from five hundred millions. Held, as it is for the most part by our own people, it has become a substantial branch of national though private property. For obvious reasons the more nearly this property can be distributed among all the people the better. To favor such general distribution, greater inducements to become owners might perhaps, with good effect and without injury, be presented to persons of limited means. With this view, I suggest whether it might not be both expedient and competent for Congress to provide that a limited amount of some future issue of public securities might be held by any bona fide purchaser exempt from taxation and from seizure for debt under such restrictions and limitations as might be necessary to guard against abuse of so important a privilege. This would enable prudent persons to set aside a small annuity against a possible day of want. Privileges like these would render the possession of such securities to the amount limited most desirable to any person of small means, who might be able to save enough for the purpose. The great advantage of citizens being creditors, as well as debtors, with relation to the public debt, is obvious. Men readily perceive that they cannot be much oppressed by a debt which they owe themselves. The public debt on the 1st day of July last, although somewhat exceeding the estimate of the Secretary of the Treasury made to Congress at the commencement of the last session, falls short of the estimate of that officer made in the preceding December, as to its probable amount at the beginning of this year, by the sum of $3,995,079 33. This fact exhibits a satisfactory condition and conduct of the operations of the Treasury.

The National Banking system is proving to be acceptable to capitalists and to the people. On the 25th day of November, 584 National Banks had been organized, a considerable number of which were conversions from State banks. Changes from the State system to the National system are rapidly taking place, and it is hoped that very soon there will be in the United

States, no banks of issue not authorized by Congress, and no bank-note circulation not secured by the Government ; that the Government and the people will derive general benefit from this change in the banking systems of the country can hardly be questioned. The National system will create a reliable and permanent influence in support of the national credit and protect the people against losses in the use of paper money. Whether or not any further legislation is advisable for the suppression of State bank issues, it will be for Congress to determine. It seems quite clear that the Treasury cannot be satisfactorily conducted unless the Government can exercise a restraining power over the bank-note circulation of the country.

The report of the Secretary of War and the accompanying documents will detail the campaigns of the armies in the field, since the date of the last Annual Message, and also the operations of the several administrative bureaux of the War Department during the last year. It will also specify the measures deemed essential for the national defence, and to keep up and supply the requisite military force. The report of the Secretary of the Navy presents a comprehensive and satisfactory exhibit of the affairs of that department and of the naval service. It is a subject of congratulation and laudable pride to our countrymen that a navy of such proportions has been organized in so brief a period, and conducted with so much efficiency and success.

The general exhibit of the navy, including vessels under construction on the 1st of December, 1864, shows a total of 671 vessels, carrying 4,610 guns, and 510,396 tons, being an actual increase during the year, over and above all losses by shipwreck or in battle, of 83 vessels, 167 guns, and 42,427 tons. The total number of men at this time in the naval service, including officers, is about 51,000. There have been captured by the navy, during the year, 324 vessels, and the whole number of naval captures since hostilities commenced is 1,379, of which 267 are steamers. The gross receipts arising from the sale of condemned prize property thus far reported amounts to $14,-896,250 51. A large amount of such proceeds is still under adjudication, and yet to be reported. The total expenditure of the Navy Department, of every description, including the cost of the immense squadrons that have been called into existence from the 4th of March, 1861, to the 1st of November, 1864, are $238,647,262 35. Your favorable consideration is invited to the various recommendations of the Secretary of the Navy, especially in regard to a navy-yard and suitable establishment for the construction and repair of iron vessels, and the machinery and armature of our ships, to which reference was made in my last Annual Message.

Your attention is also invited to the views expressed in the report in relation to the legislation of Congress at its last session, in respect to prizes on our inland waters. I cordially concur in the recommendation of the Secretary as to the propriety of creating the new rank of Vice-Admiral in our naval service.

Your attention is invited to the report of the Postmaster-General for a detailed account of the operations and financial condition of the Post-office Department. The postal revenue for the year ending June 30, 1854, amounted to $12,468,253 78, and the expenditures to $12,644,786 20; the excess of expenditures over receipts being $206,652 42.

The views presented by the Postmaster-General on the subject of special grants by the Government in aid of the establishment of new lines of ocean mail steamships, and the policy he recommends for the development of increased commercial intercourse with adjacent and neighboring countries, should receive the careful consideration of Congress.

It is of noteworthy interest that the steady expansion of population, improvement and governmental institutions over the new and unoccupied portions of our country, have scarcely been checked, much less impeded or destroyed, by our great civil war, which, at first glance, would seem to have absorbed almost the entire energies of the nation.

The organization and admission of the State of Nevada has been completed, in conformity with law, and thus our excellent system is firmly established in the mountains which once seemed a barren and uninhabitable waste, between the Atlantic States and those which have grown up on the coast of the Pacific Ocean.

The territories of the Union are generally in a condition of prosperity and rapid growth. Idaho and Montana, by reason of their great distance, and the interruption of communication with them by Indian hostilities, have been only partially organized ; but it is understood that these difficulties are about to disappear, which will permit their governments, like those of the others, to go into speedy and full operation. As intimately connected with and promotive of this material growth of the nation, I ask the attention of Congress to the valuable information and important recommendations relating to the public lands, Indian affairs, the Pacific railroads, and mineral discoveries contained in the report of the Secretary of the Interior, which is herewith transmitted, and which report also embraces the subjects of patents, pensions, and other topics of public interest pertaining to his Department. The quantity of public land disposed of during the five quarters ending on the thirtieth of September last, was 4,221,342 acres, of which 1,538,614 acres were entered under the homestead law. The remainder was located with military land warrants, agricultural scrip, certified to States for railroads, and sold for cash. The cash received from sales and location fees was $1,019,446. The income from sales during the fiscal year ending June 30, 1864, was $678,007 21, against $136,077 95 received during the preceding year. The aggregate number of acres surveyed during the year has been equal to the quantity disposed of, and there is open to settlement about 133,000,000 acres of surveyed land.

The great enterprise of connecting the Atlantic with the Pacific States, by railways and telegraph lines, has been entered upon with a vigor that gives assurance of success, notwithstanding the embarrassments arising from the prevailing high prices of materials and labor. The route of the main line of the road has been definitely located for one hundred miles westward from the central point at Omaha City, Nebraska, and a preliminary location of the Pacific Railroad of California has been made from Sacramento, eastward, to the great bend of the Mucker River in Nevada. Numerous discoveries of gold, silver and cinnabar mines have been added to the many heretofore known, and the country occupied by the Sierra Nevada and Rocky

Mountains and the subordinate ranges now teems with enterprising labor, which is richly remunerative.

It is believed that the product of the mines of precious metals in that region has, during the year, reached, if not exceeded, $100,000,000 in value. It was recommended in my last Annual Message that our Indian system be remodeled. Congress at its last session, acting upon the recommendation, did provide for reorganizing the system in California, and it is believed that under the present organization the management of the Indians there will be attended with reasonable success. Much yet remains to be done to provide for the proper government of the Indians in other parts of the country, to render it secure for the advancing settler, and to provide for the welfare of the nation. The Secretary reiterates his recommendations, and to them the attention of Congress is invited.

The liberal provisions made by Congress for paying pensions to invalid soldiers and sailors of the Republic, and to the widows, orphans, and dependent mothers of those who have fallen in battle or died of disease contracted, or of wounds received in the service of their country, have been diligently administered.

There have been added to the pension rolls during the year ending the 30th day of June last, the names of 16,770 invalid soldiers, and of 271 disabled seamen, making the present number of army invalid pensioners 22,767, and of navy invalid pensioners 712. Of widows, orphans, and mothers, 22,198 have been placed on the Army Pension Rolls, and 248 on the Navy Rolls. The present number of army pensioners of this class is 25,443, and of navy pensioners, 793. At the beginning of the year the number of Revolutionary pensioners was 1,430. Only twelve of them were soldiers, of whom seven have since died. The remainder are those who, under the law, receive pensions because of relationship to Revolutionary soldiers. During the year ending the 30th of June, 1864, $4,504,616 92 have been paid to pensioners of all classes.

I cheerfully commend to your continued patronage the benevolent institutions of the District of Columbia, which have hitherto been established or fostered by Congress, and respectfully refer for information concerning them, and in relation to the Washington Aqueduct, the Capitol, and other matters of local interest, to the report of the Secretary.

The Agricultural Department, under the supervision of its present energetic and faithful head, is rapidly commending itself to the great and vital interest it was created to advance. It is peculiarly the People's Department, in which they feel more directly concerned than in any other. I commend it to the continued attention and fostering care of Congress.

The war continues. Since the last Annual Message all the important lines and positions then occupied by our forces have been maintained, and our armies have steadily advanced, thus liberating the regions left in the rear, so that Missouri, Kentucky, Tennessee, and parts of other States have again produced reasonably fair crops.

The most remarkable feature in the military operations of the year, is General Sherman's attempted march of three hundred miles directly through an insurgent region. It tends to show a great increase of our relative strength, that our General-in-Chief should feel able to confront and hold in check every active force of the enemy, and yet to detach a well appointed large army to move on such an expedition. The result not yet being known, conjecture in regard to it cannot here be indulged.

Important movements have also occurred during the year to the effect of moulding society for durability in the Union. Although short of complete success, it is much in the right direction that 12,000 citizens in each of the States of Arkansas and Louisiana have organized loyal State Governments with free constitutions, and are earnestly struggling to maintain and administer them. The movement in the same direction, more extensive, though less definite, in Missouri, Kentucky, and Tennessee should not be overlooked. But Maryland presents the example of complete success. Maryland is secure to Liberty and Union for all the future. The genius of rebellion will no more claim Maryland. Like another foul spirit being driven out, it may seek to tear her, but it will woo her no more.

At the last session of Congress a proposed amendment of the

Constitution, abolishing slavery throughout the United States. passed the Senate, but failed for lack of the requisite two-thirds vote in the House of Representatives. Although the present is the same Congress, and nearly the same members, and without questioning the wisdom or patriotism of those who stood in opposition, I venture to recommend the reconsideration and passage of the measure at the present session. Of course, the abstract question is not changed, but an intervening election shows almost certainly that the next Congress will pass the measure if this does not. Hence there is only a question of time as to when the proposed amendment will go to the States for their action, and as it is to go, at all events may we not agree that the sooner the better. It is not claimed that the election has imposed a duty on members to change their views or their votes any further than as an additional element to be considered. Their judgment may be affected by it. It is the voice of the people now for the first time heard upon the question. In a great national crisis like ours, unanimity of action among those seeking a common end is very desirable, almost indispensable, and yet no approach to such unanimity is attainable unless some deference shall be paid to the will of the majority. In this case the common end is the maintenance of the Union, and among the means to secure that end, such will, through the election, is most clearly declared in favor of such constitutional amendment. The most reliable indication of public purpose in this country is derived through our popular elections. Judging by the recent canvass and its result, the purpose of the people within the loyal States, to maintain the integrity of the Union, was never more firm nor more nearly unanimous than now. The extraordinary calmness and good order with which the millions of voters met and mingled at the polls, give strong assurance of this. Not only all those who supported the Union ticket (so called), but a great majority of the opposing party also may be fairly claimed to entertain and to be actuated by the same purpose. It is an unanswerable argument to this effect, that no candidate for any office whatever, high or low, has ventured to seek votes on the avowal that he was for giving up the Union. There has been much impugning of motives and much heated controversy as to the proper means and best mode of advancing the Union cause, but in the distinct issue of Union or no Union, the politicians have shown their instinctive knowledge that there is no diversity among the people. In affording the people the fair opportunity of showing one to another, and to the world, this firmness and unanimity of purpose, the election has been of vast value to the national cause. The election has exhibited another fact not less valuable to be known—the fact that we do not approach exhaustion in the most important branch of national resources: that of living men. While it is melancholy to reflect that the war has filled so many graves and caused mourning to so many hearts, it is some relief to know that, compared with the surviving, the fallen have been so few. While corps, and divisions, and regiments have formed, and fought, and dwindled, and gone out of existence, a great majority of the men who composed them are still living. The same is true of the naval service. The election returns prove this. So many voters could not else be found. The States regularly holding elections both now and four years ago, to wit: California, Connecticut, Delaware, Illinois, Indiana, Iowa, Kentucky, Maine, Maryland, Massachusetts, Michigan, Minnesota, Missouri, New Hampshire, New Jersey, New York, Ohio, Oregon, Pennsylvania, Rhode Island, Vermont, West Virginia, and Wisconsin, cast 3,982,011 votes now, against 3,870,222 cast then, showing an aggregate now of 3,982,011, to which is to be added 33,762 cast now in the new States of Kansas and Nevada, which States did not vote in 1860 —thus swelling the aggregate to 4,015,773, and the net increase during the three years and a half of war to 145,551. * * * To this, again, should be added the number of all soldiers in the field from Massachusetts, Rhode Island, New Jersey, Delaware, Indiana, Illinois and California, who, by the laws of those States, could not vote away from their homes, and which number can not be less than 90,000. Nor yet is this all. The number in organized territories is triple now what . it was four years ago; while thousands, white and black, join us as the national arms press back the insurgent lines—so much is shown affirmatively and negatively by the election.

It is not material to inquire how the increase has been produced, or to show that it would have been greater but for the war, which is probably true; the important fact remains demonstrated that we have more men now than we had when the war began; that we are not exhausted nor in process of exhaustion; that we are gaining strength, and may, if need be, maintain the contest indefinitely. This as to men.

Material resources are now more complete and abundant than ever. The national resources, then, are unexhausted, and, as we believe, inexhaustible. The public purpose to re-establish and maintain the national authority is unchanged, and, as we believe, unchangeable. The manner of continuing the effort remains to choose. On careful consideration of all the evidence accessible, it seems to me that no attempt at negotiation with the insurgent leader could result in any good. He would accept of nothing short of the severance of the Union. His declarations to this effect are explicit and oft-repeated. He does not attempt to deceive us. He affords us no excuse to deceive ourselves. We can not voluntarily yield it. Between him and us the issue is distinct, simple, and inflexible. It is an issue which can only be tried by war, and decided by victory. If we yield we are beaten. If the Southern people fail him he is beaten; either way it would be the victory and defeat following war. What is true, however, of him who heads the insurgent cause, is not necessarily true of those who follow. Although he can not re-accept the Union, they can. Some of them we know already desire peace and re-union. The number of such may increase. They can at any moment have peace simply by laying down their arms and submitting to the national authority under the Constitution. After so much the Government could not, if it would, maintain war against them. The loyal people would not sustain or allow it. If questions should remain we would adjust them by the peaceful means of legislation, conference, courts and votes. Operating only in constitutional and lawful channels, some certain and other possible questions are and would be beyond the Executive power to adjust, as, for instance, the admission of members into Congress, and whatever might require the appropriation of money.

The Executive power itself would be greatly diminished by the cessation of actual war. Pardons and remissions of forfeiture, however, would still be within Executive control. In what spirit and temper this control would be exercised, can be fairly judged of by the past. A year ago general pardon and amnesty, upon specified terms, were offered to all except certain designated classes, and it was at the same time made known that the excepted classes were still within contemplation of special clemency. During the year many availed themselves of the general provision, and many more would, only that the signs of bad faith in some led to such precautionary measures as rendered the practical process less easy and certain. During the same time, also, special pardons have been granted to individuals of excepted classes, and no voluntary application has been denied.

Thus practically the door has been for a full year open to all, except such as were not in condition to make free choice; that is, such as were in custody or under constraint. It is still so open to all, but the time may come, probably will come, when public duty shall demand that it be closed, and that in lieu, more vigorous measures than heretofore shall be adopted.

In presenting the abandonment of armed resistance to the national authority on the part of the insurgents, as the only indispensable condition to ending the war on the part of the Government, I retract nothing heretofore said as to slavery. I repeat the declaration made a year ago, and that while I remain in my present position I shall not attempt to retract or modify the Emancipation Proclamation. Nor shall I return to slavery any person who is free by the terms of that proclamation, or by any of the acts of Congress. If the people should, by whatever mode or means, make it an Executive duty to reënslave such persons, another, and not I, must be their instrument to perform it.

In stating a single condition of peace, I mean simply to say that the war will cease on the part of the Government whenever it shall have ceased on the part of those who began it.

(Signed)   ABRAHAM LINCOLN.

SECOND INAUGURAL ADDRESS.

At the Presidential election of 1864, Mr. Lincoln was reëlected by a majority so large and so widely diffused as to be the most remarkable approval of the course of any administration since the reëlection of Mr. Jefferson in 1801. Even the reëlection of General Jackson was not equal to it in this respect. On the 4th of March, 1865, Mr. Lincoln took his second oath of office, and delivered the following Inaugural Address; the solemnity, the piety, and the almost tender loving-kindness of which was at once remarked throughout this country and Europe.

Fellow-Countrymen—At this second appearing to take the oath of the Presidential office, there is less occasion for an extended address than there was at the first. Then a statement somewhat in detail of a course to be pursued seemed very fitting and proper. Now, at the expiration of four years, during which public declarations have been constantly called forth on every point and phase of the great contest which still absorbs the attention and engrosses the energies of the nation, little that is new could be presented.

The progress of our arms, upon which all else chiefly depends is as well known to the public as to myself, and it is, I trust, reasonably satisfactory and encouraging to all. With high hope for the future, no prediction in regard to it is ventured.

On the occasion corresponding to this four years ago, all thoughts were anxiously directed to an impending civil war. All dreaded it; all sought to avoid it. While the ianugural address was being delivered from this place, devoted altogether to saving the Union without war, insurgent agents were in the city seeking to destroy it without war—seeking to dissolve the Union and divide the effects by negotiation. Both parties deprecated war, but one of them would make war rather than let the nation survive, and the other would accept war rather than let it perish, and the war came.

One-eighth of the whole population were colored slaves, not

distributed generally over the Union, but localized in the Southern part of it. These slaves constituted a peculiar and powerful interest. All knew that this interest was somehow the cause of the war. To strengthen, perpetuate and extend this interest, was the object for which the insurgents would rend the Union even by war, while the Government claimed no right to do more than to restrict the territorial enlargement of it.

Neither party expected for the war the magnitude or the duration which it has already attained. Neither anticipated that the cause of the conflict might cease with, or even before the conflict itself should cease. Each looked for an easier triumph, and a result less fundamental and astounding.

Both read the same Bible and pray to the same God, and each invokes his aid against the other. It may seem strange that any men should dare to ask a just God's assistance in wringing their bread from the sweat of other men's faces, but let us judge not, that we be not judged. The prayers of both could not be answered. That of neither has been answered fully. The Almighty has his own purposes. "Woe unto the world because of offences, for it must needs be that offences come: but woe to that man by whom the offence cometh." If we shall suppose that American slavery is one of these offences, which in the providence of God must needs come, but which having continued through his appointed time, He now wills to remove, and that He gives to both North and South this terrible war as the woe due to those by whom the offence came, shall we discern therein any departure from those divine attributes which the believers in a living God always ascribe to Him? Fondly do we hope, fervently do we pray, that this mighty scourge of war may soon pass away. Yet, if God wills that it continue until all the wealth piled by the bondman's two hundred and fifty years of unrequited toil shall be sunk, and until every drop of blood drawn with the lash shall be paid with another drawn with the sword, as was said three thousand years ago; so, still it must be said, "The judgments of the Lord are true and righteous altogether."

With malice toward none, with charity for all, with firmness in the right, as God gives us to see the right, let us strive on to finish the work we are in, to bind up the nation's wounds, to care for him who shall have borne the battle and for his widow and orphans, to do all which may achieve and cherish a just and a lasting peace among ourselves and with all nations.

NEGROES IN THE REBEL ARMIES.

On the 19th of March, 1865, there was a large gathering of people in front of the National Hotel at Washington, on occasion of the presentation of a rebel flag, captured at Anderson by the 140th Indiana regiment. After a speech by Governor Morton, of Indiana, the President addressed the assembly substantially as follows, directing his remarks chiefly to the subject of the then recently proposed arming of their negroes by the rebels. Mr. Lincoln's speech on this occasion was a striking exhibition of that combination of humor and sagacity which was one of the characteristic traits of his mind, and which enabled him to "put things" in such a clear, convincing, and attractive way before the public:

Fellow-citizens—It will be but a very few words that I shall undertake to say. I was born in Kentucky, raised in Indiana, and lived in Illinois, [laughter,] and now I am here, where it is my business to care equally for the good people of all the States. I am glad to see an Indiana regiment on this day able to present the captured flag to the Governor of Indiana. I am not disposed in saying this to make a distinction between the States, for all have done equally well. There are but few views or aspects of this great war upon which I have not said or written something whereby my own opinions might be known. But there is one—the recent attempt of our erring brethren, as they are sometimes called, to employ the negro to fight for them. I have neither written or made a speech on that subject, because that was their business, not mine; and if I had a wish upon the subject, I had not the power to introduce it or make it effective.

The great question with them was whether the negro, being put into the army, will fight for them. I do not know, and therefore cannot decide. They ought to know better than I. I have, in my lifetime, heard many arguments why the negroes ought to be slaves; but if they fight for those who keep them in slavery, it will be a better argument than any I have yet heard. [Laughter and applause.] He who will fight for that ought to be a slave. [Applause.] They have concluded, at last, to take one out of four of the slaves, and put them in the army; and that one out of the four who will fight to keep the others in slavery ought to be a slave himself, unless he is killed in a fight. [Applause.] While I have often said that all men ought to be free, yet I would allow those colored persons to be slaves who want to be; and next to them those white people who argue in favor of making other people slaves. [Applause.] I am in favor of giving an appointment to such white men to try it on for these slaves. I will say one thing in regard to the negroes being employed to fight for them. I do know he cannot fight and stay at home and make bread too. And as one is about as important as the other to them, I don't care which they do. I am rather in favor of having them try them as soldiers. They lack one vote of doing that, and I wish I could send my vote over the river, so that I might cast it in favor of allowing the negro to fight. [Applause.] But they cannot fight and work both. We must now see the bottom of the enemy's resources. They will stand out as long as they can, and if the negro will fight for them, they must allow him to fight. They have drawn upon their last branch of resources, and we can now see the bottom. I am glad to see the end so near at hand. [Applause.] I have said now more than I intended, and will therefore bid you good bye.

GENERAL GRANT'S CROWNING VICTORY—THE QUESTION
OF REORGANIZATION.

At last came the inevitable conclusion—Grant's crowning victory—the capture of Richmond, the surrender of General Lee's army at Appomattox Court House, and the grand crash of the rebellion. On the evening of the 11th of April, there were wide-spread rejoicings at Washington, illuminations and bonfires. The citizens assembled in large numbers before the White House, and the President made to them the following speech. He took the opportunity to set forth his views upon the reorganization of society in the so-called seceded States, and the re-establishment in them of the national authority. As his manner was he did not underrate the difficulty of the task; but he pointed out the simplest and directest means of its accomplishment:

We meet this evening, not in sorrow, but in gladness of heart. The evacuation of Petersburgh and Richmond, and the surrender of the principal insurgent army, give hopes of a righteous and speedy peace, whose joyous expression cannot be restrained. In the midst of this, however, he from whom all blessings flow must not be forgotten. A call for a national thanksgiving is being prepared, and will be duly promulgated. Nor must those whose harder part gives us the cause of rejoicing be over-looked. Their honors must not be parceled out with others. I myself was near the front, and had the high pleasure of transmitting much of the good news to you. But no part of the honor for plan or execution is mine. To General Grant, his skillful officers, and brave men, all belongs. The gallant navy stood ready, but was not in reach to take active part. By these recent successes the reinauguration of the national authority—reconstruction, which has had a large share of thought from the first—is pressed much more closely upon our attention. It is fraught with great difficulty. Unlike a war between independent nations, there is no authorized organ for us to treat with. No one man has authority to give up the rebellion for any other man. We must simply begin with and mould from disorganized and discordant elements. Nor is it a small additional embarrassment that we, the loyal people, differ among ourselves as to the mode, manner, and measure of reconstruction. As a general rule, I abstain from reading the reports of attacks upon myself, wishing not to be provoked by that to which I cannot properly offer an answer. In spite of this precaution, however, it comes to my knowledge that I am much censured for some supposed agency in setting up and seeking to sustain the new State Government of Louisiana. In this I have done just so much and no more than the public knows. In the Annual Message of December, 1863, and the accompanying proclamation, I presented a plan of reconstruction, as the phrase goes, which I promised, if adopted by any State, would be acceptable to and sustained by the Executive Government of the nation. I distinctly stated that this was not the only plan which might, possibly, be acceptable; and I also distinctly protested that the Executive claimed no right to say when or whether members should be admitted to seats in Congress from such States. This plan was, in advance, submitted to the then Cabinet, and approved by every member of it.

One of them suggested that I should then and in that connection, apply the Emancipation Proclamation to the theretofore excepted parts of Virginia and Louisiana, that I should drop the suggestion about apprenticeship for freed people, and that I should omit the protest against my own power in regard to the admission of members of Congress. But even he approved every part and parcel of the plan which has since been employed or touched by the action of Louisiana. The new constitution of Louisiana, declaring emancipation for the whole State, practically applies the proclamation to the part previously excepted. It does not adopt apprenticeship for freed people, and is silent, as it could not well be otherwise, about the admission of members to Congress. So that as it applied to Louisiana every member of the Cabinet fully approved the plan. The message went to Congress, and I received many commendations of the plan, written and verbal, and not a single objection to it, from any professed emancipationist, came to my knowledge until after the news reached Washington that the people of Louisiana had begun to move in accordance with it. From about July, 1862, I had corresponded with different persons supposed to be interested in seeking a reconstruction of a State Government for Louisiana. When the Message of 1863, with the plan before mentioned, reached New-Orleans, General Banks wrote me that he was confident that the people, with his military co-operation, would reconstruct substantially on that plan. I wrote to him and some of them to try it. They tried it, and, the result is known. Such has been my only agency in getting up the Louisiana Government. As to sustaining it, my promise is out, as before stated. But as bad promises are better broken than kept, I shall treat this as a bad promise and break it whenever I shall be convinced that keeping it is adverse to the public interest, but I have not yet been so convinced.

I have been shown a letter on this subject, supposed to be an able one, in which the writer expresses regret that my mind has not seemed to be definitely fixed on the question, whether the seceded States, so called, are in the Union or out of it. It would, perhaps, add astonishment to his regret were he to learn that since I have found professed Union men endeavoring to answer that question I have purposely forborne any public expression upon it. As appears to me, that question has not been, nor yet is a practically material one, and that any discussion of it while it thus remains practically immaterial, could have no effect other than the mischievous one of dividing our friends. As yet, whatever it may become, that question is bad as the basis of a controversy, and good for nothing at all—a merely pernicious abstraction. We all agree that the seceded States, so called, are out of their proper practical relation with the Union, and that the sole object of the Government, civil and military, in regard to these States, is to again get them into their proper practical relation. I believe that it is not only possible, but, in fact, easier, to do this without deciding, or even considering, whether these States have ever been out of the Union, than with it. Finding themselves safely at home, it would be utterly immaterial whether they had been abroad. Let us all join in doing the acts necessary to restore the proper practical relations between those States and the nation, and each forever after innocently indulge his own opinion whether in doing the acts he brought the States from without into the Union, or only gave them proper assistance, they never having been out of it.

The amount of constituency, so to speak, on which the Louisiana Government rests, would be more satisfactory to all if it contained 50,000, or 30,000, or even 20,000, instead of 12,000, as it does. It is also unsatisfactory to some that the elective franchise is not given to the colored man. I would myself prefer that it were now conferred on the very intelligent, and on those who serve our cause as soldiers. Still the question is not whether the Louisiana Government, as it stands, is quite all that is desirable. The question is, will it be wiser to take it as it is, and help to improve it, or to reject and disperse? Can Louisiana be brought into proper practical relation with the Union sooner by sustaining or by discarding her new State Government? Some twelve thousand voters in the heretofore slave State of Louisiana have sworn allegiance to the Union, assumed to be the rightful political power of the State, held elections, organized a State Government, adopted a Free State constitution, giving the benefit of public schools equally to black and white, and empowering the Legislature to confer the elective franchise upon the colored man. This Legislature has already voted to ratify the constitutional amendment recently passed by Congress, abolishing slavery throughout the nation. These twelve thousand persons are thus fully committed to the Union and to perpetuate freedom in the State; committed to the very things, and nearly all things, the nation wants, and they ask the nation's recognition and its assistance to make good this committal. Now if we reject and spurn them we do our utmost to disorganize and disperse them. We in fact say to the white man, you are worthless or worse; we will neither help you, nor be helped by you. To the blacks we say: This cup of liberty which these, your old masters, held to your lips, we will dash from you, and leave you to the chances of gathering the spilled and scattered contents in some vague and undefined when, where and how. If this course, discouraging and paralyzing both white and black, has any tendency to bring Louisiana into proper practical relations with the Union, I have so far been unable to perceive it. If, on the contrary, we recognize and sustain the new government of Louisiana, the converse of all this is made true. We encourage the hearts and nerve the arms of 12,000 to adhere to their work, and argue for it, and proselyte for it, and fight for it, and feed it, and grow it, and ripen it to a complete success. The colored man, too, in seeing all united for him, is inspired with vigilance, and energy, and daring to the same end. Grant that he desires the elective franchise, will he not obtain it sooner by saving the already advanced steps toward it, than by running backward over them? Concede that the new Government of Louisiana is to what it should be as the egg is to the fowl, we shall sooner have the fowl by hatching the egg, than by smashing it. [Laughter.] Again, if we reject Louisiana we also reject one vote in favor of the proposed amendment to the national constitution. To meet this proposition it has been argued that no more than three-fourths of those States which have not attempted secession are necessary to validly ratify the amendment. I do not commit myself against this further than to say that such a ratification would be questionable, and sure to be persistently questioned, while a ratification by three-fourths of all the States would be unquestioned and unquestionable. I repeat the question. Can Louisiana be brought into proper practical relation with the Union sooner by sustaining, or by discarding her new State Government? What has been said of Louisiana will apply to other States. And yet so great peculiarities pertain to each State, and such important and sudden changes occur in the same State, and withal so new and unprecedented is the whole case, that no exclusive and inflexible plan can safely be prescribed as to details and collaterals. Such exclusive and inflexible plan would surely become a new entanglement. Important principles may and must be inflexible. In the present situation, as the phrase goes, it may be my duty to make some new announcement to the people of the South. I am considering and shall not fail to act when satisfied that action will be proper.

NO MORE "SO-CALLED" NEUTRALITY.

The people of this country can never forget how, as soon as there appeared to be any chance of a severance and consequent destruction of the Republic, the Government of Great Britain, followed by that of France, instead of simply remaining neutral, and doing nothing to aid either the rebels or the Government, issued a proclamation of neutrality, the effect of which was to degrade a friendly nation, with whom those countries were on terms of equal intercourse, and to which they were bound by treaties recognizing its absolute sovereignty throughout its territory, to the level of a rebel power, of a few weeks' growth, which was endeavoring to destroy that sovereignty and divide that territory. Galling as this was to the national pride—and no one felt it more so than Mr. Lincoln—he yet wisely bore it without such official manifestation of resentment as would have provoked measures that must have multiplied the difficulties of the Government, and increased the sufferings and sacrifices of the people. He saw that if the nation maintained itself, this effort against its prosperity and power would only recoil against those who made it; and he so shaped the course of his Administration toward the great foreign powers that, without admitting the right or the propriety of their action, or sacrificing the dignity of the country, he could yet bend the warlike energies of the nation to one purpose, sure that if that were attained all else would be added to it. But, knowing how sensitive the people were upon this point, and being himself no less so than any of his countrymen, he, on the next day but one after the reception of the news of General Lee's surrender, April 11th, issued the following proclamation, in which he announced to foreign powers that if they continued any longer to place the national vessels of this Republic on the same footing with rebel cruisers, their own vessels would be reduced to the same level in our ports:

PROCLAMATION.

Whereas, for some time past, vessels of war of the United States have been refused, in certain ports, privileges and immunities to which they were entitled by treaty, public law, or the comity of nations, at the same time that vessels of war of the country wherein the said privileges and immunities have been withheld, have enjoyed them fully and uninterruptedly in the ports of the United States, which condition of things has not always been forcibly resisted by the United States; although, on the other hand, they have not failed to protest against and declare their dissatisfaction with the same. In the view of the United States, no condition any longer exists which can be claimed to justify the denial to them by any one of said nations of the customary naval rights, such as has heretofore been so unnecessarily persisted in; now, therefore, I, Abraham Lincoln, President of the United States, do hereby make known that, if, after a reasonable time shall have elapsed for the intelligence of this proclamation to have reached any foreign country in whose ports the said privileges and immunities shall have been refused, as aforesaid, they shall continue to be so refused, then and thenceforth the same privileges and immunities shall be refused to the vessels of war of the country in the ports of the United States, and this refusal shall continue until the war vessels of the United States shall have been placed upon an entire equality, in the foreign ports aforesaid, with similar vessels of other countries. The United States, whatever claim or pretence may have existed heretofore, are now at least entitled to claim and concede an entire and friendly equality of rights and hospitalities with all maritime nations.

In witness whereof, I have hereunto set my hand, and caused the seal of the United States to be affixed.

Done at the city of Washington, this eleventh day of April, in the year of our Lord one thousand eight hundred [L. S.] and sixty-five, and of the independence of the United States of America the eighty-ninth.

ABRAHAM LINCOLN.

By the President:

WM. H. SEWARD, *Secretary of State.*

RECEPTION OF THE BRITISH MINISTER.

Three days after issuing the foregoing proclamation Mr. Lincoln was no more. No public act or speech of his marked the brief interval. But on the very eve of his violent death he wrote one paper which exhibited the candor, the wisdom, and the kindness of his soul in a notable manner, and which showed that the proclamation which was the last to which he signed his name was instigated by no petty spite, no desire to humiliate, no wish to provoke hostile feeling. Lord Lyons had resigned, and Sir Frederick Bruce had been sent to represent the British Government at Washington. He was about to present his credentials; his reception for the purpose of presenting his letters was to have taken place on Saturday, April 15th, and Mr. Lincoln, having received an intimation of what Sir Frederick would say on that occasion, wrote out on the afternoon of the 14th his proposed reply. He never made it. The British minister did not present his credentials until some days after Mr. Lincoln's death. The speech which the President made in reply impressed the whole country and Europe by its dignity, its good sense, its candor, and its generosity. There is the highest authority for saying that this speech is the one written by Mr. Lincoln, and that being found in his portfolio, it was wisely adopted, with its writer's policy, by Mr. Johnson, and read to the British minister by a Secretary. Thus Mr. Lincoln actually stretched out his hand from beyond the grave to guide the course of the Republic which he had done so much to save, and by his services to which he earned his crown of martyrdom. The reply in question here follows :

Sir Frederick A. W. Bruce—Sir:—The cordial and friendly
sentiments which you have expressed on the part of Her Britannic Majesty give me great pleasure. Great Britain and the United
States, by the extended and varied forms of commerce between
them, the contiguity of positions of their possessions, and the
similarity of their language and laws, are drawn into contrast
and intimate intercourse at the same time. They are from the
same causes exposed to frequent occasions of misunderstanding,
only to be averted by mutual forbearance. So eagerly are the
people of the two countries engaged throughout almost the whole
world in the pursuit of similar commercial enterprises, accompanied by natural rivalries and jealousies, that at first sight it
would almost seem that the two Governments must be enemies,
or at best, cold and calculating friends. So devoted are the
two nations throughout all their domain, and even in their most
remote territorial and colonial possessions, to the principles of
civil rights and constitutional liberty, that, on the other hand,
the superficial observer might erroneously count upon a continued concert of action and sympathy, amounting to an alliance
between them. Each is charged with the development of the
progress and liberty of a considerable portion of the human
race. Each, in its sphere, is subject to difficulties and trials,
not participated in by the other. The interest of civilization
and of humanity require that the two should be friends. I have
always known and accepted it as a fact, honorable to both countries, that the Queen of England is a sincere and honest wellwisher to. the United States. I have been equally frank and
explicit in the opinion that the friendship of the United States
toward Great Britain is enjoined by all the considerations
of interest and of sentiment affecting the character of both.
You will therefore be accepted as a minister friendly and welldisposed to the maintenance of peace and the honor of both
countries. You will find myself and all my associates acting in
accordance with the same enlightened policy and consistent
sentiments; and so I am sure that it will not occur in your case
that either yourself or this Government will ever have cause to
regret that such an important relationship existed at such a
crisis.

A few hours after writing this brief speech, Abraham Lincoln received the bullet of his assassin, and never spoke again. His last act was an endeavor to soothe the resentment of his countrymen against a nation whose governing classes had seized a time of sore trial to treat this country with arrogant contempt, and to impress upon that nation the necessity of mutual respect and mutual forbearance if they desired the continuation of friendly relations between the two countries. The reader of the foregoing pages will already have thought that such was a fitting close of Mr. Lincoln's career. We mourn him, but it is for ourselves we sorrow, not for him; for he had fulfilled a great destiny and grandly absolved himself from his solemn duties. It was from a full and rounded life that the martyr to his country and to freedom was suddenly called away, leaving behind him the priceless memory of a Government conducted in the spirit of his own noble words, "With malice toward none, with charity to all, with firmness in the right as God shall give us to know the right." This land must indeed be looked upon as blessed above all others if we see soon again another President so wise, so just, so gentle, and so good.